THE LETTER CARRIER

THE LETTER CARRIER

A Novel

FRANCESCA GIANNONE

TRANSLATED BY ELETTRA PAULETTO

CROWN
NEW YORK

Crown

An imprint of the Crown Publishing Group
A division of Penguin Random House LLC
1745 Broadway
New York, NY 10019
crownpublishing.com
penguinrandomhouse.com

Originally published in Italian as *La portalettere* by Casa Editrice Nord s.u.r.l.,
Milan, in 2023.

Library of Congress Cataloging-in-Publication Data
Names: Giannone, Francesca, author.
Title: The letter carrier : a novel / Francesca Giannone ;
translated by Elettra Pauletto. Other titles: Portalettere. English
Description: New York : Crown, 2025. | Identifiers: LCCN 2024054358 |
ISBN 9780593800898 (hardcover) | ISBN 9780593800904 (ebook) |
Subjects: LCGFT: Novels.
Classification: LCC PQ4907.I266 P6713 2025 | DDC 853/.92—
dc23/eng/20241127
LC record available at https://lccn.loc.gov/2024054358

Hardcover ISBN 978-0-593-80089-8
Ebook ISBN 978-0-593-80090-4
International edition ISBN 979-8-217-08817-1

Editor: Amy Einhorn | Editorial assistant: Lori Kusatzky |
Production editor: Terry Deal | Text designer: Amani Shakrah |
Production: Jessica Heim | Copy editor: Amy J. Schneider |
Proofreaders: Sibylle Kazeroid, Alicia Hyman, and Rachel Whitten |
Publicist: Lindsay Cook | Marketer: Kimberly Lew

Manufactured in the United States of America

1 3 5 7 9 10 8 6 4 2

First US Edition

The authorized representative in the EU for product safety and compliance is
Penguin Random House Ireland, Morrison Chambers, 32 Nassau Street,
Dublin D02 YH68, Ireland, https://eu-contact.penguin.ie.

To my sister, Elisabetta.

Wherever you go, I go.

DEBORAH: Have you been waiting long?
NOODLES: My whole life.

—From *Once Upon a Time in America* (1984) by Sergio Leone

THE LETTER CARRIER

Prologue

Lizzanello

August 13, 1961

"The letter carrier has died!"

The news spread like wildfire throughout every street and alley in town.

"Yeah, right. There's no way she really croaked," donna Carmela said, emerging onto her doorstep looking groggy. Dark circles from yesterday's mascara had gathered in the wrinkles under her eyes.

"God rest her soul," said one neighbor, still in her nightgown, and crossed herself.

"They did say, didn't they? That she wasn't well?" another neighbor added from her balcony. "Hadn't been seen around in a while."

"It was her lungs, I heard," said a large woman as she swept the ground outside her door.

"Must be the letter carrier disease," said the one from the balcony. "Remember Ferruccio? He died young, too."

Donna Carmela smirked. "I guess I should go iron my Sunday best."

A few doors down, where the village ended and the expanse of olive trees began, Giovanna sat at her kitchen table crying over a postcard from May 22, 1936. She folded it in half, slipped it between her breasts, and went out.

In accordance with Anna's last will, the vigil was to be held in the pomegranate and basil garden behind her house. The mortar she'd brought with her from Liguria almost thirty years before lay next to her in the coffin. It contained two pairs of newborn socks, a pink one and a blue one, and Carlo's wedding ring, which Anna had insisted on wearing above hers. She'd said a few hours before passing that she didn't need anything else to bid the world farewell.

Roberto was dawdling by the coffin, chain-smoking Nazionali with no filters. His wife Maria was sitting in a straw chair by the casket but was unable to keep still. Her nine-month belly was making her sweat copiously. They'd promised to call the baby Anna, if it was a girl.

The procession of men and women coming to pay their respects had begun at the first light of dawn. *Good thing I made the large pot of coffee,* Maria thought, shifting positions again. A tight cluster of women entered the room led by Carmela, outfitted in a tight blue dress, French twist, and thick black eyeliner. Like a prima donna, she puffed out her chest and walked up to the casket, proudly aware of the curious glances she received, like a flame attracting moths. A kiss placed on the deceased, the handshake with Maria, the hug with Roberto: a moving performance.

Her scene was interrupted when Giovanna burst in and flung herself onto Anna, held her tight, and kissed her face for so long that everyone started to feel uncomfortable.

"Always been a weird one, that one," someone whispered.

Giovanna stood up, pulled the postcard from between her breasts, unfolded it, and handed it to Roberto, who'd just lit another cigarette.

"What is it?" he asked, turning it over.

"Read," said Giovanna, drying her eyes.

"*Best wishes.*" He stared at Giovanna, puzzled.

"Not that," she said. "Here. See?" She pointed to the top right corner of the postcard.

Roberto saw a series of minuscule words where the postage stamps must have been.

"It was your mother's idea," Giovanna explained, her voice breaking. "She was always coming up with brilliant ideas like that."

Roberto brought the postcard closer to his face, straining his eyes to decipher the writing. He looked at Giovanna in bewilderment.

"I would write secret messages to my lover and then glue the stamps on top," she explained. "We wrote to each other for years that way."

Roberto smiled awkwardly and made to return the postcard, but Giovanna stopped him.

"No," she insisted. "It's for you." She placed her hand on his. "As a memento."

"Okay," Roberto said. As he watched Giovanna hobble away, he folded the postcard in half and stuck it in his jacket pocket. An elderly woman with a puffy face and thick gray hair gathered in a side ponytail walked up and placed a vase of white flowers at the foot of the coffin.

I wonder if Uncle Antonio will be here, Roberto thought, flicking his cigarette butt to the ground. *And if he's read the letter yet.*

"Bring it to your uncle when I'm gone," his mother had said, handing him a sealed envelope.

Anna and Antonio hadn't spoken since that fateful night nine years before.

PART ONE

1

Lizzanello

June 1934

The blue bus, battered and rusty, screeched to a halt on the searing asphalt one early afternoon. A hot and humid breeze rustled the fronds of the great palm tree that stood in the middle of the deserted square. Three passengers emerged: Carlo, unlit cigar in his teeth, was dressed to the nines in a waistcoat and shiny brown leather oxfords that had come out unscathed from the two-day journey by train and bus. He smoothed his mustache, closed his eyes, and took a deep breath, inhaling his town's distinctive smell—a mixture of fresh pasta, herbaceous oregano, wet earth, and tart red wine. He'd missed it while living up north, first in Piedmont and then Liguria; recently, the nostalgia had become constant and painful, a weight on his chest. He removed his Borsalino hat and tried to fan himself with it but only managed to displace hot air—the sirocco that blew from Africa in the summer was as merciless as he remembered.

Anna discovered this as her foot hit the ground. She wore a long black dress, a sign of mourning she'd been insisting on for three years now, and was barely managing to hold Roberto, their spirited one-year-old.

Carlo held out his hand, but Anna shook her head. "I can do it," she said, unable to hide her irritation. She couldn't understand Carlo's joy and enthusiasm. He was like a child who'd finally gotten what he wanted after a long sulk. All she cared about was sleep—the journey had been exhausting. She looked at the empty square, the strange straw-yellow buildings, the faded shop signs, the gray castle tower looming above: the new backdrop to her life, so different from what she'd always known. With a pang, she realized just how far away her Liguria was, her Pigna on the hill, her chestnut forests.

"Antonio should be here by now," Carlo grumbled, looking around. "He knows the bus gets in at three." He looked up at the large clock hanging outside the town hall. "And it's three-fifteen."

"I wouldn't be surprised if the clocks moved in slow motion around here," Anna responded, wiping Roberto's sweaty forehead with her cuff.

Carlo gave her an amused look, then shook his head, chuckling; he loved everything about his wife, even her biting sarcasm.

Antonio arrived a few minutes later, out of breath, dripping with sweat, and with a strand of otherwise slicked-back hair flying loose in the hot wind.

"There he is!" said Carlo, beaming. He ran toward Antonio, threw his hands around his neck, and pulled him close—and then he jumped on him, causing Antonio to lose his balance and nearly fall.

Anna watched them laugh like children and didn't move; that moment belonged to them. Carlo hadn't let a day go by without mentioning his brother, saying, *Antonio would think this . . . Antonio would do that . . . Have I ever told you about the time Antonio and I . . .* Despite the years apart—and the slew of care packages filled with groceries and olive oil that arrived regularly from the south along with postcards, letters, and telegrams—their relationship hadn't suffered. It had only grown stronger.

Carlo took Antonio by the arm and led him to Anna.

She was struck by his resemblance to her husband, especially up close. He had a few more wrinkles and no mustache, but it was the same angular face, pitch-black irises, round-tipped nose, and a bottom lip that was a little fuller than the top one—a faithfully rendered imitation.

"This is my Anna," Carlo said, joyfully. "And this beautiful little boy is your nephew. You finally get to meet him!"

Antonio smiled awkwardly and held out his hand, which Anna shook meekly. *But his expression is different*, she thought. That had nothing to do with Carlo's sly and charming gaze. Antonio's eyes were intense and melancholic, and in that moment, they appeared to burrow into her. Anna felt herself going red and looked away. *Here we go, blushing again. Just what I needed*, she thought.

Antonio looked away too. "I'm your uncle," he said to Roberto, smiling and patting the child's head. His gold wedding band flashed in the sunlight. Still looking away, Anna handed the boy to Antonio.

"What a cutie-pie you are," he said, lighting up and taking the child under the arms.

"Just like his mama," Carlo added, caressing Anna's cheek with the back of his hand. She didn't pull away, but she was clearly not in the mood for compliments.

The bus driver, whose shirt was soaked through and sticking to his torso, finished unloading the suitcases and large cardboard box, tipped his hat, and took leave of the group. Breathing heavily, he lumbered off to Bar Castello, the only bar in the square.

Carlo grabbed the suitcases. "You get the box," he ordered Antonio, and walked off.

Anna extracted Roberto from Antonio's arms. "Careful," she said. "That box contains my most precious possessions." With a stab of embarrassment, she realized those were the first words she'd ever spoken to him.

"I'll be careful," he said. "I promise." He gently picked up the box, holding it steady at the base with both hands, and followed his brother. Anna fell into step with him. The pitter-patter of her heels on the slippery, polished cobblestones seemed to join in concert with her slightly labored breathing.

"We're almost there," Antonio assured her, flashing her a faint smile.

Carlo and Anna's house was in via Paladini, a few steps from the square. It had belonged to Carlo's maternal uncle Luigi, known as lu patrunu, the lord, because of the many acres of land he owned. He'd made money but never had any children, so he'd left everything to Antonio and Carlo: his land, houses, and a hefty sum—enough to keep them comfortable.

That blasted patrunu was the reason Anna had had to let go of her life in Pigna and leave her students for the south. She'd hated him, dead as he was.

Antonio set the box down by the entrance and rummaged through his pockets for the key. He slid it into the lock of the big wooden door and opened it wide. A wayward strip of light revealed a charming court-yard with a vaulted ceiling and honey-colored stone walls. A small round marble table stood in the middle with two wrought iron chairs. A terra-cotta vase containing a withered plant had been long since forgotten in a corner.

Carlo dropped the bags in the courtyard and started to wander around the house, up and down the stairs, examining every nook and cranny and pulling the sheets off the furniture by the fireplace. Antonio leaned against the entryway and watched him. He suddenly felt overwhelmed with emo-tion. How he'd missed his playful little brother and his wonderful bear hugs! With Carlo by his side, he'd never needed anyone else: Carlo was his brother, sure, but he was more so his best friend, his partner in mischief, the only person who truly knew him. When he'd left, Antonio had felt alone in the world. No one had been able to relieve his loneliness or bring color back to his life. Not even—he thought with a pang of regret—his wife Agata or his daughter Lorenza.

Anna looked around, holding Roberto close. *This house is too big for just three people*, she thought. The ceilings were way too high for her taste, and love didn't need all these rooms, anyway. Or locked doors, for that matter: She and Carlo had spent their first few years as newlyweds living in a three-room apartment with low ceilings, and they'd been happy—so happy. *Physical space, when there is too much of it, increases the distance be-tween hearts: What princess has ever lived happily in a castle?*

"Anna, come look at this," Carlo cried, pulling her by the hand. "Antó, you too."

He led her across the living room, through the dining room, and fi-nally into the kitchen, from where they emerged into a small garden full of pomegranate trees.

Anna smiled for the first time since she'd climbed onto the train going south. That sight was the first real sign of hope this village had given her: the red chalice-shaped flowers with their yellow corollas; the sharp, deep green leaves; the bright color contrasts; the twisted trunks—she loved it all. Maybe she could plant some basil and saturate the air with its freshness. *Enough to make us feel at home. At least a little.*

"Quel délice! Mon jardin secret!" she said in French before planting a kiss on her son's chubby cheek.

Antonio looked at her in confusion and then at Carlo.

"Yeah, sometimes my Anna comes out with a few French words. You know—"

"It's pretty common where I'm from," Anna interrupted, turning to look at Antonio. "I grew up on the border of France." Her big eyes, the color of olive leaves, were magnified by her black hair, which she kept tied in a loose braid. Her delicate, translucent skin, of a creature not of those lands, went bright red. Antonio didn't know if it was the heat or if he'd been the one to make her blush again.

Anna turned away and started gently tapping on the trunk of a pomegranate tree.

I wonder if the library has any French grammar books, Antonio thought. He'd go ask tomorrow.

————

"Well? What's she like?" That evening, Antonio's wife Agata began her relentless questioning. "How tall is she? What was she wearing? Did she like the house? What did she say? Did she seem happy?"

Antonio stood up from his armchair. "I don't know," he said, sighing. "I think so." Agata was pummeling him like hail.

"Is she pretty?" she persisted.

Was she? Antonio had never seen a woman like that. It had been like a slap in the face, and he was still reeling from it. He couldn't stop thinking about those green eyes: intense and full of light, only slightly uneven but so sweet, and framed by two gentle grooves. Then the straight, proud nose, like a Greek statue, just like her posture, solid and sure despite her slender, youthful ankles. "Normal," he answered. "I didn't really notice."

"When do you ever," Agata complained, disappointed. She would have liked a detailed report, but she'd have to make do with Antonio's monosyllabic replies.

"Go on, sit down," she urged. "Lorenza!" she yelled up at the ceiling. "Dinner's ready!"

Agata came out of the kitchen holding a steaming pot as her daughter's steps quickened down the stairs.

"Hi, Papa," Lorenza said, placing a kiss on Antonio's cheek.

He patted her on the head and hastened to ask her what she'd learned in school that day. He wanted to change the subject and hoped his daughter's presence would shut his wife up once and for all.

Agata ladled some vegetable stew onto Lorenza's plate before serving Antonio. *Those hands,* he thought. They were perpetually run-down, with scraped knuckles and nails split from too much biting. Ten years had passed since he'd first met her, and he still looked away whenever he saw those hands. "What do you expect? They're hardworking hands, these." Agata had cut him short, annoyed, the only time he'd tried to suggest she take care of them.

Anna's hands, however. He had noticed those. Manicured, smooth, soft—he could tell just by looking at them.

"Italy is a peninsula, which means it touches the sea on three sides . . ." Lorenza was saying in a singsong voice.

"When are we going to meet her?" Agata said as she sat down.

"Give them time to settle in," Antonio said, blowing the heat off a spoonful of stew.

"A welcome lunch!" Agata exclaimed, ignoring him. "That's what we need. Next Sunday!"

———

The following Sunday, Agata rose at dawn. She gently closed the bedroom door behind her to avoid waking Antonio and made her way to the bathroom. She pulled off the white nightgown that tugged at her ample hips and put on a brown cotton dress, short-sleeved and comfy, the one she'd worn the night before and had hung next to the towel. Looking at herself in the mirror, she gave her auburn hair a few quick strokes of a brush, then tied it tightly in a low ponytail and washed her face.

She tiptoed down to the kitchen and put the coffee maker on the fire. She started to chop an onion, a carrot, a celery stalk. She filled a high-sided pan with olive oil and tossed in the minced vegetables. In no time, the smell of soffritto spread through the kitchen and mingled with that of the coffee. She emptied two glass bottles of tomato passata into the pan, adjusted the salt, and covered it. She sat down for a moment to sip her coffee and go through her mental checklist for the day: She had to make the dough for the orecchiette, which she then had to fashion one by one. *Two pounds? Yes, that should be enough*—then shape the bread and cheese dumplings into compact balls, fry them, and roll them in the fragrant tomato sauce. She imagined the lunch, how it would go as she served each dish, how Carlo and Anna would react. "Mamma mia, how delicious!" Carlo would say, looping his hand in the air. "Ah, how I've missed our cuisine. And these dumplings—it's just like eating real meat!" Everyone would polish their plates with bread, soaking up every last drop of sauce, and Antonio would look at her with pride and think about how lucky he was to have such a good cook for a wife. "You have to teach me how to make these," Anna would add, looking at her with admiration. And Agata, smiling, would say that she'd be happy to. They'd be great friends—she was sure of it.

She downed the last bit of coffee, stood up, and put the dirty cup in the sink. She took some puccia bread from the pantry and started digging out the crumb.

She decided that Antonio would take care of dessert. She'd send him to pick up a tray of almond pastries from Bar Castello.

Anna and Carlo knocked on the door at twelve-thirty P.M., right on time. "Here they are," said Agata, with a flash of joy in her eyes. She untied her apron, threw it on a chair, and ran to the door. Antonio, who was sitting in his armchair reading the *Corriere della Sera*, folded the newspaper in two, stood up, and shoved his hands into his pockets.

"Welcome!" Agata said in a shrill voice, her cheeks flushed. Carlo smiled and gave her a big hug. In ten years, they'd only seen each other on three occasions, each time just for a few days: the first when he'd returned to Puglia to be a witness at their wedding, the second when he'd come to celebrate Lorenza's birth, and the third on the occasion of his father's funeral.

Anna lingered in the door holding Roberto, who was fast asleep against her shoulder.

"Anna, dear," Agata said, planting a kiss on each cheek. "Finally. I couldn't wait to meet you," she said, her voice trembling. "But please, come in." She motioned them in with her arm. "Take a seat wherever you like." She wiped away the sweat between her nose and upper lip.

Antonio came toward them. He clutched his brother in a tight embrace and greeted Anna with a raised chin.

"How are you?" he asked her, cracking a smile.

"I'm well," she said, looking around, a little dazed. "As well as can be expected, given—"

"And where's my niece?" Carlo cut her off. "She must be all grown up by now!"

"Lorenza!" Agata screamed in the direction of the stairs.

Anna made a face and instinctively covered Roberto's ears, though he continued to sleep.

"Come down! They're here!" Then, lowering her voice, she said to Anna, "I always have to call her a hundred times, this daughter of mine. She never listens!" She chuckled.

Carlo was already wandering around the room with his fingers laced behind his back, taking everything in.

"Anna, dear, don't just stand there. Sit here," Agata said, pointing at the green velvet couch in the middle of the room.

Anna thanked her and made for the couch.

"Actually, let's put the boy down first. We wouldn't want him to wake up," Agata said.

"Yes, maybe we should," Anna agreed. "Thank you."

"No worries. Come, come." Agata put an arm on Anna's back and urged her toward the stairs. "That way we can get my daughter to shake a leg."

"You didn't change a thing," Carlo said in surprise once he was alone with his brother.

Antonio still lived in their childhood home, just a few hundred feet away from Uncle Luigi's place. When their father was still alive, Antonio, with his wife and daughter, had lived there with him, sleeping in the bedroom that had become Lorenza's room. The furniture, unrefined and stodgy, was the same his mother and father had picked out before they married: the green velvet couch, now worn along the edges, was the one on which Carlo and Antonio would curl up in their father's arms on winter nights by the fire; the landscapes of olive trees their mother had painted when she was young and healthy were still hanging by the fireplace; the decorations—their father had collected all sorts of objects, especially little wrought iron figurines—remained firmly in place; and even their mother's wool blanket was still folded across the armchair by the window, where Antonio liked to sit.

"I like it like this," Antonio said with a shrug.

Upstairs, after Anna laid Roberto down on the bed and surrounded him with cushions, Agata led her down the hall to Lorenza's room and opened the door; the girl was sitting on the floor, playing intently with her stuffed doll.

"Why don't you ever answer me when I call you?" Agata chided her.

Anna walked past Agata into the room and crouched by the girl.

Lorenza stared at her, wide-eyed.

"Hi," Anna said, smiling. "I'm your Auntie Anna." She held out her hand.

The girl returned the smile and squeezed Anna's hand. "I'm Lorenza."

"Yes, I know."

"How old are you?"

"Twenty-seven."

Lorenza started counting silently on her fingers. "Eight less than Mama," she said. "I'm nine." She held up her fingers. "Like this."

"I know that, too," Anna said, smiling.

"Did you really come from far away?"

"Oh yes. Very, very far away."

"Far like America?"

Anna burst out laughing and chucked Lorenza on the cheek. "More or less," she said.

Lorenza had Antonio's and Carlo's eyes, dark and penetrating with a sparkle shining from within.

"You're really pretty, you know?" Anna said, running her fingers through her niece's hair, which was auburn, like Agata's.

"So are you. You're beautiful."

"Oh, thank you." Anna pulled her into a hug. This was exactly how she'd imagined her Claudia, her lost baby girl, if she'd had a chance to grow up.

"Well, Lorenza?" Agata prodded her daughter from the threshold, sounding annoyed. "Put your shoes on and come down, let's go. Uncle Carlo wants to see you."

Hearing footsteps on the stairs, Carlo and Antonio stood up from the couch. Antonio thought Agata looked grumpy, as if her earlier cheer had suddenly vanished. But Lorenza seemed happy to be holding hands with Anna, who was finally smiling. *She should smile more often*, he thought. *She's even more beautiful—*

"Uncle!" Lorenza screamed, running up to Carlo. He laughed and opened his arms, then picked her up and spun her around the room as she split her sides laughing.

"Slow down or she'll get queasy!" Anna warned him.

"Come on, let's eat," Agata said. "I'm going to go throw in the pasta.

'Cause it's the fresh kind, you know, you've barely put it in before it's already time to take it out."

Agata went into the kitchen, expecting Anna to follow her. Instead, Anna pulled out a chair and sat down. *Unbelievable,* Agata thought, shaking her head. Female guests were expected to help the lady of the house serve the meal. That was the rule; everybody knew it and they certainly didn't need to be reminded.

"I want to sit next to Auntie!" Lorenza said, grabbing the chair next to Anna's.

"Lorenza, come help me," Agata called to her, sharply.

"Papa'll take care of it, don't worry," Antonio said, inviting Lorenza to take her seat and joining his wife in the kitchen.

The plates were brought out and everyone sat down. Agata made the sign of the cross and with her hands together and her eyes cast down, she recited the Lord's Prayer. Carlo and Antonio set down their spoons and copied her.

"Auntie, aren't you gonna pray?" Lorenza asked.

Agata looked up.

"I'm not a believer," Anna responded, laconically.

Carlo coughed and looked around uncomfortably.

"What do you mean, you're not a believer?" Lorenza insisted, stunned.

"Let's eat," Agata interrupted. "Now. Before it gets cold."

Antonio kept his eyes glued to Anna, as if they were frozen. He looked away only when he noticed his wife staring at him in turn, her eyebrows raised. He gave her an awkward smile, took his spoon, bent over his plate, and started to eat.

———

A few hours later, in the sweet silence that follows Sunday lunches, Antonio sat in his chair with his legs crossed and his hands laced in his lap, staring at the floor and taking in the afternoon light that filtered through the closed curtains. The sound of clinking plates and gurgling water floated in from the kitchen as Agata rinsed the soapy dishes. She was unusually taciturn, yet constantly snorting. Lorenza was resting in her room.

"I'm done, finally," Agata announced, emerging into the living room looking exhausted. "I'm gonna go lie down too." Antonio came out of his daze and looked up at his wife. "Go ahead. You must be tired."

"Sure am," she retorted. "All that work for nothing."

"Why nothing? I thought it went well. Everything was delicious, as always."

"Ah, well, I'm glad to hear that. At least someone noticed."

Antonio pulled his hands apart and leaned forward slightly, his elbows on his knees. "What's the matter now, Agata?" he asked, with a hint of annoyance.

She answered with a slight snort and waved her hand as if to tell him to let it go. She walked toward the stairs but then stopped for a moment, her foot on the first step. "Well," she said, "they're right about those people from the north." With that, she disappeared behind the dividing wall.

2

The day after arriving, Anna had yet to unpack her bags. Rather, she had gone straight to her box of treasures: the raffia bag full of black Ligurian basil seeds; the white-and-gray-veined marble mortar that had belonged to her great-grandmother and then to all the women in her family; the carved cherrywood chest with Claudia's and Roberto's first pairs of wool socks—pink for her and blue for him; her mother's pearls, which Anna had received when she turned twenty-one; the lilac silk pillowcases her grandmother had sewn because, as she said, "Silk keeps your skin young and smooth"; and her books: *Madame Bovary* and *L'Éducation Sentimentale*, in their original French, and *Anna Karenina, Jane Eyre, Wuthering Heights,* and *Pride and Prejudice.*

She plucked out the bag with the seeds, went to the garden, and got to work: She dug a few dozen tiny holes, about ten inches apart, and placed two seeds in each. Given the heat in the south, she knew she wouldn't have to wait long for the first plants to sprout.

On a Saturday morning in July, she was watering those first tufts of basil when she heard a knock at the door. With a sigh, she went inside and untied the ribbon holding her straw hat in place. She wondered, *Will I ever get used to this southern heat?*, placing the hat on the table.

"Coming!" she shouted, heading for the door.

There was Agata, clutching her bag, her face shiny and red. She was wearing a straight, knee-length pink skirt. Her white blouse was all puff-balls and lace, which accentuated her ample chest.

"You're early," Anna said.

"Yes, well. I couldn't wait," Agata said, stepping inside.

Anna closed the door behind her. "Let me get dressed. I was just in the garden."

"Sure, of course, take your time, don't mind me." Agata waved her hand. "I'll just wait here and give my nephew some cuddles."

"I haven't woken him up yet," Anna said, nodding at the pram in the middle of the room.

"I'll take care of it. You go get dressed."

Anna lifted an eyebrow, then turned to climb the stairs, indolently, holding the wrought iron guardrail.

Why did I let myself get talked into going to market this morning?

She slipped out of her blue silk nightgown and pulled out a black dress. Agata had insisted on dragging her into town—had been asking her ever since she got to town—and she'd agreed by attrition. Anna had the impression that Agata's life had been an ocean of solitude before she arrived, and that her arrival was like an island finally appearing on the horizon, the only hope of salvation. Indeed, her sister-in-law gave her no rest. She visited every day, at the most inconvenient times and without notice; she always wanted to do something together—grocery shopping, a walk, the Saturday afternoon rosary, a coffee, incessant chatting. Often, she brought food. "I made enough for you," she'd say, beaming, though no one had asked her to.

Anna braided her hair and went back downstairs. The two of them left the house and walked toward the square—Anna pushing the stroller and Agata clasping her arm.

The white awnings of the market stalls filled all of Piazza Castello and the adjacent streets. The bustling background noise Anna had heard from afar suddenly came into focus and hit her hard, nearly dulling her senses. There was a loud commotion of traders calling out to potential customers, shouts, bellowing laughs, and rowdy squabbles between gesticulating shoppers.

The food stalls smelled of cacioricotta, pungent goat cheese, and spicy olives in brine—a disagreeable combination of odors, nausea inducing, especially so early in the morning. Anna picked up her pace and pinched her nose shut.

"This way," said Agata. "Come see." Her favorite stalls were in the housewares section of the market, where peddlers sold kitchen tools, home furnishings, and genuine local artisanal bric-a-brac. "I bet you'll find something here," she said. A large young man with a slight mustache and dark curly hair stood behind the first stand cheerfully touting his newly arrived merchandise: "You won't find anything like it anywhere else!" He showed them a stone vase from Lecce decorated with hand-painted yellow flowers, a thick-bottomed saucepan, and a few wooden ladles with enameled ceramic handles.

"What's that over there?" Anna asked, pointing at an unusual-looking terra-cotta object. It was shaped like a pinecone, or a bud about to bloom, with two folded leaves on the sides.

"It's a pumo," said Agata. "Do you like it?" she asked, looking hopeful.

"It's a good-luck charm," the man yelled over the general din of the market. "But only if you give it as a gift."

Anna made a face—she wasn't one to believe in charms.

"Trust me," said the man, winking. Before Anna could say anything, Agata had grabbed the pumo, paid for it, and slipped it into Anna's bag.

"This one's on me!"

Anna thanked her but didn't smile. *What am I supposed to do with this? I have no use for this ugly thing,* she thought.

They made their way through the crowd toward a papier-mâché puppet stand. Madonnas, Jesuses, and various saints were displayed in rows, upright like toy soldiers. Anna's gaze fell on a little statue forgotten in a corner: a peasant woman with a wide, billowing white dress, hair blowing in the wind and a basket of red apples in her arms. Her face was slightly chipped—the only puppet with an imperfection, among all those on display.

"I'll take that one," Anna said without hesitating.

Agata looked at her, baffled. "Why not the San Lorenzo statue, our patron saint? Look how nice it is," she said, picking it up. Anna ignored her. The man on the other side of the stall bent down, pulled out an old newspaper page from a pile at his feet, and carefully wrapped the puppet. "Try not to crush it in your bag. The papier-mâché is delicate," he said, handing her the parcel.

Soon Agata and Anna reached a heap of wicker baskets. An elderly woman with dark fuzz above her lip and hands covered in calluses was sitting on the ground, barefoot, intent on weaving a basket; she had just finished one side and was about to start on the handle. Agata greeted her warmly and struck up a conversation. As the two women exchanged a series of "By the grace of God go I" Anna stared at the old woman's feet, blackened by the earth, cracked at the heels, and with yellowed toenails. For a moment, she thought of her grandmother, who would massage her feet with milk every night at bedtime before slipping them into a pair of socks, still soaking wet. "Never neglect your hands and feet," she always said. "People notice the details first—remember that."

"This way," said Agata, grabbing Anna by the arm. They ducked down a side street to a fabric stall. The petite shopkeeper wore her hair in a bun and a green knit shawl over her shoulders. She was showing a roll of blue silk to a woman wearing a dress so tight it looked like it had been painted on. The woman's hair, full and dark, fell down her back in soft waves. But what struck Anna were her hands: not just because they stroked the silk as delicately as if it were a newborn's head but because her nails were well manicured and painted red. No other woman in Lizzanello had such elegant hands.

"Ah, our dear Agata," said the shopkeeper with a broad smile.

"This is Anna, my sister-in-law," Agata said. The woman with the red nails swung around. The blue silk slipped from her fingers. As Anna shook the shopkeeper's hand, she noticed, out of the corner of her eye, the other woman looking her up and down, staring hard.

"What do you need, my dears?"

"I need to make curtains for the bedroom," Agata said. "I'll take a few yards of white cotton and some thread to crochet the edges."

"I'm off, then," declared the woman with the red nails, finally looking away from Anna. She turned to the shopkeeper and said, in dialect, "The silk is fine; put it aside for me—I'll send my husband to fetch it later." Without saying goodbye, she turned on her heels and walked away.

"Who was that?" Anna whispered in Agata's ear, wondering what the woman might have said in a language that was so different from standard Italian, or from the dialects spoken in the north.

"Carmela," Agata said, looking uncomfortable.

"Carmela who?"

Agata gave her an abashed look. "The seamstress . . ."

"Here you go," said the shopkeeper, handing a paper bag to Agata, who paid and thanked her, promising to return soon.

Anna and Agata walked back to the busy square. "Shall we stop at the fruit vendor for a minute?" Anna said, pointing at a shop across the way that read FRUIT AND VEGETABLES. "I need a bouquet of basil. I want to make pesto tomorrow."

As soon as he spied them, a slight man with a cheerful smile greeted them at the door, tipping his cap.

"What can I get you?" he asked.

"Basil, please," said Anna. "And do make sure the leaves are whole, like last week."

"Michele, give us the freshest bouquet you have," Agata said.

"Of course," he said. He turned to the back of the shop and shouted, "Giacomino! Some basil for the outlander!" Anna raised an eyebrow, surprised and slightly displeased. Was that what people called her? The outlander? A freckled child around Lorenza's age arrived with a bouquet of basil.

"Give the basil to the signora," Michele ordered.

"Here you are," said the child.

Once out of the store, Agata asked Anna if she was in the mood to grab a lemonade at the bar before heading home. "So we can spend a bit more time together, and freshen up," she said, fanning herself with her hand. Annoyed by the prospect of making yet another stop, Anna tried not to snort, so as not to appear rude, and followed her through the crowd. They made their way through a small gaggle of women, some holding heavy bags of market spoils and others who'd rested theirs on the ground as they chatted. Anna and Agata entered Bar Castello, pushing away the rope curtain over the door. The bartender, a rotund fellow with a thick black mustache and olive skin, was drying a glass with the hem of his white apron. The walls were covered in wainscoting, above which hung a few photos of the town, a Fernet-Branca poster, and a menu written out by hand. Heavy red tablecloths were draped over the tables, and the chairs were made of wood with straw seats. On one of these lay a worn copy of the *Gazzetta del Mezzogiorno*.

"Nando, two lemonades, please," said Agata.

"Just one," said Anna. "I'll take a caffè corretto. With grappa."

Agata turned to her in shock. "Grappa?"

"Yes, grappa," Anna replied. "I've always asked for a touch of liquor to be added to my coffee when ordering at the bar."

Nando winked at her and in a booming voice said, "Same here!"

———

The next day, Anna gathered her ingredients in ceramic bowls and arranged them on the kitchen table: basil, pine nuts, kosher salt, garlic, Pecorino, Parmesan. She was missing the olive oil, but Antonio had promised to bring it by morning's end. She tied her apron behind her back and took the mortar from the shelf.

"Anyone home?" Antonio's voice filtered in from the entrance.

"Come on in!" said Anna.

"Auntie, Auntie!" Lorenza chirped, running toward her.

Anna broke into a smile, crouched down, and opened her arms. "Give us a hug, kiddo."

"Good morning!" Antonio said, walking in with a timid smile and removing his cap. "And Carlo?"

"He took Roberto to mass," she said, lifting an eyebrow.

Antonio cracked a smile. "Here's the oil. Two liters this time," he said, placing a jug on the table. The jug displayed the logo of Oleificio Greco, his oil mill, which featured a drop of oil in the shape of a leaf coming out of a tin cruet.

"Papa, can we stay and watch Auntie make pesto? Please!"

"If Auntie doesn't mind . . ." he said, searching for the answer in Anna's eyes.

"Of course not," she said, ruffling her niece's hair. Lorenza immediately pulled up a chair and knelt on it.

Antonio took a seat on the straw chair in the corner by the cupboard. No one ever sat there—it was used to store laundry for ironing.

"Let's get started!" Anna chirped. She rinsed the basil leaves and placed them on a dry kitchen towel. "Remember, you must never plunge the leaves in water," she explained to Lorenza. "Wash them like this, patting them gently with a damp cloth. Otherwise you might break them, because—you see?—they have to stay like this, intact." She put the clean leaves aside and filled the mortar with peeled garlic cloves and kosher salt. "My mother always said you need a pinch—just a pinch—of salt. No more."

Anna began to pound, drawing circles in the mortar as she worked.

Antonio watched in silence, his freshly shaven cheeks resting in his palms: Anna's hands, so smooth and soft, moved with such ease and confidence—they were the experienced hands of someone who had practiced the rite of pesto making since childhood. He'd never seen her in such a good mood. He figured she should make pesto every day if it made her smile like that.

"You must wait for the garlic to take on this consistency, see? Like a cream," Anna said. Lorenza leaned forward. "Only then can you add the basil," Anna continued, picking up the bouquet of leaves. "And another pinch of salt."

"Can I add it?" Lorenza asked.

"Yes, but just a little, like I showed you."

Lorenza reached her little hand into the salt bowl and picked up a few large grains with her thumb and index finger.

"Good job—just like that," Anna said, smiling. "And now comes the best part." She resumed pounding, working vigorously until the leaves turned into a paste and the smell of basil filled the air. "The pine nuts, Pecorino, and Parmesan. But in small doses, slowly . . . slowly." Anna emptied the bowls into the mortar, one by one. "Your arms should be sore by the end. Look at the muscles I've formed just by pounding!"

Lorenza giggled and turned to look at her father, who smiled and winked.

"And voilà!" Anna exclaimed, satisfied. Lorenza looked at the pesto in wonderment, as if she'd just witnessed some form of magic. She couldn't wait to tell her classmates about it. Every day since the arrival of her "auntie from afar," as she called Anna, she would tell her friends about the adventures, real and imagined, of her own personal heroine: One time, her auntie had seen mountains so tall they touched the sky; one time, she'd danced with the king himself; and one time, she'd touched a sick tree and cured it.

"Now we just add the oil and we're done," Anna said. "Do you want to pour it in, ma petite?"

"My little one," Antonio whispered.

"What did you say?" Anna said.

He blushed. "Ma petite . . . It means 'my little one,' right?"

Anna looked at him, one eyebrow raised. "You speak French now?"

Antonio looked down. "A little."

"How come? Did I inspire you to learn it?" She smiled.

He shrugged. "I want to understand things I don't know, that's all . . ." *I want to understand you,* he wished he could have added.

Anna couldn't have known that once she'd arrived, each night after Agata and Lorenza went to bed and the house plunged into silence, Antonio had locked himself in his study and pulled out the French grammar book he'd borrowed from the library. He stayed up late reading and underlining and only stopped when he could no longer keep his eyes open.

———

Carlo was sitting at a table outside Bar Castello with a cigar in hand, drinking the terrible house red, Roberto on his knees. What a pleasure regardless, he thought, to sit there and watch the Sunday morning bustle as people poured out of church, filed into the bakery for pastries, tossed coins to the paperboy, and walked across the square with a copy of the *Gazzetta del Mezzogiorno* tucked under their arm.

Carlo tipped his Borsalino hat and smiled at all who walked by; he knew everyone and they knew him, as if he hadn't budged from that table in ten years.

"Hey there, stranger," someone said behind him.

That voice. Carmela. He knew he'd see her sooner or later. Actually, it was funny how they hadn't run into each other until now. He'd been very busy when he first arrived: suitcases to unpack, a house to open, documents to sign at the notary, inherited lands to inspect. But the town had barely six thousand inhabitants, and it was easy to note who was around and who wasn't.

Carlo kicked out the chair beside him, smiled, and motioned for her to take it.

"I heard you were back," she said, still standing. "And I saw you in church earlier." She lowered her black headscarf to her neck.

Carmela—what a woman she'd become. When she'd blossomed, the summer she turned sixteen, the boys had launched a competition to see who would be the first to fondle her breasts. They courted her all at once, like an army laying siege: They would offer her their arm, elbow one another out of the way to sit next to her in church, buy her jam pastries, walk her home. Carlo had known her since they were children, when they lived just down the street from each other. He'd seen her cry and scream when her mother beat her, skin her knees when they played tag, and wipe away snot with the back of her hand. But that year, when he returned from summer camp in Santa Maria di Leuca to find her all grown up, confident, and breathtakingly beautiful, he'd felt intimidated and slightly annoyed. He stopped speaking to her. He just watched her from afar, studying her as if she were a new life-form, incomprehensible. He made sure to catch her eye only to quickly look away. In the end, by dint of ignoring her, he won her over. For two years he fondled her breasts and gave her furtive, passionate kisses—until the day he'd had to leave: He'd been called up to become a customs officer in Alexandria, way up north in Piedmont. But he would be back soon and marry her, he'd promised.

"This must be Roberto," Carmela said.

"Yes!" Carlo proclaimed, kissing his son on the forehead.

"What beautiful big eyes."

"Got those from his mother, thankfully."

Carmela watched the square slowly empty. Mario the shoeshine, a large man with a thick unibrow, angular features, and hair combed to one side, was sitting on the bench between the palm tree and the standing fountain, arms crossed, staring at her. She acknowledged him with a nod, then looked down and pulled her scarf back over her head. *Her hands are as elegant and beautiful as they were all those years ago,* Carlo thought, observing her slender fingers and red nails.

"And you? Any children?" he asked her.

Carmela hesitated. "Yes," she said. "One. His name is Daniele. He'll be ten in December."

"Well, you look great, you know," Carlo murmured. "You're even more beautiful than back then."

She shot daggers at him, her eyes dark and cutting. "Not enough to make you come back."

He sipped his wine and grimaced—good God was it tart, practically vinegar. Only good for salad dressing now. "You know all about that. I wrote to you," he said, setting the glass back on the table.

"Yes, yes, I know," she said, waving her hand as if to swat an insect.

"Looks like someone else put a ring on your finger, though."

Carmela felt her ring. "Well, if I had waited for you, I would have died a spinster."

"You never would have died a spinster. Not you."

"And your lady? We hardly ever see her around. What's the matter? Is our little town not to her liking?"

"Come on. Give her time, she's getting her bearings. It hasn't been easy for her, you know. Claudia, the move . . . You'll see, in time."

"Yes, I heard about the baby. A terrible loss."

"Yes," he said, pursing his lips. He took another sip of his wine. "Christ, this stuff is disgusting."

Carmela laughed. "Unlike the wine my father used to make. You liked that well enough."

"Don Ciccio's wine! Who could forget? Is he still making it?"

"Not anymore. Too tiring. He threw out his back."

"Too bad. I would love a glass of that."

"I still have a few bottles at home." She glanced at the clock on the town hall, then at Mario, who was still staring at her. "I have to go," she said.

"Maybe I'll come see you one of these days?" Carlo blurted out. "For the wine, I mean," he added, awkwardly.

Carmela forced a smile and said goodbye. She turned and walked away, knowing full well that he was watching her go.

———

Lorenza threw open the front door and walked in, screaming, "Mama, look, me and Auntie Anna made pesto!" She ran into the kitchen to show her mother the jar she was clutching in her hands.

"I already made lunch," Agata said, dismissively.

The smile on Lorenza's little face faded at once. Antonio went to her, let out a long sigh, and tried to reassure her. "We'll save it for tomorrow," he said, patting her on the head.

"I don't like that stuff. It's not from round here," Agata grumbled, dishing out the food.

Antonio already knew the pesto would go bad and that they'd end up tossing it. Anna had instructed them to eat it within the day.

"Let's go, Lorenza," he said gently. "Come help me set the table." He took the jar from her hands and placed it on the counter.

"There. Go, run along now," Agata said, drying her hands on her apron.

———

"Here we are!"

Carlo appeared in the kitchen holding Roberto, who, somewhere along the way, had collapsed into a deep sleep in his father's arms.

"The effects of mass?" Anna joked, taking hold of him.

Carlo burst out laughing. He tried to grab her from behind and steal a kiss.

Amused, she motioned to him to stop, or he'd wake the child. But after lowering Roberto into the crib, she turned and pulled Carlo into a long kiss. In all his life, she was the only one who had ever known how to kiss him like that.

The trofie with pesto—left steaming on the table—ended up being served cold that Sunday.

———

Ferragosto, the traditional worker's holiday celebrated on August 15, was hot from the first hours of the morning. Anna woke up sweating and pushed her black silk eye mask up to her forehead. Carlo's side of the bed was already vacant—she could hear him singing beyond the closed bathroom door, which he always did while shaving. She got up, sat at the vanity table, took her brush from the marble counter, and ran it through her hair, examining herself in the large oval mahogany mirror. She caressed her son's cheek as he slept peacefully in the crib and went down to the kitchen. She heated some milk in a little pot, but not too long, just for a minute; she liked it lukewarm. She poured it into a cup and went out to drink it on the bench in the shadow of the pomegranate tree. She lifted her white cotton nightgown and tucked in her ruddy, slender legs, then scooped her long, loose hair to one side. Keeping the cup firmly in her hands, she took the first little sip. Where had she been last Ferragosto? Roberto had been just a few months old, and Carlo had taken them on a little excursion, just the three of them, to somewhere near Pigna. They'd had lunch on a blanket, in the cool forest undergrowth, where the only noises were the crackling of the crickets and the chirping of the birds. From a paper bag, Carlo had produced a pisciadela, her favorite type of focaccia bread, and they'd split it in two.

Anna touched the back of her sweaty neck. *Incredible*, she thought. *I'm even sweating in the shade.* She sat back against the bench with a sigh and took another sip of milk. She realized Agata hadn't visited in days. Not that she minded. On the one hand, it was a relief that her sister-in-law had loosened her grip. But to disappear completely like that, from one day to the next? Had she upset her? She didn't think she'd been rude when, about a week before, Agata had shown up at lunchtime with a frittata made with breadcrumbs and lesser calamint. "Agata, thank you dearly," Anna had said. "That's very kind of you. But, you see, I want to be the one to cook for my family." What was wrong with that? She couldn't possibly have offended her!

"Hello, my love! Ready for the beach?" Carlo said as he walked into the garden, smelling of mint aftershave. He leaned down to kiss her and stroke her hair.

"The beach? But I don't even have a bathing suit," Anna protested.

"Not to worry! We'll improvise. I'm not going to let us stay here and die of heat," he chirped.

"And how, exactly, are we getting there?"

"By bus. It leaves in exactly fifty minutes," he said. "Antonio, Agata, and Lorenza are waiting for us in the square."

"You've already thought of everything. Why am I just hearing about it now?" Anna said, tensing up.

"Because I wanted to surprise you! You'll see, it'll be fun. Take your time with breakfast; I'll take care of Roberto."

The bus left Piazza Castello half an hour late: A crowd had formed, with people elbowing one another to get on. After protestations and invectives from those left behind, the bus driver promised to come right back for a second round.

"There's a lemonade waiting for each of you at the bar, already paid for," Carlo announced to the group that would have to wait. "So you can cool off in the meantime." With that, he climbed onto the bus amid a flurry of cheers.

"Did you hear that? That man bought us lemonade," said a mother to the young boy in her arms. He was whining from the heat.

"You paid for everyone? I don't get it . . ." Anna said.

"Indeed, I did," Carlo replied, taking a seat next to her. He waved at the little boy in his mother's arms and smiled.

Anna watched him, baffled. "But why?"

"What do you mean, why? It's a nice gesture. They have to wait in the sun, poor things."

"Yes, but what does that have to do with you? I mean, couldn't they get it themselves?"

Carlo shrugged. "That's what we do here. We always have."

"Perhaps. But to me it looks like a stupid way to throw away money."

"Don't worry about money, my love," he assured her, touching her knee. "We're not short on that. Not anymore."

"That's not a good reason to waste it."

"Auntie, I want to sit next to you," Lorenza said, emerging from the row behind and squeezing between them. Carlo chucked her under the chin. "Very well," he said, standing up. "But just this once, okay?" He winked and went to take Lorenza's seat next to Agata, who was fanning herself with a black silk-and-tulle fan. In another row, Antonio was absorbed in a book, sitting elbow-to-elbow with a young boy who was pressing his nose up against the window.

After a few miles, they came to the San Foca beach, the nearest one to town, and stopped right on the waterfront. As Anna emerged from the bus, she saw that the beach was crowded and loud. It made her want to get right back on the bus and return to the peaceful silence of her pomegranate garden.

"Can you take him, please," she said to Carlo, passing Roberto to him.

"Everything okay, my love?" he said, worried.

Anna didn't answer. She put on her straw hat, clutched Lorenza's hand, and walked with her onto the hot sand to look for a free spot. Between the people sunbathing on the ground, kids building sandcastles with buckets and shovels, and adults hitting balls back and forth with wood and leather paddles, it seemed like an impossible task. In the end, they found a free spot of sand; Carlo and Antonio sat back-to-back while Anna and Agata sat next to each other, legs off to one side, making room for the two kids in the middle. Anna felt crushed by the suffocating heat, the constantly fluctuating human horde, and the incessant chatter of the local dialect, a language that still seemed completely unattainable to her—all those words ending in U, and those Z's cropping up in the most unlikely places. But no one in her immediate vicinity seemed to mind any of that. Everyone else seemed happy to be there.

Carlo stood up and took off his pants and shirt, revealing a white-and-blue-striped bathing suit that came halfway down his thighs.

"I'm going for a swim," he announced. "Who's with me?"

"Me. I can't take this anymore. I have to cool down or I'll burst into flames," Agata said, still fanning herself. "Lorenza, let's go. Get your head wet or you'll catch your death." She stood up and helped her daughter out of her shirt, leaving her with a little yellow bathing suit with shorts.

"And you, Auntie Anna?" Lorenza beckoned. Anna stroked her head and said she'd rather stay there for the time being.

"Antonio, are you coming?" Carlo asked.

"Let me finish this chapter," he said, pointing at the page. Carlo bent down to give Anna and Roberto light kisses on their foreheads. "See you in a bit," he said. "Don't burn." Smiling, he nudged Anna's straw hat back into place. She watched him make his way to the edge of the water joking with Agata and Lorenza. As they dipped their feet in, she turned to stare at Antonio, who was still reading intently, as if nothing else existed. He must have felt her watching him, because he looked up from his novel and returned her gaze.

"What's it about?" Anna asked.

Antonio looked lost. "What?"

"The book you're reading," she said, amused.

"Oh, the book!" he gasped, blushing. "Well," he said, holding his spot with his thumb, "it's about a man who stains himself with the sin of sloth and prefers to take refuge underground, even though he envies all those who are able to act. It's called *Notes from Underground.*"

"And it's by Dostoevsky, yes, I know. I've never read any of his books."

"What do you like to read?"

Anna leaned back onto her elbows. "Jane Austen, the Brontë sisters . . ."

"You like women, you mean."

"Not only. I've read everything by Flaubert, Tolstoy. And anyway, why do you say it like that?"

"Like what?"

"In that patronizing tone. As if books written by women were of lesser value."

"No, no, you misunderstand me. I didn't mean to minimize them, believe me. I've read *Pride and Prejudice*, for example."

"Did you like it?"

Antonio shrugged. "I prefer other writers, that's all."

Just then, a boy walked by pushing a red cart while shouting, "Fresh almonds for sale!"

Anna smirked. "Why do you people yell so much?"

"You who?" Antonio asked.

"You Southerners."

Antonio smiled bitterly. "Well, not everyone." And he looked her straight in the eyes.

"Right, not you. I know. Nor Carlo," Anna said, relaxing.

"You know, I marked a passage that made me think of you."

"Of me? Why?"

"Can I read it to you?"

"Of course."

Antonio leafed through the pages until he found the right one. "Here it is." He began to read in a calm voice, "'I was tormented then by another circumstance, the fact that no one looked like me and I didn't look like anyone. I am alone, and they are everyone.'" He closed the book and looked at Anna.

"That's how you see me?" she asked, frowning.

"Is that how you feel?" Anna didn't get a chance to respond. Lorenza ran up and lunged at them, dripping with water, and screamed, "Auntie, Papa, come on! The water is beauuuuuutiful!"

3

Carlo crossed town wandering through the quiet, narrow alleyways, lit cigar in hand. The smell of tomato sauce coming from someone's open window permeated the air. He reached the door of the dressmaker's shop and knocked, whistling a tune.

Carmela opened up. She was in a floral dress and had a measuring tape draped around her neck. "You?" she said, surprised.

"You still got it?" he asked, smiling. "That bottle of your father's wine?"

"You're remembering that now?" she said, smirking. "Tràsi," she said with a sigh, stepping aside so he could enter.

Carlo obeyed and she closed the door behind him. The whole shop fit into a neat and clean little room. Everything had its place: the sewing machine, the wooden workbench, the bare mannequin in the corner, the rolls of fabric stacked on the shelf, a tower of magazines, and various tools of the trade sorted according to function into a multitude of little boxes. Against the wall, opposite the workbench, was a glass table, recently shined, with a vase of flowers and flanked by two red velvet armchairs.

"Go on, have a seat," Carmela said, pointing to a chair. "Wait here while I get the wine." She disappeared through the door that led into her apartment and returned with a bottle and a crystal glass. She poured the wine and gave it to Carlo.

He took a sip, closed his eyes, and smacked his lips. "What a pleasure to the palate." He put the glass on the table. "How are you?" he asked.

Carmela shrugged and crossed her arms. "As you see me. Always working."

"Your husband? I met him, you know. Briefly, at Nando's bar. He seems like a good man."

"He is."

Carlo picked up his glass and took another sip. "Maybe he's a bit old for you, though, don't you think? What is he—fifty?"

"Almost. But what do you mean by that?" she said, annoyed.

"Nothing, nothing." Carlo raised his hand. "Actually, I didn't just come for the wine. I just—I need to speak to don Ciccio."

"With Papa? Why's that?"

"You know about the land my Uncle Luigi left me?"

"Of course I do. Everyone knows. What of it?"

"I have to do something with it, don't I? I was thinking about producing wine. I thought maybe your father could give me some advice."

She frowned. "You'll have to ask him directly. What would I have to do with it?"

Carlo looked at the glass and swished the wine. "Before I talk to him, I wanted to ask you if he was still angry with me. Whenever I run into him, he barely says hi. Maybe I'm imagining it, but . . ."

Carmela stared at him, unyielding. "You left years ago. We've moved on—our lives don't revolve around you."

There was a knock at the door and Carmela went to open it, revealing an elderly woman with sunken eyes and a protruding mole on her chin. Several men's coats were draped over her arm.

"Ah, donna Marta . . . tràsi," Carmela said, motioning for her to enter.

Carlo put the glass down and stood up. "Good morning, donna Marta. How are you?"

"Oh, I can't complain, thank the Lord," she answered. "And you? I saw your wife with the little 'un. What a lovely woman."

Carlo smiled, then shot an embarrassed look at Carmela. "Carlo is here because he wants me to sew a dress. But he was just leaving," she said quickly.

"Yes, right." He nodded awkwardly but played along nonetheless. "Well, I'll be back when it's ready."

Carmela walked him to the door.

"Goodbye, donna Marta," Carlo said. "Goodbye, Carmela," he added, looking her in the eyes.

"My best to your family," she said, then closed the door.

Carlo walked off, cutting through a cobblestone alley that led to don Ciccio's house, about a mile away. He skirted a tuff wall beyond which he could see the foliage of some oak trees, then walked through an archway leading to an opening where a few small houses with peeling façades encircled a stone well. Carlo knocked on a green double door and waited, rocking back and forth on his heels. When don Ciccio opened the door, he looked stunned. For a moment, he stared at Carlo with his jet-black eyes, just like Carmela's. He'd put on weight over the years, evidenced by the soft belly protruding from his shirt. Even so, his arms remained as powerful and toned as Carlo remembered. His nose, slightly flattened, was covered in small brown spots and his hair, once thick and wavy, was cut short and thinning at the temples.

"Good morning, don Ciccio," Carlo said, cheerfully.

"Good day," don Ciccio mumbled, frowning. "What is it?" He clearly wanted to get to the point.

Carlo awkwardly rubbed the back of his neck. "I was hoping we could have a word."

Don Ciccio opened the door all the way and invited Carlo in with a curt gesture. He turned and led him down a dark hallway.

"And how is your wife?" Carlo asked.

"Ask her yourself." Don Ciccio took the first door on the left and walked into the kitchen, lit only by a thin ray of sun filtering in through the window. There was a strong odor of garlic and turnip greens, which were frying in a pan. Two large, bright red tomato vines hung from a hook on the wall. Gina sat knitting by the unlit fireplace. A framed photo of Benito Mussolini in a helmet and uniform was displayed proudly on the shelf above her.

"Look who's here," said don Ciccio. Carlo thought he detected some sarcasm.

Gina perked up, got to her feet, and let her needles drop to the chair. "Carlo," she said meekly, "it's been so long."

"Lovely to see you, donna Gina," Carlo said, taking both her hands in his. "I hope you are well."

"As God wills," she said.

She hadn't lost her sweet smile, Carlo thought, looking at her dimples. And she still kept her hair in a bun, as she always had, even though it was white now. Yet her skin remained tense and compact. Carmela had inherited that from her.

Don Ciccio pulled up a chair and sat down, then invited Carlo to do the same.

"Make some coffee for our guest," he ordered his wife.

Carlo laced his fingers together over the table, then changed his mind and slipped them into his jacket pocket to pull out a cigar. "Do you mind if I smoke, don Ciccio?"

Don Ciccio shook his head and Carlo lit his cigar, unleashing a cloud of smoke. The smell of spice filled the room, mixing with the pungent odor of the turnip greens. In the silence that followed, Gina served the coffee on a silver tray, in the good china, then returned to her knitting. After taking his last sip from the espresso cup, don Ciccio asked again, "What is it?"

Carlo cleared his throat. "Well, as you know, my Uncle Luigi left me twenty-five acres of land, which he'd bought before getting sick. He didn't have time to do anything with it, so I've decided to cultivate it. I'd like to plant a vineyard."

Don Ciccio placed his cup on the tray and glanced at his wife, who looked up at him. He stared at Carlo and frowned. "This is why you have come?"

"Who can advise me better than you, with your experience? I've never had a wine as good as yours, not even up north. I'm asking you to teach me everything you know, don Ciccio. Like a father to a son."

Don Ciccio looked at him for a long time, then stood up slowly and took a pipe from the mantel, where it had been sitting next to Mussolini's photo. He lit a match and heated the tobacco in the chamber. Finally, he took a puff. "Like a son, you say?" he said, exhaling the smoke.

Gina looked up again and studied Carlo with her little blue eyes.

"No. I won't teach you like a son of mine," don Ciccio said. "But like the son of Pantaleo, God rest his soul. There was a time when you could have also become a son to me. But that time is gone."

"If I've offended you, I am sorry," Carlo mumbled.

Gina bowed her head and began to knit faster. Don Ciccio walked around the table and sat down again. "I'll do you this favor," he said, spreading his arms. "I will. But know that I only do this on account of the friendship that I had with your father."

Delighted, Carlo jumped up and shook his hand. "I am grateful to you," he said. "You can't imagine how much."

After walking Carlo to the door, don Ciccio trudged back into the kitchen and sat down. Gina was still knitting, but her face was contorted, and she waited to hear what don Ciccio would say.

"There was no need to use the good china," he said. "The last thing we should be doing is rolling out the red carpet for that one."

———

"I'm thinking of cultivating Uncle Luigi's land," Carlo told the whole family that evening as they gathered for dinner at Antonio and Agata's house. "Actually, I've been thinking about it for a while."

"And this is how you tell me?" Anna said.

Carlo brushed her hand and smiled. "I wanted to be sure before talking to you about it."

She looked down and continued to eat her meat pie.

"What do you want to plant?" Antonio asked, surprised.

"Vines. I want my own wine label, like what you did with olive oil. I could ship it all over Italy, even abroad, but with my name on it," Carlo explained, hitting himself on the chest. "The wine they make here always gets sent up north and blended with theirs. It's always been that way. But we could sell it already bottled—ours has nothing to envy of those wines from Veneto or Piedmont. I know what I'm talking about, I've had them. I know ours will be better. No one here has ever dared. But now it's time to think big."

Antonio considered this for a moment, then smiled. "Yes, I think it's a great idea, Carletto."

"Good on you," Agata added, with her mouth full.

"You seem very determined," Anna said, lifting an eyebrow.

"I am," said Carlo. "Just think, 'Greco Winery.'" He made a gesture with his hand. "It has a ring to it, doesn't it?"

"But what do you know about growing vines?" Anna asked.

"I'll get help," he said, then turned to his brother. "I've already asked don Ciccio."

"Oh, really?" Agata said, stunned.

"Who's don Ciccio?" asked Anna.

"Someone who knows wine," Carlo answered quickly. He shoved a forkful of pie in his mouth.

"I'm here for anything you need," Antonio said.

"I know. Thank you, big brother," Carlo said with a wink.

"I'm here, too," Anna said, after a few seconds. "I don't know anything about vineyards. But then, neither do you. We can learn together."

A silence fell. Carlo swallowed his mouthful of pie and cleared his throat. "Don't worry yourself, my love. There's no need."

"It almost sounds like you don't want my help," Anna snapped.

Antonio and Agata looked at each other.

"No, it's not that," Carlo hastened to say. "It's that I don't want you to do something just for the sake of it. Maybe next year you can go back to teaching. Someone will surely retire by then, no? Maybe in some nearby village, or whatnot. I mean, you're always saying how much you miss school."

"I miss working. It's different," she said, vexed. "And anyway, no. At the moment, there are no openings. You know this."

Carlo sighed, put down his fork, and took her hand in his. "You have to take the time to figure out what else you want to do. Something that suits you, though. That you're passionate about. There's no rush." He kissed the back of her hand.

Antonio opened his mouth to say something, then immediately shut it.

———

The Fiat 508 Balilla, with its velvet interior and bodywork shining in the sun, zipped down the small country road at fifty miles an hour, headed for the Great Oak Tree that stood just outside Pisignano, the next town over from Lizzanello. With his foot on the accelerator and an unlit cigar in hand, Carlo was whistling a tune he'd composed on the spot.

Antonio sat paralyzed with fear in the seat next to him. "Slow down," he kept saying, clasping the door handle with both hands.

But Carlo wasn't listening. He'd wanted a car for too long. That morning, November 29, the day of his thirty-first birthday, he'd flung himself out of bed driven only by the thought of picking up his 508. He'd wanted to give himself an important gift now that he didn't have to worry about money: He withdrew 10,800 lira from his postal savings account and bought the car of his dreams without hesitation. It was the one everyone had been talking about, the one with the ad looming large in all the papers. *No longer on foot*, it said.

He'd opted for the Berlina model, with four seats and two doors, and chosen the color green because it belonged to Anna, to her eyes and her basil, even though she still didn't suspect a thing about this coup de folie, as she would no doubt call it.

He downshifted when he glimpsed the majestic, enveloping mane of the Great Oak Tree—the strongest and most ancient tree in the area— beyond the bend at the drystone wall. When he and his brother were children, their father took them there every Sunday morning. The three of them would sit on the ground with their backs against the thick trunk. Pantaleo would pull two oranges or peaches from his pockets, depending on the season, and give one to each child for breakfast. As the boys bit into their fruit, moistening their lips and fingers, their father would tell one of his tales. His favorite was the legend of the oak tree—they'd heard it countless times.

Carlo parked, and they got out of the car and sat on the soft earth, leaning their backs against the tree, like when they were young. Carlo looked up at the sky and took a few puffs from his cigar, silently. The smoke got caught in the thick leaves above, which seemed to suck it up. "Do you remember the story of the oak?" he asked his brother.

"Of course I remember," Antonio said. He started to recount it, imitating his father's booming voice and using the same words he had: "People had long believed the oak to be cursed because it was the only tree in all the realm to offer up its wood to build the cross on which Jesus died."

Carlo laughed. "You sound just like him!"

Antonio smiled and continued, gesticulating. "Its honor was only restored after many centuries. Saint Francis said, No, the oak is no traitor, as everyone thinks; rather, it was the only tree that knew it had to sacrifice itself for redemption, just like Jesus."

Carlo shook his head in amusement and recited the ending in unison with his brother: "After that, it became such a sacred tree that many Italian cities started to vie for its name. Lecce, formerly Lupiae, won out; that's why the city's coat of arms depicts a wolf under a holm oak tree."

They laughed heartily, surprised at how well they remembered their father's words.

Carlo took another puff from his cigar and closed his eyes. He didn't open them until he sensed something hovering in front of his face: Antonio was holding out an orange by the stem, pinching it between his thumb and forefinger.

"It may not be as good as Papa's, but happy birthday, Carletto."

Carlo beamed, as if he'd just received the most precious gift in the world. When he wasn't clerking at the town hall, Pantaleo tended to an orchard he'd carved out of the small stretch of land behind his house. He had trees of all types: orange, lemon, peach, pomegranate, apricot, fig, almond. It was considered one of the most luscious and colorful orchards in town. Carlo and Antonio had a fantastic time frolicking among the trees, playing tag; when one of them wanted to climb up a branch, the other would act as the ladder. For Pantaleo it was a joy to watch them both, trees and children; he loved them in the same way.

All the love coursing through his body and soul for Ada, the woman he'd married, the mother of his children, had run dry when she left him. Not that she really went anywhere; her body was still there, lying in bed at night and curled up in a chair by day. But something in her mind had been extinguished forever after Carlo's birth. It had been a difficult birth—he just wouldn't get into position—so they'd squeezed her, pushed her, cut her, and sewn her up. Tortured her. That day, they ripped the child from her body and her smile along with it—and it had never returned.

In the days when the Tramontane blew from the north, Antonio would tuck her in and warm her muff by the fire. When it was nice and toasty, he'd carefully wrap it around her freezing hands. Carlo watched his brother's loving attentions through a crack in the door, feeling at once relieved and envious of something he could never do: warm to the sight of his mother, to him a broken and empty woman. He couldn't help but blame her for her condition—he wanted to shake her and push her off that blasted armchair. Burn all the armchairs in the house. He never did forgive her, not even after she gave up once and for all, when the effort of living had become unbearable. Relentlessly in his mind he crushed her, crumpled her, balled her up into a formless mass of frizzy white hair and swollen ankles.

Sure, his father had been there to make up for the lack of motherly love, but it had mostly been Antonio who stood in for their mother. Antonio protected him, held and hugged him every day of his life, even though he was just four years older than Carlo. He was just a child too, a little man with kind eyes who cried only at night, alone and silently, hiding his head under his pillow. Carlo could hear him anyway but had never told him so.

Carlo peeled the orange and tossed the rind on the ground in front of him. He split the fruit in half and handed one part to Antonio.

He bit into a wedge and started to chuckle with his mouth full.

"What is it?" asked Antonio.

"Can you imagine? The son of a teetotaler. Making wine."

Antonio smiled. "Well, maybe that's exactly why you decided to do it."

"Revenge for all those times Papa forbade me to drink?"

"No, just to show him he was wrong."

"Then I'll make the best wine in the world," Carlo said, standing up. "A wine that even he would have liked."

He grabbed Antonio's hand and helped him up. "Do you want to try and drive back?" he asked, heading toward the car.

"Heavens, no," Antonio said, raising his hand. "It's not my thing."

———

Anna was reluctantly preparing dessert for Carlo's birthday. The last cake she'd baked was her beloved chestnut cake, her grandmother's recipe, and it had been for Claudia, when she'd turned three months old.

Lorenza had twisted her arm. She'd insisted they have a proper celebration, excited by the idea of coming together for the first time. In the end, Anna had indulged her. In this way, she thought, Lorenza was just like Agata; she could hound you until she got you to say yes. So with some effort, Anna procured two pounds of chestnut flour, some raisins, and pine nuts, and that morning, as soon as Carlo had catapulted out of bed—God knows where he'd gone in such a hurry, without even waiting to have coffee with her—cleared the kitchen table, put on her apron, gathered her hair in a silk headscarf, and pushed up the sleeves on her black dress.

She was kneading the dough when she heard a car horn start to honk incessantly. Hands covered in sticky dough, she went to the door and opened it. "Who's causing all that racket?" she shouted.

Carlo was leaning against his car, arms folded, face beaming.

Anna circled it, studying it in silence. "Well, yes. I like the color," she said in the end. "I don't even want to know how much you paid for it." But she was smiling.

Antonio, still sitting in the car, saw that Anna had flour on her chin and lower lip and felt the impulse to take her face in his hands and clean it with a kiss. The scene unfolding in his head suddenly became real when Carlo brought his face to Anna's and, with slow kisses, licked the flour from her lips. "I can't wait to taste the cake," he whispered in her ear.

"I'm heading home," Antonio blurted out, getting out of the car.

"Wait, I'll come with you," Carlo said, surprised.

"It's fine. I'm just around the corner," Antonio responded. "See you tonight," he said, almost running away.

———

It had been ten years since Carlo last celebrated a birthday in his hometown. He wanted to go overboard that night. He invited a bunch of people he'd run into in recent days: old friends, acquaintances, and even a few strangers. He ordered five gallons of red wine from the local winery and commissioned refreshments from the trattoria. "Make whatever you want," he'd told the chef. "As long as there's a lot of it."

Antonio and Agata were the first to arrive. For the occasion, she sported a burgundy suit with gold-plated buttons and wore her auburn hair in a little bun. Her lipstick matched her outfit and highlighted all the creases in her lips. Her earlobes hung down low because of the heavy gold earrings she was proudly showing off. Lorenza ran ahead of her parents and rushed up to Anna, who was wearing a black dress, even on a night like this one.

"No hug for me?" Carlo asked, tickling his niece's sides. "You know, I'm the birthday boy here." Lorenza wiggled away, giggling, got on her tippy-toes, and planted a kiss on her uncle's smooth, mint-scented cheek.

Before long, the whole town had flooded into the house. It was as if some invisible force had been standing in the way of this gathering and had finally stepped aside, unleashing a surge of people, kissing, hugging, shaking hands, and patting one another on the back. The men were taking off their hats and kissing Anna's hand, while the women pecked her cheeks. Needing a break from it all, Anna went to the gramophone and put on a song she liked very much: "Parlami d'amore Mariù." She stood there listening for a few moments, unmoving, with her back to the room of noisy people; she really wasn't used to all these manifestations of enthusiasm, but this was Carlo's day, and she didn't want to ruin it by sulking. She sighed, gathered her resolve, and turned back toward the crowd.

The olivewood table in the middle of the room was fully laden with food and jugs of wine. Agata and Lorenza were running back and forth to the kitchen, making sure nothing was missing. Carlo, with a cigar in his mouth and a glass in hand, was inviting all new arrivals to help themselves.

Anna watched him for a few moments. It wasn't unusual for her Carlo to be as bubbly as a newly uncorked bottle. It was something she'd loved about him since first meeting him. During their courtship, she could hardly get across an alley, those steep ones they had in Pigna, without him jumping out in front of her at every corner, like an illusionist. "Miss, are you following me?" he would say, teasing, even though it was obvious that the opposite was true. "You're quite persistent, don't you think?"

Anna would shake her head, amused, and continue on her way, knowing that he would do it again at the next corner. She'd fallen in love with his cheer, his spontaneity, his carefree approach to life. She'd grown up in a strict family, surrounded by cautious, rational people who were perfectly acquainted with the fashionable rules of the bon ton but who didn't know how to say *I love you*. Her parents had died without ever saying those words to her.

As the song came to an end, Anna approached the table, poured herself a drink, and went out to the garden for some peace. She sat on the bench, sighed, and in the quiet, closed her eyes and breathed in the scent of basil.

Antonio was the only person to notice her absence. He excused himself quickly from the father of one of Lorenza's classmates and joined Anna outside.

"How are you?" he asked, coming up behind her.

As he approached slowly, Anna twirled around. He stood there with his hands in his pockets.

She shrugged. "Like a fish out of water. That's how."

Antonio gripped the back of the bench.

"I used to know exactly who I was," she continued. "I had my job, my pupils, my haunts. My life, in short. But now . . . I don't even understand what people are saying."

"There's nothing wrong with that," Antonio said. "People say such foolish things."

Anna half smiled.

"But I'm sorry you feel that way," Antonio added.

They were silent for a few seconds, and then Anna spoke up. "I don't have anything new to read," she said.

"Well, that's easily solved. The library is fairly well stocked. I could take you there, if you'd like."

"Yes, I would love that," she said. She stood up and realized that Antonio's shirt collar was half up; as if it were the most natural gesture in the world, she reached out and adjusted it. "There you go," she said, pleased. "Come on, let's go back inside."

Nearly speechless, Antonio mumbled thanks. Anna's slender fingers had brushed the skin on his neck, causing him to tremble. A sort of disquiet gripped his insides. He avoided Anna's gaze for the rest of the night. When, amid applause and birthday toasts, Carlo cut the chestnut cake and bit into it with gusto, putting his arm around Anna's waist and thanking her for the cake with a kiss, Antonio quietly slipped out to the garden, sat on the bench, and gazed up at the stars.

———

The party ended in the dead of night—so late that at one point, Lorenza fell asleep on the couch and no one saw the need to wake her. Antonio and Agata left her there and walked home alone—he in silence and she in her faded lipstick, all the while complaining about having to go back and forth to the kitchen while Anna was busy having fun.

"I'll be up shortly," Antonio said, once they were home. In the semidarkness of the living room, he removed the cork from a long-necked bottle of grappa, fastened his lips to the opening, and drank in big gulps until the burning sensation of the alcohol invaded his chest and a bout of coughing shook his body. He put the bottle down and went upstairs. He slowly opened the door to the main bedroom, stripped naked, left his clothes on the floor, and got into bed. Agata was sleeping on her side. He lowered her panties. "What are you doing?" she murmured, waking up.

"Turn around," he ordered. She obeyed without protestation. He took her with his eyes closed, without looking at her, covering her mouth with his hand.

4

Agata made her big announcement during dinner that Christmas Eve. Everyone was sitting around the table, ready to raise their glasses and make the first toast of the night, when she said God had once again given her the greatest joy: She was pregnant.

From the bewildered expression on Antonio's face and his tense demeanor, it was clear that this was news to him, too.

"And you're sure?" he managed to ask, faintly.

"The doctor says I am," Agata said with tears in her eyes.

Carlo stood up and went over to congratulate her. "I'm very happy for you," he said, with a kiss on the cheek. Anna leaned forward and reached over to her from across the table. "What great news," she said, squeezing Agata's hand.

"Did you hear that, Lorenza?" Agata said, turning to her daughter, who was looking back at her in confusion. "You're going to have a little brother or sister," she explained, touching her stomach. Lorenza lit up and gave her mother a big hug, telling her how happy she was—actually overjoyed! Then she turned to see her father's reaction; he still hadn't budged an inch, as if a spell had turned him into a statue.

The memory, all too close now, of Agata's first pregnancy had paralyzed him. They had been nine never-ending, suffocating months with Agata constantly in tears, fearful of everything, either of staying home alone or of leaving the house to go grocery shopping unless someone went with her. It had been hell. Each night she struggled to fall asleep, and the days were filled with a litany of complaints because of the lack of rest. Antonio had had to watch his tongue; it took nothing to make her lose her temper. How was he going to survive it all over again, especially now that Agata wasn't so young anymore? It had been difficult nine years ago when she was pregnant, and now she was thirty-five.

"And you, Antonio?" Agata asked, sounding uncertain. "You look like a ghost." She looked at Carlo and Anna in embarrassment.

Anna and Carlo exchanged glances.

"Papa, aren't you glad?" Lorenza urged him, looking worried. "Say something."

"Yes," Antonio stammered. "Yes, of course I'm glad."

"He's so happy he can hardly speak," Carlo said, trying to defuse the situation.

Agata relaxed. "That's what it is?" she asked him, softening her gaze.

Antonio finally stood up, went to Agata, crouched next to her, and gently kissed her soft belly. No one seemed to notice the mechanical nature of his movements, as if he were following a script.

She stroked his hair. "I hope it's a boy this time," she said.

Anna raised an eyebrow but remained silent.

———

Agata lost the baby at the stroke of the third month, at the end of January.

When Antonio found her doubled over on the stairs, her nightgown soaked in blood, he understood that his wife's womb was once again empty. And from the depths of his heart, he felt relief.

When she got home from the hospital, Agata climbed into bed, clasping her silver rosary, and didn't get up for three weeks. She barely spoke, save for a mumbled prayer every now and then. She knew that this had been her last chance to become a mother again. She just wasn't ready to accept it.

Lorenza would come home from school, cross the dark, silent rooms of the house, enter the bedroom, and lie down next to her mother, who would turn the other way, listless. When Antonio returned from the oil mill for lunch or dinner, he would look in and ask if she needed anything. Agata always shook her head no and pulled her blanket up to her hairline. He would put something to eat on the nightstand with a jug of water, but she would barely touch it.

"Auntie, can you do something, please?" Lorenza begged Anna one afternoon. She'd ventured the few hundred feet that separated her home from that of her aunt and uncle, alone, to knock on their door. Anna lifted her onto her lap and hugged her for a long time, promising to help. Before then, she'd visited Agata a few times, only to be ignored. So she'd stopped going—seeing her sister-in-law like that reminded her of herself after Claudia's death: shrouded in her own pain, indifferent to the world. She understood Agata, but it hurt to see her like that.

But then there she was, early the next morning, striking the door-knocker at Agata and Antonio's house. In one arm she clasped Roberto and in the other a copy of *Wuthering Heights*. Antonio opened the door in pajamas and with disheveled hair.

"How is she?" Anna asked.

He shrugged and pursed his lips.

"I see," she said, cutting him short. "Go to work. I'll stay with her."

She went upstairs and gently opened the door to the main bedroom, allowing some light to filter in. She placed the book on the dresser and, still holding Roberto, parted the heavy curtains. Agata opened her eyes and closed them again instantly, irritated by the sunlight.

Anna placed Roberto on the armchair, picked up the book, and dragged a seat to the bed. "I know you're awake," she said.

Agata didn't answer.

Anna rested the book on her knees, opened it to the first page, and started to read aloud: "'I have just returned from a visit to my landlord—

the solitary neighbor that I shall be troubled with. This is certainly a beautiful country! In all England, I do not believe that I could have fixed on a situation so completely removed from the stir of society.'"

She didn't stop reading until lunchtime, and then she closed the book.

"Is it over?" Agata asked meekly, finally opening her eyes.

Anna smiled. "For today, yes. We'll continue tomorrow."

She returned the next morning and then every day for the following two weeks, taking care of the family.

She made lunch for Lorenza and fed some to Agata patiently. She took handfuls of Nivea cream from a blue metal container and rubbed it over the dry skin on Agata's hands, insisting on her cuticles. A few times she even forced Agata to stand up so she could wash her hair.

"Then you can go back to bed," Anna assured her.

Whenever Agata nodded off, Anna would put the book back on the dresser and quietly leave the room, keeping the door ajar. She'd stretch her back and go downstairs to make herself some coffee. She sipped it slowly, walking around the house. She tried to imagine Carlo as a child, napping on the green couch, playing on the rug, or running cheerfully from the kitchen to the living room. *He must have been such a troublemaker,* she thought, amused. She stared at the armchair by the window, where Antonio sat and where their mother had once spent her days. Carlo hardly ever spoke of her. Whenever Anna brought her up, he mumbled a few words and changed the subject. All she knew was that his mother had been absent yet cumbersome, and that upon her death, Carlo hadn't suffered all that much. Or at least, that was what he said.

Anna would sometimes make her way toward Antonio's study, but she would stop, every time, before the closed door. Her curiosity to go inside was strong, but she held back and thought of what her mother would have said: *It would be very rude to go in without permission.*

But one morning she found the door open, maybe because of an oversight on Antonio's part. She went in, treading slowly, and looked around. One wall was completely covered by a wooden bookcase, chock-full of titles. In slight disbelief, she wondered whether Antonio really could have read them all. Opposite that was a blue velvet couch and a low glass coffee table with a cup and a bottle of water. The center of the room was taken up by an elegant mahogany desk and a chair with a red cushion.

Anna sat on the edge of the seat and tentatively stroked the objects on the desk: a gold-plated fountain pen and a novel she'd never heard of: *Fathers and Sons* by Ivan Turgenev. *Another Russian*, she thought, affectionately. Next to it was an open notebook containing some neat, elegant handwriting. She leaned in to read the sentences Antonio had transcribed, probably from that novel: *Nihilists do not bend before authority nor do they accept a principle just because others might obey it*, and under that, *They were both silent, but the way in which they were silent, in which they sat together, showed an intimate complicity.* Anna reached out and touched a silver frame containing a black-and-white photo of Carlo and Antonio as children, dressed like little sailors. She smiled and brought a hand to her heart: In the photo, Antonio was serious and poised, while Carlo, standing next to him, was looking into the camera with a cheeky grin. *They haven't changed*, she thought, smiling.

———

One morning, as Anna was reading *Wuthering Heights* aloud, Agata interrupted her.

"What happened to Claudia?" she asked.

Anna felt a knot tighten in her throat. She looked up from the page and stared at her sister-in-law. Then she closed the book.

"She went in her sleep," she said flatly. "An inexplicable death, is what the doctor said."

Agata rose to a seating position and clasped her hands together.

"She was fine until the night before," Anna continued. "I gave her a bath. We played with the soap bubbles. I sang her a lullaby, and she fell asleep peacefully, in her crib, with her pink wool blanket. The next morning, she was gone." Anna looked up to hold back her tears.

She didn't say how much she'd blamed herself, certain that she'd caused Claudia's death by some oversight. She'd gone over every moment of that night, but the truth and imagined reasons had mingled together, creating a sort of impenetrable fog. Was it the bath? Was the water too hot or too cold? But no, she was certain she'd tested it with her elbow. Or maybe she hadn't burped Claudia after her last feeding? She really thought she had. Had the baby hit her little head somewhere without Anna noticing? But she hadn't cried that day or complained of anything.

"Poor thing," Agata said, patting Anna's hand. "You and I are united by the same grief now."

Anna opened her mouth to speak but didn't say a thing.

———

The forty thousand vine shoots Carlo had ordered arrived in early January: thirty-five thousand of the niuru maru variety and five thousand of black malvasia from the Brindisi area. The system of rows and poles was ready, set up according to don Ciccio's instructions. When Carlo had taken him to see the land for the first time, the day after visiting him, don Ciccio had put his hands on his hips and looked around, then out to the horizon. He'd launched into a lecture about how Carlo needed to design a system that could accommodate up to four thousand vines per hectare, if he did things right. He explained that the distance between the rows had to be at least eight feet, nine at the most, and took three strides to illustrate his point. But when he saw Carlo taking down everything in a black notebook like a diligent student, don Ciccio chuckled.

"What are you writing that for! I'll send you the skilled workers. These guys already know what to do."

So that was how Carlo came to hire some twenty farmers, most of whom had worked for don Ciccio before. They were clearly used to working hard. In just two months, they plotted the rows, arranged the wooden stakes, and tied the wiring. Meanwhile, Carlo had commissioned a sign that read GRECO WINERY from a painter with a small shop in Lecce. The writing was in elegant cursive, white on an olivewood panel. When he'd shown it to don Ciccio, full of pride, the old man had smirked.

"Those are just frills," he'd said. Carlo had been disappointed but had held his tongue.

After the bundles of shoots arrived, carried in on wide wagons, it was finally time to bed out the vines. Don Ciccio had been clear: The best time to plant them was between fall and late winter, in the resting season. During that time, don Ciccio came to the vineyard every morning to check on progress—it was the most delicate phase. He would wander through the rows with his hands behind his back, on high alert, occasionally rebuking someone. "No, this hole is no good," he'd say. "It has to be at least a foot and a half wide."

"But it is a foot and a half," the laborer would answer.

"Measure it. That's not even a foot long." And every time the farmers would see that don Ciccio was right.

Carlo stayed glued to him throughout the process, trying to learn as much as possible. But without his notebook this time.

Once all of the shoots had been planted, don Ciccio gazed at the vineyard with satisfaction.

"If all goes well, you'll see the first grapes in two years. Three at the most," he said.

"What do you mean, three years?" Carlo exclaimed in disbelief. "That many? I thought we'd be doing the first harvest next year."

Don Ciccio burst out laughing. "Yeah, right, next year. Forget about it!" he said, waving his hand. "Be patient. The shoots must follow their own cycle to become the vines you imagine. You've always wanted everything right away, you."

Carlo shot him a piqued look but was forced to swallow his disappointment; he needed don Ciccio, so and for the time being, he had to bite his tongue, even though the old man's attitude was really starting to grate on him.

"Now you have to let them grow free, without interfering," don Ciccio said. "Next winter we can start talking about the first pruning. In the meantime, you build the winery."

———

Carmela woke up from the cold. She curled onto her side and blew on her hands to warm them up. Next to her, Nicola was still sound asleep—she could tell from his heavy, raspy breathing. She reached over to the nightstand and spun the little clock to face her: it was seven A.M. and the alarm wouldn't go off until eight A.M. She decided to get up, knowing she wouldn't be able to fall back asleep anyway. She might as well get some work done, she told herself. She could hardly keep up with it all: mending and taking in all the coats being handed down from father to son, hemming flannel pants, sewing wool dresses and outfits, repairing torn quilts. She'd been working tirelessly for weeks.

As if that weren't enough, that morning she had to personally deliver Mrs. Tamburini's garments. Between walking over there, doing the fittings, and walking back, the whole thing would take up more than an hour of Carmela's time. But Mrs. Tamburini was her wealthiest client, and she couldn't possibly refuse her. The lady preferred to try her clothes on in the comfort of her own bedroom, heated by the fireplace, rather than within the damp walls of the dressmaker's shop.

After washing, getting dressed, and spraying jasmine perfume behind her ears—a perfume she made herself by soaking petals in a solution of alcohol and purified water—Carmela went to wake her son Daniele with a kiss on the forehead. She reminded him not to fall asleep again, or he'd be late for school.

Nicola opened the bedroom door and joined his wife in the living room. He was wearing blue worsted wool pajamas, and the buttons on the shirt were straining against his prominent gut. Carmela thought that if he got any bigger, she'd have to sew him new pajamas. Nicola was twenty years older than she—in about six months he'd turn fifty—and the age difference was hard to miss. His bald spot was growing larger by the day—when she'd married him almost eleven years before, he still had hair. At least, that was what she remembered, anyway.

"Leaving already?" he asked.

Carmela put on her coat and scooped out the hair caught under her collar. Her head hurt from lack of sleep and if she'd pinned her hair back the pain would only have gotten worse; she decided to leave it down for the day.

"I have to take these garments to the Tamburinis," she said hastily. "Go see if Daniele fell back asleep, as he does."

With five hangers hooked to her finger, all holding women's suits enclosed in tissue paper, Carmela set off at a brisk pace.

The Tamburinis lived in a villa just outside town. To get there, Carmela had to cut through via Paladini, the street where she'd grown up, right across from the house that now belonged to Antonio. She found herself walking past Carlo and Anna's house. Before turning right, she slowed her pace. The Fiat 508 was parked in front of the gate, and the windows were still closed with the curtains shut. She stopped for a moment and looked up at the main bedroom window. She remembered the house perfectly, as if she'd been there yesterday. As children, she, Carlo, and Antonio would go into the kitchen every afternoon for a snack. Uncle Luigi always welcomed them with a table full of delicacies, prepared especially for them: quince cakes, almond biscuits, fresh bread with orange and mandarin marmalade. And while they ate heartily, Uncle Luigi would sit there, walking stick in hand, watching them, pleased.

Carmela had always thought that one day she and Carlo would live in that house together, assuming it would be left to him. That she would become a lady, rather than wear her eyes out on needle and thread.

She imagined that beyond the window on the second floor, Carlo and Anna were still sleeping, locked in an embrace. *If it hadn't been for that woman*, she thought. *She* would be the one there, lying next to Carlo. And the room at the end of the hallway, where Carlo and Antonio would sometimes stay overnight, would be Daniele's room. They could have been a family. If only Anna hadn't gotten in the way.

The memory of that wretched letter still stung. It had taken Carlo three long pages to confess that he'd met another woman—her name was Anna—and that his heart now belonged to her. It had been sudden, as if he'd been struck by lightning—that was what he'd written. And he'd asked Carmella to stop waiting for him, because it wouldn't be right. If there was one thing Carmela didn't lack, it was pride, so Carlo's letter, which she'd never answered, had ended up in the fireplace, in flames. She would have died before letting anyone see that she'd been discarded. And while pregnant, for that matter. The only time with Carlo had been two months before, when he'd come to be a witness at Antonio's wedding. It had been a mistake for them to get together that night. But what did she know, then, about the true nature of men? She thought Carlo would return and lead her to the altar. He'd promised as much that weekend, looking into her eyes, a moment before getting on the bus that took him away again.

Watching the letter burn, with tears of rage and salt, Carmela had sworn to herself that Carlo would never know. He didn't deserve that child. Don Ciccio had settled the "incident," as her parents called it, and hastily arranged her marriage to Nicola Carlà, one of the many suitors asking for her hand. He'd chosen Nicola because he was older and seemed like the dumbest one—they could pull the wool over his eyes with impunity. Carmela had no choice but to accept the shotgun wedding without complaint. "That's how it has to be if you don't want to end up ruined," don Ciccio had said. When she'd shed a tear at the thought of marrying a man so much older than she, Gina had reassured her.

"It's six of one and half a dozen of the other, dear," she'd said, placing a hand on her shoulder. "They're all the same in the end, them masculi."

Suddenly, the bedroom curtains parted and Carmela glimpsed Carlo's outline through the window. Startled, she walked away quickly, her heels clicking on the cobblestones.

5

The librarian was a kind man with thinning hair and a gentle face. Anna thanked him and walked toward the exit, clasping a large volume of *Les Misérables* by Victor Hugo and a thinner one of *Dead Souls* by Nikolai Gogol. The first she had been wanting to read for a while, though, she thought with a sigh, it was a shame they didn't have it in French. The second was obviously Antonio's recommendation.

"It's cruel and funny at the same time. I'd really like to know what you think," he'd said. Him and his Russian writers. Anna had asked him why he liked them so much. Antonio had said that they were the best, not only at describing human suffering but also at showing compassion for it.

"They make you feel like you're not wrong, just human."

As Anna took the road home, already savoring the hours she'd spend reading on the bench in her jardin secret, especially now that the days were warm and fragrant again, she noticed a commotion coming from a small crowd gathered outside Bar Castello.

She walked up to a robust young man who was waving his stained black hands in the air.

"What's going on?" she asked. The young man spun around to look at her, his eyes wide open and his unibrow deeply furrowed. It was Mario, the shoeshine. Or, rather, Mario the *gossip*, as he was known.

"Ferruccio died," he said.

"Who's Ferruccio?"

"What do you mean, who? The letter carrier," he answered, baffled.

"He was taken by a nasty bronchitis," someone remarked.

Ferruccio. Right, she remembered. She'd seen him around a few times, walking in his uniform and with a mailbag slung over his shoulder. Anna shrugged and walked off without saying goodbye.

———

She didn't think about Ferruccio again until two days later. With some effort, she'd convinced Agata, who was feeling slightly better, to go grocery shopping with her. They'd just come out of the greengrocer's when Anna saw an ad posted on the wooden noticeboard by the great palm in Piazza Castello. JOB OFFER, it said in block letters in the middle of a white page.

"Hold on a moment," Anna said as she approached the board. Agata reluctantly joined her and started to read aloud.

April 20, 1935

Due to the tragic, premature passing of our beloved countryman Ferruccio Pisanello, the Royal Post Office calls for applications for the selection of a new letter carrier. For more information, come to the post office.

"They're already looking for a new letter carrier," Anna remarked.

Her sister-in-law nodded absently.

"Yes. But let's go now," she said, pulling Anna by the arm. "We still have to go to the milkman."

———

Winter hadn't been as rainy as Carlo had hoped, so he'd had to keep hiring day laborers to water the shoots. Even so, by spring, when the vines started to fill up with green sprouts, he could barely contain his excitement.

"They took root," don Ciccio declared, looking around with his hands on his hips, as was his custom. "You were lucky."

"I followed your advice," Carlo said.

"Then you also did a good job," he chuckled. "Now be careful, don't mess with it," don Ciccio warned. "Remember what I said: Avoid pruning in the first year."

Sure, there were those who did it, he explained. During vegetative regeneration many doubled down on the shears, but he didn't agree with that method in the least. One shouldn't bother the shoots too much.

"Now take me home. I'm tired and my back is hurting," he said suddenly as he headed toward the car.

They got back in the 508 and drove to don Ciccio's house in silence.

"Wait, let me help you get out," Carlo said, after parking in the clearing by the stone well. As don Ciccio exited the car, holding on to Carlo's arm, Carmela came out of the house. She was as elegant and neat as ever, with her hair up in a bun from which a few strands fell loosely over her cheek. Her nails were painted red.

"Hi," she said.

Carlo answered with a smile and walked don Ciccio to the door.

Carmela pressed her lips to her father's cheek and advised him to lie down for a bit, that he'd already tired himself out too much for one day.

"Sorry, that was my fault," Carlo remarked, once they were alone.

Carmela shot him a look of fake reproach.

"How are you?" he asked.

"Busy. It's wedding season."

"I hope your husband isn't feeling too neglected."

"Why should he? It's more money for the family."

"And how is your son? I saw him around town with his father. He looks just like you when you were a little girl."

Carmela looked down and curled her lips.

"Right," she murmured. "Anyway, he's fine too." She tucked a rebel lock behind her ear.

In the silence that followed, Carlo found himself staring at that lock as if bewitched. Yes, time had not weathered Carmela's beauty; on the contrary. It was clear she was now aware of the effect she had on men, which made her even more attractive.

He roused himself, cleared his throat, and smoothed out his jacket.

"I better go," he said, then headed toward the car.

Unperturbed, Carmela watched him get in, start the car, and drive off in a hurry. *As if he were trying to escape a gathering storm,* she thought. She couldn't hold back a smile.

———

Anna came home with two raffia bags overflowing with food. This always happened whenever she went grocery shopping with Agata. By dint of *And try this,* or *Sample this other thing,* she ended up buying much more than what she needed. With a sigh, she placed the bags on the kitchen table and opened the door to her *jardin secret;* she went to the bench and sat down for a moment, time enough to catch her breath. The first tentative buds on the pomegranate branches were about to bloom. Soon the garden would be full of colors again, like the first time she'd seen it.

"Look, Mama's back!" Carlo exclaimed, coming out to join her. He placed Roberto in her arms, then bent over and planted a kiss on her lips. "I have to go to the winery. They're still digging the basins, down below, and they're being a bit slow, quite frankly. Don't wait for me. Go ahead and have lunch, if you're hungry."

After Carlo left, Anna clutched Roberto tightly and sighed again. Ever since Carlo had thrown himself into the vineyard venture, she saw him little and almost always in passing. And the winery had made things worse, not just because the ruins Carlo had bought for a handful of lira required a superhuman amount of work but because she'd been cut out of that, too. She hadn't even *seen* it yet.

"I'll take you when it's finished," Carlo kept promising.

She often had lunch without him and would spend hours alone, hours that seemed interminable. Sure, she had Roberto to take care of, and she had her books to keep her company, but it wasn't enough. It had never been enough. It was hard, and she also resented that Carlo didn't want to involve her in any way, as he was fiercely protective of the entire project. He knew when he married her that she wasn't cut out for the wife-and-mother routine. She needed to work, to feel that there was more to her than house and home. All she wanted was to lend a hand while she waited for a chance to come—maybe a teaching post would become available sometime soon. But Carlo seemed to be ignoring her needs completely. She stared intently at the pomegranate buds and thought back to the post office job notice. Then her frown slowly morphed into a smile. She gave her son a little peck on the cheek and stood up from the bench. She placed him in the stroller and glanced at the bags on the table, not yet unpacked. She told herself she'd take care of them later. Now she had to take care of herself. She pushed the stroller out the door and left the house.

She walked to the square, where the post office stood a few steps away from Bar Castello, and stopped in front of the large door, which was half open. A sign with the opening hours read:

FROM 8 A.M. TO 2 P.M.

FROM 3 P.M. TO 7 P.M.

Anna pushed the stroller in and said, "Good morning."

The entire office seemed to be crammed into a single room. There was a table in the middle, two desks—one with a typewriter—a few chests of drawers, a filing cabinet, a bulletin board, a locker, and in the back, a closed door.

"Good morning," said a man sitting at a desk. He was a stocky guy with olive skin, marked features, and a thick beard. "How can I help you?"

"I read the announcement on the bulletin board," Anna replied. "You're looking for a letter carrier, right?"

"Yes, ma'am. Are you interested for your husband?"

Anna lifted an eyebrow. "No, actually I'm interested for me."

The man gave her an amused look.

"How can I participate in the selection process?" Anna continued, in all seriousness.

The man chuckled.

"You find this funny?" she said, scowling.

"Very," he responded. He stood up, opened a drawer, and took out a piece of paper, which he handed to her.

"Here's the list of what we need," he said cheerfully. "It's a title contest. Do you know what that means?"

She glared at him and grabbed the piece of paper. "Of course I do."

The man smirked and went to sit back down behind the desk.

Anna quickly scanned the list of documents she'd have to hand in: birth certificate, criminal record, certificate of good conduct, school transcripts.

As she read, a man emerged from the door at the back.

"Good morning," he said amiably. She looked up at the sound of his voice. "Do you need help?" He was young, in his thirties, with curly hair, crystal-blue eyes, and a kind, chubby face.

"I'm all set, thank you," she answered.

"The missus wants to participate in the letter carrier contest," the man at the desk interrupted, without hiding his sarcasm.

"Very good," said the man with the kind face, a little surprised. "I'm Tommaso De Santis, the director," he said, extending his hand.

She shook it. "Anna Allavena."

"Has Carmine already explained everything?" he asked.

"He gave me this," said Anna, holding up the piece of paper.

Tommaso nodded. "Exactly. When you have all your documents ready, bring them back here." He smiled at her. "You have until May fourteenth to apply."

"Thank you," said Anna, but she didn't move. She stared at the list of documents again, then looked up at the director and said, "Do you have a pen and paper? I have to send some requests, apparently. I'd best do it right away. They have to get to Pigna, in Liguria." She shot a daring glance at Carmine.

Taken by surprise, Tommaso mumbled, "Yes. Pen and paper. Of course." He went to get them from his desk and handed them to Anna.

Finally, she smiled back at him.

———

When Anna opened her eyes the morning of May thirteenth, she didn't immediately remember what day it was. She realized it only later, after watering the basil plants and as she drank her warm milk on the bench in her jardin secret. But the thought only served to annoy her. She'd never liked her birthday, never mind celebrated it. It had always been that way, even when she was a girl. Her parents would throw a party and invite her grandparents, aunts, uncles, and cousins, but she'd hide in the cherrywood wardrobe in her room the entire time and only emerge after the guests had left, which drove her mother crazy.

Still in his pajamas and with Roberto in his arms, Carlo looked out into the garden and sang, "Happy birthday to you . . ."

Anna turned and smiled at them. Carlo kissed her lightly on the lips and stroked her hair. "Happy birthday, my love," he whispered in her ear.

"The pommers," said the boy, pointing at the blossoming trees.

"They're called pomegranates," she corrected him.

It was Anna's first birthday in his hometown, and Carlo wanted it to be special. He knew that Anna didn't care, but he'd gotten it into his head that she wanted to be surrounded by family for the occasion. So he planned a surprise party and made sure everyone participated, especially Lorenza.

"I'm entrusting you with a very important task," he said to her a few days before the event. "Keep your auntie busy all the afternoon. Go for a really long walk, so me and your papa have time to decorate the garden."

Agata would take care of the cooking, preparing her unrivaled meat pie with a side of potatoes.

Anna spent the afternoon wandering the countryside with Lorenza, who forced her to stop at every field they saw to pick daisies. As she returned home with her niece, who was holding a large bouquet of flowers, she found Carlo, Antonio, and Agata standing over a table laden with delicacies, silver cutlery, crystal glassware, and lit candles, all laid out around a centerpiece of red roses. Lorenza opened her eyes wide, dropped the bouquet, and clapped her hands.

"You did an amaaaazing job!" she exclaimed.

"Why you little—You knew about this?" Anna asked her.

I should have known, she thought, forcing a smile. After all, she'd married a man who loved parties more than anything. Despite her reluctance, Carlo had always managed to pull off some kind of celebration right under her nose. The first year he'd known her, he took her to see the stars at Bordighera beach, along with two glasses and a bottle of sparkling wine. Since then, he'd surprised her each year with some new whim. Once, he even took her to dance the Charleston.

Carlo popped the cork and filled the cups.

"To Anna," he said, raising his glass.

"To Anna!" Antonio and Agata exclaimed in unison, before taking a seat at the table. Agata cut the pie in triangular slices and gave one to each guest, and then she crossed herself, interlaced her fingers, and with her eyes closed whispered a quick blessing.

As usual, between one bite and another, Antonio and Carlo started chatting away about oil and wine, while Agata launched into one of her monologues, weaving in the best town gossip. Anna always listened and nodded, even though she usually didn't know whom Agata was talking about.

Taking advantage of a moment of silence, and without addressing anyone in particular, Anna suddenly asked, "Did anyone know Ferruccio, the letter carrier?"

"Of course! Since he was a boy," Carlo said.

"May he rest in peace. He wasn't old, you know, not old at all," Agata added.

"He'd been unwell for a long time," Antonio explained.

"Yeah. Poor Ferruccio," Carlo added.

"They're looking for a replacement. The selection process ends tomorrow," Anna said.

"Mm-hmm," Carlo grumbled, with his mouth full.

Antonio began to stare at her then, wondering where the conversation was going.

After a brief pause, Anna announced, "I am also applying. Tomorrow." She took a sip of wine.

Carlo and Agata stared at her, stunned. Antonio, quite to the contrary, cracked a smile.

"My love, what do you mean? You must be joking," Carlo said, halfway between amused and worried.

"Not at all," she said, stiffening.

"But you're a woman!" Agata snapped.

"So what?"

"Come on, Anna," Carlo insisted, chuckling. "It's not a job for women."

"Says who?" she retorted.

"Anna, come on. Maybe next year you can go back to teaching. Perhaps a spot will open up. If you really want to keep busy, you could always give me a hand at the cellar—"

"Ah!" Anna snapped. "Now you want my help."

Carlo stared at her, thrown by the accusation.

"This job is just not appropriate for you," he protested, meekly.

"It's not suitable for any woman, for that matter," Agata declared.

"What's inappropriate about it?" Anna asked.

"First of all, it's strenuous," Carlo said, putting down his fork. "You have to walk around all day, rain or shine. Look at what happened to

Ferruccio . . . it was the death of him. Let's be serious. There are no female letter carriers for a reason."

"Until now," Anna said.

Silence fell. Carlo scowled as he filled his glass. Agata, eyes lowered, traced the embroidered border of the tablecloth with her finger. Lorenza really wanted to say that it was a wonderful idea, but she saw that it wasn't the right time.

"Anyway, we'll talk about it later." Carlo cut the conversation short, frowning. "Let's change the subject for now."

"And you?" Anna asked Antonio. "What do you have to say?"

Antonio cleared his throat. He looked at Agata and then at Carlo.

"Well," he answered with a shrug. "If you want to give it a try . . . I don't see why not?"

"Not you too!" Carlo growled. "Don't encourage her."

"I don't need encouragement," Anna said. "I've already decided. I've already prepared the papers."

"And when did you find the time to do that?" Carlo asked, stunned.

"While you were out working."

"They'll never take you."

Anna shot daggers at him. She banged her napkin on the table, got up, and walked away.

"Auntie!" Lorenza said, trying to stop her, but it was in vain.

———

That night, Agata made a scene once they got back home. Antonio had taken Anna's side over such a stupid, downright foolish idea. *What was he thinking, contradicting Carlo? Hadn't he heard his brother? He didn't want his wife in that job! He was her husband! Why had he stuck his nose where it didn't belong? Why was he on Anna's side every single time?*

Lorenza covered her ears and ran to her room. Without a word, Antonio slunk into his study and locked the door, leaving Agata to rant and rave on the other side of the wall.

And at Carlo and Anna's house, two plates and one glass went flying. Anna accused him of acting like an owner-husband. *It was unacceptable! She hadn't married a small-minded man—she never would have done that. Returning to the south had made him an unrecognizable imbécile!* Carlo's reaction was swift: *What did she intend to prove by getting a man's job? Didn't she realize she'd be the laughingstock of the town? Was that what she wanted for her son?*

Anna grabbed a plate that was still greasy with oil and flung it at a tree.

"Do not bring Roberto into this!"

"You want to play flying plates? Let's play!" Carlo yelled. He picked up another one and threw it against the garden wall.

"Je te déteste!" she snapped, waving her fist in the air. "Et je hais de tout mon être ce village et ses habitants!"

"Speak Italian! We're in Italy!"

To which Anna grabbed a crystal glass and hurled it straight at Carlo, barely missing his face. He touched his cheek and stared at her, incredulous.

By the middle of the night, all arguing had subsided. Antonio was asleep on the sofa in his study, a book open on his chest, while Agata tossed and turned in their bed, her eyes wide open. Lorenza, in the next room, slept clutching her cloth doll.

Anna and Carlo made love furiously until dawn.

———

The following morning, Anna turned her closet upside down. Where the hell was her yellow dress, the one with the puffball sleeves? She was certain she'd brought it. She searched for it in a frenzy, finally finding it crumpled at the bottom of a drawer. Pleased, she picked it up and held it up to her figure, against her blue silk nightgown, and looked in the mirror. She'd known her mourning would end sooner or later. She didn't want Roberto to have only dark and gloomy memories of her or think of her as a grim and sad mother. She'd always known that she would recognize the right time to throw out all her black outfits and return to dressing in color. Like a coup de foudre.

Now that time had finally come.

She went downstairs with her hair gathered in a low bun, wearing a rounded hat in the same color as the dress. She looked like an actress. Carlo, who was pacing around the living room with his hands in his pockets, stopped dead and looked at her, breathless.

"How do I look?" she asked, twirling around.

Carlo sighed.

"The yellow dress," he said, with a hint of surprise in his voice. "You look beautiful. You know that."

"That's what I wanted to hear."

"That doesn't mean I agree with what you're doing."

"I know. But that's your problem." She went to the cupboard and extracted a folder with her documents and the completed application.

"I thought there was only such a thing as *our* problems. Was I wrong?"

"Apparently."

"Anna," he murmured, taking her hand. "Do you really want to do this?"

She pulled away from his grasp, grabbed her bag from the coatrack, and opened the front door.

"I presume it's pointless to hope for a 'good luck' from you?"

Carlo did not answer.

"Fine," Anna said. She clasped the folder under her arm and closed the door behind her.

She walked to the square and soon arrived at the post office. A moment before she entered, she heard someone calling her. She turned around to see Antonio walking toward her, accelerating his pace, holding the *Corriere della Sera* in one hand.

"What are you doing here?" Anna asked.

"I was at the bar, and I saw you," he said, a little out of breath. "You're . . . you look good in that dress."

"Thank you," Anna said, smiling. "I was just about to go in." She pointed at the office.

"Of course, of course," he mumbled. "Go ahead." As she turned to go, he added, "Good luck!"

Anna turned around for a moment and smiled at him, then crossed the threshold of the post office. She thought of Carlo's words: *They'll never take you.* She would prove him wrong. Big-time.

———

In that exact moment, Carlo was impatiently knocking on the door to the dressmaker's shop.

Carmela opened and stared at him, stunned.

"May I come in?" he asked.

"Always," she said.

6

Six Months Later

Anna left the house early in the morning. She was wearing the blue, red-collared uniform cloak that came down to her ankles, the cap with the inlaid crest of the Royal Post Office, and flat black pumps on her feet. She put the leather mailbag over her shoulder and set off.

"Good morning, Madam Letter Carrier," said her neighbor. Still in her nightgown, and with a wool jacket draped over her shoulders, the woman was briskly sweeping her slice of the sidewalk, which measured no more than six tiles or so.

Anna returned the greeting by lifting her cap. "Good morning to you."

She came to the square just as it was beginning to come alive. Michele was loading crates of oranges onto the sidewalk; Mario was sitting on a stool on the corner, shining the shoes of a well-dressed man in a fancy hat. The barber, in his white apron, was smoking a cigarette outside his door, waiting for the first clients of the day. Anna headed for Bar Castello and went in.

"The usual?" asked Nando amiably.

She nodded, peering at two old folks sitting at a table. They were playing briscola, but they stopped dealing the cards to stare at her, whisper something, and elbow each other.

"Here's your coffee," Nando said. "Corrected with grappa."

Anna drank it in one sip, still staring at the two men, who hadn't taken their eyes off her. They were no longer talking—their mouths were hanging wide open. She smacked her lips, savoring the alcoholic aftertaste on her tongue.

"Thank you, Nando," she said, leaving the coins on the bar. It amused her to know that after she'd left, the usual comments would follow. It was as if she could hear those two men lamenting the fact that a woman could enjoy a drink so early in the morning.

"Now I've seen everything," she'd heard them say, once.

She entered the post office and greeted Tommaso, who reciprocated with a smile, then Carmine, who stroked his beard and shot her the usual skeptical glance.

She opened the door to the back room and greeted the telegraphists, Elena and Chiara. The "young ladies," as everyone called them, since neither of them was married. The first was a large, jolly woman with a wide face and a long tongue who lived with her older sister, who was also without husband. Chiara, the younger of the two, was a slip of a girl with thick glasses and a sweet smile who took care of her elderly mother. *It's my job, as the daughter,* she explained once, pointing out that her two brothers already had wives and children to look after.

"I brought a cake," Elena said. "Come on, have a slice with us. It's almond."

Anna asked if she could wrap up a slice; she would take it with her in the mailbag and enjoy it later.

She went to the large table in the middle of the office and began her daily ritual of sorting the correspondence based on neighborhood.

Among the letters, packages, and telegrams was a white envelope. The address read *Giovanna Calogiuri, Contrada La Pietra, Lizzanello (Lecce)*. No mention of a sender, just the post office from which it had been sent and the date. Next to that was a stamp featuring King Vittorio Emanuele III; the letter had been mailed from Casalecchio di Reno, in the province of Bologna.

"Where is Contrada La Pietra?" Anna asked, turning the envelope over in her hands.

"Who's sending mail to Contrada La Pietra?" Carmine asked, surprised.

"I don't know. There's no sender."

Tommaso came over and read, "Giovanna Calogiuri."

"You mean Crazy Giovanna?" Elena piped up, appearing in the doorway.

"Who is Crazy Giovanna?" Anna asked.

"Someone who's out of her mind," said Carmine.

"Nah, she's just a bit strange. Sometimes I see her grocery shopping in town," Tommaso said.

"Strange my foot. She's as dumb as they come," Elena said. "In school, she was the only one who still couldn't read after three years. The teacher always made her kneel on chickpeas behind the blackboard. He'd slap her hands with a ruler."

"Then eventually she just went mad," Carmine continued. "She would get these demonic fits and throw everything in the air—books, notepads, chairs. They had to kick her out of school. And a good thing they did."

"Then there was that whole thing with the guy who became a priest . . ." Tommaso muttered.

"Yes, well, that was the final blow! And then she locked herself up there, in Contrada La Pietra, with her dog. Her mother, a saint of a woman, God rest her soul, probably died of heartbreak for all the trouble her daughter gave her. But Crazy Giovanna got lucky: she was an only child, so she got all the money donna Rosalina had squirreled away from her job as a cook for the Tamburinis. I bet that woman doesn't even bathe. When she comes to town, you can smell her from a mile away," Elena said, holding her nose.

Anna lifted an eyebrow. A little dazed by all that gossip, she asked if someone could just please explain how to get to Contrada, as she was already late. She learned that Giovanna's house was on the edge of town, where the olive trees grow; this was going to be hard work on her poor feet. She knew that that night she'd have to soak them in warm water longer than usual. She couldn't say how many miles she'd walked in those first six months; all she knew was that the soles of her feet were covered in calluses and constantly hurt.

She slipped the letter into the back of her bag; it would be the last stop of the morning. She slung the mailbag over her shoulder and left the office. As soon as she stepped out, she saw Carlo standing outside Bar Castello, absorbed in reading the paper with a cigar between his teeth. They hadn't seen each other yet that morning. He had been in the bathroom as she was leaving.

Anna glanced at her watch. Antonio had given it to her when she got the job, back in May. She loved the watch. It had a black leather strap and a rectangular dial with Arabic numerals. It was unusual but simple, just as she liked it.

I really don't have time to stop and talk to Carlo, she thought. Nor had she any desire to. She'd see him later at home. What difference did it make? Since her birthday, all they did was squabble over the smallest things. *They'll never take you.* Carlo's words still rang in her ears even though she'd patently proven him wrong.

Her level of education had made all the difference: The other two candidates hadn't advanced past fifth grade. He should be proud of her. She'd done it, for heaven's sake! Yet Carlo didn't even seem to care; he had known that she didn't listen to him, she did things her way, and yet he still couldn't forgive her for it. He ended up pointing his finger at her along with everybody else. She felt like everyone—with their chorus of *You'll never make it, But you're a woman, It's not a job for women*—was just waiting to see her fail. To restore the order of things.

Anna felt a sudden sense of fatigue and quickly crossed to the other side of the street.

Carlo looked up from his paper, lighting his cigar as he noticed her walking away. She wasn't that far; he could have just called out her name to make her turn. But he didn't—because Carmela was waiting for him, and he was already late. He folded the paper, dropped it onto a table, and walked to his car.

He drove to the corner near Carmela's house and stopped there for a moment; once he was certain that Nicola's car was gone, he turned onto her street. Carmela had assured him that her husband left very early to take their son to school before going to work, but Carlo always peeked. He parked on a little side street, a dead end where no living soul ever passed except for a colony of stray cats. He got out of the car and continued on foot. He found the door ajar, like every morning. He pushed it, entered, and closed it behind him.

"It's me," he said.

Carmela came down the long hallway in her white silk nightgown and lunged in to kiss him.

"You're late," she said.

"Forgive me. Roberto had a tantrum this morning, and it took me longer than usual to bathe and dress him. I dropped him at Agata's and came straight here. To you," Carlo lied, hugging her hips.

———

Anna began her morning rounds with Giuseppina, a woman who kept her white hair in a low ponytail and who spoke in a shrill voice. Once a month, she received news of her son Mauro, who had gone to try his luck in Germany. It seemed like he really had succeeded, judging by the money he sent her on a regular basis. Giuseppina was a widow who couldn't read or write, so it was up to Anna to go inside, sit down and drink burnt coffee she would have gladly done without, and read the letter, enunciating each word, starting over once or twice each time. Giuseppina would shower genuine gratitude on Anna and shake her head and say, "You're such a good person, Mrs. Anna. I wonder why everyone always speaks so ill of you."

Then it was on to Angela, a slender nineteen-year-old girl with a kind smile who received a new gift from her suitor every week. She'd clap her hands, happy as a clam, and open the package while Anna was still stand-ing at the door. The gift always consisted of some small, delightful wooden figurine: a train car, a jewelry box, a heart-shaped pendant, a key.

"He's a woodworker, you know. He has a shop in Lecce," Angela ex-plained, full of pride.

The following stop was Mr. Lorenzo, a gruff man with sad eyes and a grizzled, knotty beard. Whenever he saw Anna coming, he'd greet her with the fascist salute, which she invariably refused to reciprocate. Each time, Mr. Lorenzo sent his mail back to the sender, a man who shared his last name. The scene was always the same: Mr. Lorenzo grabbed the postcard—a different image of Rome each month—took one look at it, sneered, and said, "I don't want it. Take it away."

———

As Anna was walking away from Mr. Lorenzo's house, Carlo was lying on Carmela's bed, smoking, taking slow and measured puffs. Still naked, Carmela got up and opened the window to let air into the room; she knew the spiced smell of smoke would have to disappear completely before Nic-ola's return. She got back into bed and lay down on her side, resting her head on her hand.

"You're beautiful," she said to Carlo.

He exhaled smoke from the side of his mouth and stroked her arm listlessly.

"You too."

Carmela reached a hand under the sheet.

"I have to go," he said, without too much conviction. "Don't you have work to do?"

She pulled her hand back, indignant.

"Of course I have work to do. I always work, don't I?"

She sat up, retrieved her nightgown from the nightstand, and slipped it on, turning her back to him.

"What happened to my pants?" he asked.

"How would I know? Look under the bed."

Carlo leaned over. The pants were there, inside out. The business cards he had been hiding in his pocket were now scattered across the floor. He got up and started to gather them quickly.

"What are those?" Carmela asked.

"Nothing."

"What do you mean, nothing? Show me." She grabbed a card out of his hand.

"'Anna Allavena. Letter carrier,'" she read aloud. "She has business cards now? We all know who she is. Is she worried we're going to forget?" she said, aiming for sarcasm, but a voice crack betrayed her.

"Give it over," Carlo said, stiffening. He put it in his pocket with the others. "It's none of your business," he added, in a serious tone.

"Far be it from me . . . To each their own cross to bear," she said, waving her hand. She slipped her shoes on.

"No cross. Just business cards. Nothing wrong with that."

"Sure. Nothing wrong with having a ball and chain that does whatever she wants and behaves like a man."

"Anna doesn't behave like a man. What are you talking about?"

"Doesn't she? Actually, I bet she's the one who wears the pants in the family, not you. That's what everyone thinks anyway. She even has a little drinking habit, I've heard. Ask Nando about the grappa she guzzles down every morning. *You* can't keep her under control. That's what people are saying."

Carlo said nothing. He quickly put his clothes on, adjusted his hat, and left the room without saying goodbye.

He opened the front door and looked left and right. Once he was sure the coast was clear, he quickly walked toward his car, full of rage. Instead of heading toward the vineyard, though, he took the road to the oil mill.

He parked in front of the entrance, by the turquoise tin sign that read GRECO OIL MILL in block letters. He entered and gallantly tipped his hat to Agnese, the secretary. She'd been working for Antonio for at least six years and was always bent over a pile of paperwork, pen in hand, and glasses on the tip of her nose held in place by a gold chain.

"Is my brother in? May I?" Carlo asked. Without waiting for a reply, he opened the door to Antonio's office.

"Good day, big brother," he said, his cigar held tightly between his teeth.

Antonio looked up from his ledger and broke into a smile.

"Come, come," he said as he stood up.

Carlo walked up to Antonio and gave him a big hug, then took his face in his hands and planted a kiss on his forehead.

"Look how beautiful you are!" he said, laughing. Antonio looked particularly relaxed that morning. Maybe it was his freshly shaved face or his hair, which was neatly combed back and shiny with wax.

"Did you go see Fernando?"

"Yes, early this morning. But I think he put in too much gel this time," Antonio said, touching his slightly hardened hair.

Carlo pulled out a chair from Antonio's desk and sat down. The *Corriere della Sera* was open to a page showing the picture of a memorial statue. The engraving read *November 18, 1935—XIV. In memory of the siege so that the enormous injustice committed against Italy, to whom civilizations on all continents owe a great debt, shall be remembered for centuries to come.*

Carlo grimaced. "What a fool," he said, nodding at the paper.

"A dangerous fool," Antonio added. "He's going to rain hell down on Ethiopia, especially after the 'enormous injustice' of the League of Nations sanctions."

"Anyway," Antonio continued, sitting down. "Why have you come?"

Carlo shrugged and took a drag from his cigar. "Do you know what people are saying in town? Have you heard the rumors?"

Antonio sat back in his chair and sighed. "No. What are they saying?"

"That I'm a laughingstock."

"Don't be ridiculous!" Antonio chuckled.

"It's true. They say Anna's the one who wears the pants, not me."

"Oh yeah? And who says that?"

Carlo became pensive. "Carmela."

"Ah, well, if Carmela says so. A more than reliable source," Antonio teased him.

"I know she's right. I feel them, you know, the looks people give me."

"No one's looking at you, come on."

"Yes, they are, I'm telling you. I know what they think of me. And of her."

Antonio became serious.

"And what should they think? That she earns an honest living? An unforgivable crime, to be sure," he said.

Carlo shook his head. "You make it sound easy."

"Because it is, Carletto."

"Sure, it's easy to be progressive with other people's wives. I'd like to see you in my place."

Antonio interlaced his fingers over the desk. He wanted to say that he would give anything to be in Carlo's position even for one day. How many times had he imagined lying silently in bed watching Anna sleep, stroking her loose hair on the pillow, tracing the contours of her face with his finger and saying *Antonio's here, I'll take care of you.*

"She's making me look ridiculous, and that's the truth," Carlo growled. "Did you know that she drinks a shot of grappa every morning at the bar? It's only natural that people should talk."

"Let them talk. What do you care?"

"No, Antonio. These are *my* people; this is my *home.* I have a business here. Of course I care."

Antonio stood up, stuck his hands in his pockets, and went over to the window.

"And about her? Do you care about her?" he asked, looking outside.

"What kind of question is that!" Carlo tensed up. "Would I be here talking about it if I didn't? She's my wife."

Antonio looked at him again, this time with a hint of sadness in his eyes.

"Well then. If you care, you should be the first to stop dragging her through the mud."

Carlo looked away.

"There is only one thing you should be doing right now," Antonio said, looking back out the window.

"And what would that be?" Carlo asked, crossing his arms.

"Protecting her," Antonio said in a faint voice.

———

It was long after midday when Anna finally turned onto the road that led to Contrada La Pietra.

Giovanna lived in a farmhouse with a red roof, surrounded by countryside. Its shutters were closed, as if no one had lived there in a long time. When Anna opened the wooden gate, a German shepherd ran up to her, barking. She crouched down and reached her hand out, palm up; the dog stopped barking and started to sniff her, then lowered his ears and sat down in front of her.

"Cesare! Come back here!" a woman yelled from the doorway. Then she saw Anna. "Who is it?"

"A letter for Giovanna Calogiuri," Anna said, walking toward the house.

"That's me."

She doesn't seem at all crazy, Anna thought once she was in front of her. Sure, her hair was disheveled, and she had probably been wearing that brown wool dress for God knows how many days, but there was something elegant about her face: big hazel eyes, long eyelashes, pale skin, full lips, high cheekbones. And she certainly didn't stink.

"This is for you," Anna said, handing over the envelope.

Giovanna didn't budge.

"It's yours. A letter," Anna insisted.

"You must be mistaken."

"But you said you're Giovanna Calogiuri, right?"

"Yes."

"Then there's no mistake. Here."

"What am I supposed to do with it? I can't read."

"Well," Anna said, thoughtfully. "If you want, I can read it to you. It wouldn't be the first time."

Giovanna bit her lip, doubtful.

Finally, she said, "Come in."

The house was neat and respectable and smelled of mothballs. The furniture was sparse, and the place was undoubtedly run-down. Several kitchen tiles were chipped, the pink cotton curtains were frayed at the bottom, and a crack on the wall went all the way from the ceiling to the baseboard. But Anna thought the house seemed welcoming, safe.

"I'll make you a coffee," Giovanna said.

"I'd love that, thank you." Anna sat down and placed the mailbag on the kitchen table. She pulled out the slice of cake she'd been saving from that morning, that Elena had wrapped in a cloth napkin.

"So, *you're* the outlander." Giovanna addressed her familiarly now, maybe without even realizing. She turned to look at Anna and smiled at her.

"In the flesh."

"I'm sorry." Giovanna blushed, realizing how crass her phrasing had been.

"No, no, there's no need. I know what people call me."

Giovanna grimaced in embarrassment. "The uniform suits you," she said, before turning on the burner.

"Oh, thank you," Anna said, pleased. "I think so too."

They drank the coffee in silence and shared the slice of cake while Giovanna's dog Cesare snored at their feet.

Anna looked at the time. "Can I open it now?"

Giovanna nodded and bit her lip again.

The envelope contained a page folded in half, with light blue doodles at each corner. Holding the letter with both hands, Anna began to read:

Dear Giovanna,

I hope this letter finds you well. First of all, I want to
apologize for not writing sooner, but it hasn't been easy here.
Don't think I haven't thought about you. But, you know, as
we've talked about, it was necessary for some time to pass and
for there to be enough distance between us. I can't get my last
image of you out of my mind, your tears, your desperation.
You don't know how much it pains me to think about it. I
hope you've found peace in your heart.

Know that I love you and always will.

I wish you much serenity. I will pray for it to be so.

Don Giulio

Anna looked up and saw that Giovanna's face was streaked with tears.
"Are you okay?" she asked, placing a hand on her arm.

Giovanna stood up, grabbed a kitchen towel stained with sauce, and
dried her face with it.

"I do have a question . . ." Anna hesitated. "Why is he sending you a
letter? Doesn't he know that you can't read?"

Giovanna blew her nose. "No. I was too embarrassed to tell him."

"Oh, but it's nothing to be ashamed of. It's never too late to learn how
to read."

"Not for me."

"It's true for everyone. Trust me."

"Not for me," Giovanna said again. "I can't see them—the words."

Anna made a puzzled face. "I can help you. To see them, I mean. I was
an elementary school teacher."

"No!" Giovanna yelled decisively, wringing her hands.

"Well, if you still want to respond to him, you can dictate the letter
to me."

Giovanna bit her lip and looked away.

"If you change your mind, you know where to find me," Anna said. She stood up, put her mailbag back over her shoulders, patted Cesare on the head, and left.

She couldn't have known then how many shoes she'd eventually wear out by walking that road.

7

Late one February morning, a few months after their first meeting, when the sky was gray and dense, Giovanna showed up at the post office. She timidly peeked through the door and stood there stock-still, wringing her hands.

Tommaso and Carmine exchanged glances. Anna was sitting at the table emptying her mailbag of the outstanding letters of the day, among which was the latest postcard for Mr. Lorenzo, this one depicting the Fountain of Trevi. Someday she'd ask him why he persisted in sending back the postcards he received from his brother—the mysterious sender, as she'd discovered.

"Good morning, ma'am," Tommaso said to Giovanna. "Can I help you?"

Anna looked up.

"Giovanna?" she exclaimed, stunned.

Elena immediately popped out from the back room and positioned herself to listen in from behind the open door.

"I'm ready," Giovanna declared, raising a hand to adjust her hair, which she'd gathered as best she could.

"For what?" Anna asked. She hadn't thought about that day in Contrada since her initial offer.

Giovanna lowered her head, clearly disappointed.

"To answer," she whispered. She looked like someone who, on the contrary, had tormented herself every day and night since their meeting, before making her decision.

"Of course," Anna said, pulling up a chair. "Forgive me. I remember now. Of course I remember."

"What's happening?" Tommaso asked.

"Oh, nothing. Giovanna wants to dictate a letter to me, right?" she answered, turning to look at her.

Giovanna nodded and bit her lip.

"She wants to dictate a letter," Elena whispered to her colleague, who was bent over writing. "Did you hear that?"

"Yes, I heard," Chiara grunted, without looking at her. She simply pushed up her glasses, which were sliding down her nose.

"I wonder to whom. Let's hope the letter carrier tells me everything later, or else," Elena declared, keeping her voice down.

"Come with me," Anna said. "Let's grab a seat at the bar. I'll get pen and paper." She pulled a brownish piece of paper out of a drawer in a wooden chest.

"Tommaso . . . Do you mind if I take off for half an hour?"

He gestured not to worry, that she could go ahead.

They crossed the road to Bar Castello and Anna pointed at an outside table. Giovanna took a seat, looking around nervously.

"Everything okay?" Anna asked.

"Yes, yes," she mumbled.

Anna placed the piece of paper on the table, took out the pen, and said she was ready.

Giovanna hesitated. "First, promise you won't tell anyone."

Anna placed a hand on her arm. "I promise. It will stay between you and me."

Giovanna nodded and finally smiled. Her big hazel eyes lit up. *Yes, she really was beautiful,* Anna thought.

Giovanna started to dictate in a trembling voice. Her cheeks turned red as she dictated to Anna how much she missed Giulio's kisses and that "special touching" under the sheets that made her feel as light as air and put fog in her eyes.

Anna wrote without blinking, serious and focused.

"Do you think I'm a bad person?" Giovanna asked, suddenly stopping.

Anna looked up from the page. "A bad person? Why should I?"

"Because of what I'm saying," she said, biting her lip.

"Listen," Anna said. "If a man were saying this, would we be here talking about it?"

———

Agata was walking on the other side of the square with a neighbor, carrying a canvas bag full of flour.

"Isn't that your sister-in-law?" the neighbor asked, nodding at Anna.

Agata turned and saw Anna and Giovanna laughing heartily, looking intimate and cheerful. She felt a stab of jealousy: Anna had never laughed with her, in all the time since she and Carlo had moved to Lizzanello. Plus, since she'd become a letter carrier, she acted like she was better than everyone else. Anna never had time for her anymore, not even for grocery shopping. Not once.

"The madwoman and the outlander. What a pair," the neighbor said, adding insult to injury.

Agata puffed up with resentment and thought back to the previous Saturday afternoon rosary circle, when she'd had to take her sister-in-law's side to defend the family's honor against her friends. Apparently, Carlo's morning "visits" to donna Carmela had become an open secret.

"Well, when a woman gets her feathers up like that, it's only natural that her man should step out," the women all agreed, between an Our Father and a Hail Mary. Agata retorted that it would be better if everyone looked in their own home rather than judge others, putting an end to the discussion.

Now she hardened her gaze as she watched Anna and Giovanna.

"Like two peas in a pod," she agreed with her neighbor, taking her by the arm.

———

Anna folded the letter in half and promised Giovanna she'd send it the following day. Don Giulio hadn't left a return address, but she knew where to send it. How many parishes could there be in Casalecchio di Reno?

As soon as Anna returned to the post office, she found herself under assault.

"Well?" Elena prodded her, following her around.

"Well, what?"

"Tell us everything. Who was Miss Crazy writing to?"

"First of all, can you stop calling her 'Miss Crazy'? She has a name."

Elena stared at her, baffled. "But we've always called her that." She turned to Carmine for support.

"To us she is and will always be Miss Crazy," he said bluntly, stroking his long beard.

Anna shook her head and started to gather her things.

"Come on, give us something. It'll stay between us colleagues," Elena insisted.

"I'm not going to tell you anything."

"What's the matter, you don't trust us?" Elena said, frowning.

Anna looked up at the ceiling and grabbed her mailbag.

"That's enough," Tommaso said from his desk. "She's right; it's a private matter."

"Thank you, Tommaso," Anna said. She waved goodbye as she left the office.

"What's her problem?" Elena complained.

"I told you she wouldn't tell you," Carmine said with a shrug.

Elena continued to stare at the door resentfully.

"I even gave her a piece of cake," she grumbled finally, returning to her seat.

———

Don Giulio's response arrived three weeks later. Anna bolted to Giovanna's even though her mailbag was bursting with letters. The unscheduled stop would cost her at least an extra hour of work, but she didn't care; Giovanna's anticipation had become hers, too, and she could hardly wait.

Giovanna came to the door half asleep, still wrapped in a wool shawl. Cesare approached wagging his tail.

"Were you sleeping?" Anna asked her. She greeted the dog with a pat on the head.

"Yes, but don't worry," she answered.

"It's here!" Anna exclaimed, waving the envelope in the air.

"Come on in. I'll make some coffee."

A shadow fell across Giovanna's face as she took the coffee out of the cupboard.

"What's that face for? Aren't you happy?"

"It depends on what he wrote."

"We don't even know yet! Hey, how about I open it?"

Giovanna gave up on the coffee and placed the container back on the shelf. She sat down and started to bite her nails. Cesare lay down at her feet.

Anna tore off one side of the envelope and pulled out the letter. She opened it, cleared her throat, and started to read.

Dear Giovanna,

I was surprised to receive your letter, since I had intentionally left out a return address. Anyway, I read it carefully, more than once. And I want to tell you that I haven't forgotten either. How could I? Those are extremely precious memories that I carry with me every day and that warm my heart.

Don Giulio

P.S. It would be best if you didn't send me such—how can I put it?—passionate letters. Prying eyes are all around.

"I don't know if I understood him correctly," Giovanna said, visibly confused. She tore off a cuticle with her teeth.

Anna became thoughtful and started to drum her fingers on the table, then was struck with inspiration.

"Here's what we'll do," she said, beaming.

"What are you talking about?"

"I have an idea. Tomorrow, though. There's no time now," she said, smiling mischievously.

She returned the following afternoon with a black-and-white postcard of Piazza Castello and a bundle of ten-cent stamps.

The plan was to make the "passionate" words so small that they could be hidden under the stamps. All Giulio would have to do was moisten the stamps to remove them and uncover the words.

"But how will he know? That he has to remove the stamps, I mean," Giovanna asked.

Anna had thought of everything. "You'll send him a separate letter with instructions a few days before he receives the postcard. We'll just write, 'The postage stamps conceal more words than one might think, if one only knows where to look.' If he's not a complete idiot, he'll understand what to do. And if I'm right, as I suspect, he'll answer with the same method. Wanna bet?"

Spring had come. Carlo knew it as soon as he smelled the air on that clear and sunny Easter Sunday. He'd decided to take Roberto to mass that morning; it had been a while since he'd spent some time alone with his son. He had seen him very little over the past few weeks—one year had passed since he'd planted the vines, and the first pruning had completely absorbed him. The Greco Winery was now bustling with laborers who started at dawn and remained hunched over the shoots with shears in hand until dusk. Don Ciccio showed up only once, on the first day of pruning, and stayed for less than an hour. He just explained to Carlo how it was supposed to go, and that this was a delicate phase that would determine the quality and quantity of future grapes.

"Figure out the rest yourself," he added, gruff as usual.

Thus, Carlo learned that everything depended on how many buds were pruned. More shoots left on the vines meant a more plentiful production, but it also led to a lower sugar content and a smaller concentration of aromatic compounds. The ideal plan was to keep no more than two buds on each plant, the ones tough enough to grow into a trunk. As Carlo supervised the work, he realized that some of the laborers—usually the younger and least experienced ones—would cut the good buds with the most sap, leaving the weaker ones on the vine. He would reprimand them immediately. Their humble apologies came just as swiftly.

Now Carlo dressed Roberto in his Sunday best, a blue jacket with matching pants, white shirt, and silver tie.

"Look at Papa's handsome little boy," he said, squeezing his son's rosy cheeks. Roberto responded with a joyful giggle as Carlo brought a finger to his lips. "Mama's sleeping," he murmured.

He slinked up to the bedroom and gently opened the door. Anna was lying on the right side of the bed, her hair strewn across the pillow and a black silk mask over her eyes. He stared at her for a moment, holding his breath. She was so perfectly beautiful, he thought. He suddenly felt crushed by the weight of the world, the gaping distance that had formed between them, and the height of the wall they'd erected with each fight. The last one had taken place just the night before, causing dinner to go down the wrong pipe for both of them. He'd provoked her, just for the fun of getting on her nerves. He knew how important it was to Anna that they only speak Italian at home; she'd categorically forbidden the use of dialect, and if Carlo let slip a word, she'd chide him instantly.

"Not in front of the boy, please."

Yet for the entire length of that dinner, he'd taken it upon himself to teach his son words in his local dialect, encouraging him to repeat everything he said from atop his wooden high chair. When Anna ordered him to stop, he upped the ante, clapping every time Roberto got the pronunciation right.

Thinking back on it, he felt a deep sense of shame. He'd been stupid and childish. Maybe she was right when she said the south had made him an imbécile and a réactionnaire.

As he stood there leaning against the doorjamb watching her sleep, for the first time, he feared he'd lost her respect over these past few months. Even just the thought of that prospect felt intolerable.

He closed the door and returned to his son's room. He picked him up and slowly carried him downstairs.

They arrived at the San Lorenzo church early for the ten-thirty A.M. mass. As they walked in, Carlo dipped his fingers in holy water before crossing himself. Up by the main altar, in all its intricate baroque splendor, the organist was taking his seat. Carlo walked the tiled floor of the central nave that ran parallel to two side aisles with smaller altars, and chose a pew on the center left, which was reserved for men, next to the sepulchral monument to Giorgio Antonio Paladini, the ancient lord of Lizzanello. Within a few minutes, the church was full. Carlo spotted don Ciccio's family heading toward the front pews. Gina was holding on to her husband's arm while Carmela and Nicola walked side by side. Daniele, their son, was one step behind them. They soon took their seats: don Ciccio, Nicola, and Daniele on the left, and Carmela and her mother on the right.

When it was time for communion and the organ began to play, Carlo picked up Roberto and got in line at the altar. In that moment, Daniele came out of his pew, followed by his father and grandfather. He and Carlo ended up standing right next to each other.

"Good morning, don Ciccio," Carlo whispered, smiling.

The elder man reciprocated with a chin lift.

"Finished with the pruning?" he asked, just as quietly.

"Yes, all done," Carlo said. "Let's hope for the best."

"Hello, Carlo." Nicola shook his hand. "Daniele, say hello to Mr. Carlo," he ordered.

The boy turned around and doffed his hat. "Good morning," he said, reluctantly.

Amused, Carlo put his hand on the boy's shoulder. "How's it going, young man?" he asked.

Don Ciccio became uncomfortable and looked away.

"Can you get a move on?" came the hoarse voice of a man in line behind them.

Carlo, Roberto, and Daniele in front, and the other two behind them, walked the few feet that separated them from the priest, proceeding in small steps.

Carmela had remained seated next to her mother, waiting for the men's turn to end and the women's turn to begin. Her gaze was fixed on Carlo and Daniele as they walked together, her heart hammering away in her chest. If the organ had stopped playing, everyone in the church would have heard it.

It was the last Monday in April, and the post office was all abuzz. After a whopping eight years of engagement, Tommaso would be getting married to Giulia, a frail and shy girl from a good family, the only child of a local landowner. He'd brought a tray of almond pastries and popped a bottle of sparkling wine; although it was only eight in the morning, everyone gladly had a drink. When Anna walked in, everyone was standing in front of an almost polished-off tray of sweets, glasses still in hand. Lorenza was with her, wearing her school uniform—a black skirt and white shirt with a dark collar. For months she'd been pestering her auntie to show her where she worked, and Anna had finally relented. Provided she could take her to school right after, no complaints.

"What a lovely young lady," said Tommaso. "How old are you?"

"Eleven!" Lorenza exclaimed.

"That's Antonio's daughter—don't you recognize her?" Elena said. "She's the carbon copy of her mother." She turned to Lorenza. "You should have seen your mother at your age—you two are identical."

"You know my mom?"

"Of course I know her. We were classmates, as girls."

"What do you mean she looks like Agata? Aside from the hair, that is?" Anna objected. "Can't you see she has Antonio's handsome eyes? His smile?"

Elena studied the girl with her arms crossed. "Meh, maybe. She's all Agata to me. What do you think, Carmine?"

"I don't know. It's not like I can remember Antonio's eyes, with everything I've got going on."

"You grumpy old man," Elena sighed, dismissing him with a wave. "How your wife puts up with you, I'll never know."

"You should see how I put up with her," Carmine chuckled.

"Eleven . . ." Tommaso said. "Do you know what you'll do after elementary school?"

"Of course she does," Anna said proudly. "She's getting ready for the middle school entrance exam. Then she'll go to the classical high school and then to university."

There had been a bit of an argument about it at home. Agata wanted her daughter to go to a three-year trade school.

"At least you'll learn a skill," she'd argued, but Antonio had no doubt Lorenza would be going to college. She'd be the first Greco with a college degree; he'd been dreaming about it since the day she was born, and no one in the world was going stand in the way. With that, Agata, who'd rarely seen her husband so determined, had acquiesced, but not without grumbling at length. She'd been raised on bread and practical sense: What was the point of studying all those years if you were just going to work yourself into the ground anyway? Plus, what she really wanted for Lorenza was a good husband. That was true security, when it came to feeding mouths.

"The classical high school. Very good," Tommaso praised her, stroking her cheek.

At the unexpected gesture, Lorenza immediately blushed and lowered her head.

Anna took her by the hand and walked her around the office, quickly explaining everyone's roles. Lorenza, as usual, started hammering her with questions:

"What's this scale for?" "What's in this chest of drawers?" "Whose desk is this?" "What's the vault for?"

Anna answered each question patiently.

"Now sit quietly for a moment," she said. "Auntie has to fill up the mailbag."

"Come over here with us," Chiara said to Lorenza, reaching for her hand. Lorenza followed her and Elena to the telegraphy office while Tommaso sat down at his desk and Carmine opened the front door to indicate that the post office was open for business.

Once the mailbag was full, Anna closed it, slung it over her shoulder, and went to the back room.

"Okay, I'm ready," she said. "Let's go."

Lorenza was sitting on the desk dangling her legs while Chiara explained how a telegraph worked. With every electrical impulse, she told her, a sequence of lines and dots was created. It was called Morse code. Her job was to decode it and translate it into words.

"Like magic!" Lorenza exclaimed, opening her eyes wide.

"Yes, a sort of magic." Chiara smiled sweetly.

From one post over, Elena sighed and mumbled that she didn't see anything magical about her job.

"Let's go, ma petite," Anna said, helping her niece down from the desk. "Or you'll be late and so will I. There's even a letter for your papa today."

———

Before going to the oil mill—the last stop of the day—Anna knocked on Angela's door; she had a small box to deliver. She pulled it out of her bag and weighed it in her hand, noting that it was extremely light. She shook it gently to guess its contents. She wondered what Angela's tenacious suitor had come up with this time. Angela welcomed her with her usual radiant smile, took the box from her hands, and, as always, opened it on the spot. Suddenly, she opened her eyes wide and slowly pulled out a carved wooden ring. She immediately slipped it onto her finger.

"It's my size," she said gleefully, showing her hand to Anna.

"It's very nice," Anna said, examining the ring. She looked up at Angela. "I'm pretty sure he's about to give you a real one."

The girl shrugged and gave a flirtatious grin. "My mother says the same thing."

It was almost lunchtime when Anna arrived at the oil mill. Agnese greeted her with a smile. "You can give it to me," she said, holding out her hand for the letter. But Anna said she'd rather deliver it in person. She knocked on the door to Antonio's office and waited for him to answer.

"Come in!"

"A letter for you!" she said, waving the envelope in the air.

Antonio jumped to his feet, dropping the folder that was open on his desk.

Anna burst out laughing.

"What a nice surprise," he said, going toward her.

"For you," she said, handing him the envelope.

Antonio took it and, without looking at it, placed it on the desk behind him. He invited Anna to sit down.

"How are you?" he asked, taking his seat in the chair in front of her. He glanced at her wrist to see if she was still wearing the watch he'd given her. He felt comforted when he saw that she was.

Anna shrugged.

"I'm fine, although your brother hasn't been making my life easy. It's a constant battle, as if he wants to make me pay for my choice every day," she sighed.

Antonio looked down.

"I don't understand what got into him," Anna continued, frowning. "He doesn't seem like the Carlo I know. He's so obsessed with what these people think . . . but why?"

"He'll get over it," Antonio said. "That's Carlo for you. When he gets something into his head . . . that's all he can think about. It becomes a sort of challenge for him. It could be a while before he relents."

She nodded.

"Yes, I know full well," she said. "I saw it right away, that your brother was stubborn. He courted me for more than a year. Just think, at first, I couldn't even stand him. I liked someone else."

"Is that right?" Antonio said in surprise, feeling a pang of jealousy.

"Yes. His name was Amedeo. He was a painter. A good-looking guy."

"And then?"

"And then your brother came into the picture and resolved to . . . take him out. Him and all the other suitors."

"Why—you had a lot?" Antonio smiled.

She shrugged. "A few."

She shifted her weight in the chair.

"But I made him wait a long time before I let him kiss me," she said, puffing up with pride. "My cousins kept saying, 'Don't play too hard to get,' 'Don't let someone like Carlo get away.' And do you know what I'd say to that?"

Antonio shook his head.

"That he should watch out that I didn't get away!"

"Can't argue with that," Antonio said, his voice cracking.

"I wish he could understand how important this job is to me," Anna added, becoming serious. "You understood right away. Why does he still not get it?"

Antonio stood up and stuck his hands in his pockets. "Do you want to come see my favorite place?" he asked suddenly.

She stared at him, curious. "What place?"

"It's not far. It's just above our heads," he said, pointing at the ceiling.

They went out the back door and emerged into an open space surrounded by high walls with flaking plaster.

"Where are we?" Anna asked, looking around.

"Come," Antonio said, leading the way.

They took an alley that ran alongside one of the walls, so narrow that they had to walk in single file. From there they climbed a long stone staircase that led to the oil mill's terrace.

"Look," Antonio exclaimed when they reached the top.

Anna took a few steps forward. From there she felt like she could hold the entire town in her hands; she recognized the church, the square, the castle, and saw people walking along, as tiny as ants. "You can see the post office, too!" she said.

"And behind us is the sea." Antonio placed his hands on her arms and slowly turned her toward the view.

Anna looked out in the distance. A strip of water cut the horizon in half.

"It's beautiful here," she said. "It's so peaceful."

"That's why I come here every day."

Anna smiled at him and then looked back at the sea. Just then, a gust of wind ruffled her hair, causing a lock to fall loose from her braid. She closed her eyes and let the breeze caress her face.

Antonio stared at her with his head slightly tilted. He imagined tracing the profile of her body with his finger as it stood out against the sky; he listened to the silence of that exposed yet intimate place, and realized they had never been so alone together, sheltered from everything.

In a sudden decision, he took her face into his hands and gently placed his lips on hers. It was a long, sweet kiss.

When he opened his eyes, Anna moved away and brought a hand to her mouth in shock, processing what had happened.

In a daze, Antonio stepped back until he was leaning against the railing behind him.

"Anna, I'm sorry," he said in a strangled voice.

She looked at him in horror. Without a word, she strode toward the staircase and disappeared from sight.

8

Since that morning on the terrace, Antonio hadn't been able to sleep. He tossed and turned in bed, sweating and in the grip of an inexplicable hunger for air. He felt like his breath had run aground in his chest and couldn't come out. The first time it happened, he thought he was about to die. He sat up in bed and with fear in his eyes, shook Agata awake. She made him lie down on his back and, as if she knew exactly what to do, squeezed his hand and ordered him to blow air out of his mouth while counting to ten.

"Pretend that you're trying to make your breath cross the room from wall to wall," she said. After a few long exhalations, which gradually became deeper, Antonio finally calmed down.

These last few weeks had been the worst of his life. With a stab of pain, he tried to avoid Carlo, but every time he looked him in the eyes, he had to hide his discomfort with a forced smile, which made him feel like a bastard, a traitor, the most despicable thing. He stopped getting coffee at Bar Castello every morning so as not to risk running into Anna as she arrived at the post office; he invented work-related excuses to arrive late to Sunday lunches with the family and leave as soon as possible. But it was all for naught: He still felt like a caged animal, forced to run around in circles without rest. The few times he'd caught Anna's eye, he hadn't seen any kind of spark or quiver—as if nothing had happened. It was as if she'd imposed an iron, almost militant discipline on herself to erase every moment of that blasted morning. To the point where he came to wonder if he'd dreamed it, if that kiss only existed in his head. He went over the events in his mind again and again, thinking back on every word that was said, every look, every move, trying to give them meaning—yet all the fragments remained scattered at his feet and there was no way to put them back together again. He wanted to run away, recover far from everyone and not be forced, at every turn, to face his guilt.

An acquaintance, Enrico, gave him a brilliant solution after he ran into him in Lecce, at the chamber of commerce. It was May 10, 1936, the day after Mussolini proclaimed the Empire of Italian East Africa: after Eritrea and Somalia, Ethiopia, too, had fallen to the fascists.

Enrico owned a construction company and was excitedly telling Antonio that he'd just obtained a colonial pass from the police. He would set sail from Brindisi in early June on a steamer headed to Asmara, the capital of Eritrea. Several other local businessmen were also moving there after deciding to expand their activities to the Italian colonies.

Antonio saw a way to get out of the problem of his own making.

The thought of leaving for Africa, the farthest place he could imagine, had crept into his mind slowly and then forcefully, until it became the only choice that gave him some solace. He could export his oil to the Italian colonies, set up a business there. He'd be away for a while, enough time to allow him to feel normal again. So, without a word to anyone, he applied for an emigration pass and underwent the bureaucratic process to obtain permission to leave. Once his professionalism, moral integrity, criminal record, political allegiances, and bill of health were established, he too received a colonial pass and the authorization to conduct business in Ital-

ian East Africa. He'd set out with a small shipment of oil and if business
with Asmara took the right turn, as he hoped, he'd send for more supplies.
Agnese was the only person who knew about the trip. It would be her job
to ship the goods and take care of the oil mill in his absence. Antonio had
no doubt about her discretion and loyalty.

He decided he would tell his family only a few days before his trip,
after it was too late for them to stop him.

———

"The cellar is finished. Will you come see it?" Carlo asked Anna out of the
blue one Sunday morning as she was drinking her warm milk in the garden, her eyes resting on the blossoming branches of the pomegranate
trees. She knew him well enough to see that this unexpected request
meant one thing only: Carlo had finally laid down his arms. He'd never
been great at uttering the word *sorry:* When he felt sorry, he preferred to
show it with actions, he always said.

"Yes," Anna said without looking away from the trees. "I'll come."

Carlo smiled and, for the first time in months, brushed her cheek
with the back of his hand.

"Take your time. I'll go help Roberto get dressed," he said.

"You're skipping mass today?"

"Yeah. I don't think anyone will mind," he said.

He had no desire to run into Carmela or submit to her dirty looks and
silent requests for an explanation regarding his behavior as of late. He'd
cut back on his morning "visits," and now it had been over a week since
he'd seen her; though she didn't know it yet, he'd decided he would stop
going altogether. He was relieved with his decision. Carmela had started to
make demands and sulked whenever he didn't tell her what she wanted
to hear, or if he happened to mention Anna one too many times, or if he
left her bed too quickly, which had been happening increasingly often.
The truth was that he didn't want that life anymore; while he'd initially

felt like he was giving Anna her rightful punishment—even though she was completely in the dark about it—now he just felt guilty. He was ashamed of having fed her to the town wolves, of allowing them to disparage her, of minimizing their love in the eyes of others.

They climbed into the 508 and instead of taking the road to the cellar, Carlo asked her if she felt like having a caffè corretto with him at Bar Castello.

Anna looked at him with concern.

"Is this another provocation?" she asked.

He turned to her. "No, really," he assured her, taking her hand. "I'd like it to become our ritual, from now on."

She studied him for a moment, then gave in to a smile.

"Did you hear that, Roberto?" she said, turning her head to look at her son, who was sitting in her lap. "Papa wants a drinky."

Carlo parked the car in the square, which was already packed with people, and as he and Anna got out, he thought he sensed glances, nudges, and murmurs. They made their way through the crowd toward the bar, each holding Roberto by the hand as he skipped along between them.

Nando came over in a white apron that stretched over his belly and greeted them as cordially as ever.

"What can I get ya?"

"The usual," Anna said, leaning against the bar. "But for two," she added, turning to Carlo.

The same two old folks were still there, sitting at the same table, as if they were cardboard cutouts that Nando set up every morning and stored in the closet at night.

Anna clinked her cup against Carlo's.

"Santé," she said, drinking her coffee in one sip.

The old folks cast a quick glance at them and lowered their heads, returning to their game of briscola.

Carlo noticed her only once they were back at the car and he was about to open the door. Carmela had been standing across the crowded square the entire time, in front of the church, stiff as a board, her black veil over her head. She was holding on to her husband, who was engaged in conversation with a group of men.

She was staring at Carlo with fire in her eyes.

Carlo looked away and got in the car.

Once out of town, on the road to the winery, Anna lowered the window and let the wind soothe her face. She suddenly felt comforted, as if she'd escaped some kind of danger. *Every piece must fall into place,* she thought, watching the fields of olive trees pass by as if they were in a relay race. *Nothing irreparable has happened,* she kept saying to herself. What happened with Antonio had been a flash of madness and weakness; the most reasonable thing to do was minimize it, tear it to pieces, and toss it into the wind. She was certain he felt the same way and that there was no need to talk about it. They'd both move on and soon forget about it. They had to—there was no other way.

"Here we are," Carlo exclaimed, turning right. He stopped the car in the clearing outside the winery and pulled the emergency brake.

"Come see Papa's kingdom," he said cheerfully, helping Roberto out of the car. Then he reached for Anna, who took his hand and set out with them under the warmth of the late-morning sun.

Carlo opened the wooden gate and they went in. Anna was immediately struck by the vaulted ceilings, but she especially liked the smell of tuff rock that permeated the room.

"This is the bottling room," Carlo explained, drawing circles with his arms. "That's where the corking machine will go. This is where we'll store the empty bottles," he said, pointing at another corner of the room. "And over here," he continued, dragging her to the next room, "we'll attach the labels."

He opened a door. "And this is my office." It was a small room with a desk, a chair, and an empty bookcase.

"Some stuff is still missing," he added.

Anna kept looking around in disbelief.

"Come on, let's go downstairs," he said. They went down to the cement vats. "The wine will ferment in here," he explained, crouching by a vat.

"What can I say, Carlo? This place is . . . yours. You did a good job," she murmured, looking around.

"Do you really like it?" He was beaming.

"Yes, really."

"And there's one more thing," he continued. "No one knows. And I wanted to surprise you once it was bottled. But actually, there's no reason to wait."

"What are you talking about?"

"About Donna Anna. That's what we're calling the first label. The first wine to be issued by the Greco Winery."

Anna teared up.

"You're serious?" she asked with a smile.

"Very serious," Carlo declared, enchanted by his wife's joy.

Anna gently touched his cheek. Then she kissed him.

"Donna Anna!" Roberto parroted in his cute little voice.

———

Don Giulio's reply arrived with the roses' full bloom.

When Giovanna saw the postcard, which depicted Piazza Maggiore in Bologna, she burst out joyfully laughing, with her big hazel eyes filled with light. Cesare, infected by her cheerfulness, jumped up on her, wagging his tail.

Under Giovanna's impatient gaze, Anna took a wet sponge, wrung it well, and dabbed at the stamps; then, with the tip of a knife, she pried them away, starting with each corner. As expected, a few words appeared.

"Well?" Giovanna urged her. "What does it say?"

Anna hesitated.

"I'll read it to you, but on one condition," she said. "That you let me teach you to read and write."

Giovanna's face darkened. "You know I can't," she said, shaken.

"That's not true. Let me try, at least."

"I told you. I can't see the words. Everything looks confused . . . like a big black blob."

"I know what to do," Anna said. "Just trust me."

Giovanna bit her lip and gave her a resigned look.

"Excellent," said Anna, perking up. "We'll start tomorrow."

"Now you read?" Giovanna asked.

"Now I read." Anna winked at her.

The words don Giulio had concealed revealed a man full of passion, the man with whom Giovanna had fallen in love and whom she now recognized again. He certainly hadn't held back on the "inappropriate" thoughts away from prying eyes. Even Anna, not a prude by a long shot, blushed at them.

> I feel split in two. My thoughts are sinful and claw at me in
> the night like a beast I can't contain. I let myself be devoured,
> and when I wake, I ask God for forgiveness. Write to me
> again. Tell me your most sinful thoughts.

That day, Anna left Contrada as the sun was setting. The entire way home, she brooded over the whole chastity matter and what nonsense it was. In her ideal world, priests would be able to marry and start a family or declare their love like everyone else. Wasn't theirs a job like any other?

She thought at length about how to help Giovanna. She had no idea why she couldn't "see the words," as she said. In all her years as a teacher, she'd never seen anything like it, so she searched for the answer in the medical manuals she found in the town library. Even there, she found no answers; Giovanna's challenge seemed to be nameless, a disorder no one had investigated. She had no choice but to rely on instinct. She told herself that if her friend saw words crowding on the page like a flock of birds, the only thing left to do was to hold them still. She procured a piece of rectangular white card stock and cut out a window that was two inches long and as tall as the lines in a book.

―――

The next day, she knocked on her friend's door with two copies of *Pride and Prejudice*: one was hers, worn from reading it over and over, and the other was borrowed.

She sat in front of Giovanna and explained how these afternoon lessons would unfold and warned her that from then on, they would be daily.

"I'll read out loud, very slowly, and you will follow on your copy, isolating each phrase as we go along using this card stock. See that little window? That's what it's for."

"But . . . we'll read the whole thing?" Giovanna asked with dismay, turning the book over in her hands. Cesare came up and started to sniff the book with curiosity.

"I guess we'll see!" Anna replied.

―――

Carmela looked in the mirror one last time. She was wearing a dress she'd made for the occasion, copied from a model she'd cut out of *l'Eco del Cinema*. It was an ultramarine dress with light blue flowers, a knee-length pleated skirt, three-quarter sleeves, and a white belt that cinched her waist. She also put on a little boiled-wool cloche hat in the same color, applied lipstick, and dabbed a layer of powder on her face. Finally, she slipped a yellow envelope into her purse and left the house, looking like someone ready to deliver a death blow.

She made a beeline for Carlo's house, taking side alleys to avoid crossing the square. She walked across the courtyard to the front door and knocked.

Carlo opened up, still in his pajamas. When he saw Carmela, he went white in the face.

"Why are you here?"

"If Mohammed won't go to the mountain . . . Ease up, I know she's not here at this hour. Can I come in?"

"Of course not. Have you gone mad?" Carlo said, casting a glance over her shoulder. The lines on his face hardened, creating deep grooves in his forehead she'd never noticed before. Carmela peeked beyond the door and saw Roberto sitting on the rug playing with a wooden horse.

"What do you want?" Carlo said.

She stared at him disdainfully. "You're the best, aren't you? At disappearing? You disappeared twelve years ago, and now here you go again. What, you think everyone is just here to serve your every whim? And then keep quiet about it? Well, I'm going to talk, this time."

Carlo leaned against the doorframe.

"Carmela, it had to end sooner or later," he whispered, casting another glance at the road.

"And you decided that on your own. From one day to the next. As always."

"There was nothing to talk about. What good would that have done?"

"Of course. You come into my house, take what you want, and say 'see you later.' You did the same with my father—you asked him for help and then didn't give him anything for his trouble."

"Don't worry about don Ciccio. I know how to pay him back."

In that moment, they heard the clatter of hooves on the cobblestones; a man was driving a mule-drawn cart down the road perpendicular to theirs.

"You can't stay here, Carmela."

"I'm going, I'm going," she grumbled, with a gesture of impatience. "But first I have to give you this," she said, pulling the yellow envelope from her bag.

"What is it?"

"Open it."

Carlo took it, opened the flap, and pulled out a sepia-colored paper folded in half. It was a birth certificate. *Daniele Carlà.* Under that was a date of birth: December 16, 1924.

"What is the meaning of this? Why did you bring me your son's birth certificate?"

"For a businessman, you're not so great with numbers." She started to count on her fingers, "April, May, June, July, August . . . shall I go on until December?"

"I don't understand," he mumbled.

"It's not that hard, Carlo. You'll get it."

"Carmela, what are you trying to say?" he asked, raising his voice as he slowly caught on.

Behind him, Roberto stopped playing and looked up at his father.

"Papa, thirsty," he whined.

Carlo turned to look at him, bewildered.

"Go help your son, go on," Carmela said, smirking. She took the certificate from his hand, turned on her heels, and walked away. She didn't care how angry Carlo got or for how long. The only thing that mattered was the certainty that from that day on, whenever Carlo looked at her, even from afar, he would see the mother of his child. Of his firstborn son. He would no longer be able to ignore her. And that was enough.

At least for now.

———

Carlo spent the following days seized by an unusual weakness in body and spirit.

He tried to remember the few times he'd run into Daniele: the first time he saw him, in town with Nicola; the morning he stopped by don Ciccio's house and found him there with his grandparents, doing his homework; the time he saw him furtively light a cigarette with some friends behind Bar Castello. Oh, and on Easter Sunday, in church, as they walked side by side to the altar. He'd always looked at him with indifference, as a person of little consequence.

Now he knew how to explain those looks don Ciccio would give him, his hostile comments, those sentences Carmela left dangling, as if she were forcing down the rest. A sudden wave of anger rose in his chest: don Ciccio, Gina, Carmela . . . they'd orchestrated everything, they'd pulled the strings for all those years, and he was nothing but a puppet. How could they have kept him in the dark? And Nicola? Was he in on the farce? Who else knew?

Exasperated one morning while driving to the vineyard, Carlo suddenly veered toward the oil mill and, once in front of the door, started honking his horn nonstop.

Antonio threw open the door.

"You have a subtle way of announcing yourself," he joked. When he noticed his brother's gloomy expression, he quickly became serious.

"Get in, we have to go somewhere," Carlo said, hurriedly.

"Where?"

"I'll show you."

"But . . ." Antonio hesitated. "Did something happen? Do I have to worry?"

"No. But let's go."

"Let me alert Agnese." Antonio went inside and came out again with a jacket folded over his arm.

Once Antonio had climbed in, Carlo stepped on the gas pedal and took off with a screech.

"Are we in a hurry?" Antonio asked, clutching the door handle.

"No," Carlo said, keeping his hands stiff on the wheel and his gaze fixed on the road.

"Then slow down. At least we'll get there alive."

Carlo drove to the school, then pulled over and turned off the engine.

"Now what are we doing?" Antonio asked.

Carlo opened the glove compartment and pulled out a cigar. He brought it to his lips and lit it.

"Now we wait," he said.

A few minutes later, Daniele arrived and joined a group of classmates by the school gates.

"There he is," Carlo exclaimed.

"Who now?"

"Daniele. Down there."

"Carmela's son?" Antonio asked, tentatively.

Carlo blew out smoke.

"Right. *Carmela's* son."

"Carlo, I'm not following. Why are we here?"

"Do you think he looks like me?"

Antonio stared at him, flabbergasted.

"Like you? Why should he—"

"Look at him," Carlo said sharply. "Do you see any resemblance? To the Grecos?"

Antonio leaned forward and studied the boy through the windshield.

"No, Carletto," he said finally. "None at all."

"Yeah," Carlo mumbled with his eyes pinned on Daniele, who was standing with his hands in his pockets and laughing with another kid.

"Must have been easy to fool everyone. He's the spitting image of Carmela, lucky for her."

Antonio turned to stare at him in shock.

"Do I understand what you're implying correctly?" he asked.

Carlo tapped his finger on his cigar and a cylinder of ash fell to the floor. Then he started the 508 and turned right.

"She wants me to suffer, the bitch," he hissed.

"And you're sure it's true?"

"Yes. The dates coincide. It happened when I came down for your wedding. Daniele was born in December."

"Who else knows?"

Carlo shrugged. "As far as I know, Carmela's parents. I don't know about Nicola."

"Will you tell Anna?"

"Are you kidding? No."

Antonio hesitated. "What will you do?"

"Nothing," Carlo said. "What can I possibly do?"

"Aren't you worried she'll tell Anna?"

Carlo took a drag from his cigar. "She won't. She's built her life on a huge lie to save her and her family's honor, and she can't destroy it all now. She's not that stupid. And don Ciccio would never let her anyway."

"So then why did she tell you? Do you think she wants something from you?"

"No. She just wants to torment me. I know her. But it won't work on me. Children belong to the people who raise them. As far as I'm concerned, that kid is Nicola's son."

Antonio nodded and looked down. He knew exactly what was happening: Carlo was distancing himself, building a wall of bricks made of fake indifference. That was his way of protecting himself, of standing up to the force of life's terrible blows. That was what he'd done with their mother, too, by pulling and pulling at the ties that bound them until they snapped for good.

Once they arrived back at the oil mill, Antonio sighed deeply, frowned, and announced that he also had something to say.

"I've decided to leave, Carletto. I'm going to Asmara with some other businessmen. I'm going to try to set up an oil trade with the colonies, and to do it I'll have to stay there for a while. You're the first person I've told. I set sail in ten days."

He said it all in one breath, tripping over his words and without looking Carlo in the face.

Carlo was dumbfounded. "Just like that, out of nowhere?"

"No, I've been thinking about it for a while."

"And why have you never mentioned it?"

"It was just an idea . . ."

"Yeah, right. You've already planned everything. How long will you be away?"

Antonio shrugged. "I don't know. The time it takes for them to get to know my oil. It might go badly and I'll be back right away, who knows."

"It seems like you were almost afraid to tell me," Carlo said, frowning. "That's why you've been so odd lately."

Antonio's heartbeat sped up.

"No, it's just . . . I didn't know how you'd take it."

"Well, I'm surprised, I'm not going to lie. But what can I say—if you want to do this and you're happy, big brother, then I'm happy too!"

Antonio's face relaxed. "Really?"

"Of course! Actually, it's good that you want to expand."

"Yeah," Antonio said, forcing a smile. "I guess I'm more afraid of Agata and Lorenza's reaction. I don't think they'll take it well. Plus, I don't know. I'm sorry to leave you alone now of all times, with this whole thing . . ."

Carlo put his hand on Antonio's shoulder and squeezed it.

"Don't think about me. I'm fine. Truly. As for Agata and Lorenza, well, they'll understand," he assured him. "And if not, I'll help you explain it to them. It's just a work trip. It's not like you'll be gone forever, right?"

Antonio felt his heart skip a beat. There had never been secrets between them before.

If only I didn't love you so much, he thought. *If only.*

———

That evening, when Antonio came home, the table was already set. Agata was in the kitchen wearing a white apron tied around her ample hips, stirring something in a copper pot with a wooden spoon. He greeted her with a hand on her back. She planted a quick and moist kiss on his cheek and told him to call Lorenza, as the soup was almost ready.

Antonio went upstairs and gently opened the door to his daughter's room. She was sitting at her desk drawing in a notebook with a sharp pencil.

"Ma petite," he said.

Lorenza giggled.

"That's what Auntie calls me." She jumped out of her chair, ran up to him, and pressed herself against him.

"Are you hungry?" he asked her, stroking her hair.

She nodded.

"Let's go, then. Dinner's ready. Let's not keep Mama waiting."

They went back downstairs just as Agata was bringing the soup to the table. They sat down and Agata crossed herself. She joined her hands together and recited grace, devoted but quick—it would be a shame to let the soup get cold.

Antonio looked at his wife and then at his daughter; they both radiated cheer that evening. Agata smiled as she got up to pour soup into Lorenza's dish. *She seems so different when she smiles,* Antonio thought. While he watched her, he saw with absolute clarity how Agata was a part of him, of his story. He certainly cared for her; she was the mother of his daughter. Yet there was a *but.* There had been from the start. A cumbersome *but* that both of them, from a certain point on, had pretended not to see. Agata had been the first woman to tell him she loved him—she had wanted him and so she pursued him until she got him. Antonio, for his part, had simply let himself be chosen. His brother had recently gone away, and he felt terribly alone. Agata seemed like a decent alternative to solitude.

"Love can be learned," she told him. "And you'll learn. Until then, mine will be enough."

But it hadn't been enough—he never learned to love her. They had a sort of tacit agreement now, and they both knew that if one of them broke it, their lives would be reduced to rubble, along with whatever good they'd managed to build together in the process, in spite of everything.

Antonio knew that the words he was about to utter would shatter the harmonious family portrait that had formed in that moment. Like the bucolic landscapes his mother had hand-painted that were hanging on every wall in the house. He was moments away from extinguishing the smiles on his wife's and daughter's faces, causing their features to tense up, their muscles to harden. Still, he didn't feel guilty about leaving them both alone.

He dumped the words on the table in one breath.

Agata stopped dead, put her spoon on the napkin by her dish, and hid her hands under the table.

"How long will you be gone?" she asked in a cracked voice, after a long pause.

"As long as necessary."

"Papa, but Africa is faaar away."

"It's a whole other world," Agata mumbled.

"Can't you take me and Mama with you?" Lorenza asked.

Antonio took her hand and, borrowing Carlo's words, tried to reassure her. It was just a work trip; it wasn't like he was going away forever.

"But you already have a job here," Lorenza said. "Why do you need another one?"

"What are we going to do without you? Who will I rely on if something happens to our child?" Agata complained.

"Why should anything happen?"

"And just like that, out of the blue, you take off in ten days and I'm just hearing about it now. Do Carlo and Anna know?"

"I told Carlo. I guess Anna knows by now."

"Papa, don't go." Lorenza was squirming in her seat.

"Listen to your daughter," Agata muttered. "Will you at least consider her?"

"I'll be back soon," he said, trying to comfort them. He stroked Lorenza's head. "And I promise to write every week."

"Swear?" Lorenza asked, with a sad look on her face.

"I swear."

"Don't swear," Agata said, frostily. Then she stood up and brought her steaming dish back into the kitchen.

———

On the morning of June 22, Antonio grabbed his brown leather suitcase and placed it by the front door. He peeked into the kitchen. Agata, her eyes swollen from crying, was filtering ash from the pot of water in which she'd boiled the laundry and pouring the remaining water into a bowl. She would use it later to wash her and Lorenza's hair. Antonio felt a vague sense of nostalgia and tenderness, but he wasn't able to say anything. He went back into the living room, picked up the suitcase, and closed the door behind him.

He walked to Carlo's house; his brother would drive him to the port in Brindisi in the 508.

Anna opened the door. She looked at him and then at the suitcase.

"Carlo's almost ready," she said.

"There's no rush. I'm the one who's early," Antonio said.

Anna crossed her arms and sighed. "Will I see you again soon?" she asked.

Antonio looked up and stared at her intensely, without a word.

Anna blushed and looked away.

In that moment, Carlo joined them, out of breath. As always, he smelled of minty aftershave.

"Here I am, big brother. I'm ready," he exclaimed. He got in the car and Antonio placed the suitcase in the trunk while Anna, standing at the door, watched them both with an inscrutable gaze.

In the end, all she said was "Safe travels." She went back inside without giving Antonio a chance to answer.

9

Tommaso's wedding was held on a Sunday morning in July, in the church of San Lorenzo. It was a simple and intimate ceremony—just as he had wanted it. They had to be careful not to further strain the delicate heart of his sweet Giulia. But the townspeople could not resist the urge to peek at the wedding gown, which was why a phalanx of neighbors had positioned itself to await the newlyweds as they exited the church.

Anna recognized Giuseppina, who beamed at her and waved hello. *She always seems so happy so see me,* Anna thought tenderly. A moment later, she noticed two fascist squadristi congratulating Tommaso's in-laws, with whom they seemed thick as thieves. Anna hardened her gaze and stared at them, annoyed. Must they wear those blasted black shirts at weddings, too?

Giulia's gown, designed and sewn by Carmela, was romantic and soft, with long sleeves and a draped neckline framed by little pearls, which also adorned the skullcap she wore atop her long blond hair. She was holding a bouquet of calla lilies. Whispers started to dart across the square:

"She's so elegant. She looks like a real princess!"

"That girl has always been graceful."

"Shame about her health, poor thing."

Tommaso's eyes were bright and clear like the sea on a summer morning. His curls, stiffened by an excessive amount of gel, formed a sort of crown. No one had the heart to suggest that the newlyweds weren't truly happy and in love, even though some folks on the other end of the square were already betting on how long that happiness would last.

Tommaso and Giulia left for their honeymoon on the Amalfi coast the following day. They would stay there a week. Carmine would stand in for the director, not just because he was the longest-serving employee but also because he was the only man in the office.

With the summer heat, Anna retired her winter uniform and donned a light one in blue cotton and short sleeves; plus, with great relief, she stopped wearing her thick black stockings, a change Carmine was quick to point out.

"You represent the Royal Post Office. You can't go around with bare legs, like your mama made you," he scolded her.

"How about this," Anna replied, as she stuffed her mailbag with letters. "I promise to put them back on as long as you wear them, too."

Chiara burst out laughing and quickly covered her mouth with her hand. Elena put her hands on her hips and raised her eyebrows in the mistaken assumption that her gesture would act as a warning. Anna didn't even look at her.

That morning, she learned that there would soon be another wedding to celebrate: the one between Angela and her devoted woodworker. When she knocked on the girl's door to deliver a white envelope with no sender instead of the usual package, Anna couldn't help but notice a gold ring with a small diamond on her finger.

"You were a part of this story, you know," Angela said unexpectedly, with shiny eyes. "When I tell my children, I can't not talk about the lovely letter carrier who brought their father's gifts to me every Tuesday."

She added that after the wedding, she'd be moving to Lecce, to the house her future husband had bought for them, a stone's throw from his workshop, and that she was truly sad that she would not be seeing her again.

Anna just smiled, embarrassed. Then, from her jacket pocket, she pulled out a business card and gave it to the girl.

"So you can show your kids," she said.

Giovanna's lessons continued. Aside from Sundays, Anna went to Contrada every day between four and six o'clock in the afternoon. As Anna had hoped, the novel was a perfect reflection of Giovanna's romantic disposition, and she jumped every time she saw Elizabeth and the charming Mr. Darcy appear on the same page. Her desire to find out whether they'd get married was her greatest motivator. Slowly but surely, Giovanna kept reading on her own after the end of each lesson. Initially, she'd advance by just a few lines, but after two months, she found that she could read a whole page by herself.

Writing, though, was much more difficult for her. Anna started to have her write the postcards to don Giulio, sitting next to her and helping her spell out each word. If the message was particularly long, it could take days.

In his last postcard, don Giulio had informed her that he'd be visiting his family in late August and that he'd be very pleased to see her again. Assuming she wanted it too, he'd specified.

———

Antonio's first letter arrived on the eve of San Lorenzo, along with the shooting stars. That morning, when Anna read the address and recipient— *Lorenza Greco, via Paladini 43, Lizzanello (LE) Italia*—her breath got caught in her chest for a moment. She flipped over the envelope and saw the sender. Yes, Antonio had finally written, after a weeks-long silence.

Anna wanted to open the envelope and read the letter before everyone else; she knew how to peel off the flap and close it again, making it appear intact. She lingered on the thought for a few minutes while standing at the big table in the post office, staring at the envelope and at Antonio's handwriting, so clear and elegant.

The chimes of the clock on the town hall ringing nine o'clock were enough to dissuade her. As if she'd been slapped in the face, she shook her head and thought, *What am I thinking?* She quickly slipped the envelope back in the mailbag and headed straight to Agata and Antonio's house.

Anna stood in the middle of their living room watching Agata tear off one side of the envelope and pull out two letters. There was a brief one to her and a much longer one to Lorenza. She scanned her husband's words with thirsty eyes, then collapsed in a chair, as if the letter itself had exhausted her.

"At least he's alive, the swine," she said.

The lack of news from Antonio had stressed Agata's nerves to the breaking point. While she told everyone she saw in town that he'd probably died or drowned in the Red Sea, whereupon she would take on the devastated look of a newly widowed woman, at home she snapped over the smallest thing, and her favorite target was inevitably Lorenza. Whatever her daughter did, or didn't do—an unmade bed, a slight tardiness, a cup forgotten on the table after breakfast—threw her into a rage. Lorenza was the fuse that made Agata explode. And every time, Lorenza's eyes would tear up; keeping her head down, she'd tightly press her lips together to keep from sobbing.

"What did he say? Is he okay?" Anna asked, barely able to contain the emotion in her voice.

Agata folded both letters and put them in her dress pocket.

"He's fine," she said, sourly. "We're here, me and his daughter, going through hell because of him. But anyway," she said finally, standing up with a sigh, "who cares about us?"

Anna scowled.

"Well," she said, "we're here, too. It's not like you're alone."

"Cold comfort that is," Agata said, turning her back on her.

Anna shook her head and walked toward the door.

"Oh," Agata added without turning around. "He says hi. To you and Carlo."

That day, after lunch, Lorenza arrived at her aunt and uncle's house panting and clutching the letter.

"It's here, Auntie!" she exclaimed, running up to Anna and jolting awake Roberto, who'd been sleeping on the couch.

"I know." Anna smiled. "I was the one who delivered it to your mom."

"Go on, read it," Carlo urged her, sitting on the couch next to his son, who simply turned over and fell right back to sleep.

Lorenza sat down next to her uncle while Anna stood and crossed her arms in front of her. Then she opened the letter, handling it with the tips of her fingers as if it were made of crystal, and started to read it in her high-pitched little voice.

> My dear, sweet Lorenza,
>
> Here I am, finally. I know that I'm unforgivably late, but I assure you that I had perfectly valid reasons to not write sooner. I hope you don't think it was because I didn't want to, and it pains me to imagine that you feel neglected. More than anything, I'm ashamed of not having kept my promise of writing every week. I promised it lightly, I see that now—I didn't have the slightest idea of what I'd find upon my arrival. I apologize from the depths of my heart, my dear daughter. Do you forgive me?
>
> Your papa is well. I'm staying in a warm, welcoming boardinghouse. It's called Casa degli Italiani and from my window I can see the opera house, an architectural marvel!

You would love it. Outside it is a shell-shaped fountain surrounded by two imposing staircases that lead to the entrance. Just last week I went to see a play by Pirandello, *Non si sa come*. I loved it and couldn't stop thinking about it for days. When I return, I'll take you to see it at the theater. You're a big girl now.

Asmara is in constant evolution and expansion, and I've already established several contacts with local restaurants and hotels, which I visit daily to bring samples of my oil. Two restaurants on Corso Italia, the main thoroughfare in the city, have already ordered a supply for the next few months. Isn't that great news? I hope you'll be as happy about it as I am.

I don't know when I'll be back; there's still a lot of work to be done here.

I'll try to write more often, but meanwhile, tell me how your summer is going. Have you been to the beach? What books are you reading?

Try to listen to your mother and don't upset her.

I love you,
Your papa

"He seems to be doing well," Carlo said, spreading his arms and standing up.

Lorenza stayed seated, bowed over the letter she held tightly in her hands.

"Something wrong, ma petite?" Anna asked, coming closer.

"What does he mean he doesn't know when he'll be back?" she asked faintly.

"It means business is going well," Carlo comforted her. "Don't worry. He'll be back before school starts. And he'll bring you a great present, you'll see!"

Anna sat next to her and pulled her in close.

"It's okay," she whispered. "Actually, you know what we'll do? Stay for dinner tonight and we'll make pesto together. I need my best helper," she said with a smile.

Lorenza looked up at her suddenly and beamed. But then she became sad.

"We'll invite Mama too, right?" she asked, almost fearfully.

"Obviously," Carlo cut in. "Tonight, we'll all celebrate your papa's first sale together," he added cheerfully.

———

The following morning, Anna left home earlier than usual—at that hour, the neighbor wasn't even out sweeping the sidewalk yet—and made a beeline for the library. She crossed the square, which was still empty except for Michele, who was unloading large watermelons from a cart. Anna picked up her pace and scurried in through the library's open door. She asked the nice man at the desk if they had a copy of *Non si sa come*. He looked hesitant and asked who the author was. Luigi Pirandello, she told him.

The man stood up and headed for the theater section. It was ten whole minutes before he returned with the book. That entire morning, as she walked from house to house, emptying the mailbag as she went, she couldn't think of anything but the book in her bag and why Antonio had loved that play so much, to the point where he couldn't stop thinking about it. She couldn't wait to start reading it on her bench in her *jardin secret*.

That afternoon, Anna read avidly, without stopping, until dinnertime, when the garden became tinged with the colors of twilight. Pirandello's play told the story of a man who gave in to his passions and lay with his best friend's wife, only to suffer from extraordinary guilt. His remorse for that impulsive, wretched act became so great that the man wanted to be punished at all costs.

Only when she reached the last page and closed the book did Anna understand the real, hidden reason why Antonio had left. Like the main character in the story, he, too, had sought punishment and had found it by running off to the farthest possible place from her and Carlo.

———

School started in late September, but despite Carlo's optimistic forecast, Antonio did not return. He sent Lorenza a few lines where he wished her a good school year and urged her to study hard and become the best in the class. Regarding his return, though, not even a vague promise. Lorenza was about to start junior high school, the one that would allow her to go to the classical high school and then to college, a dream Antonio had nurtured for her since she was little. As Carlo drove her to Lecce in his 508 for her first day of school, Lorenza looked out the window frowning, thinking that if her papa hadn't come home to her for such an important occasion, it meant that this dream didn't mean anything to him anymore.

She started to spend all her afternoons at her aunt and uncle's house. It was as if Agata was breathing in poison and exhaling it onto Lorenza. Now she couldn't even stand the way her daughter chewed her food.

"Can you stop that racket, once and for all? Eat like a good Christian, not like a beast!" she kept saying, exasperated.

With her heart pounding, Lorenza tried hard to keep her mouth sealed shut and chew quietly.

Then there was the matter of homework, which had turned out to be extremely demanding. Not only did Agata not know how to help her, but she didn't have the slightest desire to try.

"Were it up to me, I'd have found you a job," she snorted. "It was your father's idea to send you to junior high. Now he's not here and who knows when he'll be back. Do it yourself!"

So it was up to Anna to help Lorenza, and luckily, she had almost all her afternoons free, since Giovanna was reading just fine on her own. How moved she'd been when Elizabeth finally accepted Darcy's proposal!

Anna and Lorenza's afternoons together filled them both with joy:

Anna helped Lorenza with her homework and then corrected it; made her a snack with bread, jam, and pomegranate juice; and on some evenings, after a long day of school, she drew her a bath with Marseilles soap petals and combed her hair.

There was only one thing that could ruin Anna's mood and make her fly off the handle—the glorification of fascism, which always came up, especially in Italian homework.

"Unacceptable!" she exclaimed one day, scrolling through the topics Lorenza could choose from for her essay.

In a singsong tone, she read through the prompts: *"Why I'm a little Italian, Which fascist works do you admire most? From Vittorio Veneto to the March on Rome, a martyr and a hero of the recent Italian-Ethiopian war.* You know fascism is wrong, right?" she said.

Lorenza looked down.

"Mm-hmm," she mumbled, a bit dubiously.

"Your father would tell you the same thing if he were here."

"My teacher likes the Duce, though—" Lorenza tried to retort.

"Your teacher is an idiot," Anna interrupted.

Lorenza looked at her in confusion. "But everyone in school likes the Duce."

"That doesn't mean it's right." Anna sighed and changed to a more reasonable approach. "Obviously you can't say these things to your teacher. Or to anyone else, got it?"

"I have a question, Auntie," Lorenza said. "Is Papa not coming back because he doesn't want to be with my mama anymore?"

Anna swallowed and hesitated at length before answering. " No," she said, stroking Lorenza's cheek. "Your Papa's there for work. You know that. He's doing it for you, too. Especially for you."

"But I didn't ask him to."

"He'll be back soon, don't worry, ma petite."

"How do you know that?"

"I know your father."

And as she said it, Anna wondered if that was really true.

———

One morning in late October, Giovanna walked out the wooden door of the library holding a copy of Flaubert's *Sentimental Education*. She thought about how many stories she'd missed over the years, so certain of her inability to read. Yet all she had needed was Anna's stubbornness to show her she had been wrong. Now she wanted to make up for lost time and devour stories until she overdosed on them. Sure, she still made a lot of mistakes, especially when writing, but the little card stock window was now a distant memory.

"Hey there, friend!" Anna popped up behind her, looking flawless in her blue winter uniform. "What have you got there? Let me see."

Giovanna bit her lip and handed her the book.

"Ah, you took my advice! It's a masterpiece, you'll see." Anna smiled. "No one has ever been able to describe love's great expectations, and disappointments, better than Flaubert." She looked at Giovanna pointedly, with a hint of regret in her eyes.

Giovanna looked at her feet and took the book back.

"He'll come next summer, I can feel it," she murmured. "I know you don't believe it anymore, but you'll see. He'll come."

Anna nodded uneasily.

"I have to go. See you later? Are you bringing the pomegranates for juicing?"

"Of course," Anna said.

As her friend walked away, Anna couldn't help but hear the two women muttering on the bench behind her.

"Wasn't that one a dimwit? How is she reading now?"

"Nah, she's just pretending. When someone's bent, you can never set them straight."

Anna took a deep breath, turned around, and stomped over to the two women.

"Oh, good morning, Mrs. Letter Carrier," they said.

"The only dimwits I see here are the two of you," Anna said. Then, indifferent to their stunned expressions, she turned on her heel and left.

"What a temper, that outlander," one woman said, shaking her head.

———

The months flew by during Antonio's absence, and in all likelihood, more would have passed if, on the last day of October, Agata hadn't sent a telegram to her husband.

Lorenza is sick. Come home immediately.

Antonio packed his bags quickly, announced his return via telegram, and left the very next day. When the steamer left the port of Asmara, he stayed on deck to stare at the city as it got smaller and smaller. Everything that had happened to him in those months suddenly seemed to belong to someone else, to a man who had lived there, and lied there, in his stead. As the ship crossed the Red Sea, he understood that he would never again set foot in Africa. But he also knew that the time away had not eased his pain. He would find it intact, and inexorable, upon his return.

Lorenza had nothing more than a common fever and she'd recovered long before Antonio touched land.

So I lied, Agata said to herself. For a just cause. At least it brought him home.

10

Seven Months Later

That summer, it seemed like all the single young women in town had conspired to wed at the same time; between the end of summer and the start of spring, the San Lorenzo churchyard had become a carpet of rice grains, as no one ever bothered to clean up between one wedding ceremony and another.

Carmela's workload tripled. The dress she'd made the year before for Giulia had been so widely admired that orders had taken off. Her dressmaker's shop became a revolving door of future brides searching for their dream gown, "like the one for the padrone's daughter." These were feverish weeks; Carmela would wake up at four in the morning, fill her biggest moka pot (the six-cup one), and sip her coffee little by little, making it last until lunchtime. As Nicola and Daniele slept like logs behind the door that separated the dressmaker's shop from the house, she drew sketch after sketch, still in her nightgown, until opening time. She always kept hold of a copy of *Moda Illustrata*, the magazine from which she took inspiration for her own designs.

Sometimes, at dawn, she would hear Daniele stumble down the stairs, cross the kitchen, and stop in front of the shop door. He would peek in, his hair disheveled, wearing nothing but his underwear and white under-shirt, then sit quietly next to her, crossing his arms on the table and rest-ing his chin on them. He would stay there watching her, focused and curious, while Carmela's pencil danced on the page, tracing laced bodices, soft trains, and sheer sleeves.

"Mama, I don't want to go to school anymore," Daniele said one morn-ing, out of the blue. "I want to do what you do."

Carmela stopped dead, pencil in midair, then slowly placed it on the table. "What do you mean you don't want to go to school?"

Daniele looked down.

"I'd rather work with you," he said, almost in a whisper.

"That won't be possible."

Daniele hesitated. "Why not?"

"You really need to ask me that? You're a boy, and if you *really* must leave school to start work, that's fine by me, but you have to leave to find a *tough* job, one a man would have."

Daniele looked at her, disappointed.

"Let me try, at least? I've been designing dresses in my notebook. Wanna see?"

"No," she said curtly. "I don't want to see any such thing. Sewing is not for boys. I'll find you a job, to be sure, but I don't need to hear another word of this nonsense. Now buzz off—I've got work to do."

That unexpected request unsettled Carmela, causing her to worry for the rest of the day. What had gotten into him? A boy at a sewing ma-chine? And he'd been designing dresses, too? He'd been coddled for far too long. He wasn't Nicola's son, but he'd inherited the same mild tem-perament of the Carlà side of the family. She had to do something, and quick, to make him drop those eccentric ideas.

She went to her father and asked him to hastily find a job for his grandson.

"Hard labor is what he needs. Or he'll end up in a skirt," she declared dramatically.

"Ask his father to put him to work," don Ciccio said matter-of-factly.

Carmela smirked. "Nicola barely even works himself."

"I mean his real father."

She looked at him, stunned.

"With all due respect, dear father, have you gone mad?"

Don Ciccio shrugged. "Why not? Don't you know how many folks want to work for the Greco Winery?"

"And what would he do there? Let's hear it. Be their personal servant?" she said, standing tall. "Over my dead body will I let him soil his hands in Greco dirt."

"Dirty hands can be washed," don Ciccio said. "Money's going to be swirling around that place, and plenty of it. *He's* thinking big," he emphasized, spreading his arms. "Don't you want your son to get a piece of it?"

"And how is he supposed to get this piece you speak of?" Carmela asked with false curiosity. "It's not like *he* owes us anything."

Don Ciccio stood up from his chair and took the pipe from the mantel. He calmly lit it and took a meditative puff. He remained silent for a few seconds, then, impassively, said, "You, my dear, are underestimating the power of blood."

"What blood!" she growled. "That guy doesn't give a damn about Daniele. Plays dumb. Disappears and forgets. That's Carlo Greco for you— do you think I don't know him?"

"You shouldn't have told him. You were impulsive and foolish, like all females," don Ciccio scolded her. "But since it's done, use it. Put the kid right in front of him, so he has to see him every day. It will make things different than now; he barely knows what he looks like. He can start off as a simple laborer—he's still a pipsqueak anyway, not even two hairs on his chin yet. And you'll start to see a change in Carlo. Give it time."

Carmela stared at him, dubiously. "See what kind of change? You think he'll give him the vineyard?" she asked with a bitter laugh.

"No," don Ciccio said seriously, blowing out a cloud of smoke. "He can't leave that to him, we know this. But in the end, he'll give him something. And it won't be a small slice of the pie. Trust what I say, I know how things go. Blood always wins."

She hardened her gaze.

"You ask him then, to take Daniele on," she said adamantly. "I'm not going to beg him for any favors."

———

With a cigar in his teeth, Carlo was crouching in the vineyard watching the farmers busy with the green pruning, the one done in summer. In September—Carlo could hardly contain himself; he'd been waiting for three years—they would harvest the grapes. He'd already commissioned the label for the Donna Anna, and of the various options the artist had given him, he'd chosen the image of a bright red rose in bloom.

He stood up, stretched, and just then saw don Ciccio coming toward him. Startled, he waved hello.

"Don Ciccio, what a surprise! Did you walk all this way in the sun? You shouldn't tire yourself." His tone was friendly, but it betrayed a certain puzzlement.

Don Ciccio said he wasn't a worn-out old man just yet and invited Carlo to take a walk with him among the vines. He was curious to see how work was progressing.

They set off into the vineyard. Don Ciccio was looking around intently, stopping now and then to direct the laborers: "Don't cut too close to the crown buds—leave at least a few inches." "Get these leaves off here, they'll crowd out the grapes."

Once they were far enough, among the untrimmed plants at the back, don Ciccio resolved to talk.

Carlo lit his cigar and listened with a mixture of apprehension and resentment, shifting his weight from one foot to the other.

"The kid needs to cut his teeth and learn what it means to work hard," don Ciccio said. "To prove his mettle and character, to become a man. You know? His father Nicola is not so good at teaching him anything manly."

Carlo felt his legs turn to ice.

"But why here of all places . . . with all the vineyards in the area?" he argued meekly.

Don Ciccio took a few steps back, stuck his hands in his pockets, and turned away from Carlo.

"My father, God rest his soul, always said that there is nothing in this world worse than ingratitude," he said.

"Oh, but I am grateful to you for your help, don Ciccio. You know that," Carlo hastened to point out.

Don Ciccio turned and fixed his eyes on him. "This is what I ask for the service I provided," he said, spreading his arms to take in the vineyard. "You would refuse me?"

Carlo ran a hand through his damp, sweaty hair. Then he put his hands on his hips, frowned, and looked to the horizon.

"If this is what you ask of me . . ." he mumbled, defeated.

"Very well," don Ciccio said with a sly smile. "He'll start tomorrow morning." He was about to head back when Carlo, with a brief sprint, stepped in front of him.

"Allow me one last word," he said, this time with confidence. "I hope you don't underestimate me to the point of thinking me a fool. In my eyes, your grandson will be a laborer like any other. He bears the name Carlà."

Don Ciccio looked at him and said mockingly, "He has his father's name. Whose else?"

———

That summer Lorenza ceased to be a girl. As soon as she saw streams of blood running down her legs, she started to scream, terrified.

"What are you going on about? It's just your time of the month. You're a woman now—good for you," Agata said after finding her in the bathroom.

She handed her a stack of cotton rags cut out of an old white sheet and showed her how to put them in her underwear, advising her to replace them at least every two hours.

"Or you'll stink, and people will want to stay away from you," she explained. Then she started to list all the new behaviors Lorenza had to adopt during her "days of blood": no touching plants and flowers or she'd make them wilt, give a wide berth to bread dough or it won't rise, and stay clear of wine or it'll turn to vinegar.

When Lorenza reported all this to her aunt, Anna laughed so hard she almost cried.

"Why are you mocking me?" Lorenza said, gloomily.

"It's not you I'm mocking! You're sure your mother said all that nonsense?"

"I'm sure," Lorenza said, bowing her head.

"It's nonsense, don't believe one bit of it."

"So why would she say those things?"

"They're beliefs as old as time. Totally unfounded. Come with me, I'll show you." She took Lorenza's hand and walked her to the garden.

"Touch my basil," she ordered.

Lorenza instinctively took a step back. "Auntie, I wouldn't want—"

"Quit fussing and touch it. Go on."

Tentatively, Lorenza approached the bush.

"Go ahead, touch it," Anna said. "So you'll see yourself that it won't wilt. On the contrary," she added, looking amused, "when we finish here, we'll go down to the cellar. You know the one, right? Where your uncle keeps the wine? And you can touch all the bottles."

———

The days of blood took on a whole new meaning when, at the end of her first year of junior high, Lorenza found out she had failed both Latin and Greek.

"See?" Agata said, waving the report card in Antonio's face. "And she barely passed in the other subjects. I told you we should have sent her to trade school. But who listens to me anyway?"

Lorenza, sitting on the green couch with her fingers interlaced, bowed her head, devastated.

"I'll find a professor to tutor her," Antonio said calmly. "She'll be fine." He smiled at his daughter, but it fell into a void.

Since returning from Africa, Antonio had felt like an unwanted guest in his own home. No open arms had been there to welcome him, aside from Carlo's; his brother was the only person who seemed happy to see him. Agata, for her part, immediately consigned him to sleeping on the couch in his study.

"Alone you left me for months, and alone I want to stay," she said, without even looking him in the eye.

Without a word, he went to the chest and retrieved clean sheets and a lumpy pillow, on which he still slept even now. His wife didn't let a day go by without directing venomous remarks at him.

"You'll have to make do with the food we have here," she would say as she brought his plate to the table. If Antonio happened to stay late at the oil mill and come home late for dinner, she'd greet him with a sarcastic "He still thinks he's 'over there' in a hotel."

When he told Lorenza he'd take her to a play at the Politeama Theater in Lecce, Agata wondered out loud, piqued, "Why did you get the theater bug 'over there,' of all places?"

Whenever she talked about Africa, she just said "over there" and made a face.

Antonio always made an effort to respond calmly and kindly, but instead of appeasing Agata, this would just set her off even more.

But what hurt Antonio the most was the profound change he saw in Lorenza. Whenever she met her father's eyes, she'd suddenly look down; she no longer ran up to him when he came home from work, and she seemed to watch her every word, as if she lived in constant fear of making a mistake. But what hurt him more than everything else was that she no longer said that everything was "beauuutiful." She no longer got excited about anything.

With a pang of regret, Antonio realized how much his absence had affected the lives of his wife and daughter. A chasm had opened between them. And his attempts to bridge the gap had, so far, been fruitless.

The oil trade with Asmara had continued for a few months after his return, steadily, until one day in late winter his oil shipment was returned to him along with a long letter. Anna delivered the letter to his office.

She stood there staring at him, with a quizzical gaze, waiting for him to open the envelope. *This is our first time being alone again*, Antonio thought. On other occasions, other family members had been present, but aside from a few friendly exchanges, the two of them had not yet talked properly since his return. But one look into the green of Anna's eyes was all it took for him to realize that no place on Earth would ever be far enough to escape what he felt for her.

"Of course I read the name of the sender. Who's Lidia?" Anna asked, getting to the point.

Antonio looked away, muttering that it was the owner of a restaurant he'd done business with.

"Liar."

"Why the unpleasant tone?"

"Is this woman the reason you wouldn't come back, the reason you abandoned your daughter?" she prodded him. "Do you have any idea how much Lorenza suffered?"

"I didn't abandon anybody!" he bellowed.

"Be honest, Antonio."

He sighed, sat in the armchair by the window and looked out, narrowing his eyes.

Anna sat down in the armchair in front of him and crossed her arms against her chest.

"I'm listening," she said.

"It was . . . nothing," Antonio responded in a whisper.

There had been a woman, he admitted sheepishly, and it was Lidia, yes. He met her the day he disembarked in Asmara. In the throes of hunger, he'd walked into the first restaurant he found on Corso Italia, and that's where he first saw her. She was the young daughter of two settlers from Veneto who'd moved to Eritrea in 1930 to open a restaurant-theater, La Piccola Venezia, mostly frequented by Italian immigrants. Lidia was the waitress: She'd just turned twenty-two and was a rare beauty, with long, blond, curly hair; freckles dotted across her face; and a big, genuine smile.

"Do you love her?" Anna interrupted him, agitated.

Antonio stared at her as he grappled with the question . . .

"Love? Don't be silly . . . I didn't love *her*, anyway," he said, standing up again. "I told you. It was nothing."

He didn't tell her the rest, and would never tell anyone, not even his brother.

Antonio had behaved very badly toward that young woman, and now he felt deeply ashamed. Night after night, he'd seduced her, reciting poems by authors she'd never heard of. He made her fall in love with him and like a ravenous beast had ended up devouring everything Lidia freely gave him—her young body with its smooth skin, which had never known the touch of a man, and the unconditional love that followed. Her devotion to him—although Antonio felt nothing for her but a confused tenderness—ended up becoming a balm for the deep wound inflicted from his kiss with Anna. There, thousands of miles from home, Antonio saw that he could be whoever he wanted to be, free from scars or pain. In no time, he assumed another identity and became, by all appearances, Lidia's official fiancé. In this life, he wasn't married, he didn't have a daughter, he wasn't hopelessly in love with his brother's wife . . . he was just a man without a family who had come to Asmara to seek his fortune. And no one could ever say otherwise. He made Lidia promises he would never keep and commitments to her parents he already knew he wouldn't honor. He was willing to do anything, even build a castle of lies, to keep hold of the relief he felt, to break away from the pain that consumed him. But he knew his sudden departure had broken her heart.

"I hope it was worth it, at least," Anna remarked, irritated.

"Even so, what does it matter to you?"

Anna did not reply.

"Why did you stop braiding your hair?" he asked after a moment of silence, catching her off guard.

Her long, raven black hair fell soft and loose over her shoulders. She gave him a dazed look, then recovered. "I like it better this way," she said.

"Me too." Antonio smiled. "Don't braid it again."

———

"Good morning, Mr. Carlo."

"Goodbye, Mr. Carlo."

That was how Daniele would address Carlo whenever he saw him arrive at or leave the vineyard. Carlo reciprocated with a chin nod and a hint of embarrassment, then immediately turned his back on Daniele and started a conversation with someone else. Initially, Carlo had hoped the boy would give him a reason—any reason—to let him go; not even don Ciccio could object to him firing his grandson if he turned out to be a slacker. Then he could finally be free of that burden. Seeing Daniele every day, with that sweet, fresh face and those kind eyes looking out through long, luscious lashes, made it harder for Carlo to hold on to his reservations about hiring the boy.

But Daniele proved to be a tireless worker and was well-liked by all— there was always someone at the morning break yelling, "Come on over, young man! Have some of my sandwich!"

He learned quickly and performed his tasks with uncommon diligence for a boy his age. He already knew how to be a man in this world, contrary to what don Ciccio had to say about it, Carlo thought, and a vague sense of pride began to form.

———

On August 9, the summer substitute arrived at the post office to relieve Anna for two weeks.

"Did you hear that, Carmine? Our very own letter carrier is going on vacation to Gallipoli. Ah, lucky those who can afford it," Elena said as Anna left, slapping a fake smile on her purple face.

Before going home, Anna stopped by the library to take out a book to bring on vacation. After wandering among the shelves, glancing at various book covers, she was drawn by Goethe's *Elective Affinities* and by the crucial question it asks: What happens to a couple of elements if a third one comes into play?

The next day, the whole Greco family left for the beach, stacking their luggage on the roof of the 508. Carlo had rented a charming villa by the beach, with an elegant veranda and three bedrooms, one for him and Anna, one for Antonio and Agata, and the last one for the two kids. It had taken a good amount of effort to talk Agata into it; she didn't want the vacation to sound like a reward for Lorenza. She'd failed in two subjects and had been grounded until the end of summer, as far as Agata was concerned. As usual, Antonio patiently tried to mediate, all the way up until a few hours before the departure time. In the end, he managed to extract an assent from his wife, on the condition that Lorenza bring her books and limit her presence on the beach with the others to two hours in the morning and two in the afternoon—she'd spend the rest of her time locked in the house, studying Latin and Greek.

"I'm warning you, Antonio—if your daughter fails her makeup exams this September, I'm done sending her to school," Agata said, determined to have the last word.

Anna tried to convince Giovanna to join them, but nothing could be done. Anna had tried her best to sway her, enticing her with the imagery of swimming at sunset when the sun dove into the Ionian Sea, walking on the cool sand early in the morning, chatting on the veranda until the dead of night. But all in vain. Giovanna had declined kindly but firmly—don Giulio would come see her that summer, she was sure of it, and she didn't want to accidentally miss him.

The days in Gallipoli were calm and weightless, made up of long swims, naps on the warm sun-kissed sand, lunches on the beach with peaches and melon, sunset strolls among the town's narrow alleyways, and intimate evenings on the veranda, caressed by a light breeze and with a view of the boats returning to port in the light of the moon.

Agata's nerves seemed be easing up, too. She started to address her husband without hostility and without bringing up "over there," which she'd been obsessing over for months. Even her attitude toward Lorenza softened.

"That's enough studying, for today. Go freshen up," she'd say, peering into the room where Lorenza sat on the bed with a book open in front of her. Most of the time, she even offered to cook for everyone.

"You go on. I'll take care of things in here," she'd say, and shoo everyone out with an authoritative nod.

Anna loved to wake up before everyone else, when the sky was just starting to lighten up and the house was still absent of voices and laughter. She would heat up the milk for less than a minute and take her cup to the veranda; there, she'd sit back in the chaise longue and dive into *Elective Affinities*. Every morning, Antonio would happen to join her with his book (that summer he was reading Chekhov), waking up at the same time every morning. It was if he'd been listening for her steps and decided to follow her once he heard them. Without a word, he would sit in the chaise longue next to hers, smile at her, and then open the book to where he'd left off. He would stay and read with her like that, sharing the silence and peace of the first hours of the day. The house started to become lively only after an hour, when Carlo's youthful laugh would ring out from the kitchen along with the sound of cups clattering as Agata pulled them off the shelves.

"Good morning!" Carlo would then burst out, popping onto the veranda, smiling, before bending over to give Anna a light kiss and then turning to tickle his brother's sides.

"Good morning, Carletto," Antonio would say, laughing. Then he would close his book and go inside.

"Let me see if the coffee's ready," he'd say, leaving his chair to Carlo.

———

Two days before Ferragosto, Giovanna heard a knock at the door. Cesare started to bark, but he stopped suddenly when she opened the door.

Don Giulio, dressed in a black tunic and white collar, cracked a smile. He was clean-shaven, a little weathered and gaunt in the cheeks, but as handsome as Giovanna remembered: slender features, big, dark eyes, and a slightly upturned nose.

She brought her hands to her face and started to jump with joy.

"Hi, Giovanna."

She threw her arms around his neck and held him close. "I knew you'd come," she said, her voice trembling.

She looked at him and went to kiss him, but he stopped her, placing a hand on her mouth.

"Let me take off my cassock first," he said, in a serious tone.

She stared at him bewildered, then mumbled, "Of course, of course. Come in."

For the rest of the afternoon, they surrendered to love while don Giulio's black cassock and white collar sat folded carefully on a chair.

Curled up in a corner of the bedroom, Cesare stared at them with sad eyes.

11

December 1938
The Last Christmas Before World War II

Carlo bought a six-foot pine tree. On the morning of December 8, he rose early and went to wake up Roberto while joyfully singing "Tu scendi dalle stelle." But it was a holiday, so Roberto pulled the covers over his head and grumbled that he wanted to sleep a little longer.

"Ten minutes, not more," Carlo said jovially, ruffling his son's hair. Then he went downstairs and lit the fireplace.

When Roberto joined his father, a good half hour later, Carlo was sitting at the foot of the great pine tree pulling Christmas decorations out of boxes: papier-mâché figurines for the nativity scene, wreaths, colorful orbs, wooden snowflake ornaments, a golden tree topper.

"There you are." Carlo smiled at him. "Just the person I was waiting for."

Father and son started decorating the tree while the fire crackled in the hearth. Roberto passed the decorations and Carlo, halfway up a wooden ladder, carefully arranged them on the tree. Every so often, he'd climb down, take a step back, and proclaim, "No, we have to move that red orb higher up . . . and we need to take down a few snowflakes. See how they're all up there and there's nothing down below?"

When Anna came home at lunchtime, she found them there, still decorating the tree.

"Papa, come on, it's fine," Roberto grumbled. "It's the fifth time you've moved that thing around."

Anna smiled.

Carlo was holding a wooden angel. It was the last ornament, and he just couldn't find the right spot for it.

"Give it here," Anna said, amused. She took the angel and placed it front and center in the middle of the tree, between a white orb and a red one.

"It's perfect here," she declared.

Carlo observed it and nodded, doubtfully.

Roberto collapsed onto the couch. "We're done, finally," he said. "I'm so tired."

"Too bad you're tired," Anna said with a sly smile. "I wanted to take you and Lorenza to the movies to see a cartoon . . . I guess it'll just be her and I. You can stay here and rest."

Roberto immediately pulled his head up.

"Actually, I'm just a little bit tired," he said.

Anna and Carlo exchanged glances and smiled.

———

When they got to the Olympia theater, Anna stopped in front of the movie poster, pointed at it, and asked her son, "What does that say?"

Roberto moved in closer and easily read, "*Snow White.*"

"Very good!" she said with pride.

Roberto had started elementary school in September, even though Anna had already long since taught him the alphabet.

"*A* for Anna, *B* for Basil, *C* for Carlo . . ." she'd repeat every time she had the chance.

"Let him learn with the other children, when the time comes," Carlo would interrupt her, annoyed.

"Why, if he can get a head start?" she'd say, then continue, "*D* for Dog, *E* for Easy, *G* for Greco . . ."

By the time school started, Roberto already knew how to write his name in block letters, without going outside the lines.

All three of them loved *Snow White*. Roberto came out of the theater excited, singing "Heigh-Ho!," and imitating the walk of the seven dwarves. He carried on like that the whole way home as Lorenza split her sides laughing and Anna shook her head, amused.

"Vaudeville is what you should be doing," she teased him.

"I wish a prince came and woken me, too . . ." Lorenza sighed.

"*Had come*," Anna corrected her.

After a few steps, she added, "Why? Are you asleep like Snow White?"

"I'm not," Lorenza murmured, embarrassed. "I just mean . . . well, anyway, that I also once dreamed of a prince who"—she hesitated—"had come to save me."

Anna stopped dead. Concerned, she took her niece's arm and gently turned her to face her. Roberto noticed they'd lagged behind and stopped walking.

"There is only one person who can save you," Anna said to Lorenza in a serious tone. "Do you know who that is?"

Her niece looked at her, almost fearfully, and shook her head.

"It's you," Anna said, pointing right at her. "Only you can save yourself. There is no prince who can help you, believe me."

Lorenza became gloomy and walked on with her head bowed. She found those words alarming; ever since she could remember, her mother had always said that a woman only becomes whole after finding a husband and settling down, that it's the man who saves and protects her, and that if you're born female, you'll never get anywhere on your own. Her classmates felt the same way. Studying was just a way to find the best possible prospect, they would say, coquettishly. For them, "later," what they wanted to do when they "grew up," was to have a nice house to clean and maintain, a good husband who could provide for them, and healthy children to raise. She'd never heard them wish for anything else when talking about the future. As for her, she always felt one step behind her peers; for the second year in a row, she'd barely passed, and would have to retake Greek and

Latin. That summer, too, she'd had to study instead of enjoying the long, carefree days of having fun in the sun. She felt her father's disappointed gaze constantly upon her, although he tried not to show it. Instead, he persisted in paying Professor Gaetani, who was now retired, to get those ancient languages into her head, though to her, they seemed useless and often incomprehensible. She also felt ugly, unlike her classmates; every time she saw her face covered in pimples in the mirror, she felt like shattering it. She avoided it as much as possible, picking up her pace whenever she passed one. Even Auntie Anna had stopped telling her she was beautiful.

———

Like every year, in the weeks before Christmas, the post office was gearing up for the holidays. Countless cards, letters, packages, and baskets of homemade delicacies going to faraway loved ones needed to be processed. Anna knew that for the whole month, the big table in the middle would be overflowing with trays of mustazzoli, fish-shaped almond cakes, those strange Christmas sweets that looked like little gnocchi covered in honey and toasted almonds, whose name she still struggled to pronounce— purcidduzzi or purceddruzzi?—and still more cups of coffee and bottles of limoncello, which Elena made herself. She was also the one who played host, offering food and drink to whoever walked in.

"Come on in, grab a sweet," she'd say, pointing at the table.

Carmine had put on some weight lately, but this didn't stop him from constantly getting up to pour himself a drop of limoncello and grab a sweet. Tommaso would shoot him a reproachful look whenever he returned to his post with his mouth full. The only thing that had gotten bigger about Chiara were her thick lenses. She was never even tempted by the almond pastries and would remain in the telegraph room working with her head down.

"Come on, take a break and come join us," Elena would say. "This girl. I just don't get her. She's always so sad," she'd add, dispirited.

"I'm not sad in the least," Chiara would shout from the back room.

Their days were full and tiring. Anna sped around town like a spinning top, always in a hurry to pick up or deliver everything on time. It wasn't unusual for her to work into the afternoons.

That year, Giuseppina received the best gift she could have ever wanted. Her son Mauro had returned to Italy from Germany, where "the air had turned poisonous with that Hitler guy," with a wallet thick enough to remodel the house.

"Come in, Mrs. Letter Carrier, meet my son," Giuseppina said. She'd been standing at the door waiting for her, and as soon as she saw her walk by, she'd called her in a booming voice.

"Anna was such a dear," she had told her son earlier that day. "She gave a voice to your words all this time—like Ferruccio used to do."

Mauro shook Anna's hand and thanked her profusely, adding that if she ever needed anything, she could knock on their door.

Anna smiled in embarrassment and said that there was no need to thank her, that she was just doing her job. But Mauro insisted on giving her a package of Lebkuchen, traditional biscuits from Nuremberg.

"You're going to love 'em!"

Mr. Lorenzo, on the other hand, continued to salute Anna with a raised arm, even though she persisted in not reciprocating. But that year, after taking the latest postcard from her, he hadn't given it back. His brother had written that he had had enough, that it was time that they go back to celebrating Christmas together, like a family, whether he wanted to or not. He and Renata would be arriving in time for Christmas Eve dinner.

The man was so upset he read the message out loud.

"Is Renata your niece?" Anna asked, secretly hoping to finally solve the mystery of the rejected postcards.

"No," he grumbled.

"Oh, I'm sorry. I thought—"

"Renata was my girlfriend," Mr. Lorenzo said, bitterly. "They ran off together one night, like thieves, years ago."

Anna was shocked.

"I'm sorry," she stammered, mortified. She wished him goodbye and a merry Christmas, even though she didn't think it would do much good. As she set off, she was shaken by a strange sensation, something undefined that wavered between relief and guilt.

———

Daniele's first scattered facial hairs had sprouted. The older workers at the vineyard teased him affectionately.

"You're no pickney no more. You're a man now, you are," they chuckled, chucking him under the chin or patting him on the back. He smiled, but he hated those little hairs above his lip from the depths of his heart. They were horrible to look at and they constantly itched.

Whenever he came home from the vineyard with his pay in his pocket, he'd rush to his room and put half of it in a metal box, which he kept at the back of his closet. In a year and a half of work, he'd managed to gather a good stash, though it still wasn't enough. He wanted to buy a Singer, like the one his mother used in the dressmaker's shop. That same metal box also contained his notebook with the patterns. Every night after dinner, he'd hastily say good night and withdraw to his room, where he'd spend hours drawing elegant dresses. When he was certain his mother had left on some errand, he'd sneak into her shop and leaf through the latest issue of *Moda Illustrata*, or retrieve fabric scraps she'd thrown into the trash.

Sometimes, in the evenings, Carmela would open the door to the dressmaker's shop, lean against the frame with her arms crossed, and ask him, "How was today?"

"Fine," he'd say dismissively, with one foot on the staircase leading to the bedrooms.

"Was Mr. Carlo there today?"

"Yeah, obviously. He's always there."

"Is he still treating you well?"

Daniele always nodded and Carmela would make do with that mute response. He never told her just how nice and generous Mr. Carlo always was to him. Sometimes he'd give him a few extra lira with his daily pay and wink at him as he handed over the money, as if it was their little secret; during the two harvests they'd done, Carlo had even entrusted him with one of the most important tasks: checking that the grapes were all intact and healthy before being poured into the tubs for the pressing, and getting rid of spoiled ones when necessary.

Once the Donna Anna had finally been bottled, Mr. Carlo had proudly presented him with a bottle.

"Let don Ciccio taste some," he'd said.

Daniele had never seen a wine that color; it was a translucent pink, elegant and sophisticated.

"It's good," his grandfather had declared upon tasting it. Then he'd sniffed it at length, taking in the fruity perfume of cherries and wild strawberries.

———

For Christmas Eve dinner, the Greco family gathered at Anna and Carlo's house. This time, Giovanna finally decided to join them.

"I'm not going to let you spend Christmas alone again," Anna had told her. "You'll come to ours, and I don't want to hear any excuses. Bring Cesare along if you want."

Anna and Carlo spent the afternoon cooking; he prepared the broth while she worked on the dough and filling for the tortellini. As a second course, they would have Agata's famous meat pie, which she'd insisted on bringing. Just before the guests arrived, Carlo put "Un'ora sola ti vorrei," by Nuccia Natali, on the gramophone; reached for Anna, who looked radiant in a long blue satin dress; and started to dance with her slowly, holding her waist with one hand and a lit cigar in the other.

Once most of the guests had arrived, Carlo uncorked a bottle of Donna Anna and poured each person a glass. Everyone—some sitting on the couch, some sitting by the fireplace, others standing—raised their glasses to the Christmas of 1938.

Lorenza had brought a copy of *A Christmas Carol* and was curled up on the couch reading out loud to Roberto, who listened with his head resting on her shoulder. Excited by all those people, Cesare was constantly wagging his tail and roaming about the house, stopping to sniff whomever he could find, hoping for some petting.

Anna grabbed Giovanna's hand as she strolled in late, rushed her upstairs, and ordered her to sit at the vanity table.

"Tonight, you'll need some lipstick and a drop of perfume. It's a party," she exclaimed.

She applied cherry lipstick to Giovanna's lips and, squeezing the bulb on her perfume bottle, sprayed the scent behind her ears and on her wrists. Carlo had given it to Anna for her birthday. He'd had it specially made by a perfumer in Lecce and, of all the scents the man had suggested, Carlo had chosen the one with base notes of musk and sandalwood.

"Voilà! Look, you're beautiful," Anna said.

Giovanna leaned forward and stared at her reflection in the mirror. Her eyes seemed to sparkle, highlighted by the red of her lips and the silver brooch on her chest. If only Giulio could see her now. A few days before Christmas Eve, he'd sent her a postcard with the picture of a little girl sitting at a window and marveling at the falling snow. It came with a package containing a silver brooch in the shape of a flower and a note that said *Wear it and think of me.* When Anna and Giovanna went back downstairs, the others were already seated at the oval dining table: Carlo at the head of the table, Antonio and Agata to his left, Lorenza and Roberto at the other end. Anna sat to Carlo's right and invited Giovanna to sit next to her.

Agata joined her hands together, closed her eyes, and started to recite the Our Father. Everyone copied her except for Anna, who sat still and absently massaged the back of her neck with one hand. After the "Amen" and the sign of the cross, Carlo stood up and filled everyone's bowls: two ladles of tortellini soup each.

"Giovanna, that lipstick looks good on you," Antonio said.

Giovanna blushed and bit her lip.

"Thank you," she said in a cracked voice.

How lovely to be here with them, she thought, gazing at the real family in front of her, admiring the decorated tree, the lit fireplace, the presents to unwrap, and soaking in the laughter and all there was to eat. She turned to Anna and looked at her with teary eyes.

"What's wrong?" Anna asked her, looking amused.

Giovanna, by way of an answer, lunged in to hug her.

Agata raised her eyes to the sky, but no one noticed.

At the stroke of midnight, they all gathered around the tree to exchange well-wishes and presents. Carlo opened another bottle of Donna Anna. While everyone was busy unwrapping presents and packages, making a joyful mess of it all, Antonio quietly ducked under the tree and grabbed a rectangular package wrapped in golden paper.

"Pour toi," he said, handing it to Anna.

She smiled at him, sincerely.

"Merci," she said, and unwrapped it.

Lorenza, who was sitting on the rug admiring the silver hairbrush she'd received from her aunt and uncle, started to watch the scene surreptitiously.

"*Gone with the Wind,*" Anna read on the book cover.

"I've just read it. I liked it very much," Antonio explained.

"What did you like about it?"

He thought for a moment.

"The main character, Scarlett, reminds me of you," he said, finally.

Anna bowed her head into the book, her lips curling into a smile.

"And also," Antonio continued, "I liked the fact that she always finds the strength to start over, even after the war."

He couldn't have known how dramatically prophetic his words would be.

The Christmas of 1938 would be the last one in peacetime for many years.

For the Greco family and for the whole world.

PART TWO

12

Seven Years Later

"We interrupt this programming to report the extraordinary news . . ."

Anna dropped the rag on the kitchen table, among the dirty dinner plates, and marched into the living room. She crouched by the radio, which was on the console table, and turned up the volume.

"The German armed forces have surrendered to the Anglo Americans," the announcer was saying, his voice cracking with joy. "The war is over. I repeat: The war is over!"

"Carlo!" Anna yelled at the stairs.

He peeked over the top of the staircase, with his toothbrush in hand and a trickle of toothpaste running down the side of his mouth. It was still strange to see him without his mustache; he'd shaved it off one day saying, "I don't want it anymore. It reminds me of Hitler."

"What's going on?" he asked, looking worried.

Anna stood up and smiled at him. "The Germans have surrendered," she said, pointing at the radio.

Carlo dropped his toothbrush, ran down the stairs, and flung himself at Anna, grabbing her by the hips and lifting her into the air.

"Put me down!" she protested, laughing.

But he continued to hold her and, with his head flung back, he exclaimed, "Do you know that you're even more beautiful from this angle?"

"Can't say the same for you, with that toothpaste on your face," she said, laughing. "Here, let me clean it off." He put her down and she started rubbing away the toothpaste with the tip of her thumb. "There. Now you're clean." And she stroked his cheek.

"Let's go tell Roberto!"

"Tomorrow. He's probably asleep by now."

"Maybe he's still up reading."

He grabbed Anna's hand, and they went upstairs. He slowly opened the door to Roberto's bedroom. A faint light came from the lamp on the nightstand, which Roberto kept on all night. The boy was sleeping on his back, with his head turned to one side and a copy of *Topolino* open on his chest. He was twelve years old now, but his face was still smooth and rosy like that of a small child. He'd grown into a miniature copy of Anna: the same thick black hair, the same green eyes, the same linear profile. His smile and mischievous gaze, though, those were all his father's.

"Come on, let's leave him alone, he's sleeping so peacefully," Anna whispered.

"As you wish," Carlo said, somewhat disappointed, and closed the door.

As they went back downstairs, they heard chatter coming from outside. They rushed to the living room window. People were pouring onto the streets to celebrate. Some were shouting, "It's over! It's over!" Some were laughing, some were crying, some were hugging, and some were knocking on the doors of sleeping households and screaming, "Come out!"

Anna and Carlo exchanged glances. He grabbed his overcoat from the coat hanger, threw it on over his pajamas, and squeezed Anna's hand, and they went out.

They ran straight to Antonio and Agata's.

Carlo knocked persistently until he saw a light go on in the study. A few moments later, Antonio, sleepy and in his pajamas, opened the door and stared disconcertedly at his brother and sister-in-law as they stood there, hand in hand. He glanced behind them, taking in the upbeat commotion invading the streets, and finally asked, "What the hell is going on?"

"While you were sleeping peacefully, the Germans raised the white flag," Carlo said, with an even bigger smile.

"But . . . really?"

"It doesn't seem real to me either," Anna said.

"Who's here at this hour?" came Agata's alarmed voice. She came down the stairs and joined her husband at the door. She was wearing a pink nightgown and a matching nightcap, from which white locks poked out haphazardly. Her auburn hair had long since turned white while two deep wrinkles had made their way down the sides of her mouth to her chin, giving her a perpetually despondent look. "What is it? Has everyone gone mad?" she added, noticing the disorder in the streets.

"The war is over, Agata," Antonio said, his eyes tearing up.

Agata squeezed her husband's arm and crossed herself. "Thank God," she murmured.

"Hey, come on, let's go wake up Nando and get him to open the bar. We need to drink!" yelled a gleeful man on the street. A small crowd immediately followed him.

As if just remembering that she was wearing her nightgown in front of all those people, Agata instinctively took a step back inside.

Anna only thought about it once she and Carlo turned to head home—the light in the study turning on and Antonio opening the door right after, in his pajamas, looking like he'd just been wrenched from sleep.

"They don't sleep together anymore?" she asked Carlo out of the blue.

"Who, my love?" he said, wrapping himself in his coat.

"Your brother and Agata."

Carlo shrugged. "It's none of our business," he said.

"Obviously not. I was just curious," she said, pretending not to care all that much.

———

Anna stepped out of the house and took a deep breath. The air smelled of springtime and wisteria, especially at that time of the morning. She closed the front door; grabbed the handles of her bike, which was leaning against the rock wall; and pushed it out to the street.

"Good morning, Mrs. Letter Carrier," came the neighbor's greeting, right on cue, as she persisted in sweeping her small portion of sidewalk. Anna reciprocated, slightly lifting her cap, then climbed onto the Bianchi Suprema, the women's model she'd bought for nine hundred lira in 1940, the year Fausto Coppi won the first Giro d'Italia. Since then—and with great relief for her poor feet hardened by years of walking back and forth on the cobblestones—she'd used it every single day. Especially for work. That bike had helped her deliver all the telegrams from the Ministry of War calling young men to arms. She'd watched so many of them pack up and leave, while their families despaired. Some had never come back, and it was not always known when or how they might have died; others bore the signs of the war on their bodies and spirits and would never be able to erase them. Anna heard that some, while on leave, had burned themselves with boiling water to avoid returning to battle. Every time a draft telegram arrived, Anna would scan it, heart pounding, and only once she ascertained that neither Carlo's nor Antonio's name was on it would she bring a hand to her chest and sigh with relief. *None of Carlo's peers have been called yet,* she'd think, reassured that it couldn't be his time yet. *And it's not like they're going to draft Antonio, at forty-one years old,* she'd think right after, feeling a weight lift off her chest.

And how many letters from the front she'd had to read to parents, sisters, wives, or girlfriends as they sat there, weary and shattered. Anna had never even met many of those young men. Sure, maybe she'd caught someone's eye around town, but she wasn't sure. But their words, their letters—she still remembered those perfectly. There was Giuseppe, a worker from the Greco Winery who'd been sent to fight in Russia and who didn't write to his wife Donata about the war but only of his dreams.

When night fell on the freezing, foul hideout in which he slept, he dreamed of being home with her, of their life composed of small habits, and his newfound realization that those were the things he missed the most. Francesco, the youngest son of the couple that managed the tobacco shop where Carlo bought his cigars, always thanked his parents for the tobacco they sent him and begged them for more; it was the only way to get an extra ration, he explained, since he bartered it for bread with his fellow soldiers. *Mama, I'm always, always hungry* was the inevitable conclusion of his letters. Pietro, who was a builder in his civilian life, wrote to his sister Maria from Ukraine, where he and his squadron had walked along the Donets River for more than a hundred miles, seeing prisoners in a valley occupied by the Germans. Men piled on top of one another with machine guns pointed at them, starving and exhausted, soiling themselves and smelling like beasts. *If that happens to me, I'd rather die,* he'd written. Andrea, who helped his father at the cheese stand at the market on Saturdays, always asked his longtime love, his Annunziata, to not be overcome with sadness, telling her the war would end one day, in one way or another, and promising that upon his return, they'd party every day.

Anna pedaled to the square, which was still pleasantly empty and quiet at that hour, and headed for Bar Castello. She got off her bike and looked at her watch, the one with the rectangular face that Antonio had given her in May 1935 and that she hadn't taken off since; for once, she was early and could indulge in the luxury of drinking her coffee sitting down. She leaned the Bianchi against the wall and sat at an outside table, observing those bustling around her. Fernando was smoking his morning cigarette and leaning against the door of the barber shop; Michele's wife, a slender woman with strong arms, was unloading a heavy-looking case of oranges onto the sidewalk. Sadly, the corner usually occupied by Mario the shoeshine, his hands always stained with grease, was empty and always would be.

"Woe betide anyone who takes my spot, 'cause I'll be back!" he'd warned everyone before leaving for the front.

With a smile, Nando brought out her caffè corretto, and Anna blissfully inhaled the pungent scent of the grappa. He put a hand on her shoulder in a fatherly manner and went back inside. He'd lost a lot of weight in the war years; the old white apron now needed to be tied twice around his waist.

Anna was enjoying her last sip when she spotted Elena's heavyset figure pop out from one of the alleys into the square, near where the fabric lady set up every Saturday. She was walking slowly and morosely toward the closed post office. All she ever did recently was complain about her ankles, which she said had grown as big as melons and made every step painful. With a sigh, she pulled the key out of her purse and opened the door.

Anna caught up with her, pushing her bicycle.

"Did they kick you out of bed this morning?" Elena exclaimed, stunned.

"I didn't sleep much—I wonder why," Anna said, placing the mailbag on the table.

"You're tellin' me," Elena remarked, removing her wool coat. "I've been sleeping badly for ages. Sometimes I still hear them in my ears, those sirens."

Chiara arrived a few moments later. She'd remained a slip of a thing, still with those thick lenses, but now she smiled a lot more. She'd fallen in love with a doctor, people were saying, the "new" one that had come to town during the war and who'd cared for Chiara's mother until the end. Elena was constantly making sly jokes at Chiara's expense, trying to learn more, but she was wasting her breath; she couldn't pry a single word out of Chiara's mouth.

Carmine came in with his head bowed, limping slightly. He'd had to shave his beard when he was called to fight, but now it had grown back, bristly and full of white hairs. He never talked about the few days he'd spent at the front. All that was known in town was that he'd left with the shoeshine and that on August 30, 1942, Carmine had saved himself and Mario had not. They were both on the *Sant' Andrea* oil tanker as it set sail from Taranto, heading for Greece, when twenty English planes bombed the ship, which caught fire and sank to the bottom of the sea. Carmine had come home with a burnt foot and his bad temper completely intact. He mumbled a greeting and went straight to his desk. When Elena asked how he was, he touched his beard and said, "Normal, how am I supposed to be?" Which meant he hadn't yet had his second coffee of the day.

Tommaso was the last to arrive. He smiled kindly, wished everyone a good morning, and went to his desk, clutching his leather briefcase. Anna often thought that the director's eyes looked smaller every day. His bright and lively gaze had long since disappeared, ever since the night the war took what he loved most in this world: his Giulia. The heart of that fragile girl, whom he'd loved so much, hadn't withstood the latest air-raid siren that had snatched her from her sleep. She died on the way to Antonio's oil mill, which by day was used for reserving oil portions with ration cards, and at night became the safest bomb shelter in town. When that terrible fifteen-second howl began, followed by as many seconds of silence, people would run there, breathless, wrapped in coats that barely covered the men's pajamas and the women's nightgowns. They'd spent so many nights pressed up against one another, under heavy wool blankets. Only the children managed to fall back asleep, cradled in their mothers' arms, while the adults looked at one another with terror in their eyes and strained ears, waiting for the worst.

And now the worst was over.

Anna finished filling her mailbag, went out, mounted her bicycle, and set off. She'd only gone a few feet before a horn sounded behind her.

She put her foot on the ground and turned around. Antonio pulled up next to her and rolled down the window.

"Need a ride?" he joked.

"No, thanks. I don't trust your driving," she retorted, smiling.

Antonio laughed. "Can't argue with that!"

He'd had to get his license the year before, after Carlo gave him his 508. He didn't need it anymore, since he'd bought a nice, shiny black Fiat 1100.

"You better sell it. Don't give it to me. What am I going to do with it?

You think I'm going to learn to drive now, at forty-five years old?" Antonio tried to refuse, but Carlo wouldn't hear reason.

"I can't watch you go everywhere on foot. Please," he'd insisted.

"But I like walking, really," Antonio had replied. But in the end, he gave in. "I'm only going to use it if I have to," he declared.

And he'd kept his word. Most of the time, the Fiat 508 stayed parked in front of his house—he only started it if he had to leave town.

"Where are you off to?" Anna asked.

"I'm heading to the winery."

"Let me know if you get there alive," she said. She waved goodbye and resumed pedaling.

Antonio chuckled and turned right. Once at the winery, he parked in the large clearing where the carts that transported the grapes from the vineyard were kept.

He pushed the heavy wooden door open and looked inside. "Carlo?" he called.

"I'm down here!"

Antonio went down the stairs to the basement, which housed the cellar with the cement vats. *It is always so cold down here*, he thought with a shiver.

Carlo was talking to a short, elderly man with hollow, wrinkly cheeks who was wearing overalls and a cap on his head.

"Antonio. Over here," Carlo said, waving his hand. "This is Franco. I told you about him, right?"

"Yes, of course," Antonio replied, shaking Franco's hand.

"We finally reached an agreement," Carlo explained, satisfied. He placed a hand on the man's shoulder.

"So it seems," the other answered.

The deal concerned the sale of a few hectares of land not far from the Greco Vineyard. Carlo had set his sights on it some time ago—he wanted to expand the vineyard.

He needed to produce more wine, since business was finally going well. It hadn't been at all easy to continue production during the war. Many workers had been called to the front, and although some of their wives took their places in the fields, the labor force hadn't sufficed—plus the difficulty of finding glass bottles had forced Carlo to slow production.

And that was the new normal until the Americans had come. On September 11, 1943, while the north was still in the hands of the Germans, the king was on the run toward Brindisi, where the Allies had landed, in addition to Taranto. The entire country was adrift. Carlo immediately understood that this could be a good opportunity, the one he'd long been waiting for to "make the jump," as he called it. He told himself that someone had to supply alcohol to American soldiers as they trudged through this war, so why not him? He would have bet anything that those foreigners had never tasted wine as good as his. So he prepared a case of Donna Anna and loaded it into his Fiat 508.

"Where are these going?" Daniele had asked. Carlo had promoted him to manager after the previous one had been sent to fight in the north.

"To Brindisi, my boy," Carlo said, sitting at his desk writing a note to go with the wine. "We're taking them to the king himself!" he'd added with a laugh, twirling his index finger in the air. "It's just a taste. If I'm right, we'll be sending plenty more cases."

Daniele had looked puzzled but hadn't asked anything else.

Sometime later, three soldiers showed up at the winery in a jeep. An officer shook Carlo's hand and introduced himself as the U.S. Army's supplies commissioner. In broken Italian, he thanked him for the kind offering, which they'd received, and drunk, with much pleasure. Now he'd come to meet the man who produced such extraordinary wine, pink and bright, that smelled like . . . cherries and strawberries, he said in English. Carlo smiled in response and took the three soldiers to visit the winery, while Daniele, by his side, joined in every so often, mostly with gestures, to explain the phases of the wine-making process. After the tour, the officer nodded with satisfaction and ordered a large supply of Donna Anna for the American troops.

"I knew it!" Carlo had exclaimed as soon as the jeep left.

In a flash of enthusiasm, he took Daniele's head between his hands and planted a kiss on his hair. The boy was flushed at first, but then he let himself get carried away by the euphoria, laughing along.

Franco said goodbye to the brothers by lifting his hat.

"I'll let you know when the notary can see us," Carlo said to him before he disappeared up the stairs.

"So, big brother," he said, turning to put an arm around Antonio's shoulders. "What brings you here?"

"I haven't seen you in three days," Antonio said. "I missed you."

"What a big softie," Carlo teased him, pinching his cheeks.

Daniele poked his head into the cellar.

"Mr. Carlo?"

"What is it, my boy?"

"I'm heading to the vineyard. The corking machine is all set."

"Very good. Yes, go ahead."

But Daniele hesitated, looking at Antonio.

"Mr. Antonio," he said then, clearly embarrassed. "Can I ask how Lorenza's doing? I haven't seen her around in a while."

"Ups and downs," he said, sticking his hands in his pockets.

"I bet," Daniele replied, sadly. "Maybe one of these days I could take her to the movies, with her friends. To get her mind off things . . . Obviously, with your permission." He looked down.

"It's kind of you to think of her," Antonio mumbled. He let the request fall into the void.

"Don't worry, she'll be fine," Carlo butted in. "You're kids. This, too, shall pass, at your age."

Daniele nodded doubtfully, said goodbye, and headed for the stairs.

"Don't forget to say hello to your grandfather," Carlo yelled after him. "And tell him I'll come see him as soon as I can."

———

Daniele and Lorenza had become friends in March 1943, when Daniele's best friend Giacomo, the fruit vendor's son, fell in love with her.

"Did you see how hot Antonio Greco's daughter got?" Giacomo would say, elbowing Daniele whenever he saw Lorenza walk past the shop. Sometimes he'd whistle at her and signal for her to come over.

"Shh! Come on, is that how you get a girl's attention?" Daniele would chide him, lowering his friend's arm with an amused look. Giacomo would take a piece of fruit from the nearest crate and hand it to Lorenza, holding it out in his palm.

"Only the best fruit in town for the most beautiful lady," he'd say. She'd smile, embarrassed, take the fruit—sometimes a nice, juicy orange, other times a mandarin or a pear—and thank him. After she left, Giacomo would continue to stare at her in a daze. It was as if all the freckles on his face were smiling along with his eyes.

Daniele had indeed noticed that Lorenza, Mr. Carlo's niece, had blossomed into a beautiful young woman. He remembered her from when she was a child. Obviously, they ran into each other often, but even though they were almost the same age, they'd never really talked. She'd grown taller and her hips had gotten rounder; her shiny auburn hair cascaded down to her backside and the pimples that had once covered her face had disappeared, leaving just a few small scars that could only be seen up close. Plus, her eyes were exactly like Carlo's when he smiled, Daniele thought; they gave off the same sparkle, as if they were lighting up from within.

Giacomo began to court her shamelessly. On Sunday mornings, he'd park himself on the bench in the main square and wait for her to appear. If she wasn't with her mother or aunt, he'd sneak up behind her.

"Good morning to the most beautiful lady," he'd say, doffing his cap. "Can we walk you home? Me and my friend here?" he'd add, pointing at Daniele.

"But it's just around the corner," she'd say, amused.

"So what? Around this corner today, around that corner tomorrow..." Giacomo would say with a smile. So all three of them would set off, with

Daniele hanging back by a few feet. But Lorenza's voice still rang out clearly. He heard her talking to Giacomo about her day, her classmates, of when the war would be over, but especially of what they taught her in school—the love story of Paris and Helen, the rivalry between Achilles and Hector, Ulysses's long journey home . . . Giacomo would walk alongside her, looking at her adoringly, without saying a word.

"I never tire of listening to her talk. Does that mean I'm in love?" he'd ask Daniele later, after Lorenza returned home.

One afternoon in May 1943, she'd invited them to the movies with two of her most respectable-looking classmates, who had come from Lecce that day so they could all do their homework together—or so Lorenza had said. But Daniele had immediately understood, given the suggestive glances between the girls, that that was just an excuse, and that the outing had been designed and orchestrated down to the last detail. They went to the afternoon showing of *Un Pilota Ritorna*, by Roberto Rossellini. Lorenza chose a seat in the back row and with one glance hinted to Giacomo to come sit next to her. Daniele ended up sitting between the two other girls, whose names he no longer recalled. Later, he realized he remembered hardly anything about the movie. He'd been distracted the whole time, trying to see what was happening two seats away from him. He heard Giacomo and Lorenza giggle and murmur while her friends tried to catch one another's eye and wink, as if to say *Did you see that?*

At the point in the movie where Massimo Girotti says to Michela Belmonte, "You're everything to me," over the roar of bombs falling in the night, Daniele saw that his friend had taken Lorenza's face in his hands and had placed his lips on hers.

Their love story continued to the sound of stolen kisses in alleyways as Daniele acted as the lookout, conspiratorial glances in the square or at the shop, and clandestine meetings, like when Lorenza told her parents she was going to study at a friend's house and got on a bus to Lecce, on which Giacomo was also traveling, though at an appropriate distance. That afternoon—Giacomo later confided to Daniele—he and Lorenza had made love in a straw hut in a field just outside Lecce. It had been her first time, and she'd been so happy she'd cried. As he held her, Giacomo recounted, lying naked and trembling, he had thought, *I'm going to marry this one.*

A second later he'd declared: "Sunday I'm coming to talk to your father."

Lorenza had pulled him in closer. "It's all I ever wanted," she told him.

The last time Daniele and Lorenza saw Giacomo was on the morning of July 2, that same year. It was a Friday, and two days later, Giacomo was supposed to go to Lorenza's house to ask for her hand.

"Have you ever been to the feast of the Visitation of the Madonna, at Salice Salentino?" Giacomo had asked them both while stacking fruit crates at the shop.

Daniele was sitting on the sidewalk and Lorenza was standing, holding the bag of cherries she'd just bought, the second in two days.

"I've been going since I was little," Giacomo explained. "My ma was born there and my grandparents still live there. There's this big fair, where you can get anything you want. Let's all go together next year!"

That day, right as the fair was getting under way, an American B-24 bomber detonated right outside Giacomo's grandparents' home, a farmhouse in the open countryside where the whole family was having lunch.

The only survivor was Giacomo's mother, the fruit vendor's wife, and all she could remember was the devastating roar and the out-of-control animals from the fair, who had fled in panic, stomping and trampling over people and things.

The whole town attended the funeral. Sitting in the crowded church, Daniele struggled to hold back his sobs; next to him, Carmela, irritated, kept whispering that he had to stop, that nobody wanted to see a boy cry in public.

When Giacomo's and Michele's coffins were carried out of the church and the procession to the cemetery slowly got under way, Lorenza had unhooked her arm from her mother's, walked up to Daniele, and hugged him. As Carmela watched them, unsure of how to interpret the gesture, he'd placed a hand on her back and breathed in the subtle smell of laundry in her hair.

Still hugging him, Lorenza had started to sob and then, unexpectedly, let out a cry so desperate that Daniele felt like he could see it spread throughout the streets and squares of the entire town.

———

That evening, after the funeral, Daniele returned to the little house he'd moved into some time before. His paternal grandmother had lived there, a shy and sweet woman who'd passed away at the start of the summer of 1940. He was certain that she had let herself die so as not to see another war. The place was small—with only two rooms—the walls were always covered in mold, and in the winter, it seemed impossible to heat it. But Daniele wouldn't have traded it for anything. It was his first real home, a place he could come to after his job at the winery and design clothes and sew in peace, away from his mother's gaze. He had gathered enough savings to buy a Singer, which took up the center of the eat-in kitchen. Rolls of fabric in various colors and patterns were stacked in a corner. After he'd stopped to test their textures at the fabric stall at the Saturday market for the third time in a row and still hadn't bought anything, the woman with the hair bun had leaned over slightly, smiled complicitly as if she'd understood everything, and whispered, "Come see me at home, young man. So you can browse in peace."

The wardrobe in the next room, where he also kept his bed, contained three elegant dresses that no woman had ever worn.

He sat at the table and opened his notebook of patterns to a blank page. He couldn't shake the image of the funeral and the feeling of Lorenza holding him, desperate and inconsolable. He picked up his pencil and started to sketch a dress. For her.

13

The night before June 2, 1946, the outfit Anna had chosen was hanging on the wardrobe door. She would cast her very first vote while wearing a basil green suit. The jacket was fitted around the waist and the knee-length skirt was flared at the hem. A billowy pink rayon blouse completed the look.

She had done her part to ensure that this moment would finally arrive. One day in October, two years ago, while reading the paper, she saw an appeal from the Union of Italian Women, which had formed a pro-vote committee in Rome ahead of the 1946 administrative elections. She immediately felt euphoric, eager to do something. She grabbed a piece of white paper and copied out the text of the petition in her graceful and rounded handwriting. The Union was calling all women, in all of Italy, to sign it.

> We the women of Lizzanello demand that the National
> Liberation Committee give us the right to vote and the
> eligibility to stand in the next administrative elections. We
> hold that exclusion from such a right would leave women in
> the position of unjust inferiority to which fascism had

relegated us, not only within the State but also compared to women in all civilized countries. Fascism and its deranged war policies destroyed our homes, scattered our families, and placed us in undue harm at work, in raising our children, and in the daily fight for survival. We fought fascism and the German oppressors alongside our men and displayed tenacity and courage during the difficult months of the occupation. We feel that in so doing, we've earned the right to participate fully in the reconstruction of our country.

We therefore ask that our legitimate aspiration be taken into account by the men in government and that the women of Italy finally be granted the justice and equality that are the basis of every truly democratic society.

The following day was a Sunday. While Carlo and Roberto slept, Anna went down to the living room, picked up the little wooden table by the door, and left.

"Do you need a hand, Mrs. Letter Carrier?" asked her neighbor's grandson, a scrawny child, when he saw her set off with a ream of paper under her arm and a table in the other hand.

"No, thank you, I've got this," she said with a smile. She set up the table next to the bench in Piazza Castello and placed the paper on top, the copied text on one side, and the blank pages for gathering signatures on the other.

Although it was early, she'd attracted curious glances from people loitering outside the bar, from those going to church, and from all other passersby.

"What's that outlander up to now?" The question bounced from mouth to mouth, the locals still calling her that name after all these years. An elderly man with a cane was the first to approach her for a peek. He was wearing pants and a white shirt and gave off a light scent of damp wool.

"What's that?" he asked in a cavernous voice, pointing at the table with his cane.

"A call for signatures," Anna explained cheerfully. "We're asking the government to give women the vote. It's a national initiative."

The man scowled.

"Can I read it to you?" she asked, picking up the paper. "You can take a seat here." She pointed at the bench, where the man sat down somewhat reluctantly, placing both hands on the knob of his cane.

Just then, Nando arrived followed by some customers from the bar. Then came two women with black scarves on their heads who were heading, arm in arm, toward the church of San Lorenzo.

"Bah, you people just want to turn the world upside down," the elderly man grumbled, once Anna had finished reading. He leaned on his cane and stood up.

"Why, you think it's been right side up this whole time?" she retorted, resentfully.

But he gave no reply. He turned his back on her and walked to the bar, followed by a coterie of men, all shaking their heads.

"Don't mind him," Nando said, with a grimace. "That guy's wife can't even leave the house without his permission."

"I'd like to sign that," said one of the two women timidly.

Beaming, Anna handed her a pen.

"Please, right here," she said, showing her the blank page.

Every afternoon after work, for several weeks, Anna set up her little table in the square. She stopped women on the street, or waited for them to approach her, curious, and read them the petition, often explaining its meaning in simpler words. Finally, she'd hold out the pen. People asked the most bizarre questions.

"Is it legal? It's not like the police are going to come looking for me at home, right?"

"Bah, I don't believe it, but I'll do it anyway."

"I'll sign, but I'm sure not going to tell my husband. And neither are *you*, letter carrier, got it?"

Carlo had promised his "unconditional" support from the start, even though he'd steered clear of the table.

"We're about to bottle. I really can't get away from the winery," he said as an excuse. Antonio, on the other hand, joined her in the square after a few days with a cardboard sign that read SIGN HERE TO GIVE WOMEN THE VOTE.

"I thought it could come in handy," he said, looking down at the cardboard. "It's a bit rudimentary, I know—"

"It's perfect," Anna cut him off, with a big smile. "Put it right here in front."

Antonio set it on the ground against the table leg.

"Why don't you stay and give me a hand?"

"If you want, sure, with pleasure."

"Yes, I want."

From that afternoon on, every time he could, Antonio joined her at the stand, imitating everything she did. Every so often, she'd stop dead and stare at him intently.

"What is it?" he'd ask, feeling watched.

"Nothing," she'd say, blushing.

Within a few weeks, they'd gathered several hundred signatures, including those of women Anna knew personally: Giovanna, Agata and her friends from the rosary, Lorenza, Elena, Chiara, her neighbors, Antonio's secretary. Even Carmela had approached the stand, wearing a fitted dress and lipstick that matched her nails, and asked, "Where do I sign?"

At the beginning of January 1945, Anna put the signatures in a yellow folder and, thoroughly pleased with herself, addressed it to the *Ad Hoc Committee of the Union of Italian Women, via 4 Novembre 144, Rome.*

———

Anna decided to cut her hair the night before the vote. Moving slowly so as not to wake Carlo, she sat at her vanity table and looked at herself in the mirror in the feeble light of her lamp.

She stroked her long black hair, interwoven with a few silver threads; divided it into two sections, letting each one fall to her chest; took the scissors from the marble top; and, without looking away, gave her hair two blunt cuts, first on the left and then on the right, at the base of the neck. She rinsed her hands in a water basin, ran them through her hair, and finally pulled her curlers from a drawer and wrapped her strands around them. Then she went to bed.

The next morning, Anna woke up at dawn, sat back down at her vanity, and started undoing her curlers one by one. Her hair fell to the sides of her face in soft waves. Carlo woke up as she was adjusting them with her brush.

In the feeble light that filtered through the curtain, he looked at his wife, rubbed his eyes, and sat up, leaning on his elbow.

"Anna!" he suddenly screamed at the door. "There's a strange woman in our bedroom. She has terrible, horrific intentions!"

Anna turned around laughing. "You're such an idiot."

"You look really good, you know." Carlo couldn't take his eyes off her.

"Merci!" she said, still brushing her hair.

"Come here," he said, patting his chest. "The polling stations can wait a little longer. I can't."

They had decided to all go and vote together. Anna headed toward Agata's house and knocked on the door. Agata opened in a huff, her cheeks all red.

"Are you okay?" Anna asked, stepping inside.

Agata closed the door.

"If only. I'm catching fire," she replied, fanning herself with her hand.

"Yup, my ma was right," she said, walking toward the kitchen with Anna in tow. "Aunt Flo is a punishment when you've got it and also when you don't."

"You're not dressed yet?" Anna exclaimed when she saw Lorenza in her nightgown, sitting at the kitchen table dipping her biscuits in milk.

"I've been trying to drag this lazybones out of bed for an hour. I've been ready for a while now," Agata complained. "What did you do to your hair?"

"I cut it. Do you like it?" Anna said, twirling a ringlet with her finger.

"I don't know. It's strange," Agata said, frowning. "I have to get used to it."

"Has Antonio already left?"

"Ten minutes ago."

Anna nodded. She turned back to her niece.

"Lorenza, come on, hurry up. Giovanna is waiting for us."

"I'm not coming," Lorenza said, sounding annoyed.

"What's that supposed to mean?"

"I couldn't care less about voting."

"She doesn't want to study, she doesn't want to vote, she doesn't want to work," Agata sighed.

"Lorenza, don't be ridiculous. This is an important day for you, too," Anna scolded her.

"Maybe for you. Not for me."

"How dare you," Anna exclaimed. "If you don't come, you insult yourself most of all. Go get dressed. Now!" she ordered, extending her arm. Lorenza stood up, grumbling.

"I set out a nice outfit for you on the bed!" Agata yelled after her.

Since Giacomo died, Lorenza had plunged into a seemingly endless inertia. She didn't want to go to college anymore.

"I'm an adult now. I decide," she'd insisted.

Antonio had tried to change her mind, but it had been no use talking to her, encouraging her, or telling her about the future she'd be missing out on by not studying.

"And your dreams? What happened to those?" he once prodded her.

"That wasn't my dream, it was yours," she said, harshly. "If there's one thing I've learned, it's that you can't find happiness in books."

"You're wrong," Antonio said.

"Oh yeah? Then tell me, since you read so much: Are you happy? It really doesn't look like it."

"You're angry and you're in pain. I understand that, I do," Antonio said, kindly. "But think about it a little longer, please. It makes me very sad to see you abandon your . . . *our* dream."

"Maybe you were too busy to notice," Lorenza continued, hostile. "But I'd found my own dream. With Giacomo. And this damned war took it away from me."

Lorenza now stared at the clothes on the bed: a black pleated skirt and a pale yellow silk blouse with a little bow at the neckline. She sighed and sat on the edge of the bed. It was one of her Sunday outfits, the same one she would have worn that Sunday, to become Giacomo's betrothed, when her happy life should have begun. And now? Who or what was she, without a man to love her? She jumped up, opened the wardrobe, and pulled out the first dress she got her hands on. A common one, for everyday use, would do fine.

Giovanna was waiting at the gates of the elementary school, where the polls were being held. She was looking around anxiously, clasping her black purse.

For her alone, the war had brought the only thing she'd ever wanted. In 1943, don Giulio escaped Emilia Romagna in northern Italy and took refuge in the south, even though none of his family members were around anymore for him to stay with. The partisans were targeting priests, especially between Bologna, Modena, and Reggio Emilia, and many had been killed. He showed up at Giovanna's door in secular clothing, with a threadbare bag over his shoulder, a worn face, terrified eyes, and an untamed beard.

"Help me," he begged. "Keep me here with you."

She opened the door to him and for a few weeks, Giulio holed up there. He stayed until he found an opening as vice parish priest in Vernole, his hometown, some ten miles from Lizzanello. He was assigned a little house next to the church. But every afternoon, after the last mass, he'd mount his bike and ride for miles on back streets and through fields to reach Contrada La Pietra. Some nights he'd get back on the bike and return to Vernole; when he was too tired, he'd stay and sleep at Giovanna's and leave before dawn. Although no one had ever seen them together, rumors in town had started to circulate. Giovanna realized it from certain furtive glances she got when she visited Anna or went grocery shopping.

"No shame. I mean, really," she heard someone mumble. But she didn't care in the least.

Anna ran to her friend while Agata held back a little, locking arms with Lorenza.

"Bah, I really don't understand you, ungrateful daughter. I set out such an elegant outfit for you," Agata scolded her for the umpteenth time since they'd left the house. "What are people supposed to think? That we don't have nice clothes?"

"Are you happy?" Anna asked Giovanna, giving her a big hug. "Today is a special day."

"If you're happy, I'm happy," she replied, as mild-mannered as ever.

"Come on, let's go in," Anna exclaimed, with a sweep of her arm.

Inside the polling booth, her heart beating, Anna touched the ballot with the tip of her finger, and then, to make the moment last, she slowly traced a cross on the symbol for the republic, which comprised the head of a woman wearing a turreted crown framed by laurel and oak leaves.

Once outside, she looked up at the sky, curled her lips into a smile, and took a deep breath. What a memorable day—she'd cherish it forever.

"Let's all go to the bar," she said cheerfully. "My treat."

Giovanna accepted the invitation gladly and took her by the arm.

"I want an almond pastry," she exclaimed. So they set off, followed by Agata and Lorenza.

Various groups of people had gathered in the clearing in front of Bar Castello. Some were railing against the monarchists, some were just having a good time, some were smoking, and others were toasting with wine. Children played all around them, running after a ball and making a racket.

A few kids were playing behind the bench, including Roberto, who had his hair combed back and was wearing a button-down vest over his white shirt. Next to him a petite girl with delicate features stared at him adoringly. Every so often, Roberto would reciprocate the glance and smile at her bashfully.

"Who's that?" Anna asked.

"Who do you mean?" said Agata.

"That one, next to Roberto."

"That's Fernando's daughter," Lorenza replied. "The youngest of the three."

"What does she want from my son?"

"Oh, leave him be!" Agata exclaimed. "At thirteen he's starting to feel the itch. It's normal."

"What itch?" Anna said, irritated. "He's still a child. The only thing he should be thinking about are his studies."

Later, at home, I'm going to give him a good talking-to, you bet, she thought as she resumed walking.

Suddenly, she heard someone behind them shout, "Lorenza!"

Everyone turned at the same time to see Daniele running toward them, waving.

Lorenza pried herself away from her mother's arm and went toward him.

"It's good to see you. How are you?" he asked, slightly out of breath.

Lorenza shrugged. "So-so. Some good days and some less good."

"I always ask about you—"

"I know. My Uncle Carlo tells me. Thank you."

"You seem thinner since the last time I saw you."

Lorenza looked down. "You think? I haven't noticed."

"Just looking at you, I think I got the measurements wrong . . ." Daniele muttered, almost to himself.

"Measurements? What measurements?" Lorenza asked, perplexed.

Daniele blushed. "For your dress."

"What dress?"

"It's . . . a present."

"For me? You bought me a dress?" she asked, bewildered.

"Not exactly. I made it myself. But I'm still really slow and I only have so much time."

"Hold on. Since when do you sew?" Lorenza asked, folding her arms over her chest.

"Actually, I like designing them more. The clothes, I mean—more than sewing them. I carved out this really small workshop area in my house, but nobody knows."

He brought a finger to his lips, as if to say to keep it to herself.

"Well, now I'm curious."

"Lorenza, come on!" Agata called her. "We're all waiting on you here."

"Coming!" she answered, turning toward her mother.

"Listen . . ." Daniele continued. "If I invite you to the movies again, will you say yes this time?"

Lorenza smiled. "I'll say yes . . . if you let me see your workshop after. And especially my dress!"

"Lorenza!" Agata insisted.

"I have to go," she said, clearly annoyed.

"Next Sunday?" he asked with a hopeful look in his eyes.

"Okay. Next Sunday," Lorenza replied. "Let's meet in front of the Olympia." She picked up her pace and joined the others.

Suddenly, she noticed her father and his brother.

"Look, it's Papa and Uncle Carlo!" Lorenza exclaimed, pointing at them. After she ran into Daniele, her mood had noticeably improved.

Carlo and Antonio were sitting at a table outside Bar Castello with two well-dressed, distinguished-looking men.

"Here come our beautiful ladies," Carlo greeted them, taking a puff from his cigar.

Antonio stood up and went to get more chairs.

"Here," he said, setting them up around the table. When he pulled the chair out for Anna, he asked her, in a whisper, "Um . . . your hair?"

"What, you don't like it?" she asked, a little offended.

"I didn't say that . . ."

"Very well," one man said, standing up, followed by the other. "We'll leave you to your family. We'll continue our discussion tomorrow."

"Certainly," Carlo said, shaking their hands. Antonio said goodbye with a chin lift.

"What discussion?" Anna asked.

Carlo and Antonio exchanged glances.

"Should we tell them?" Carlo whispered with a sparkle in his eye.

"It's not like we can keep it a secret forever—"

"What do you have to tell us?" Agata butted in.

Carlo stuck his cigar in his teeth and spread his arms.

"Look at me," he exclaimed.

"Yes, yes. You're incredibly handsome, we know," Anna joked.

Giovanna giggled and covered her mouth with her hand.

"Thank you, my dear," Carlo said, stroking Anna's face. "No. Look at me closer. Sitting before you is a future candidate for mayor of Lizzanello."

"Seriously?" Anna was stunned.

"Seriously."

"How did you come up with that idea?"

"They came to me," he said, nodding at the two men walking away. "They say I can win. Tomorrow, they're taking me to meet the provincial secretary to talk about the details."

"Ah, sure, since going into business with the Americans you've become a big shot, someone who can win votes," Agata teased.

"Sorry, but the provincial secretary for which party?" Anna asked.

"Christian Democracy."

Her face clouded over. Lorenza couldn't help but notice her father's eyes rest on her aunt and tacitly ask, *Why are you sad? Are you okay?*

"It's really great news," Agata said, glancing at her sister-in-law.

"It absolutely is," Carlo said, excited. "And now I'm going to get some wine for all these beautiful ladies!" he shouted, twirling his finger in the air.

"I'll come with you," Antonio offered, pushing his chair out. "I'll help you carry the glasses."

"Don't forget the almond pastries," Giovanna said.

Carlo moved aside the rope curtain and saw Carmela standing at the bar with her husband. His joy instantly vanished.

"Nando! A bottle of Donna Anna and six glasses, please," Antonio said.

"You're celebrating?" Carmela asked, looking Carlo straight in the eye.

"We're toasting our women," Antonio said, trying to get his brother out of an uncomfortable situation.

Nicola mumbled that it was a good idea, that this day was special for them all, and that it should be celebrated, no doubt.

"How's don Ciccio?" Carlo asked.

Carmela shrugged. "He is how he is. He doesn't get out of bed anymore. He says he feels like he's got knives poking into his back."

"I'm sorry. Please give him my best."

"He's always glad to hear from you," she said.

Carlo nodded and started to drum his fingers on the counter as he waited for their order.

Nicola checked the clock and said that he and his lady really had to get going.

"Good day to you," he added. He picked up his hat and headed for the exit.

Carmela followed him apathetically. But as she walked past Carlo, she brushed his arm with her shoulder.

———

On the following Sunday afternoon, Lorenza arrived late at the Olympia. Daniele was waiting for her, leaning against the wall with the sunlight illuminating half his face. His cap was tilted to the side and he wore a checkered shirt and dark pants held up by suspenders. For a moment, Lorenza was breathless; Giacomo also used to wear caps and suspenders. And he'd had that same checkered shirt . . .

Before joining Daniele, she glanced at the film poster: *Sciuscia*.

"Sorry. Have you been waiting long?" she asked, with a slight smile.

He pushed himself off the wall immediately.

"No, don't worry, not at all," he said.

They went in and stood in line for their tickets.

"What's it about? The film, I mean," Lorenza asked.

"I don't know much about it. I read something quickly in the paper; it's about two kids that work as shoeshines in Rome."

Lorenza turned up her nose—she would have much preferred a love story.

"You know, I'm kind of excited about the idea of you seeing the dress later," Daniele said suddenly.

"It still seems weird, this thing," she said.

"What thing?" he asked, pulling out his change purse.

"The fact that you design clothes . . . Giacomo never told me."

"That's because he didn't know," Daniele explained, bashfully. "It's always been my little thing. If my mother knew . . ." he added, with a smirk. He turned to the ticket vendor. "Two, please."

"Why?" Lorenza inquired.

He shrugged and took the tickets. "She thinks it's not for men," he said, heading into the theater.

"That's nonsense," she said indignantly. "Is that why you never told Giacomo, either?"

"I dunno. Maybe," Daniele said. Then he moved the red curtain aside for Lorenza.

A few hours later, Lorenza was sitting on Daniele's love seat, looking around.

"It's cozy, though," she said into the other room, where Daniele had gone to retrieve the dress from the wardrobe.

"I think so too," Daniele said. A moment later, he came back into the kitchen holding a hanger with a blue dress with yellow inserts, a wide skirt, no sleeves, and the stitching still visible.

"The sleeves are missing and the skirt needs to be hemmed a bit—it should come to your knee . . . And then I want to add some round buttons, here on the bodice, and a belt around the waist," he explained in one breath.

Lorenza smiled tenderly at him.

"But to finish it, I have to measure it properly," he added.

"I'll try it on right away," Lorenza said, standing up. She took the hanger from his hand.

"You can go into the bedroom," Daniele said, nodding toward it.

Lorenza walked in and only partially closed the door behind her.

Daniele pulled a chair out from under the table and sat down to wait, resting his elbows on his knees and tapping his foot.

"Everything okay?" he asked after a minute.

"Yes, yes," she answered. "I'm just taking my clothes off."

Daniele nodded. Then he slowly leaned back until he could glimpse Lorenza through the crack. He could see the sinuous lines of her hips and her long, smooth auburn hair falling over the rounded curve of her breast.

He felt a sudden stir in his abdomen and an instinctive desire to possess her. He jumped up from his chair and poured himself a glass of water. He drank it all in one gulp and then poured some more, drinking it quickly, as if he were trying to douse the flames inside him.

"You're right, maybe it's a little big," Lorenza said, opening the door, wearing the dress.

Daniele swallowed and, his cheeks crimson, responded that, yes, true, it was at least one size too big.

"I'll take it in right away," he said.

14

"Vote Carlo Greco for mayor! Choose Christian Democracy!" roared the voice from the loudspeaker mounted onto the Fiat Topolino as it roamed around town nonstop. Anna ended up running into it on every street while delivering mail on her Bianchi, as if the two men on board were following her. She couldn't even escape the chant by ducking down a side alley—on the contrary, it felt like the voice became even more booming and obsessive as it bounced off the walls of the houses.

Speaking of walls, they were covered in electoral posters in which her husband's name towered over the cross emblem of the Christian Democratic Party. WITH THIS VOTE YOU WILL SECURE YOUR WELL-BEING, they read. Or: VOTE FOR HONEST AND COMPETENT PEOPLE TO RUN YOUR TOWN. VOTE FOR CHRISTIAN DEMOCRACY.

As if that weren't enough, whenever she stopped to deliver the mail to someone, they would say, "Congratulations to your husband, Mrs. Letter Carrier."

"Please do tell Carlo I'll be voting for him."

"He'll win, I'm sure of it."

And so on. Anna did her best to smile and thank people, even though what she really wanted was to smash the loudspeaker and rip up the posters one by one. *Why did he have to run for Christian Democracy? What the hell?* she thought, increasingly irritated.

"I'm not going to put my cross on the Christian Democracy's cross," she told Carlo after he had brought home a stack of electoral pamphlets fresh from the printer's, giddy as a boy.

"What's that now?" he asked, in the tone of someone who suspects a joke.

"Come on. I'm serious."

"You won't vote for your husband for a stupid matter of principle?"

"It's not just a matter of principle," she exclaimed. "Over my dead body will I ever vote for the Catholics."

"It's me you'll be voting for, not the Catholics!"

"If you want my vote, then change parties."

"Do you hear yourself? And who would you vote for? Let's hear it."

"The Communist party! Do you know how many people in the Union of Italian Women are communist? Well, so am I!"

"And when might have you become one, because I sure haven't noticed. At night, while I was sleeping?"

"Communists care about women's rights!"

"And you think I don't care about you ladies? Are you serious?"

"I don't when you say 'you ladies' in that tone . . ."

"I'm sorry I'm not a woman. I'm sorry I said 'you ladies,'" Carlo said sarcastically, raising his hands.

"I'm sorry too, Carlo. But I'm not changing my mind."

"So you won't support me? You've decided?"

"I won't do anything to harm your chances. But you can forget about my vote."

"Then you can forget what it's like to sleep next to your husband," he said furiously, leaving the room.

That night he started sleeping on the living room couch.

Even Roberto, who'd always steered clear of their squabbles, sided with his father. "Do you think it's normal for you not to vote for Papa?"

"'Normal.' How you love to throw around that word."

"And you, Maman? What did normality ever do to you?"

"Oh, let's hear it, since when do you get to decide what's normal?" Anna challenged him, hands on her hips.

"I could ask you the same question," Roberto replied, placing his hands on his hips to mimic her.

Antonio and Agata, meanwhile, got to work to support Carlo's electoral campaign, ramping up in the few weeks before the vote. Antonio joined his brother as he went door-to-door, participated in party meetings, and handed out flyers; Agata visited her rosary friends and her neighbors to make sure they'd vote "the right way."

Even at the post office they hardly spoke of anything else. According to their predictions, Carlo would win by a landslide.

"Unfortunately!" Carmine remarked. "Know that I'm giving my vote to the socialists, not your husband!" he added, pointing at Anna, who was forced to bite her tongue, even though she would have very much liked to agree with him. Elena, on the other hand, immediately declared herself an enthusiastic supporter of Carlo. She was telling Anna how after all, even the new priest, don Luciano, before every "Ite, missa est," reminded the faithful congregants that only Christians and democrats could defend freedom and the future of their children.

Inevitably, she'd conclude, "You'll be the mayor's wife, can you believe it?"

Only Chiara's announcement was able to briefly divert attention from the topic. One morning, she arrived with a tray of pastries that looked bigger than her and, bashfully, announced she'd gotten engaged to her doctor and that the wedding was set for the following spring. She'd stay with them for just a few more weeks, until Christmas, and then she'd resign.

Elena, Carmine, and Tommaso immediately congratulated her, while Anna shot her a dubious look and didn't move.

"Why should finding a husband keep you from working?" she asked loudly, causing a silence to fall over the office.

Chiara bowed her head timidly. Then she repositioned her glasses on her nose and responded kindly but firmly.

"For me it's no sacrifice at all, to stop working. I want to be a good wife and it's a big commitment that requires a lot of time. I'm happy—don't worry about me."

"I would have done the same thing in her place, you know," Elena cut in, biting into a pastry. "What do you think? If I'd had a man to take care of me, do you know how fast I would have shot out of here?"

Anna stared at them and was about to respond when a thought crossed her mind: *If Chiara is leaving, we need a new telegraphist.*

And who better than Lorenza? It could give her a boost, bring her out of the inertia she'd fallen into. She would suggest it that very day. And Antonio would surely be grateful, she thought, happy to have had the idea.

———

"Can you talk to her, please? Can you talk some sense into her?" Carlo said, pacing back and forth in Antonio's office.

"You know what Anna's like . . . she won't listen to anyone," Antonio replied from his armchair.

"She listens to you. She always does. I swear I'm not letting her off the hook this time."

"The more you dig your heels in, the worse it gets. It's like you don't even know her."

"Would you put up with this?" Carlo asked, exasperated, only to answer his own question right after. "No, you wouldn't put up with this!"

"I don't know, Carletto," Antonio sighed. "What does it matter in the end? You have the votes of the whole town. Anna's vote certainly won't make the difference."

"That's not the point," Carlo grumbled, placing both hands on the desk. "She's my wife. Her vote counts more than the others."

"But if she doesn't want to vote Christian Democratic, it's not like you can force her."

"Antó, are you on my side or hers?" Carlo asked, irritated.

"I'm not on anyone's side."

"Imagine that. And here I was, thinking my brother was on mine."

"I mean, yeah, Carletto, of course I am."

"Then talk to her. Help me?"

"Okay, okay. I'll try," Antonio said in defeat, raising his hands but thinking, *Why don't I ever say, "Nope, leave me alone this time, deal with it yourself"? Why?*

The next day, he lay in wait outside the post office, timing his arrival to when he knew Anna would be finishing her shift.

"Antonio, what are you doing here?" she said, surprised, as she came out of the office.

"I was nearby and wanted to come say hi," he answered casually.

"Glad you're here," Anna said, grabbing the handlebars on her Bianchi and pulling it off the wall.

"Walk with me?"

"Did something happen?" she asked, suspiciously.

"No, like what? I told you, I was nearby so I figured I would wait for you."

Anna studied him. Then she started walking, pushing the bicycle alongside her.

He picked up the pace to keep up with her and they crossed the near-empty square—it was lunchtime, and people had already gone home to eat. He followed her as she turned left, passing Michele's closed shop, and mentally went over the argument he'd prepared: how to start, the words he would use to convince her without irritating her too much, the answers to her objections.

Exasperated by that prolonged silence, Anna stopped and grabbed his arm. Looking him straight in the eye, she finally said, "Come on. Out with it."

Antonio snorted. "It's for Carlo."

"I knew it."

"He can't swallow it."

"Yes, I've noticed," she exclaimed, and started walking briskly again, causing the wheels on the bicycle to slip on the cobblestones.

"Don't get mad, wait," he said, running after her. "Come here, let's sit down for a moment, please," he added, taking her hand.

Anna stopped dead, blushed, and stared at Antonio's hand holding hers.

"There, let's sit here," he suggested, dropping her hand and pointing down a narrow alley at a stone step on an abandoned house.

Anna leaned the bike against the wall and sat down.

"Well?" she prodded, crossing her arms.

Antonio sat on the step. "Well." He took a deep breath. "Do you remember how you felt when you decided to become a letter carrier and Carlo wouldn't stop hounding you?"

"I'm not hounding him," she interrupted, piqued.

"Please listen for one second," he said, covering her mouth briefly with his hand.

The gesture made Anna open her eyes wide, but she didn't move.

"What I mean," Antonio continued, "is that you know full well what it feels like when the person you share your life with isn't on your side."

"Fine, but I'm not standing in his way," she retorted.

"I know, Anna," he assured her, softening his voice. "But he's still disappointed. For him, your support is more important than anything. He can't do it without it."

She looked down. "What am I supposed to do? Go against my principles?"

"Yes. For once, yes."

"But it's not fair!" she exclaimed, resentfully. "Should I pretend to be someone I'm not? It's like being in a cage. Do you have any idea what it feels like?"

Antonio stood up suddenly. He stuck his hands in his pockets and kicked a pebble.

After a long silence, Anna looked up at him.

"I'm sorry. I really am . . ." she said.

"What are you sorry about?" he asked, in a harsh tone.

Anna stood up and went to him. She put a hand on his cheek and looked at him intensely. Antonio closed his eyes and rested his cheek on her palm, then lifted his hand and closed it around Anna's.

When he opened his eyes, their gazes met again. They looked at each other in silence for a long time. Then Anna pulled her hand away, grabbed her bicycle, and left, pedaling fast. Antonio watched her, distraught, until he saw her turn right onto via Paladini. Only then did he walk away.

That evening, as Lorenza was setting the table and Agata was bringing a wooden spoonful of steaming bean soup to her lips to test it, Antonio locked the door to the oil mill and walked briskly to the Olympia theater. He arrived out of breath and went in without even looking at the film poster.

"The movie started a while ago," the ticket boy warned him.

"Doesn't matter," Antonio responded, handing him some change. He walked into the dark theater as Anna Magnani was taking her bobby pins out of her hair, looking beautiful on the big screen in a fur-lined robe. He sat in the last row, two seats away from Melina, a war widow with a slender, almost childlike figure, thick eyebrows, and very black curls. Left alone and without a cent, she'd started to turn tricks. Everyone in town knew that they just had to sit in the back row at the Olympia.

Melina turned to Antonio and nodded slowly.

———

Hundreds of bottles were about to be filled with Donna Anna, vintage 1946. Once again, part of the yield would end up in the United States; the ties forged between Lizzanello and America in the fall of 1943 had been going strong ever since. Carlo had decided to print the labels for those bottles in English—which, in these parts, had never been done before—and he was just about to head to Lecce to pick them up from the press when Roberto stopped him.

"Papa, can I come with you?" he said as he sat upside down on the couch, head dangling over the carpet and legs in the air. "I've finished my homework. I'm bored."

"I don't see why not," Carlo said. "Go on, get in the car."

Drystone walls flanked the road to Lecce on both sides. Beyond them, expanses of olive and fruit trees dotted the countryside, along with large farms and typical pyramidal pagghiare constructions, where farmers stored their tools. That day, the sky was clear and the pungent smell of wild chicory that grew alongside the walls filled the car.

Carlo drove to Porta San Biagio, one of the ancient access points to the city, and parked by the two pairs of baroque columns framing the ornate door, above which rose two stone wolves and the coat of arms of King Ferdinand IV of Naples.

They walked along the cobbled streets, passed through the door, and continued to the print shop, located in an alley to the left of the church of San Matteo.

"This is a strange church," Roberto said with his head tilted backward. "See, Papa? It's convex below but concave on top," he explained, pointing.

Carlo stopped for a moment and looked.

"Yeah, it is strange. Your mother would like it," he said with a touch of sarcasm. He carried on walking while Roberto followed him, turning back every so often to look at the church again.

Carlo stopped in front of the sign that read COMMERCIAL PRINT SHOP and went inside. The small shop had a vaulted ceiling and smelled of ink. Large posters of lyrical operas that had been staged at the Politeama Theater were plastered on the walls. He picked up the brown paper pack of labels that had been readied for him and stuck it under his arm.

"Come on, let's get a pasticciotto at Caffè Alvino in Piazza Sant'Oronzo. It's the best in the city," he said to his son.

As they walked, Carlo rested his hand on Roberto's shoulder. After a few hundred feet, they got to a coffee shop that looked out onto the stone square, in the center of which towered a column with the statue of the patron saint. They sat at an outdoor table in front of the Roman amphitheater, whose ruins had been uncovered only a few years before in 1940.

Behind the amphitheater rose an imposing building, the Istituto Nazionale Assicurazioni: Mussolini had inaugurated it in the 1920s.

"On the other hand, Mom would not like that big building at all," Roberto said. Carlo made no reply.

They ordered two pasticciotti, plus a coffee for Carlo and a lemonade for Roberto.

"When do you think you'll make up, you and Mom?" Roberto asked, sinking his teeth into the pasticciotto and getting lemon cream all over his lips.

Carlo leaned against the rigid back of the metal chair, lit his cigar, and inhaled the first puff.

"Ah, that's why you keep bringing her up. Well, it certainly isn't up to yours truly," he said. "But don't worry about it; it has nothing to do with you."

"Yes, it does. So long as I live in the same house as you," Roberto retorted. "I can't stand seeing you grumpy all the time. Couldn't you resolve it like adults, for once?" He wiped his lips with a napkin.

Carlo looked at him, surprisingly amused, and thought that Anna had raised him to be just like her, a straight shooter, bordering on insolent. He'd grown so much in the past year, as if he'd waited for the end of the war to make the jump. He was almost as tall as Carlo now, and his angelic voice, with its high tones, had disappeared who knows where.

"We'll do our best to please you," Carlo said, smiling.

As they headed home, Roberto asked Carlo before he turned onto their street, "Can I come with you to the winery?"

"But you never want to come," Carlo said. "You always say you get bored there."

"Fine. If I get bored, I'll tell you and you can take me home," Roberto chuckled. Carlo smiled and turned in the other direction.

As he pulled up to the winery and got out of the car, with the pack of labels under his arm, Carlo was warmly greeted by the workers.

Roberto followed him, slightly surprised by all that coming and going. "That wasn't there before," he said, pointing at the corking machine.

"Yes, you're right," Carlo said. "Come, I'll show you." He handed the labels to a passing errand boy and went to the machine.

In that moment, Daniele came up from the cellar wearing a cap and with a pencil stuck behind his ear.

"Good afternoon, Mr. Carlo," he said.

Carlo spun around and felt his legs go weak; this was the first time he was in a room with both his sons, something he had never thought would happen with Roberto being at the winery so infrequently. No doubt they'd already seen each other before, in church or in town, but they were never classmates, nor had they ever played together—Daniele was almost twenty-two years old and Roberto was just thirteen. Carlo was certain they'd never spoken to each other. He couldn't swear to it, but he felt it in his gut. And now they were about to. Like two perfect strangers meeting for the first time.

"This is Daniele Carlà, our site manager," he told Roberto.

Daniele smiled and held out his hand. "Hello."

"Hi, I'm Roberto—"

"Yeah, this is Roberto, my son," Carlo cut in, a bit too hastily.

The boys didn't seem to notice.

"Do you know how this works?" Roberto asked Daniele, pointing at the corking machine.

"Yes, of course. Do you want me to show you?"

Carlo crossed his arms in front of his chest and watched his boys as his heart pounded fast. Daniele took one of the empty bottles lined up nearby, ready to be taken to the cellar, and placed it at the base of the corking machine.

"You see?" he explained, as Roberto watched him attentively. "This is where you fit the stopper. Then you push this lever to stick it into the bottle and remove the air."

"It doesn't seem hard. Can I try?"

"Sure," Daniele said. "Be careful not to hurt yourself. I'll help you." He gently placed his hands on Roberto's and guided them on the corker machine until the stopper went straight into the neck of the bottle. "See? Good job!"

Roberto looked up at him and smiled, pleased with himself.

They'd already climbed back into the 1100 when Carlo told Roberto he had forgotten something inside and turned the car around. Once he made sure no one was around, he slipped the empty, unmarked bottle from the corking machine—the one his sons had just closed together—took it into his office, and hid it in the bottom drawer of his desk.

———

The final rally of the campaign was held on November 22, two days before the election. A little stage had been set up in the middle of Piazza Castello. The flag with the Christian Democracy symbol waved under the gusts of the Tramontane wind.

A man wearing a long black coat open over his large belly, and with thinning hair ruffled by the wind, stepped up to the microphone and announced that Carlo Greco would soon be arriving.

Anna looked around, wondering why Antonio and Agata weren't there yet. Roberto, arms crossed and eyes fixed on the empty stage, was by her side.

"Maybe they're already here but can't see us," Anna thought out loud, casting her gaze over the crowded square. Not far away she spied Chiara, clutching her fiancé's arm as he towered over her by several inches. She noticed Elena too, near Bar Castello, chatting and laughing with her sister. Everyone else seemed to be accounted for.

"Where the heck are they?" she grumbled.

"I can go look for them if you want," Roberto said.

"Sure, go on."

As her son walked off, Anna noticed Carmela making her way through the crowd to a spot under the stage. Her son and husband were behind her. A fur stole was effortlessly slung over her right shoulder, covering part of her tight red wool dress with its three-quarter sleeves and knee-length skirt. Topping off the outfit was a small-brimmed hat made in the same fabric and matching lipstick. *She looks like she's going to a gala, not a rally,* Anna thought. Carmela shot her a glance and greeted her with a chin raise. Anna reciprocated courteously, then moved her gaze back to the stage. She wondered if Carlo had chosen the pinstripe suit. She'd left him as he was staring at two outfits laid out on the bed, a pinstripe suit and an iron-gray one. He was tense—he kept smoothing back his hair while looking at those suits as if his life depended on which one he chose.

"Wear the pinstripe one," Anna had suggested, with the sole aim of freeing him from that impasse.

"Do you think it looks better?"

"Sure. What matters is what you say, right?"

"You're right," he admitted. "I'm worrying too much."

"Yup. I'm going. See you there." She put her coat on and was about to leave the room when he stopped her, grabbing her by the wrist.

"Hey, wait a minute," he murmured.

"What is it?"

"I wanted to thank you again for changing your mind. I know what it means to you, and I'm really grateful and—"

"Maman, I found them!" Roberto's voice tore her away from that memory.

Antonio and Agata were walking toward her. They were arm in arm, or rather, Agata was clasping her husband's arm with both of hers. Agata's elegance stunned Anna; she was used to seeing her without a hint of makeup, hair brushed haphazardly, and in flower-patterned muumuus. But that day she was sporting mauve lipstick, an elaborate hairdo acheived with the use of many hairpins, and even a gold-plated brooch of a leafy stem with a blooming flower pinned to her brown coat. Lorenza reached them a minute later, looking around as if she were searching for someone.

She was wearing a long-sleeved blue-and-yellow dress that was cinched at the waist with a belt that separated a button-up bodice from a wide, knee-length skirt.

"You look beautiful, ma petite," Anna greeted her with a smile. "Is that a new dress?"

"No, a friend of mine—Cecilia—gave it to me. It doesn't fit her anymore, not since she had her baby."

"Cecilia who?" Anna asked, looking confused.

"Of course, an old friend from school, the one that lives in Lecce," Agata answered. "And sure, it's nice enough," she continued, "but she'll catch a cold! I told her to dress warmly, with this wind."

"I'm not cold," Lorenza protested.

Apparently, I'm the only one who didn't get all dolled up for the occasion, Anna thought, looking down at her very simple green wool dress.

"How's Carlo?" Antonio asked, trying not to look Anna in the eyes.

"A bit nervous, understandably," she said.

"He'll do great," Agata said, pleased. "Look how many people came to hear him."

"There he is," Lorenza said suddenly, beaming.

The small group immediately turned toward the stage, but it was still empty. Lorenza broke off and went to meet Daniele, who saw her and ran toward her.

"You're wearing it, finally. It looks great on you!" he said, taking her hands.

"I adore it wholeheartedly," Lorenza said.

"It's beautiful because you're the one wearing it," he said. "I'll make you more! All the ones you want!"

"I think I'll need them—office clothes, actually. Next week I'm starting a telegraphy course."

Daniele looked at her in confusion. "Telegraphy?"

"Chiara is getting married, and Auntie Anna asked me if I wanted to take her place, so . . . I'm going to try," she said, smiling, and shrugged.

"Well, that's good news, right?" he asked.

Agata, who was watching the scene unfold from afar, smiled knowingly.

"That's the kid that works with Papa," Roberto said. "Daniele, the site manager."

"You know him?" Anna asked.

"I met him a few days ago, at the winery. He's nice."

"He's a good kid. They all say so, right, Antó?" Agata asked.

Antonio was also keeping his eyes fixed on Lorenza and Daniele. But he wasn't smiling.

"Antó?" Agata called him. "Are you listening to me?"

"Yes . . ." he mumbled absently.

"I would be very glad if he and Lorenza . . . I mean, you know," Agata said with a mischievous grin.

"What nonsense. Please," Antonio snapped.

Agata was dumbstruck. "What did I say?"

Anna shot Antonio a puzzled look. *He's not usually one to use that tone . . . What's eating him?* she thought.

In that moment, a roar of applause erupted in the square. Carlo was stepping onto the stage in his pinstripe suit. He waved at the audience and approached the microphone.

"Dear friends and countrymen, I'm happy to see so many of you," he began, his voice cracking with emotion.

The morning of November 24, in the voting booth, Anna picked up a pencil and paused for a long time, staring at the ballot.

Then she marked a cross on the symbol for the Communist party. No one would ever know, aside from her. And that was all that mattered.

That night, Carlo started sleeping beside her again.

15

Five Months Later

The latest issue of *Oggi* was open on the dressmaker's workbench. With her glasses mounted on her nose, a fresh coat of lipstick, and her thick hair gathered into a bun, Carmela was bent over the page, engrossed in an article on the Fontana sisters. She looked at the picture of the three-story Roman building where they had moved their high-fashion house. What a dream that would be, she thought, to own a real atelier, a spacious one, instead of this damp hole-in-the-wall in which she was forced to work and that she'd had to carve out of the stables attached to the house.

Two quick, light knocks on the door tore her away from her fantasies.

"I'm coming!" she said, closing the magazine with a grumble.

She opened the door, but the "Good morning" she was about to say died in her throat.

Anna and Giovanna were standing before her.

"Hello, Carmela. May we come in?" Anna asked amiably.

With all the calm she could muster, Carmela managed to mumble, "Trasìti."

Once the two women were inside, she ushered them to two armchairs.

"Have a seat," she said, leaning against the table behind her with both hands. "How can I help you?"

"We would like you to make us some pants," Anna said.

"Like that actress has," Giovanna added.

"Which actress?" Carmela asked.

"Katharine Hepburn," said Anna. "Do you know her?"

"Of course I know her," Carmela said, cuttingly.

"Well, we want the same pants she wears."

Carmela pursed her lips and narrowed her eyes into slits.

"Hold on, I think I have it here somewhere . . ." She started to rummage through the magazine clippings she kept on a shelf. "Here it is," she said after a few moments. She showed the two women the picture of Hepburn in high-waisted, wide-leg pants, which were paired with a black blouse with rolled-up sleeves. "Like this?"

"Exactly!" Anna confirmed, beaming.

Carmela placed the cutting on the table. "I have to take your measurements," she said, trying to hurry them along. "Who do I start with?"

"With me," Anna said, standing up and unzipping the side of her skirt.

"What are you doing?" Giovanna said, agitated.

Anna stopped. "I'm undressing . . ."

"But why?"

Carmela frowned. "How else am I supposed to get her measurements?"

"But I don't want to get undressed in front of her," Giovanna protested, pointing at Carmela and standing up.

Anna went up to her and placed a hand on her arm.

"What's the matter? It'll just take a minute," she assured her. "Isn't that right?" she asked Carmela.

"Yup, nothing to it," Carmela said impatiently.

Giovanna was crazy then and is crazy now, she thought, shaking her head. *As I always say, when someone is born round, they don't die square.*

"Sit down, don't worry," Anna said, placing a hand on her cheek.

Giovanna looked at her with tears in her eyes and nodded. She sat down again.

Anna finished unzipping herself, then slipped out of her skirt and her nylon stockings, remaining in her underwear.

Carmela couldn't help but linger on the diaphanous skin of her legs, her tapered thighs, and her slender ankles. *Like those of a chicken*, she thought.

"Stand here," she ordered Anna, pointing at the center of the room and grabbing a measuring tape. She lifted her sweater, made her put her arms out, and measured first her waist and then her hips. She marked the numbers—twenty-six and thirty-seven inches—in a notebook open on the table next to the copy of *Oggi*. Then she crouched to measure the circumference of her thigh, her knee, and her ankle. Finally, she positioned the measuring tape at the height of her waist and let it unfurl down to her heel.

"I'm done with you," she said. "You can get dressed."

"See how easy that was?" Anna said with a smile, turning toward her friend.

Giovanna bit her lip and slowly stood up, while Carmela studied her with a mixture of pity and irritation. In the end, she managed to take the necessary measurements from Giovanna, who stood there with her cheeks burning the whole time. Then they moved on to selecting the fabric and color of the pants. They both wanted soft cotton, maybe in a nice, light beige.

"Minimum ten days. I have to finish up some other work first," Carmela warned them as she walked them to the door. "You can bring the money when you pick them up."

As soon as she closed the door, Carmela leaned against it heavily and let out her breath, only then realizing that she'd been holding it tightly for the duration of that unexpected visit.

It was a warm day in early April, and Anna took Giovanna by the arm.

"I'll walk you home," she said, heading toward Contrada La Pietra.

They strolled in silence for a while, but in the end, Anna couldn't help but ask, "Why were you so ashamed of getting undressed?"

Giovanna bowed her head. "Because of Giulio. He gets mad if someone sees me when I'm not fully dressed."

"Even the seamstress?" Anna said, stunned.

"I don't know. I think so. He always says that my body is his and his alone."

Suddenly worried, Anna took a few moments to respond.

"Well, that's just not true. Your body is yours and no one else's."

"Not even Giulio's?"

"No. Not even Giulio's."

They walked a few feet in silence, side by side. Then Anna stopped dead, shaken by an intuition, and turned Giovanna toward her. "I'm going to ask you something now. Promise me you'll answer honestly."

Giovanna looked at her with disappointment. "I've never lied to you."

"I know," Anna assured her, taking her hand. She took a deep breath, hesitated, and then went for it. "Giulio has never forced you to do anything you didn't want to do, right? With your body, I mean."

"I don't . . . I don't understand you."

"In bed," Anna specified, getting straight to the point. "Is there anything that you do together that bothers you or hurts you?"

"No . . ." Giovanna whispered.

"Are you telling me the truth?"

Giovanna bit her lip and nodded.

"I have to go home," she said. She pulled her hand back, planted a light kiss on Anna's cheek, and ran off.

Left there in a lurch like that, in the middle of the street, Anna watched Giovanna walk away and thought bitterly about what had just happened.

She knew that Giovanna had told her a lie.

———

"Good morning, donna Gina," Carlo said, removing his Borsalino hat. "Is don Ciccio able to see me?"

"Good morning, *Mr. Mayor*," Gina greeted him, somewhat harshly. "It's been a while. We'd forgotten what you looked like."

"You're all too right, donna Gina," he apologized, holding his hat between his hands. "But I'm only finding the time now. It wasn't for lack of inclination."

She stared at him warily.

"Tràsi," she said finally.

She closed the door behind him, motioned for him to wait in the entryway, and went to make sure her husband was awake. There was always a pungent odor in that house, Carlo noticed with a grimace of disgust. Like burnt garlic. Gina returned after a few minutes.

"He says he'll see you now," she mumbled, and led him down a long, dark hallway. She stopped in front of the slightly open door to the bedroom and before entering, she cautioned, "Don't tire him out. He doesn't even have the strength to sit up anymore, because of the pain."

Carlo nodded and assured her this would be a brief visit.

The room was almost completely dark; only a faint light filtered in through the closed shutters. Carlo groped his way forward, trying not to bump into the furniture. He identified the profile of the wrought iron bed frame and then the bulge of don Ciccio under the covers.

He stopped at the foot of the bed and mumbled, "Good morning, don Ciccio . . . it's Carlo. How are you?"

Don Ciccio let out a wheeze.

"As God wills," he said.

"Your wife told me you no longer get out of bed."

"To go where?" don Ciccio chuckled bitterly. "I can't walk no more."

"I'm very sorry . . . If there's anything I can do . . ."

"Nothing to be done." Don Ciccio cut him short. "Rather, tell me: How's the winery? Are things coming along well? Are you still selling to the Americans?"

"Sure am. It's all going for the best, thank God. I also planted the

Primitivo, bought the durmast barrels, and carved out another cellar. I hope to bring you some soon—the first red from my winery."

Don Ciccio was silent for a few seconds.

"You need a whole lot of patience with red wine," he said.

"And I've got it."

"Are you here for my blessing?" don Ciccio scoffed, letting a wheeze slip out.

"No," Carlo said. "Actually, I'm here about a delicate matter."

"What would that be?"

"I must speak to you about my"—he stopped and corrected himself—"about your grandson."

"Did he get up to something?"

"No, no, on the contrary. Only good things."

"So what's the problem?"

Carlo hesitated, grasping onto the wrought iron bed.

"It's about him and my brother's daughter," he said. "Lately, they've been spending a lot of time together."

"Go on," don Ciccio hissed.

"Antonio, my brother, is worried. The last thing he wants, God save us, is to see his daughter married to . . ." Carlo paused. "To her cousin."

"Your brother knows?"

"He's the only one."

Don Ciccio let out a grunt. "Too many people have come to know about it."

"I trust Antonio as much as I trust myself. You don't have to worry about him. He hasn't said anything and he never will. I give you my word."

"Go on," don Ciccio said again.

"Well, I've thought about it a lot, about what to do. And maybe I've found a solution: I need someone to take care of business at the winery in New York. It could be him. He could go away for a while, I mean. Just the time it takes to—"

Don Ciccio let out a raspy laugh, followed by a bout of coughing. "This is your solution?" he asked, once he'd regained his composure.

"It's well known: Far from the eyes—"

"Right," don Ciccio interrupted. "Who knows that better than you."

Carlo ate his heart out but didn't answer. "I only ask whether you have anything against me sending the boy" was all he said.

"For how long?"

"A few months."

"Have you told his mother?"

"No, I wanted to speak to you first."

There was a long silence. "Well, it couldn't hurt him," don Ciccio said finally. "A change of scenery, to see another world."

"Your words are a comfort to me, don Ciccio. I didn't doubt your wisdom—"

"But don't get any illusions that it'll work," don Ciccio interrupted him, harshly. Then, with a sigh, he added, "Now go. I'm tired."

Carlo bade him goodbye and exited into the hallway. Gina was sitting nearby in the kitchen, in front of the window. He had the impression that she spent entire days like that, waiting for her husband to call for her. Without a word, she stood up and walked Carlo to the door.

As soon as she closed it, don Ciccio's voice rang out, imperious in spite of everything, "Gina! Bring Carmela to me! I have to speak to her!"

———

Carmela sped down the street in a state of fury, causing her purse to swing rhythmically as the Tramontane wind raged, implacable, blowing locks of her hair—which she'd tied up hurriedly—across her face. She hadn't even looked in the mirror that morning, but she didn't care.

She reached the town hall and practically ran inside.

"Donna Carmela, where are you going?" the doorman shouted after her.

"I must speak to the mayor," she said sharply, hurrying past him while looking straight ahead.

"I don't know if he's busy . . . Let me check, first," the doorman begged while running after her.

For Carmela it was as if the man didn't exist. She reached the door with the brass plate that said MAYOR, grabbed the handle, and shoved the door open. Carlo was sitting at the desk, bent over a mountain of papers, cigar in hand. He jerked his head up.

"Mr. Mayor, I apologize," the doorman gasped, running in after Carmela. "The madam didn't give me time to warn you. She says she must speak with you."

"Yes. With some urgency," Carmela added, clutching her purse to her chest.

"Thank you, Giuseppe. Please let Mrs. Carlà in, don't worry," Carlo said with a wave.

The doorman excused himself and went to leave, but not before shooting a nasty look at Carmela, who couldn't have cared less.

"Well?" Carlo asked, standing up. "What's going on?"

"What's going on is that I'm about to stick these nails where the sun don't shine," she said, opening her hand and putting her red nails on display.

"That's quite a threat," Carlo said, sitting on the edge of the desk. He took a puff from his cigar.

She came up to him so that her face was an inch away from his. "Don't joke with me," she threatened him.

"And what have I done to you?"

"Daniele is not going to America. Do you hear me?"

"You spoke to don Ciccio," Carlo sighed.

"I spoke to him, yes," she barked. "So you can both forget about sending my son to the other side of the world."

"Can we talk about this calmly?"

"There's nothing to talk about. My son stays where I say he stays." Carmela patted her chest. "And that's final."

Carlo sighed and sat back down at his desk.

"It's just for a few months. It's not like he's going off to war! It's a big opportunity for him, you know."

"Shut up." She stopped him, bringing her finger to her lips. "You're done charming me with your words. Those days are gone!"

"I wasn't trying to charm you," Carlo said. "I just want you to understand that it's not the tragedy you imagine. It's just a trip, Carmela. We need him to take care of a few things."

"We who? Your family, not mine. It's not Daniele's fault if *that girl* makes eyes at him," she said scornfully.

Carlo did his best to hold back. "Listen, it's up to Daniele. He's twenty-two years old. He doesn't need your permission. I bet he'll be happy to do it. I know him."

"*You* know *my* son? *You?*"

"More than you know," Carlo said gravely, looking her straight in the eyes.

"Well, I'm glad to hear it," Carmela said sarcastically, her voice suddenly cracking. She looked away and crossed her arms.

Carlo continued to watch her in silence; he knew that when she bit her lower lip like that, she was trying to hold back tears, proud as she was. Seeing her like that triggered a surge of tenderness in him.

"Listen," Carlo said, softening his voice. "I'm not just sending Daniele to New York to keep him out of trouble, but because he's good at what he does! He really is good, and he's great with people. I'm certain he'll close some great deals over there. I trust him."

Carmela looked at him again.

"I'll also pay him well, of course," Carlo continued.

"How well?"

"What he deserves."

"My son deserves the best."

"And the best is what he'll get."

She instantly regained her usual haughty composure.

"If that's how it is," she said.

———

Anna was waiting outside for Lorenza, grasping the handles on the Bianchi and repeatedly glancing at her watch. When her niece finally arrived, she pushed the bike forward, walking fast as Lorenza picked up her pace to reach her.

"Sorry I was late, Auntie," Lorenza said. "Again."

"I noticed," Anna replied.

"It's just that Mama forgot to wake me up this morning."

"What, at twenty-two years old you're still not able to wake up on your own?"

"I won't be late tomorrow, you'll see."

It was the same thing every morning: a litany of ridiculous excuses and half-hearted promises. Anna was no longer sure it had been a good idea to offer her that job. Lorenza seemed persistently lazy, as if she didn't care about anything.

"You don't have to do this, you know. You can always look for another job, something you really like," she'd told her several times.

But Lorenza just shrugged. "Bah, I don't know what I like" was her answer. "A job is a job is a job."

For the post office, on the other hand, Lorenza's arrival had been a real treat. On her first day, they'd all crowded around her with great fanfare and many congratulations.

Even grumpy old Carmine had exclaimed, "Finally! It was about time we got a breath of fresh air in this office."

Meanwhile, Elena was almost in tears.

"I still remember when you came here years ago . . . you were this high!" she said with a chuckle.

Well, Anna thought, pushing her bicycle along. *Maybe she doesn't like the job, but she certainly can't say she wasn't well received.* Elena in particular had taken her under her wing from the start, having understood that with Lorenza, she could prattle and gossip at will. Unlike with Chiara, who "you didn't even notice if she was there or not," as she'd said once, with a snort. Anna often saw Elena and Lorenza bent over magazines commenting on the appearance of some actor; recently, they'd gotten into those weeklies that published romance novels and still frames from films, and all they did was sigh and elbow each other as they read them.

One person's reaction did surprise Anna, and it was the director's. Soon after Lorenza's arrival, Tommaso had started using a remarkable amount of cologne, to the point where he left a lingering trail of it as he walked by. He'd also stopped using gel and now sported soft, rebel curls, which made him look decidedly younger than his forty-plus years. Every so often, he'd stand up from his desk, poke his head into the telegraph office, and ask Lorenza, with a smile, "Everything okay?" He sometimes even opened the door for her, displaying a gallantry he'd never shown before, or, if he was going to Bar Castello, he always offered to bring her something: "Would you like a coffee? Or a sweet?"

"Yes, please," Lorenza would answer, smiling. "Both."

He was also rather tolerant of her mistakes; distracted as she was, it wasn't rare for her to misspell something when transcribing or to omit a word.

"Hmm, something's not right," Elena would say, studying the text of the telegram. "I think you skipped something here, see?" And she'd point at a space between two words.

In those cases, it wasn't rare for Tommaso to come running.

"Come on, what's the matter . . . Add a word yourself, as long as it makes sense," he'd say.

Lorenza would blush while Elena simply obeyed, but not without giving Tommaso a puzzled look. He was a kind and available man, true, but at work he'd always been unyielding. At least until then.

That morning, Anna left the office with a half-empty mailbag. She mounted her Bianchi and passed two elderly women standing at the fountain, where they were filling up a large glass bottle. She skirted around the castle walls, turned right at the tower, and took an uphill cobblestone street. She lifted herself off the seat and pedaled firmly for a few hundred feet, until the road leveled out again and she could sit down.

She took a left down an alley overlooked by small balconies with rusty iron railings, where she saw a pair of large women's underwear hanging out to dry.

Anna stopped, opened her mailbag, and pulled out a white envelope. *Marilena Cucugliato, Vicolo della Torre, 4, Lizzanello (Lecce).* She looked around for the street number but couldn't find it. She saw the one, the two, the three, and even the five and six up ahead. Only the four was missing, as if it had been skipped. A lean man looking sleepy in his pajamas came out onto a balcony and lit himself a cigarette.

"Excuse me, you!" Anna called out.

The man exhaled the smoke and looked down at the road.

"Can you tell me where number four is? I can't find it."

"You're looking for the perfumery? It's there, at the top of those stairs," he said, pointing at an opening in the opposite wall, where a stone staircase began. Anna hadn't even seen it.

She thanked the man, left the bicycle, and went up the stairs.

"Pinch your nose shut, or she'll knock you out, that one, for all the perfume she wears," the man shouted after her, chuckling.

The passageway was narrow and dark and smelled like mold. After a dozen steps, Anna arrived at an archway and hit the doorknocker twice. A robust woman in her sixties opened the door. She was wearing a baggy blue wool dress that gave off a scent so alcoholic that Anna felt slightly faint. The woman's voluminous gray hair was tied in a ponytail that fell to the side of her puffy face.

"Are you Marilena Cucugliato?"

The woman nodded.

Anna handed her the envelope and tried to leave—she could barely breathe.

But the woman said, "Lucky you, for being so skinny. I can only barely pass through."

She pointed at the stairs. Anna smiled courteously and again tried to leave, but the woman held her back.

"Would you like a coffee? Nobody ever comes up here." She smiled.

Anna hesitated, but then she remembered that her mailbag wasn't full that day, so she wasn't in much of a hurry. She figured it couldn't hurt to say a quick hello to this woman who had eluded her awareness all these years.

Happy as a clam, Marilena ushered her into the house and closed the door. The interior had nothing in common with the dark and narrow entryway. Each wall was covered in pink wallpaper and little framed pictures depicting various types of flowers. There were also vases with real flowers scattered throughout the house: on the entryway cabinet, on the living room table, on the chest against the wall. The woman invited Anna to take a seat in a red velvet sitting room and returned a few minutes later with a tray holding two steaming cups of coffee.

As Anna waited for the coffee to cool down, she glanced at the woman, who was still staring at her, smiling.

"I see you like flowers," Anna said finally, just to say something.

Marilena looked around, holding her coffee cup with both hands.

"Oh, them. But those are my friends!"

Anna shot her a puzzled look.

"No one listens as well as flowers, you know?" the woman went on. "I speak to them every day. I confide in them memories of my youth, my fears, my small joys and regrets. Especially the regrets." She paused. "As one would expect from good friends, flowers never judge you. Do you have them? Real friends?"

Anna took a sip of coffee.

"I have a very dear friend," she said. *And she's the only one I have*, she thought.

"Keep her close, then," the woman said. "You know, I also had a very good friend, once . . ." She stood up slowly and placed the cups on the tray. "But then . . ." She sighed.

"I really must go," Anna said, standing up. She thanked Marilena for the coffee and headed for the door.

She went down the stairs, emerged back into the sunlight, and got on her bike. The balcony where the man had been standing was empty.

———

Daniele nearly fell off his chair when he heard the news.

"Really, Mr. Carlo? You're not pulling my leg?"

Him in America. Him, Daniele Carlà, in New York! He kept looking at Carlo in awe, like a child with an enormous, unexpected present. New York. The skyscrapers. The lights. The fashion he'd read about in magazines. He agreed to it on the spot, without even thinking about it. His job was to find new clients in America, Carlo told him, strike while the iron was hot. He'd start at the Italian bars and restaurants in a place they called Little Italy.

"It means 'piccola Italia,'" he explained. "Only Italians live there. You won't have any trouble communicating, don't worry."

He would be taking a load of Donna Anna along with him on the transatlantic ship. And he didn't have to worry about money, since it would all be on Carlo's dime, obviously. He'd hand Daniele a pretty sum ahead of his departure, and once there, he'd regularly send him money. If Daniele was up for it, he could leave at the end of the month: The *Saturnia* was setting sail on April 27 from the port of Naples. Carlo would take care of gathering the necessary documents in time.

"They owe me more than a few favors," he said with a wink.

"Thank you for your trust in me, Mr. Carlo. I won't let you down," Daniele replied, holding out his hand. Carlo smiled and shook it, then instinctively pulled the boy into a hug. Daniele went red in the face and gawked, embarrassed.

"I know," Carlo said. "You've never let me down."

Daniele couldn't wait to tell Lorenza. He imagined her joy at the opportunity he was being given, at the extraordinary trip he'd make, and at all the stories he'd be able to tell her when he got back.

Instead, he was met with an avalanche of anger that nearly knocked him out.

"You're abandoning me too, I knew it! You don't care about me at *all*. You only think of yourself, like everyone else. Go on, just go to the other side of the world!" she exclaimed melodramatically as she paced back and forth in Daniele's little house.

All his attempts to comfort her, to swear to her that he loved her, that he'd be back soon, were ignored.

"I don't believe you. I don't believe in people who leave," she declared, letting herself fall onto the couch, exhausted.

Daniele knelt and took her hand in his, begging her to see things as they were, not as she feared them to be.

"Wait," he said finally. He grabbed a powder-pink fabric cutting off the floor, cut a strip with his long pointy scissors, and rolled that between his fingers until it took on the shape of a ring. Then he looked Lorenza in the eyes and gently placed it on her ring finger.

"Do you believe me now?" he asked.

Lorenza hinted a smile and nodded.

And thus, four years after his friend's death, Daniele shed what remained of his guilt and allowed himself to finally kiss the girl he loved.

———

Anna looked at herself in the mirror, pleased with what she saw, singing along with "La barchetta," by Nilla Pizzi, which was playing on the radio. "Guarda lassú in alto mare c'é una barchetta piccina, ad ogni ondata s'inchina quasi dovesse affondar."

Yes, the pants fit perfectly. She had to admit that Carmela had done an excellent job; she'd commission more, in different colors. She did the last button on her black half-sleeve blouse and pulled her mother's pearl necklace from an engraved wooden jewelry box. She reduced it into two circles and put it around her neck, over her shirt.

"La barchetta in mezzo al mare deve andare assai lontan, ma per farla navigare ci pensa il capitan," she sang in a slightly louder voice, twirling.

Roberto looked into the bedroom and leaned against the doorframe, watching his mother with surprise.

"Comme tu es belle, Maman!" he said. "And those pants?"

She turned around, smiled brightly, and put her hands on her hips in a movie star pose.

Roberto laughed heartily.

In that same moment, in the farmhouse in Contrada La Pietra, don Giulio had gotten hold of a large pair of scissors and was about to tear Giovanna's pants to shreds as she curled up on the bed with her hands on her face, sobbing uncontrollably. Cesare sat on the floor, watching her and whimpering.

"Pants are for women of ill repute!" don Giulio declared, impassively.

He started cutting.

16

"The keys, do you have them?" Carmela asked, blocking her husband's way.

"What keys?" Nicola asked, sinking into the living room sofa.

"To your mother's house."

"Yes," he mumbled. "Daniele gave them to me. Why?"

"Give them to me," she ordered, putting out her hand. "I have to clean it and air it out. It's been closed up for more than two months."

"I've already taken care of it," he tried to assure her. "I go sometimes. I open the windows. I give it a sweep."

Carmela crossed her arms over her chest.

"You? I've never seen you pick up a broom in your life. Gimme, come on." She held out her palm again.

"Really, there's no need," Nicola reiterated. "I'll take care of it. It's my mother's house, isn't it?"

"Actually, it's Daniele's house now. And what belongs to my son belongs to me. So, will you give them to me, or do I have to take them by force?"

Nicola sighed deeply, put his weight on an armrest, and pushed himself up with a heave, going all red in the face. *He's only recently turned sixty-two, but it's as if he carries around at least twenty more years with him,* Carmela thought. All that fat, which deeply disgusted her, caused him to struggle with the simplest of movements. At night, he snored so loudly that she'd sent him to sleep in Daniele's old bedroom.

Nicola headed toward the coatrack in the entryway, rummaged through his jacket pocket, and finally pulled out a set of two keys.

"Here they are. This little one is for the gate, and this is for the main door," he explained flatly.

"Thank you," she said, grabbing them out of his hand. "Was that so hard?" Then she took her purse off the coatrack and announced, "I'm going."

Once at the house, Carmela opened the gate and crossed the small garden to the entrance. She walked through the unkempt grass that scratched at her knees—she should send someone to cut it, she thought—turned the key in the lock, and opened the door. The inside was pitch-dark and the stench of humidity was suffocating. Carmela left the front door open and pushed open the shutters on the window that looked out over the garden. In the light of day, she saw the white sheets that covered the furniture, a crusty cup in the kitchen sink, and the coffee maker still on the stove; a broom and dustpan brimming with dust bunnies were leaning against the wall.

Hah! He really did sweep, she thought. *But he didn't even empty the dustpan.*

She shook her head and caught sight of the black leather shoes Daniele wore for special occasions sitting in a corner. She placed her purse on the counter, pushed up her dress sleeves, and, sending up a cloud of dust, removed the first sheet, revealing a two-seater couch and a coffee table. She balled up the sheet and went into the garden to shake it properly, then went back inside and draped the clean sheet back over the couch.

Carefully, she lifted the second sheet, which was covering something in the center of the room.

What she saw left her breathless.

A sewing machine and a workbench emerged in a cloud of dust. Carmela let the sheet fall to the ground as she observed the scene in front of her: The large basket on the table contained fabric scraps, colorful threads, thimbles, a pincushion and one for needles, two carefully folded measuring tapes, and a wooden ruler.

Disconcerted, she sat down and started to turn those objects over in her hands, one by one, as if they were clues in a treasure hunt.

That's why Nicola didn't want to give me the keys. He must have known everything, the wretch!

She jumped to her feet and went to the bedroom. She opened the shutters and then the wardrobe. On the left, she recognized Daniele's clothes: his Sunday outfit, his shirts, his pants, his jackets; on the right, though, was a stack of rolled-up fabric. And women's dresses were hanging from the rod.

Carmela pulled one out and studied it. A red wool dress with a knee-length skirt, adorned with a fur collar fastened with a round pin. She placed the dress on the bed and took out another; it was a spring model with black-and-white checks, fitted at the waist and with a button-down bust.

She took them all out, one after the other, even the unfinished ones whose sleeves were still attached with many colorful pins. She then spied a familiar metal box in the back of the wardrobe. Daniele had always kept it in his room as a child, but she'd never managed to open it; it was always locked. She picked it up with both hands and tried to lift the lid, which this time yielded, revealing a stack of black notebooks, the same kind she used for her sketches.

She sat down on the bed, among the pile of clothes, and started to leaf through the notebooks, gawking at every page. Daniele's drawings were surprisingly beautiful. More beautiful than hers, she thought with a touch of resentment. Evening gowns, elegant formal dresses, everyday clothes in vivid colors . . . not to mention styles Carmela had never seen, not even in fashion magazines. She felt cheated for having been kept in the dark by her son and her husband, and at the same time annoyed that Daniele hadn't listened to her. On the contrary, he'd done as he'd pleased. He'd been mocking her all this time, making her believe he'd let go of that absurd idea of designing and sewing clothes, like a girl.

He's such a liar, she thought, resentfully. *After all, blood doesn't lie . . . and his is Greco blood.*

She hung the clothes back in the wardrobe and closed the door. Then she placed the notebooks back in the box and slipped it into her purse.

———

"This heat is killing me," Elena complained, fanning herself with a folder. "It's like an oven."

"Want some water?" Lorenza asked.

"Yes, do you mind getting some?" Elena said, looking drained.

Lorenza didn't get a chance to leave the room before Tommaso looked up from his desk, smiling, and asked, "Do you need something?"

"Just getting a glass of water for Elena," she said, and walked toward the shelf where they kept the glass bottle and stack of cups. She noticed that the bottle was almost empty. "I'm going to the fountain," she said, turning to Tommaso. "Be right back."

"Take your time," he said.

Lorenza stepped out into the street as the weight of the heat clamped her throat. She went straight to the little fountain in Piazza Castello and started to fill the bottle, holding it with one hand. As the fresh water came out, she looked around distractedly. When her gaze fell on Bar Castello, she saw them. Her father and Auntie Anna, who had left the post office a few minutes before. He handed her a book and she lifted a hand off her handlebar to take it. She stared at the cover for a few seconds, then looked up at Antonio and smiled, saying something. He looked at her with his head slightly tilted to the side, as if afraid to let something slip. After a brief conversation, Anna slipped the book into her mailbag, mounted her bike, and pedaled away slowly. He put his hands in his pockets and stood there staring at her until she turned right, disappearing from view.

"Are you trying to run the whole town dry?" a passerby reproached Lorenza.

She looked down at the fountain and saw that the bottle was over-flowing.

"I'm sorry," she said, quickly closing the tap. The woman shook her head and continued on her way, grumbling.

"Everything okay? You took a while," Tommaso said when Lorenza returned to the office.

She put the bottle back on the shelf.

"Yes, of course," she said abruptly, filling a glass.

"Finally. I was about to melt away," Elena sighed, taking the water.

Lorenza sat down at her post and for the following two hours, retreated into a silence as dense as the day was hot. She couldn't erase the image of the sweet smile she'd seen on her father's face as he spoke to Auntie Anna. She'd never seen him smile at her mother like that . . . or at her. She tried to distract herself by thinking about Daniele but ended up feeling even more alone.

Since he'd left, he'd only written her one letter, in which he described in detail a bunch of things she couldn't understand—skyscrapers that lit up the night in the big city, walking across a mile-long bridge so beautiful it appeared to be floating above the water, going inside a large statue of a woman holding a torch. At the end of the letter, Daniele had told her that they'd go there together one day, to New York, and that she, too, would see all the extraordinary things that existed beyond the ocean.

The truth was that such a letter, so full of enthusiasm and wonder, had hurt her and annoyed her. She wanted to hear that Daniele was overcome with longing for her, unhappy and disappointed by such a distant and different world.

"What's wrong? You're quiet today," Elena said.

"Nothing," Lorenza replied apathetically.

"Are you thinking about your beloved?" she goaded her, smirking.

Lorenza didn't answer. Instead, she jumped up and walked over to Tommaso's desk. "Can we go get a coffee?" she asked.

He looked at her, surprised. Then he smiled. "With pleasure," he said. "My treat."

———

Anna stopped, placed a foot on the ground, and pulled a handkerchief from her jacket pocket to dry the sweat off her forehead and neck. The heat that morning was draining. She couldn't wait to go home, dunk her head under the cold water spout, and spend some time reading. Earlier that day, Antonio had lent her his copy of a novel called *A Time to Kill* by Ennio Flaiano, an author Anna had never heard of before. He'd recently won an important literary award, Antonio told her.

"I'd like you to read it," he added. "I underlined some phrases . . . If you want, you can also underline the ones that strike you the most, and then we can talk about them."

Finally, she delivered the last letter of the morning: the energy bill for an elderly woman who was deaf in one ear and to whom Anna had to read every line item—consumption sum, government tax, meter rental, stamp duty—three times before the woman was satisfied that there had been no mistake. Anna closed the empty mailbag and glanced at her watch. Yes, she had time to stop by Contrada La Pietra. So what if she had to brave the heat; she had to take advantage of the hours when don Giulio was away at the parish.

She hadn't seen Giovanna in two weeks. Maybe she was mistaken, but it seemed like her friend had been avoiding her for some time; she no longer visited her in town as regularly, and Anna rarely found her at home when she stopped by. On those few occasions when they'd seen each other, Giovanna had seemed quiet and uncomfortable, as if she couldn't wait to leave. The last time Anna had gone knocking at the farm in Contrada, Giulio had come to the door. Anna had been surprised to find him there in the middle of the afternoon.

"Giovanna is resting," he'd said with a stiff face. He hadn't even invited her in.

"At this hour?" Anna had said, lifting an eyebrow.

"She has a headache."

"Okay, I guess I'll come back tomorrow."

"Don't bother coming back to visit *us*," he'd said. Then he'd pointed his gaze at Anna's pants. "If she wants to, she'll be in touch." And he'd shut the door in her face.

When Anna arrived at Contrada, she decided to take a different approach. She opened the gate and whistled for Cesare, but he didn't show up.

She went up and knocked on the door. "Giovanna, are you there? It's me."

It was a good few minutes before Giovanna decided to open the door.

"Finally!" Anna exclaimed, irked. "You're still alive, then."

"Yes. *I* am," she said in a whisper, retreating into the house.

Anna followed her and placed her mailbag on the table. "What do you mean?"

"Cesare."

"When did it happen?"

"Two weeks ago."

Anna put her hand on her hip and looked at her, vexed. "And you're telling me now?"

"I'm sorry, I didn't think about it," Giovanna said. "Would you like a coffee?"

"Don't worry about the coffee. Will you tell me what's the matter? You disappear, you don't tell me Cesare died—"

"I didn't disappear. I'm here, aren't I?" Giovanna said, looking down.

"Look me in the eye," Anna ordered her. Giovanna slowly raised her head.

"I'll ask you again: Will you tell me what's the matter? Did I do something to you?"

"No." Giovanna pulled out a chair and sat down.

"I don't believe you. I know something's up," Anna insisted.

Giovanna wrung her hands, then went to the sink and filled a chipped glass with water.

"Why are you trying to take me away from Giulio?" she asked.

Anna looked at her, astonished. "Me? What are you talking about?"

"You're the one who said those things, about my body. That it's not his. You even accused him of hurting me."

"I didn't accuse anyone. I just asked you a question. And regarding your body being yours, well, I stand by that. But I don't understand: What's your point in bringing all this up now?"

"I talked to Giulio about it. He explained that it's not like you say. That you can't understand what he and I have, and that you're just saying these things to take me away from him. Why? You don't want me to be happy?"

"Why did you tell him? You shouldn't have."

"He doesn't want there to be secrets between us."

Anna closed her eyes for a moment and rubbed her forehead with her fingers, as if she'd suddenly come down with a throbbing headache.

"And he got mad because of the pants," Giovanna continued.

Anna opened her eyes. "What's the matter with pants now?"

"He says they were your idea," Giovanna said, gripping her glass. "That I never would have thought of it."

"Is that why I've never seen you wear them? He doesn't want you to?"

"He cut them up."

"And you let him?"

Giovanna shrugged. She drank the last sip of water and placed the glass on the table.

"I don't believe it . . ." Anna murmured under her breath.

"It's true!" Giovanna exclaimed, with a hostility she'd never displayed before. "It was your idea. You're the one who brought me to the seamstress. I didn't even want them."

"What are you talking about? You know that's not true. You were so happy—"

"You always make me do the things you want to do," Giovanna almost shouted.

Anna stared at her, disconcerted.

"I see," she said in a low voice. She picked up her mailbag and went to the door. She knew her friend wouldn't stop her, that she'd let her leave without protestation. That wasn't her Giovanna. She felt deeply unsettled about the power Giulio had over her, the way he was able to distort reality, his frightening ability to put thoughts and words in her head. *He explained that . . . he says that . . .*

"I'm very sorry about Cesare," Anna said as she left, closing the door behind her.

She rode back to town with a lump in her throat and intolerable sadness in her heart.

———

As that week of infernal heat came to an end, the Greco family decided to spend Sunday at the beach.

"Lucky you, I wish I could go for a swim," Tommaso had said from his desk, listening as aunt and niece talked about their beach trip while at the office, and how they couldn't wait to go on Sunday.

Lorenza had turned to him and shrugged.

"Wanna come?" she said. "We'd love to have you. Wouldn't we, Auntie?" she added, looking at Anna.

"Yes, of course," Anna said, hesitantly, casting a questioning glance at her niece. But Lorenza ignored her.

"Good," she said, turning back to Tommaso. "Then we'll see you at eight. Outside my house. You know where it is, right?"

They squeezed everything—food, drinks, swimsuits, changes of clothes, books, magazines, towels, and beach chairs—into their two cars and left Lizzanello in the early morning.

"Are you going to be able to keep up with me?" Carlo yelled out to his brother, sitting at the wheel of his car in sunglasses and with a cigar in his teeth. Anna was sitting next to him, laughing. Roberto, who'd always hated rising early, was lying in the back seat with his eyes closed, sulking.

Antonio pulled his Fiat 508 next to Carlo's car and retorted, "If I can remember to shift into second gear, yes, I might just."

Carlo burst out laughing, as did Agata, who was sitting in the car next to Antonio. In the back, Lorenza and Tommaso looked at each other and smiled.

It was very early, so the San Foca beach wasn't busy yet. The group laid out their towels by the water's edge and opened the foldable wooden chairs, sticking the legs into the sand. Agata, Anna, and Lorenza found a cabana and changed into their bathing suits.

"On three, everyone in the water!" Carlo shouted after quickly stripping down to his trunks.

"Papa, I'm tired," Roberto grumbled, lying on a towel with his arms over his eyes.

"I'll wait a little longer," Anna murmured, leaning back onto her elbows.

Carlo put his hands on his hips and looked at them, lifting an eyebrow. "Is that so?" he said. In a fit of passion, he picked Anna up and ran toward the sea while she thrashed and begged him to put her down, laughing all the while. Finally, he threw her into the water. She emerged after a few moments, coughing and laughing at the same time.

"Now it's your son's turn," Carlo said, heading for Roberto, who jumped up and started to run.

"I'm going to get you!" Carlo shouted.

"Poor thing, leave him alone," Agata intervened, chuckling.

Finally, Carlo managed to catch his son by the hips, pick him up, and throw him in the water as everyone laughed.

"Funny guy, your uncle," said Tommaso, who was sitting on a towel next to Lorenza, his arm resting on his knee.

"Yeah, he's always been a clown."

"You're not going in?"

"In a bit," Lorenza said, pulling a copy of *Bolero* magazine out of her bag.

"I think I'll go in right now, actually," Tommaso said, standing up. He unbuttoned his short-sleeved shirt and took it off, then removed his pants and undershirt until he was wearing nothing but a pair of dark blue swim trunks that came halfway down his thighs.

Lorenza peeked over the magazine and couldn't hide her surprise: Tommaso had broad and confident shoulders, well-defined biceps, and a lean, shapely body. He caught her staring at him and smiled timidly. Lorenza blushed and hid her face in the pages of *Bolero*.

Antonio walked toward the sea and stopped at the edge, crossed his arms in front of his chest, and let his feet sink into the surf up to his ankles. Roberto came out of the water toward his uncle.

"It's so cold," he said, shivering.

"Go sit in the sun," Antonio said, giving him a pat on the back, then turning to look out at the horizon.

Carlo dove into the water and started to swim with wide strokes.

"Sometimes I wonder where he gets all that energy." Anna's voice made Antonio turn around. And there she was, by his side, and he couldn't help but think that the green in her eyes seemed to have turned fuller and brighter that day, as if her irises had absorbed all the colors of the sea.

"And to think that as a child he was afraid of the water," Antonio said, amused. "It took me a while to make that go away. And look at him now, he's like a merman."

"I'm worried about Giovanna," Anna said out of the blue.

Antonio was startled. He stared at her, suddenly very serious. "Why?"

She told him about having seen her a few days before, about her harsh words, how it appeared that Giulio had taken possession of her mind and body, about the destroyed pants, and how all of it had left Anna upset and dispirited.

"He's a dangerous man. I wish she would just leave him," she concluded.

Antonio pursed his lips. "It's not so simple. She's in love with him, isn't she?"

Anna shook her head. "No, she's not in love. She's subjugated, it's different. How could I not have noticed what kind of a man he was? And to think that I even encouraged her." She gave the sand a little kick, lifting a pile of grains.

"It's not your fault," Antonio said. "How could you have known?"

"I could have . . ." she responded in a whisper.

"I don't see how."

"I should have seen it, since those first letters. It was all written between the lines."

Antonio smiled ruefully. "That's how it often goes, doesn't it? What is truly important is found between the lines. But not everyone can see it. Or maybe they prefer not to."

Anna looked down and traced a circle in the sand with her toe. Then she looked back up at Antonio.

"*No one knows how,*" she said.

Antonio looked at her, disoriented.

"Pirandello's play, the one you mentioned in your letter? I read it. At the time."

"You never told me . . ." Antonio's voice cracked.

She shrugged. "That was also a message between the lines."

She looked at him intensely.

Antonio stared at her but wasn't able to say a word because in that moment, Carlo reached the shore and joined them.

"The water is beautiful," he said to Antonio, slicking back his wet hair. "Dive in, big brother." He splashed some water onto him.

"I'm going, I'm going," Antonio said, holding out his hands to defend himself from the splashes. He took a few steps forward and dove into the sea with a little leap.

"Will you give me a kiss now?" Carlo said, pursing his lips comically.

"No," Anna said, smiling. "That way you'll learn not to throw me in the water against my will."

They joined the rest of the group and Anna lay down on a towel.

"How's the water?" Agata asked as she peeled a peach with her knife.

"Cold," Anna said, closing her eyes.

Carlo sat down next to Lorenza, patting himself dry with a towel.

"Hey, Uncle, you're getting me all wet!" she protested.

He chuckled. "I think the main character of"—he peeked at her magazine—"'A Light in the Darkness' could use a dip, sad as he is." He chucked her lightly on the shoulder. "Where's Tommaso?" he asked.

"He's there, swimming," Lorenza said, nodding at the sea.

"He's totally smitten, isn't he."

"Who is smitten?" she asked innocently, blushing.

"You dare to ask me who? Your nice director, that's who."

"He's just like that. He's nice to everyone."

"Yeah, right." Carlo smiled.

"And even if he is interested, I'm not," Lorenza added, becoming serious.

"Why not? He's a good guy. Respectable. Good character. And he's not bad to look at, either."

"I'm waiting for someone else, you know that," she said, cutting him short.

Carlo couldn't help but grimace. "Daniele?"

"Yup."

He stood up and started to dust the sand off his calves.

"Did he ever write to you?" he asked with all the ease he could muster.

"Just that one time. And to you?"

Carlo hesitated, then decided to lie. "Yes, plenty."

"Ah," Lorenza said, surprised. "And what does he say? How is he?"

"He's well. Working hard and enjoying the city. He's meeting loads of new people."

Lorenza bit her lower lip. "Did he ask you to say hi to me?"

"Actually, no," Carlo said, feigning regret. He studied his niece's face hoping to find at least a vague trace of disappointment.

"No matter," Lorenza said. She sank her face back into the pages of *Bolero*.

"Where the heck is he going?" Agata exclaimed.

Antonio had swum out to sea and now looked like a small speck on the clear water.

As she stared at the sea, Agata started to peel another peach.

"His arms and legs are going to give out," she muttered.

Anna, who was lying next to her with one arm on her face to protect it from the sun, turned to look at her.

"Oh, you'd fallen asleep?" Agata asked.

"Yes," Anna said with a yawn. She sat up. "What were you saying?" she asked, rubbing her face.

"Nothing, nothing."

Anna rummaged through her purse, pulled out a book, and placed it on the beach towel. Then she continued to search.

"I wonder where my pencil went," she mumbled to herself, her face buried in her bag.

Agata glanced at the cover of the book. "Ennio Flaiano . . . *A Time to Kill*," she murmured. It took her a few seconds, but then she recognized it; it was the same book she'd seen in Antonio's study the week before, when she'd gone in to dust. Yes, it was the *very* same copy, with that small coffee stain in the corner.

In a fit of irritation, Agata tossed the peach pit. A memory emerged, forceful and painful. When she was expecting Lorenza, she'd had to spend the last few months of her pregnancy in bed, as per doctor's orders. Antonio would lie next to her and read her novels to pass the time. At one point, though, she'd confessed that she couldn't take it anymore—she didn't want to hear all those made-up stories about people who'd never existed. She asked him to tell her real ones, rather, about people she knew. What was happening in town?

"Tell me, whatever happened with Nando? Has his wife taken him back?"

"Is Michelina getting married or not?"

"And did Cosima's son get a job or is he still lounging at home all day?"

Antonio had looked at her and shaken his head. No, he didn't know anything about life in town.

"What does it matter to you, what happened to Nando or Cosima?" he exclaimed later. "These stories are much better, more compelling, more real than what's real! They help you understand so many things, they make you think . . ."

Agata had turned away and closed her eyes without responding.

Since then, he'd never tried to read a book to her again. *Nor have I ever asked him to*, she thought, with some bitterness. She remembered that Anna, too, had started to read her a book when she was ill after losing the baby. It hadn't helped her feel better that time, either. *They fill their heads with words and then they can't find the right ones to console people*, she thought.

"You even bring those to the beach? You're both such bores," she said out loud, bitterly. She took the last bite of her peach and lay down with a sigh.

Anna looked up from her book and stared at her in confusion.

"I'm sorry, are you talking to me?"

Agata closed her eyes without answering.

17

"Look, Mama, Elizabeth and Philip."

"Who?" Agata asked with a frown.

"The Princess of England, Mama! She got married."

Lorenza was having breakfast at the kitchen table, still in her night-gown. She was reading an article in *Oggi* that described the wedding of Elizabeth Windsor and Philip, the Duke of Edinburgh. Enraptured, she ran her finger across the photographs. The crowd welcoming the newly-weds as they exited Westminster Abbey, the greeting from the balcony at Buckingham Palace, the ivory silk dress embroidered with pearls and crystals and with a thirteen-foot train.

Agata came over holding a rag and leaned in to take a look. "That's her, the princess?" she asked, turning up her nose.

"At my wedding, I want a train as long as this one," Lorenza said, dreamily.

"What, are you some kind of royalty?" Agata said with a snicker, pick-ing up the empty cup. "Go get dressed, come on, or you'll be late for work." She placed the cup in the sink with the other dirty dishes from breakfast and shook her head.

"So what? I want a dress everyone will remember."

"First wait for the proposal, then you can worry about the dress."

"As soon as he's back, Mama. He promised."

Agata waved her hand in the air, as if to say they were just words in the wind.

"What, you don't believe me?" Lorenza said, annoyed.

"Men's promises are like the Tramontane," Agata said. "Three days, they last." She held out three fingers.

"Not Daniele's," Lorenza defended him.

"Oh yeah?" Agata threw the rag over her shoulder and leaned back onto the sink. "And why isn't he back yet? I wonder who he found, in America. Listen to me. You have to forget about that one. Now you're still at a marrying age and soon you won't be," she said, emphasizing her point with a wag of her finger. "The boys will start looking at the young fresh ones, and no one will want you anymore."

Lorenza felt her heart beat faster and faster, and suddenly she was inundated by an anger that seemed to come from very far away.

"You're the one no one wants anymore," she hissed, pushing back her chair. "Not even Papa," she added in a whisper, before leaving the room.

Agata felt a sudden vertigo, as if she'd received a slap in the face. She pulled a chair out from under the kitchen table and slowly sat down. It was as if an enormous cloud of gnats were swarming around her eyes, obscuring her sight and hearing. She tried to take a deep breath and then a second and a third.

"Antonio," she murmured, but her voice died in her throat like the flame of a spent match. In that moment, she completely forgot that her husband wasn't home; only half an hour before, Antonio had drunk his coffee and said goodbye to her with a kiss on the cheek, as always. It was the only kiss of the day, the only physical contact Antonio now granted her and that she always waited for, each morning. As soon as she woke up, she'd go to the bathroom and wash her face with a Palmolive soap bar, then she'd go downstairs, make coffee, and set the table with the cups and spoons. When Antonio came to kiss her cheek, he'd find it soft and perfumed, and she hoped that, after all these years, he'd still think that the smell of his wife's skin was pleasant.

Agata tried to stand up, putting her weight on the back of the chair, but the dizziness forced her to sit down again. She heard Lorenza come down the stairs and open the front door. She listened for a few seconds, waiting. But her daughter's goodbye didn't come that morning.

Lorenza walked out with her heart full of rage but also gripped with guilt. The words she'd flung at her mother were sharp blades that had wounded her deeply—she knew this well. She was tempted to turn back and ask for forgiveness, but her resentment for her own pain got the best of her and drove her onward.

Yes, it was true, she thought, as she approached her aunt and uncle's house. Daniele wasn't back yet, but in the past few months, after a silence he'd blamed on work, he started to send her many letters. The only thing he ever wrote of was New York, of the friends he'd made in Little Italy, of new clients, of the deals he'd closed, making Carlo proud of him. It hadn't been at all difficult to sell Donna Anna; a single glass would win anyone over. What he hadn't told anyone except for Lorenza was that he was attending a tailoring workshop in a basement on Mulberry Street three nights a week. It was run by Marisa, a jovial woman from Campania who always had a joke at the ready and who sewed men's clothing for a store on Fifth Avenue. He'd even sent Lorenza a photo. It featured him dressed in an elegant pinstripe suit with the jacket tapered at the waist, wide shoulders with pads, a silk handkerchief in his pocket, a tie, and a hat *like the one Humphrey Bogart wore in* Casablanca, he'd explained. *Do you like the jacket? I designed it and sewed it myself!*

As soon as the workshop was over, in December—the letter said— he'd be back. He'd even confessed his intention to stop working for the Greco Winery. He was grateful to Mr. Carlo, he always would be, but it was time to follow his dreams. He'd open his own tailor's shop in Lecce and he and Lorenza would go and live there together. As long as she still wanted that. He ended every letter with *I love you, my little Lorenza.* He wrote plenty of words, rivers of them, but he also left out the one that really mattered to her: *marriage.* Lorenza wanted to understand him and be happy for all the wonderful things that were happening to him, but in truth, she couldn't help but resent him for not choosing to stay, for not giving up the trip to New York because he preferred—*wanted*—to be with her. He was just like her father many years ago, when he had left for Africa even though she'd begged him not to go.

In a few months, I'll be turning twenty-three, she brooded, *and I'm the only one of my friends who has yet to marry.*

Some of them were even pregnant with their second child. And she? What did she have to show for her life? She still lived with her parents, in the same room where she'd slept as a child, in the same pink sheets with embroidered edges. When would she have her own house to take care of?

As usual, Anna was waiting for her at the front door. She was wearing her uniform jacket over her pants. They were all she wore now, and she'd had a whopping five pairs made in different colors and fabrics.

"Why the long face?" Anna said to Lorenza, furrowing her brow. "What happened?"

"I had an argument with Mama," Lorenza said.

Anna set off, pushing her bike. "Do you want to tell me about it?"

Lorenza was tempted to vent, but then she thought of her mother and felt a pang of pity for her. Always bitter, always sad, always alone . . . a loneliness that at the end of the day was hers, too. No, she didn't want to reveal the weight she was carrying to anyone, least of all Auntie Anna.

"I don't feel like it now," she said, without looking at Anna, and kept walking.

Just like every morning, Tommaso's face lit up when the two women walked into the post office. He wished Lorenza a good morning with a broad smile, then followed her with his eyes until she opened the door to the telegraph office. It was impossible not to notice it, but up until that moment, Lorenza had chosen to ignore the underlying desire Tommaso possessed for her.

But that day, as she sat down at her desk, she realized that Tommaso was perfect "marriage material," as her mother would have said. He wasn't and would never be a romance novel hero, impulsive and passionate, but in exchange, he could be counted on for a "worry-free life," another expression Agata used, which meant being treated with respect inside and outside the home, conducting a dignified existence, and having the financial security of an honest and secure job.

Anna didn't notice when Tommaso had approached her holding the paper.

"They're showing *Angelina* at the theater," he said.

"The one with Magnani, right? I saw the poster," Anna said, pretending to be busy.

"Why don't we go one of these nights? All of us, I mean," Tommaso suggested, looking around, lingering on Lorenza for a moment.

"Yes, good idea," Anna said, slinging her mailbag over her shoulder.

"How about Saturday?" she said as she walked out.

———

Aside from Carmine, who'd declined the invitation with a grumble, they all went to the theater together that Saturday—the postal workers and the entire Greco family. The theater was packed, so they looked around for empty seats: Carlo and Roberto went toward the front rows, Elena and Agata chatted away, making their way to a few empty chairs on the other side of the stalls, and Lorenza and Tommaso, who were trailing behind, walked side by side, taking their time. Anna came in last with Antonio, who immediately locked eyes with Melina, who was sitting in her usual spot at the back. She was playing with a lock of her curly hair, twirling it in her fingers. She greeted him with a suggestive smile.

"Do you know her?" Anna asked.

"Who?" Antonio said, blushing.

"What do you mean, who? The woman who smiled at you," Anna said, nodding toward her.

But Melina was already looking elsewhere.

"You must be mistaken; nobody smiled at me," Antonio stammered.

"Perhaps . . ." Anna said, uncertain.

Carlo raised a hand and motioned for Anna and Antonio to join him.

Agata and Elena had found two seats on the right side of the theater, and Elena was waving her arms to signal to Tommaso and Lorenza that there were two more spots, one of which was at the beginning of the row. Once they'd reached them, Tommaso shot a look at Elena and she immediately understood the silent message; she moved inward, freeing up the seat next to Lorenza's. But she made no effort to hold back a giggle.

During the movie, Tommaso was extremely nervous; he was moving around so much in his seat that someone behind him grumbled, "Hey, stay still a minute, will you? Were you bit by a tarantula?"

"What's wrong, are you uncomfortable?" Lorenza whispered.

"No, no," he said, waving a hand. "Everything's fine."

When the lights came back on and the room started to empty, Elena took Agata by the arm and joined the others so that Tommaso and Lorenza could walk to the exit alone.

"So, did you like it?" Tommaso asked.

"Very much," Lorenza said. "You know, I was thinking she's just like my aunt."

"Who? Anna Magnani?"

"Yes, but I don't mean physically," Lorenza explained, sounding melancholic. "The character. Women like them are special. Such spitfires . . . they aren't afraid of anything." She was sure that if her Auntie Anna had been in Anna Magnani's place, she would have also campaigned to give poor people homes to live in.

"You're special, too," Tommaso said.

Lorenza slowly shook her head.

"I mean it, you know."

She hinted a smile. "You're sweet to say that."

"I've thought it ever since you arrived in the office . . . it's as if you brought a spark of light into my life—I'm sorry," he said, embarrassed. "I'm not good at these things. It's been a long time since I—"

Lorenza placed a finger on his lips. "I know," she whispered, softening her gaze, just before pushing aside the red curtain.

———

That November, for his forty-fourth birthday, his first since becoming mayor, Carlo threw a party in grand style with music, dancing, and baskets of cigars. He hired a small ensemble from Lecce, which he paid handsomely, and which included piano, trombone, saxophone, and violin. That year, the Donna Anna bottles were sporting a new label to celebrate the tenth year of production. It said DONNA ANNA ANNIVERSARY next to the logo with the blooming rose. For the occasion, the composition was slightly changed. The site manager who was standing in for Daniele had suggested decreasing the percentage of Negroamaro and increasing the Malvasia. An exceptionally fresh wine had come of it, with a unique bright rosé color and embellished by the scent of rose petals. Carlo served rivers of it to his birthday guests.

Walking around the packed living room, Anna couldn't help but notice how different this party was from the others in years past. Carlo used to invite the *regular* people of Lizzanello, including farmers, workers, and traders. This time, he'd sent invitations to his political party's friends and supporters, some of whom came from Lecce. City council members also came, with wives and children in tow, as did the priest, don Luciano, who brought the apologies of the bishop, who was being held up by a previous engagement. *This is more than a party. It's almost like an exercise in alienation*, Anna thought.

Carlo moved about the room merrily, cigar in hand, stopping to talk to everyone. Every so often, he'd drag Antonio into the mix. He'd search for him among the crowd with his eyes and, as soon as he spotted him, he'd call him over loudly.

"Have you met my brother?" he'd say, with a hand on Antonio's shoulder.

Agata sat hunched on the couch, fingers intertwined in her lap, staring at the crackling fire and sometimes looking up at Lorenza and Tommaso, who were talking intensely as they sat next to each other on the couch in front of her.

Suddenly, Carlo waved his hand and asked for silence. The orchestra stopped playing and everyone crowded around him.

"Ladies and gentlemen, I hope you're having a good time," he exclaimed. "Judging by the empty bottles, I'd say you are!" He smiled.

"A toast to our mayor!" a man shouted, holding up a glass.

"Happy birthday!"

"Many happy returns!"

"Thank you, thank you all," Carlo said. "I'm very happy to have you here tonight to celebrate with me. But now . . ." He paused to study the small crowd. "Now I'd like to ask my beautiful wife to share the first dance of the night with me." He raised his glass in her direction.

Dozens of eyes turned to Anna. She curled her lips into a poorly executed smile. *Carlo and his flourishes,* she thought.

He whispered something into the pianist's ear and the first bars of "Amado mio" filled the room. He walked up to Anna with a charming, mischievous smile, took her by the hand, and led her to the center of the room. As people stepped out of the way, he held her by the waist and started to dance, looking her in the eyes.

"Would you like to dance too?" Tommaso asked Lorenza.

"Now?"

"When else?" He smiled.

"I'd like to dance, but in a bit," she said, trying not to seem rude.

In that moment, Carmela walked into the room on Nicola's arm. Lorenza stiffened and inched away from Tommaso. Why hadn't her Uncle Carlo warned her that Daniele's parents would be there? She went to go say hi but then stopped herself, shaken, having noticed that Carmela's dress looked just like one of Daniele's models. She remembered when he'd shown her the design, full of pride.

"It's an evening gown," he'd said. "For special occasions." It had a fitted bodice that was cinched at the waist and a wide, flared skirt that came down to the calf.

It can't be, that's absurd, Lorenza thought. It must be a coincidence, she told herself. Surely Carmela had copied it from one of her magazines. *Carmela doesn't know about his secret workshop.*

The song ended and Carlo made a funny bow to thank his audience for the deafening applause. Then he took Anna by the hand, approached two men and their respective wives, and started chatting with them.

"Happy birthday, Mr. Mayor!" Carmela's shrill voice made Carlo jump, forcing him to turn toward her.

"Papa sends his best wishes. He very much appreciated the new bottle of wine you sent him," she continued, unconcerned with having interrupted his conversation.

"He said that when you're ready to go see him, he'll tell you in person what he thinks."

"I'm glad," Carlo said. "I'll stop by for sure, in the next few days."

"What a beautiful dress," one of the wives said to Carmela.

"You like it?" she said. "It's my own creation."

The woman looked surprised and congratulated her. The other one said she would love to have one just like it.

"Yes, it's very beautiful," Anna admitted, after observing it carefully.

"Thank you, Mrs. Letter Carrier," Carmela said, beaming.

"Please excuse me, but I still have to introduce Anna to a few people," Carlo said. Having grabbed his wife's hand, he dragged her toward a man he introduced as the provincial secretary for Christian Democracy. Anna shook the man's hand without much enthusiasm. He asked how construction of the new school was going, and Carlo, pleased, said the project had just been approved by the council and that work would soon commence.

"And what will you do with the old building?" the man asked.

"We are considering various proposals," Carlo said. "They're all on my desk, waiting to be examined. But after the party," he concluded with a smile.

Anna became pensive. She looked straight ahead for a few minutes as the conversation taking place before her became a sort of distant murmur.

"I also have a proposal for what to do with that old building," she exclaimed finally.

Carlo and the man turned to her in surprise.

"What would that be, my love?" Carlo asked in a tone that belied both curiosity and fear.

"One might call it a . . . Home for Women," she explained, lighting up. "A place where the door is always open, where a woman can find shelter when she's in trouble. I'm thinking, for example, about young mothers without a husband or a job, about those who are alone, about women who don't know how to escape violent men . . ." She paused to think. "We could help them in a concrete way, protect them, and maybe give them an education, teach them a trade. I mean, everything they'd need to fend for themselves."

Scenes of her life with Giovanna passed before her eyes. Her struggles with reading, her isolation, the stigma the entire town had imposed on her for so long. The physical and mental pain her relationship with don Giulio caused her. Her inability to ask for help. They hadn't spoken since that morning in July. She'd seen her in town a few times, at a store or leaving the library, but something in her eyes, in her gait, her mannerisms, had prevented Anna from approaching her. She feared that Giulio would find out and punish her. How many women like Giovanna were out there? How many stories of cruelty, suffering, and abandonment were hiding under the placid façade of that town?

"A Home for Women . . ." the man repeated. But from his tone it was impossible to tell whether he thought it was a feasible project or true madness.

"My wife is always keeping me on my toes," Carlo said, slightly embarrassed. "This idea is entirely new to me, for instance."

"It's new to me, too. I just thought of it now," Anna said. "But you can be sure that I'll write a compelling proposal, *Mr. Mayor,*" she concluded with a smile.

———

"That sky is ripe for snow," Elena said, peering out the window. Gusts of Tramontane winds were incessantly shaking the leaves on the great palm tree.

"I wish," Anna sighed, as she slipped letters and bills into her mailbag. "I haven't seen snow for—" She stopped to make a quick mental calculation. "Thirteen years."

"It won't snow this year, either," Carmine declared resolutely.

"The expert has arrived," Elena teased him.

"It would be nice, though, to have a white Christmas," Tommaso said.

"Lorenza, a letter for you!" Anna exclaimed, examining a sepia-colored envelope with the United States Air Mail logo.

Lorenza jumped up from her chair, pushing it back loudly. Her eyes lit up with joy as she ran to Anna, took the envelope, and returned to the back room smiling, closing the door behind her. She didn't notice Tommaso, who had looked up from his desk behind her and followed the entire scene with a desolate expression.

Lorenza sat down, ripped open the side of the envelope, and pulled out a piece of paper folded in half. As she unfolded it, the sight of Daniele's rounded and slightly crooked handwriting was enough to make her heart beat faster.

She sat back in her chair and started to read.

My little Lorenza. Little and beautiful Lorenza.

How was your morning today? Did you manage to get to work on time? My adorable and incorrigible sleepyhead . . .

What a beautiful photo you sent me . . . You have such a sweet expression. You look more and more beautiful every time I see you. Is there a limit to beauty, or are you destined to surpass it? I put the photo on my nightstand so that you're the first person I see when I wake up every day and the last one I say good night to.

What's happening there? Tell me something nice. Something that makes you happy. Did you celebrate Carlo's birthday? I wrote him a letter wishing him a happy birthday—I hope he got it in time!

I have good news and less good news. Where should I begin? Let me think. Okay, I'll start with the good news.

Marisa saw my sketches of men's clothing and she liked them a lot. She showed them to the owner of the store, Mr. James, and guess what? He wants to sell them in his shop, at least a few. He pays well . . . Let's see how it goes, he said.

I know what's stirring inside your little head right now. Breathe. Remember that I love you. And that I want to be with you. And that I'm doing all this for us and for our future.

Is that better?

Okay.

Now the not so good news. I can't come back right away. Not for Christmas, as I'd promised. I'll need a bit more time to create the collection. I can't say no—the opportunity is too important. I know you'll understand.

Don't be disappointed or sad, please. The very thought of that makes me feel sick. Our time together has only been postponed. Don't be afraid. Understood? DON'T BE AFRAID. I love you. You and no one else. We've survived apart for these seven months, we can do it for a little longer, I know we can!

Respond right away, please. Tell me that everything is okay.

Lorenza put the letter on the desk and realized her hands were trembling. Her heart was still beating fast, but now it was due to rage. *No, he doesn't really love me,* she thought. *He won't be back. He is a liar too. Like all of them. Like my father.*

18

A nna draped her wool shawl over her shoulders, poured warm milk into her cup, and went to sit on the bench in the garden. The first moments of the day, punctuated by her little rituals, were her favorite. Only there, in *her* spot and in the absence of noise, could she feel truly peaceful and be able to put order to her thoughts.

The day before, she'd seen Giovanna walking through town with her head down, looking despondent and defeated, and for a moment—but maybe she was mistaken—it seemed like her friend had looked up in search of her eyes.

"Bonjour, Maman." Roberto suddenly came up behind her and leaned over to smack a kiss on her cheek.

"Bonjour, mon chéri," Anna said, stroking his arm. Roberto sat next to her on the bench, his hair tousled and his eyes swollen from sleep. He pulled his knees up to his chest and rested his head on Anna's shoulder. He was fourteen years old now, but he sometimes still acted like a child with her.

"What were you thinking about? Engrossed as you were . . ." he asked in a sleepy voice.

Anna placed her lips on the edge of her cup and took a sip. "About Giovanna," she said finally.

"Do you miss her?"

"Yes. A lot."

Roberto pulled his head up and looked at her. "Go tell her, then, no?"

"She already knows. I hope."

He raised an eyebrow, just as she did when she was vexed. "If you don't tell her, how is she supposed to know?"

Anna smiled bitterly. "It's not that simple. It's like . . . how can I explain? Well, it's like she's fallen under a spell. And I don't know the formula to reverse it."

Roberto pursed his lips and thought for a moment.

"Well," he said, "maybe it's one of those spells that only disappear with another spell, an even stronger one."

Anna shrugged. "I don't know . . . if that's the case, I really don't know which it could be."

"I think it's all the love you feel for her. The stronger spell, I mean."

Anna smiled at him and ruffled his hair. "What a wise son I have," she said.

He stood up and stretched his arms.

"I know," he said. "Papa always tells me that. That I'm wise like him," he added, with one of his father's happy-go-lucky smiles.

"Oh, well," Anna said slowly, standing up to head back inside. "Your papa is very intelligent. And also clever. But *definitely* not wise."

Later, while Anna was pedaling the Bianchi under a cloudy and windy sky, she thought back to her son's words. Maybe he was right: She just had to go to Giovanna and tell her she missed her. Remind her that she loved her, every day if she had to. *Maybe in the long run, a good spell really can reverse a bad one,* she concluded.

Lost in thought, she traversed the road to the edge of town for the last delivery of the day. She stopped in front of a dilapidated house with peeling plaster and a wooden door that was heavily worn in multiple spots. A very tall man with tanned skin and muscular arms came to the door. Beyond him, Anna spied a carpet of tobacco leaves and a woman with two children, a boy and a girl, who were sitting on the ground, legs splayed, placing the clean leaves in a cardboard box. Anna handed the man a telegram. He took it, made a quick motion of dismissal, and closed the door.

Anna climbed onto her bike to return to town, but then she stopped and looked at her watch: It was one o'clock and don Giulio would almost certainly be at the parish. She turned back and made a beeline for Contrada La Pietra, riding against the wind.

When Giovanna opened the door, there was no need for words. As soon as she saw Anna, her big hazel eyes filled with tears and her body, which seemed thinner and extremely frail, shook with sobs.

Anna felt unending tenderness, like she'd never felt for anyone before. For a moment, she thought of her little Claudia, so fragile and helpless. Then she hugged Giovanna with all her might.

"I'm sorry," Giovanna said, still sobbing, curling up in Anna's arms like a child. "You were right."

"It's okay, I'm here now. Calm down," Anna murmured. She patted Giovanna's head but stopped when she realized she'd just touched a patch of exposed scalp, as if the hair had been torn out. She pulled away with a worried expression and turned Giovanna toward her; yes, there was a hole in Giovanna's mane.

"Was it him?" she hissed.

Giovanna sniffled. "No," she said. "I did it."

The night before, sitting naked on the bed and looking lost, she'd started to tear her hair out. She continued even when Giulio clamped her arms down and screamed at her to stop. Not long before that, he'd entered the bedroom in his cassock and collar and had ordered her to undress. While Giovanna took her clothes off, he also stripped down, then he grabbed her wrists and tied them with a ribbon while Giovanna tried in vain to wriggle out. He tied her ankles in the same way. Then he pushed her onto the bed and took her violently. In tears, Giovanna swore to Anna that it had never happened before.

Anna stared at her with a steely gaze, and then she grabbed Giovanna's hand and led her into the house.

"You have a travel bag, right?" she asked.

Giovanna looked around in bewilderment. "Yes. I think it's under the sink . . . I can't remember."

Anna started looking for it everywhere. She looked under the sink and under the bed; she opened all the cupboards and drawers and finally found it rolled up inside a chest in the bedroom. She opened it, put it on the bed, then went to the wardrobe and started to throw her friend's few clothes into it along with her coat, undergarments, and underwear.

"What are you doing?" Giovanna asked in a trembling voice, hugging herself.

"I'm not leaving you here," Anna said, filling the bag. "You're coming to stay with me. I won't take no for an answer."

Silently, they took the road into town. Giovanna walked with her head down, constantly wiping away her tears with the back of her hand. Anna pushed her bicycle alongside her.

Once at home, Anna opened all the windows in the guest room, made the bed with lavender-scented sheets, put Giovanna's things in the closet, and handed her a brand-new bar of Marseilles soap still wrapped in paper.

"Go take a nice hot bath," she said. "The towels are in the top drawer. Take your time. I'll wait for you downstairs."

Sitting on the bed with her eyes fixed on the floor, Giovanna simply nodded.

As soon as Anna left the room, Giovanna picked herself up and went to the chest of drawers. She found the linen towels carefully folded without a crease. She was about to pull one out when she noticed an object in the corner of the drawer.

Oh, it's a pumo. I haven't seen one of these in a long time, she thought, turning it around in her hands. The small, delicate porcelain flower had collected dust. She remembered that her mother Rosalina had had one too, and that she kept it on display on the kitchen table.

"It's a good-luck charm—woe betide you if you break it!" she always said. Giovanna caressed the pumo, scooped it up in her arms like a babe, and set it on top of the dresser.

———

Later that day, Anna peeked into the bedroom while Carlo sat in front of the mirror, undoing the knot on his tie.

Quietly, she told him what had happened.

"Giovanna will stay with us for a bit. I don't know for how long. You don't mind, do you?" she concluded.

"Of course not," he said. "She can stay as long as she wants." He removed his tie with a sigh of relief and started to fold it onto itself.

"I swear, I would choke him with my own hands," Anna said, folding her arms.

"I know you're fully capable of it, my love," he said.

"Oh," he continued, as if he'd only just remembered in that moment. "The old school will be demolished. We discussed it yesterday."

"What will they replace it with?"

"We'll move the Saturday market to that spot, making it permanent. Everyone will get their own wooden stall. It'll be a sort of constant fair. The traders proposed the project, all together, and the council voted unanimously in favor."

Anna made a disappointed face. "What a shame, though. My project would have been much better. If only I'd had more time to obtain all those documents . . ."

"You're surprised? It's the bureaucracy of this country," Carlo said. He stood up and gently pulled Anna toward him. "I'm sorry about your Home for Women," he whispered. "But believe me, you avoided a big disappointment and a lot of work for nothing. I know the men on the council. They never would have voted for such a . . . modern idea."

Anna frowned and was about to ask him if he, too, agreed with those men, but just then they heard someone knocking on the front door, intense and furious.

"Who could it be at this hour?" Carlo wondered, frowning.

"Who do you think?" Anna said.

They went downstairs and opened the door to find don Giulio. He was clearly furious.

"What do you want?" Anna said.

"Giovanna is here, isn't she?"

"That's none of your business."

"You better leave," Carlo said.

"Giovanna!" don Giulio screamed, trying to push his way in.

Carlo grabbed him by the arms and pushed him away. "Out of my house!"

"Giovanna!" don Giulio kept yelling.

"Carlo, close the door, please," Anna said.

Carlo tried, but don Giulio blocked it with a foot. "I'm not leaving until she comes to talk to me."

Suddenly, Giovanna appeared at the top of the stairs, barefoot and in her nightgown.

"There you are!" don Giulio yelled. "What were you thinking, leaving home like that?"

"Giovanna, go back to your room," Anna said. "Please."

Giovanna could barely breathe. She kept standing there stiff as a beam, grasping the handrail.

"Let's go home, come on," don Giulio ordered.

Giovanna stepped back. "No," she whispered.

"Did you hear that?" Carlo said. "Giovanna's staying here. And now leave or I'll kick you out on your ass."

"I'm not budging from our house. Understand?" don Giulio continued, without looking away from Giovanna.

"That is not your house," Anna said.

"Giovanna, I'll wait for you at home," he said.

"Then you're going to be waiting forever. If you try to go near her again, I promise I will report you, if it's the last thing I do," Anna threatened, pointing a finger at him.

"Hear that?" Carlo said.

Don Giulio loosened his collar and stared at Giovanna in disgust.

"You crazy woman—people were right about you," he said, before finally leaving.

Giovanna tightened her grip on the handrail and bowed her head.

———

Lorenza did not answer Daniele's letter. He wrote to her again, at Christmas, a telegram that Elena transcribed in her minute handwriting. It wished her happy holidays and begged her to write him at least a few lines. Lorenza balled up the telegram and threw it into the scrap paper bin.

Driven by a desire for vengeance, she invited Tommaso to dinner on Christmas Eve at her aunt and uncle's house. That evening, she adopted an almost flirtatious attitude toward him. She sat next to him at dinner; she laughed at his jokes; she gave him suggestive smiles and long, intense looks. She even bought him a gift: a dark gray felt hat with a medium brim. Under the great pine tree, which Carlo and Roberto had decorated, as they did every year, Tommaso unwrapped the package, happy and surprised to receive a gift. Lorenza pulled the hat out of the box and exclaimed, "Go on, try it on!" She placed it on his head and took a step back.

"I knew it," she said finally. "You look great in hats. Promise me you'll start wearing it right away."

It went without saying that after that, Tommaso wore it every single day.

In the run-up to New Year's Eve, he asked her to a Saturday afternoon movie. They went to see *Miracle on 34th Street*, during which Lorenza touched his hand a few times. Then one Sunday morning, he asked Agata if he could take Lorenza for a ride in his Fiat Topolino. He promised to bring her back in time for lunch, she didn't have to worry. Agata immediately agreed—she liked Tommaso and didn't hide it. *He is a good man,* she thought, *someone you can really rely on, unlike that other one.*

On that sunny and windless morning, Lorenza waved goodbye to her parents with a broad smile while Tommaso opened the car door for her. They headed to the beach, where he bought freshly caught urchins from a fisherman. They ate them sitting on a bench by the sea, scooping up the pulp with some bread. After getting back in the car, Tommaso took off his hat and surprised Lorenza with a kiss, which she thought was a bit too wet and suffocating and yet somehow also very sweet.

The following Monday, at the post office, they exchanged long looks filled with tenderness and an awkward energy.

Elena leaned across her desk.

"What happened between you and the director?" she prodded Lorenza, giggling. "I saw you, you know?" she said, flashing her eyebrows.

Lorenza smiled and shook her head. "Actually, something did happen."

"And your nice American boy? He's always sending you telegrams, poor thing. At least answer him . . ."

Lorenza's face suddenly darkened. "He can stay where he is, as far as I'm concerned."

The following Sunday, Tommaso took her to lunch at a trattoria in Lecce, where they ate fried bread with cheese and drank an entire bottle of Donna Anna. They took a brief walk to Piazza Sant'Oronzo and right there, under the statue of the patron saint, Tommaso pulled a red velvet box out of his pocket and got down on one knee.

Lorenza looked at him, breathless. For a moment, she felt the urge to run, to escape to anywhere that wasn't that place and that moment, in that corner of the piazza, there with Tommaso.

But when she saw him on one knee, looking up at her with those desperately adoring eyes—eyes that promised her devotion, that said *I'll never leave you*—Lorenza said yes and let herself be drawn into a hug.

Tommaso insisted on getting the family together the very next day, so they could make the big announcement. He seemed incapable of containing his joy, but at the same time, he seemed anxious and fragile, as if he worried that she might take back her yes and return the ring, saying *I'm sorry, I was wrong. It's not you I want. I never wanted you.*

Lorenza let Tommaso talk her into inviting them all to dinner at his house. She came up with an excuse to ensure that everyone would make it. "He says he wants to thank us for the dinner on Christmas Eve."

He still lived in a house owned by Giulia's family: After her death, his in-laws had insisted he stay. "You're like a son to us now," they'd said, hugging him.

When Agata arrived, she looked around, stunned. The house wasn't very big, but it was thoroughly lavish: Persian carpets covered the entire floor in every room; there were walnut and velvet couches, satin curtains, ebony tables with marble tops, golden frames on the walls . . .

"What a beautiful house," Agata said, sitting on the living room couch while Antonio took a seat in an uncomfortable-looking chair with carved wooden armrests.

"Certainly not thanks to me," Tommaso chuckled. "My in-laws decorated it . . . my former in-laws," he added, embarrassed, and shot a look at Lorenza.

She replied with half a smile and started to wander around the room listlessly, running her fingers along the marble, touching knickknacks and the fabric on the sofas, and peeking at the family portraits hanging on the walls.

Tommaso went up to her as if he'd read her mind.

"If there's anything you don't like, you can change it however you want," he whispered to her. "The only thing that matters is that you're here with me."

Lorenza smiled gratefully. She didn't like anything about the place. Everything seemed old, oppressive, and presumptuous. It felt like living there would require wearing a ball gown every day.

Anna arrived a few moments later with Carlo, Roberto, and Giovanna.

"This house isn't you at all," Anna said right away, as she took her coat off.

"I know," Tommaso said, looking at Lorenza. "But it'll change soon enough." He invited everyone to move into the dining room. "I hope you're hungry," he said. "I've been cooking for four hours."

"I'm impressed!" Agata said, trying to get up from the couch. Roberto held out his hand and she leaned on it as she stood up. To Roberto she mumbled, "He even knows how to cook!"

Once they were all seated, Tommaso uncorked two bottles of red wine with no label and filled everyone's glass. Carlo took a sip. "It's good," he remarked. "It's a Primitivo, right?"

"Yes, I got it on tap from the osteria," Tommaso explained. "And your red? When will we be able to taste it?"

Carlo placed his glass on the table. "Well, it's still early."

The dinner unfolded in a calm and festive mood. After each course, Agata kept saying how wonderful everything was. And Tommaso—Lorenza noticed—had a talent for conversing with everyone and showing interest in what people cared about. He turned out to be thoughtful without being sappy.

Before dessert was served, Lorenza, who'd been sitting next to Tommaso, gave him a meaningful look. He leaned in toward her and whispered, "I'll take care of it, don't worry."

He went into the kitchen and came back with a big cake with chocolate frosting and put it in the center of the table.

"I didn't make this, though, let's be clear," he said. "It comes straight from the pastry shop."

While everyone took their slice, Lorenza got up and went to stand by Tommaso at the head of the table. He placed his arm around her waist and looked at her in a very sweet way.

Agata immediately curled her lips into an impatient smile and started to wriggle in her seat.

"I'm so happy to give you this news . . . You can't imagine how happy," Tommaso began. "Lorenza and I—well, we're getting married."

Agata let out a cry of joy and clapped her hands.

"Oh, my dear Lord!" she exclaimed. She stood up and ran to hug her daughter and then Tommaso. Antonio went over to shake the hand of his future son-in-law.

"I'm glad it's you," he said. Then he looked at Lorenza.

"So, this is who you have chosen?" he asked. She nodded and smiled. Antonio pulled her into a hug, cradling her in his arms. "I'm happy for you," he whispered into her ear.

Carlo congratulated them both, happy as a clam, then poured another glass of wine for everyone.

"A toast to the betrothed!" he cried. Roberto shook Lorenza's hand and then Tommaso's. Then it was Giovanna's turn; she approached Lorenza with her eyes brimming with tears.

"Weddings have always made me cry," she stammered in a cracked voice.

Amid the laughter, confusion, and hugs, Anna remained frozen in place.

And Daniele? Your true love? What about him? she wanted to say, then and there, in front of everyone. She wanted to cut short those expressions of joy that seemed too hasty to her, too unfair. She desperately tried to make eye contact with Lorenza, but it didn't take her long to realize that her niece was intentionally avoiding her gaze. Nearby, Carlo and Antonio were staring at each other with knowing smiles.

Strange, Anna thought, lifting an eyebrow. She thought she'd seen relief in their faces. But no, she must be mistaken.

———

On the morning after the dinner, Lorenza was late meeting Anna, as usual.

"Good morning, Auntie," she greeted her distantly.

"Good morning," Anna said.

They set off in silence.

"I couldn't wait to be alone with you. I wanted to talk to you," Anna said finally.

"Why? Do you want to apologize for last night?" Lorenza said dryly.

"I'm sorry. You know I struggle to—"

"Yes, we all know," Lorenza interrupted. "It no longer surprises us, as you can see."

Anna stared at her, frowning. "Why are you so harsh?"

"You're asking me? All you had to do was stand up from that chair and show a modicum of happiness for us."

"I would have if I thought you really were happy."

"And who told you I'm not?"

"Lorenza . . ." Anna said with a sigh. "I've known you since you were a child."

"Well, I'm all grown up now, and I've changed, if you haven't noticed."

Anna stopped. "And Daniele? You're just going to give up on him?"

"Do you see him anywhere?" Lorenza said, holding her arms out. "Where is he? Certainly not here. Not with me."

"You know he'll be back. Why do you want to deny yourself the joy of marrying a man you love?"

"You're wrong. I don't love him. Not anymore."

"Liar," Anna said, softening her gaze.

"Tommaso is the right man for me," Lorenza said decisively. "He's a good man, who will always stay by my side."

"But you're not in love with him," Anna said. "You know that."

"I care about him very much," Lorenza snapped.

"That's not reason enough to marry someone. I also care about Tommaso. He's my friend. But I wouldn't marry him for that."

Lorenza smirked and started walking again, but Anna stopped her, grabbing her by the arm. "Don't rush into this, please. Think it through. Decide with your heart."

Lorenza pulled her arm away abruptly. "I've already decided," she said.

An hour later, in the telegraph office, Lorenza composed a telegram to Daniele.

I've stopped waiting for you. I love another. I'm getting
married in May. Lorenza.

As soon as she sent it, she felt empty. In that moment, she realized
she'd only said yes to Tommaso because she wanted Daniele to know
about it. She wanted him to suffer at the thought of having lost her and to
pay for his absence. But the satisfaction she thought she would feel soon
turned to ashes.

19

Don Ciccio died in his sleep on the night of April 28.

At midnight, the bells of the San Lorenzo church began to ring in mourning. The vigil was set up in the bedroom. Gina sat by the casket, silently shedding tears and gently caressing her husband's wrinkly cheeks. She'd dressed him in his best outfit, a sand-colored suit with a blue shirt and red tie. Nicola sat next to her, holding her hand.

Carmela was shuffling back and forth between the bedroom and the kitchen; she greeted those who came to offer their condolences, received the trays of pastries and bags of coffee they brought as gifts and placed them on the kitchen table. Gina's sisters, who'd come from a nearby town, kept two coffee makers on the stove at all times, the big twelve-cup one and the smaller three-cup one, so that coffee would always be ready for anyone who wanted it.

Carlo entered the crowded house and took off his hat. He walked down the hallway as people whispered, "Good morning, Mr. Mayor." He entered the bedroom, approached the coffin, and stared at a lifeless don Ciccio, whose face remained contracted in a grimace of pain. Carlo would never tell anyone, but the truth was that he couldn't really feel sad about his passing. On the contrary, he felt a vague sense of relief, even though he couldn't quite explain why. He made the sign of the cross and lightly kissed the coffin. He shook Nicola's hand and leaned over to hug Gina, who sniffled and wiped away a tear when she saw him.

"Where's Carmela?" he whispered to Nicola.

He looked around the room. "Try the kitchen."

Carlo found her there, drinking coffee and leaning against the sink. She looked tired.

He hesitated, then put a hand on her arm and squeezed it. "I'm very sorry," he said. "How are you?"

Carmela drank the last sip of coffee and put her cup down. Then she stood up straight, smoothing out the bodice on her black dress.

"At least he's not suffering anymore," she said.

Carlo nodded and twirled the hat in his hands. "Is there anything I can do to help?"

She looked at him thoughtfully, pursing her lips. "Actually, there is something. I can't get away from here."

"Anything, tell me."

"I need you to alert Daniele."

"Yes, of course," Carlo said. "I'll do it right away."

He put his hat back on and headed to the post office.

"Uncle!" Lorenza greeted him in surprise. "What are you doing here?"

"I'm here to send Daniele a telegram. I have to tell him his grandfather passed."

Lorenza's face stiffened. Then she looked down, grabbed a pen, and ripped off a piece of paper. "Go ahead," she said, affecting indifference.

She transcribed the text of the telegram into Morse code and sent it.

"Done" was all she said.

The last time she'd communicated with Daniele had been in early March. He'd answered the telegram about her wedding with a message saying,

Why are you doing this to us?

She'd decided to ignore him, letting the days go by in silence, like a punishment. Then he'd sent her another one:

Don't do anything silly. Wait.

Then another:

Why did you stop trusting me?

Until the last one, where he'd written:

I won't bother you anymore. Congratulations.

Daniele responded immediately. First, he sent Carlo a message, thanking him for the notice, and then he sent one to his mother. It was up to Lorenza to transcribe them both. The second one said,

I'm sorry about Grandpa. I don't know when I can return. I'll do my best, promise.

Lorenza stared at those words and couldn't help but sneer at them. She really had made the right choice by not waiting for him. Her mother was right: Daniele's promises had always been Tramontane promises.

———

"Well?" Agata asked. "Did you see the Colosseum? What did you eat? What was the weather like? Was the hotel okay?"

Lorenza and Tommaso were sitting next to each other on the couch, holding hands. Agata had organized a dinner with the whole family to celebrate their return from their honeymoon. She'd prepared her famous meat pie. They were all seated around the newlyweds and Tommaso was chattering away, excited by the beauty of the capital, its majestic monuments, and the extraordinary history that permeated the city. Lorenza simply nodded and said, "Yes, indeed," or, "It's true."

The wedding had taken place two weeks before, on a cloudy day with no light. After a sleepless night, Lorenza had sat down on the bed to stare at her wedding dress, which was hanging over her wardrobe door. It was the dress Agata had worn on her wedding day.

"Finally, the time has come," she'd told Lorenza when she showed it to her, with a tremble in her voice and tears in her eyes. It had a flared skirt, a short train, an embroidered bodice with long, lacy sleeves, and a shoulder-length veil that needed to be set in place with a bejeweled comb. It was very different from Elizabeth's dress, Lorenza thought. But also from the one Daniele had drawn in one of his black notebooks long ago, which he'd described to her in detail, down to the satin bodice, heart-shaped neckline with broderie anglaise, mother-of-pearl buttons, and full, floor-length skirt.

She'd shaken her head as if to shoo away the thought. Agata had walked into the room with a festive group of women who'd come to "prepare the bride." One helped put her hair in a bun, another ironed a crease into the skirt of her dress, another knelt to put on her shoes. In that whirlwind, Lorenza let herself be dressed, brushed, and done up like a doll. And was enormously comforted by it.

Anna was the only woman in the family who had not been present.

"I'll see you in church," she'd told Lorenza the night before. "If you should change your mind at the last minute, don't be afraid," she'd said. "Go ahead and call the whole thing off."

On the one hand, Lorenza had found everything to be a lot easier without the weight of her aunt's reproachful looks. On the other, Anna had been the only one to ask her if she was happy. No one else, not her mother nor her father, and certainly not her Uncle Carlo, had taken a moment to check on her since the day of the announcement at Tommaso's house. *It's probably for the best,* she thought.

And now? Now that she finally no longer slept on the pink sheets with embroidered edges? Now that she had a husband and a house to take care of—did she feel happy?

As if she'd uttered these thoughts out loud, Lorenza felt Anna's questioning eyes upon her. She squeezed Tommaso's hand and he gave her an adoring look.

"And we spent the last day just walking around the city center," he continued. "But we missed so many things! Yes, we'll definitely go back to Rome. Won't we, Lorenza?"

"It must be so beautiful," Giovanna said. "How I'd love to go there myself one day, to Rome."

"And who says you can't?" Anna said. "We can go whenever you want. You and me."

Sitting in the chair in front of them, Agata shot them both a glance that was somewhere between indignant and scandalized.

"We better sit at the table," she said, getting up and heading to the dining room.

Everyone followed her. Carlo placed both hands on Roberto's shoulders and playfully pushed him forward. "Smell that? It's the call of your Auntie Agata's pie!" he exclaimed, sniffing the air. Antonio chuckled, took Tommaso by the arm, and joined the others.

Anna didn't move until everyone had left the room but Lorenza. She approached her and whispered that she had to talk to her. "I'm coming. Go on ahead," she said to Giovanna, who was waiting for her.

Lorenza crossed her arms over her chest. "What is it?" she asked dryly.

Anna cleared her throat. "There's something you need to know, and it's best if I tell you myself, right now."

Lorenza frowned. "What happened?"

"Well, while you were gone, Daniele sent another telegram to his mother."

"Why are you telling me this? I don't care."

"I think you do," Anna said. She pulled a piece of folded paper out of her cleavage. "For once, Elena was discreet, don't worry. I copied it for you."

Lorenza stared at her for a long time, and then she took the piece of paper and opened it. Anna reread it in her mind along with her niece; she knew it by heart, for all the times she'd read it.

> I managed to take care of everything here. I bought my ticket. I arrive the morning of June 5 in Naples. Please ask Carlo to come pick me up with the car.

Lorenza's breath turned into a gasp.

"Are you okay?" Anna asked, placing a hand on her arm.

Lorenza bit her lower lip so forcefully that her eyes filled with tears.

———

Anna walked into the bedroom and saw the suitcase open on top of the chest at the foot of the bed. It was still empty.

Carlo was kneeling by the wardrobe, rummaging through the drawers.

"What are you looking for?" she asked.

"The striped blue tie. Have you seen it?"

Anna lifted an eyebrow. "What do you need a tie for?"

"What kind of question is that?"

"Go on, move over." She bent down and rifled through the drawer. "Here it is," she said, pulling out the tie. "It was right under your nose."

Carlo took it from her and placed it on the bed.

Anna crossed her arms and stared at him. "You seem nervous. Is everything okay?"

Carlo took a beige suit from the wardrobe, observed it for a moment, then nodded and put that on the bed too.

"Yes, yes," he said. "I have to drive for several hours. That would make anyone feel anxious, don't you think?"

Anna didn't answer. She simply watched him fill his suitcase, bring it outside, and load it into the back seat of his Fiat 1100.

"Got everything? You're sure?" she asked in a slightly sarcastic tone.

"I think so," Carlo said, in total seriousness. "It's only one night any-way. I'll just buy whatever I need there if I have to."

He closed the car door. "Where's Roberto? He's not coming down to say goodbye?"

"I think he's taking a bath. He's going to the movies tonight with his friends, from what I understand."

"All right. Say goodbye for me," he said, somewhat disappointed.

Anna went up to him and adjusted his jacket collar. "You'll see him tomorrow. Or were you thinking of sailing off?" she joked.

Finally, Carlo's face relaxed. "If I did, I'd take you with me." He kissed her, got in the car, and left.

Anna went back inside. Giovanna was sitting on the couch reading *Crime and Punishment*. "This book is hard," she said, scowling and looking up at Anna. "It's giving me a headache."

Anna smiled and sat down next to her. "Antonio gave it to me years ago," she said. "How come you chose this one? There are many other books you would like more, I'm sure of it," she said, pointing at the book-shelves behind her.

Giovanna turned the book around in her hands. "Because of the in-scription," she said.

She opened it to the first page and read:

The greatness of this novel lies in its message that every culprit, no matter how shameful, deserves compassion.

Happy reading,
Antonio

She put the book on the couch.

"Do you think so too?" she asked Anna. "Do you think we should have compassion for those who wrong us?"

Anna placed her arm on the headrest and curled up her legs.

"I don't know," she said, after a few moments. "Maybe compassion goes hand in hand with remorse. I don't think I could feel that for some-one who doesn't display a hint of regret."

Giovanna nodded and seemed to be reflecting. Then she said, "Do you think I could ever feel compassion for don Giulio? If he showed remorse, I mean."

"He doesn't need your compassion. He already has it from God," Anna said, sarcastically.

"I mean for real," Giovanna insisted. "If he—I mean, if he were to tell me that he was wrong, that he has repented—"

"Would you believe him?"

"I don't know. I think so."

"You'd be wrong. People like him don't change from one day to the next. They probably never change."

Giovanna smirked. "He might still be waiting for me . . ."

Anna shook her head and took Giovanna's hand in hers.

"Don Giulio never went back to Contrada."

"How do you know?"

"I went there a few times. To check. All his stuff is gone."

Giovanna bit her lip.

"You don't have to go back, if you don't want to," Anna assured her, as if she'd read her mind. "You can stay and live here, if you want."

Giovanna's face instantly brightened. "You're sure Carlo doesn't mind?"

"Of course not! He likes having you around too."

It was true. Nobody minded Giovanna's presence in the house. She was unobtrusive and discreet, thoughtful without being invasive.

"But if my presence starts to weigh on you or on Carlo or Roberto, you have to tell me—"

"Nonsense." Anna cut her short. "You don't weigh on anyone at all."

This was also true. She and Carlo provided for Giovanna financially and did so without effort, as her added needs were minimal.

Anna had tried to find her a job, but it had turned out to be such an impossible and painful undertaking that she hadn't even found the cour-age to tell Giovanna, fearing she might hurt her feelings. For weeks she'd approached shopkeepers in town, asking if they needed workers. The few who had said yes had immediately recanted when they heard the job was for Giovanna.

"Mrs. Letter Carrier, I respect you and Carlo, but that woman—just no," the tobacconist had said.

"Please, nobody will come here anymore if they see that woman in here" had been the haberdasher's response.

"Come on, only respectable people work here," a grocer had said.

"Understand?" Anna said again. "Don't ever think that your presence is a burden."

"Thank you," Giovanna whispered, drawing Anna into a hug. "You're the best friend in the world."

Anna smiled and slapped a kiss on her cheek. Then she stood up from the couch. "Come on, let's go make dinner," she said. "Tonight you and I are going to party."

As Giovanna started to mince the garlic, Anna went down to the basement where Carlo kept his small collection of wine.

"We need Champagne," she muttered, searching among the French wines. "Hmm . . . Not this one, or this one," she kept saying, after peeking at the labels. A moment before finding the Champagne, she saw a bottle that seemed out of place; it looked like a Donna Anna, but it had no label and it was empty, as if it had never been filled. Yet the cork was fully inserted. *How odd,* she thought. Then she shrugged and put it back where she'd found it.

As soon as Roberto went out, Anna popped the Champagne. "I'm sure Carlo won't mind. At least I hope not." She filled two glasses, but then the two women ended up downing the whole bottle while sitting barefoot on the rug.

Anna put "La Vie en rose" on the gramophone and held out her hand to Giovanna, inviting her to dance. Giovanna accepted, amused, and started to move around awkwardly until Anna, at the end of the song, plunged her into a dip, causing them both to fall to the ground, one on top of the other.

Lying on the floor, the two women looked at each other and burst out laughing until they cried.

———

The next morning, Carlo left the hotel in Piazza Orefici, near the port of Naples, and went to pick up the Fiat 1100, which he'd parked on a side street. It was such a hot day that he had to take off his jacket and push up the sleeves of shirt, panting. Once at the port, he continued on foot until he reached the Molo Angioino, where the *Saturnia* was set to land.

He found a seat and pulled a cigar from his pocket. He wiped the sweat off his forehead and loosened the knot on his tie.

"Can hardly breathe in this heat, eh?" he said with a pained expression to a man sitting nearby.

Then he lit his cigar, and at the first puff he started to cough. When the man saw that the cough gave no sign of relenting, he went to Carlo and offered him a drink of water from his bottle. Carlo gulped it down.

"Thank you," he said, handing the bottle back to the man.

"Is it over?" the man asked.

"Yes, yes," Carlo said. "Thanks again."

The imposing, majestic *Saturnia* entered the port around midday.

Carlo joined the horde of people gathering to witness the docking operations. When the passenger disembarkation finally commenced, he got on his tippy-toes to look over the sea of heads in front of him. More than half an hour passed before he saw Daniele emerge at the top of the ladder. His heart beating fast, he started to elbow his way through the crowd to get closer.

Daniele saw him and nodded. *My gosh, he's changed,* Carlo thought, heading toward him. Not his face, which still looked as tender and disarming as ever, but his attitude, his gait. He seemed so confident, determined, inhabited by all the new things he'd seen and experienced and that he was now bringing home with him.

"My boy," Carlo greeted him with open arms.

"Hi, Carlo," Daniele said with a smile.

He put his suitcase down and hugged him.

20

"Knock-knock," Anna said cheerfully, rapping her knuckles twice on the open door to Antonio's office.

"Hi!" he said, taken by surprise as he put a cardboard binder back on the shelf.

Anna walked in and closed the door behind her.

"I brought your book back," she said, opening her mailbag. She pulled it out and handed it to him. It was *The Woman of Rome* by Alberto Moravia.

"Well? Did you like it?" he asked.

She sat in the chair by the window. "You know I'm prejudiced against men who think they know what a woman thinks and feels and are sure they know how to write about it."

"Hmm," Antonio said, sitting in the chair in front of her. "I deduce that you did not like it."

"I wasn't finished," Anna said.

"Forgive me, you're right," he apologized, raising his hands. "Go on, please."

"As I was saying, in this novel, Moravia does it surprisingly well. I underlined a lot more passages this time."

Antonio smiled and started to leaf through the book, lingering on a sentence that had been underlined twice in pencil. He brought the book closer to his face and read, "'If you despised me, the fault was yours and not mine.'" He nodded. "Yes," he commented, keeping his eyes on the page.

"And there are many more. You'll find my usual notes next to them."

Antonio looked up. "I'll have something to look forward to tonight, then," he said, smiling, and closed the book.

"And now? What shall we read?" Anna asked.

"You choose the next one."

"Deal," she said. Then she glanced at her watch. "Oh, it's late." She stood up and headed to the door. "Oh, one more thing," she said, turning toward him. "Have you spoken to Lorenza recently?"

"Why? Did something happen that I don't know about?"

"No, no." Anna waved her hand. "It's just that I was wondering how she seemed to you. Since Daniele came back, I mean."

"Why are we talking about this?" Antonio asked, bewildered. "It's all water under the bridge. She's a married woman now."

Anna lifted an eyebrow. "You're sure about that? You really haven't noticed? You, who always notices everything?"

"What should I have noticed?"

"She's sad, Antonio. Terribly sad. How can you not see that? She knows she's done something incredibly foolish. She acted on impulse, for revenge, and now she's dug her own grave. I tried to warn her—"

"Daniele is not the right person for my daughter," he hissed, jumping up from his chair. "Things went the way they were supposed to go."

"How were they *supposed* to go? What do you have against the boy? This isn't the first time you've reacted this way when his name came up. Even that day, at Carlo's rally . . . Is there something I need to know?"

His jaw dropped, but he quickly regained his composure.

"No, of course not," he murmured, sitting behind the desk. He placed his elbows on the table and interlaced his fingers. "I just think that for Lorenza, given her restless and needy nature, and her desire for affection, a more mature man is best, someone settled, who can give her a sense of security. That's all."

Anna observed him. "How absurd," she said.

But Antonio did not respond, so she opened the door and left, wagging a quick goodbye with her fingers.

She left the oil mill irritated by Antonio's refusal to hear reason and resumed her delivery route. The following stop was the Tamburini villa, just a few hundred feet away. Anna pedaled up to a sort of hill immersed in greenery, then got off her bike and continued on foot. The Tamburini home was a historic building with a long stone balcony, large windows with velvet curtains, and a double staircase leading to the main entrance. A man in a straw hat and armed with a pair of shears was bent over some bushes in the garden that surrounded the house. Anna took one of the staircases and tapped the doorknocker. She pulled out an envelope that was closed with a wax seal. *Must be an invitation to one of their rich-people parties*, she thought, turning it around in her hands.

In that moment, the door opened and a young girl with an extremely serious, almost fearful expression appeared. Her hair was done up in a bun and she was wearing a white apron over a black dress with a wide skirt.

Anna didn't know her, but she wasn't surprised; it seemed like the Tamburinis' maids never lasted very long and there was always another girl ready to take the place of the one who'd . . . left? Got fired? *But this one really is so young!* she thought. *How old could she be? Twelve? Thirteen? She should be in school, not polishing silverware!*

"Who is it!" thundered the voice of a woman from inside.

The girl jumped. "It's the mail, madam," she said, turning slightly.

"Bring it to me now!" the woman ordered.

The girl bowed and murmured, "Thank you, Mrs. Letter Carrier. Good day," and quickly closed the door. For a few seconds, Anna remained motionless in front of the closed door, feeling a sense of unease that, then and there, she couldn't quite name.

———

Since the day Daniele had set foot back in Lizzanello, everything seemed shrunken. Had the buildings always been so low and the streets so narrow? He wandered around town, weighing it with new eyes. It took him some time to get used to that setting again, to regain familiarity with those places.

Who knows if he would have felt that way if Lorenza had been there to embrace him? If she'd waited for him, as she'd promised. In the first weeks, he tried to steer clear of the main square, the post office, and the street on which she now lived with another man. He spent a lot of time at home, lying in bed, staring at the ceiling with his hands crossed over his chest. From time to time, he'd go to the Greco Winery to say hi and lend a hand. Carlo had offered him a new role designed especially for him: he wanted him to become the winery's sales manager, given the excellent results he'd obtained in New York. He'd talked to him about it on the return trip from Naples.

"You can sell, my boy. You're a natural. Now take a few days off. When you're ready, the winery will be here waiting for you," he'd said. In that moment, Daniele hadn't found the courage to tell him that he had other plans now. He hadn't said anything about the success of his men's suits, of the enthusiasm of the shop owner on Fifth Avenue, of the fact that he'd offered him a long-term collaboration, and that he'd refused it. What had seemed so natural, so right, in New York had now become something to hide again, to be ashamed of. His mother's words had started to buzz in his ears as soon as he got back: *Sewing is not for boys.*

He'd only gone to see his parents once, for dinner, the day after his return. He'd found them stubbornly unchanged, trapped in the same roles. His mother the executioner, with her rude and arrogant ways, and his father the victim, who made himself smaller and smaller as he bowed his head. After they'd finished their meal, while Carmela was making coffee in the kitchen, Daniele had leaned toward Nicola and quietly asked him, "Papa, did you reorganize my wardrobe? I can't find my metal box, the one with the notebooks. Did you move it somewhere by any chance?"

Nicola had gawked and stammered that he didn't know anything about it, he hadn't touched a thing.

"I have your precious box," Carmela said, returning to the dining room with the tray of steaming cups.

Daniele jumped up from his chair. "You went through my stuff? In *my* home?"

"Calm down," she said, placidly, sitting down. "I know your secret now."

Daniele turned to Nicola, whose eyes were now glued to the floor. "Papa . . . I asked you to do *one* thing. One! Why did you let her in?"

But Nicola didn't answer.

"I have to admit that you're a pretty good liar," Carmela cut in, and took a sip of coffee.

Daniele stared at her, frowning. "Give me my sketches back. Now!"

Carmela put the cup down, smacking her lips.

"Too late," she said. "I've already made them. All of them."

"What did you do?" Daniele couldn't believe it.

"A favor! That's what I did," she said, raising her voice. "Can't you see how ridiculous you look? Do you want people to think you're a pansy? Grow up and quit it with all of this. You have a man's job now, thanks to your grandfather, God rest his soul. Imagine where you'd be if I'd waited for this one to sort things out," she said with a smirk, indicating Nicola. "From now on you're going to take things seriously and *only* think about the winery," she concluded, tapping a finger on the table.

Dispirited, Daniele looked at his father, who continued to stare at the floor. Then he fixed his eyes back on his mother.

"I . . . I have no words to describe what you are," he murmured, in a cracked voice. He threw the door open and never returned to his parents' house.

But he did go to his grandmother's house every day, and more often than not, he'd stay for lunch. "It's so lovely to have you back here," she'd say, reaching her wrinkled hand across the table. "We've missed you so. Especially your grandfather, even though he was never very good at saying things like that."

Daniele would squeeze her hand and smile. "I'm here now, Grandma."

"Would you please go and buy me a basket of cherries?" Gina asked him on one of those mornings. "I don't feel well enough to do it myself." She picked up a fan and started to wave it in front of her face. "It's too hot."

Daniele hesitated, then said, "Of course, Grandma, I'll take care of it."

And it was on that morning, as he was thanking the fruit vendor and walking away with the bag of cherries, that he finally saw Lorenza. She'd just come out of the post office. A moment later, Tommaso joined her and placed an arm around her shoulders. Daniele grasped the bag and froze in place, watching her cross the square toward the bar. As always, she was even more beautiful than the last time he'd seen her, though he couldn't help but notice a certain melancholic, almost resigned expression, which she carried around consistently now. The polar opposite of her husband, who walked next to her looking radiant, as if he felt like the luckiest man in the world.

Tommaso smiled at a man who was standing outside the bar, who waved him over. The two of them started talking about something that Lorenza was clearly not interested in, because she started looking around with a bored expression.

Until she noticed that Daniele was staring at her.

She went stiff and stared back at him, her mouth falling open. They looked at each other for just a moment, but it felt like it lasted forever. Neither of them lifted a hand in greeting; neither of them took a step toward the other. They both stayed motionless, holding their breath, until Tommaso said goodbye to his friend and placed a hand on Lorenza's shoulder. She gasped slightly, looked down, and walked away with her husband.

———

Roberto opened the pale wooden cupboard, pulled the record out of its paper sleeve, and positioned it on the record player, which he'd just bought with the savings from his allowance—it was the latest model on the market. A swing tune spread through the room and Roberto started to dance with his eyes closed.

"What is it?" Carlo asked, sitting in a chair by the fireplace, reading the paper.

Without stopping, Roberto opened his eyes. "'Il mago dello swing' by Aldo Donà," he said.

Carlo looked at him, amused.

"You're a good dancer. You must have gotten it from me," he said, raising his voice to be heard over the music.

Anna walked in just then, holding the sheets she'd just gathered from the balcony. Roberto went to her, took her by the hand, and dragged her into the middle of the room. The clean sheets ended up on the floor.

"You want to dance now? With all the things I have to do!" Anna protested. But she was smiling.

"Shut up and dance, Maman," Roberto said.

Anna stepped up to him and started to imitate him.

"Like this now," he said, bringing his leg back and rotating from the hip. Anna laughed, gave Carlo a brief glance, and tried to imitate the movement.

"Very good!" Roberto exclaimed. "Isn't she really good, Papa?"

Carlo nodded with a smile. "She's the best," he said.

When the record came to an end and the music stopped, Roberto bowed to his mother.

"Put it on again," she said, breathless, with her hands on her hips. "I want to dance it with your father." She turned to Carlo with a mischievous smile.

He grabbed the sides of the armchair with both his hands and stood up with a slight shortness of breath.

"Come on, old man," she teased him. "Come here."

"Who are you calling old man, you bad girl!" Carlo joked, raising an eyebrow. He grabbed her by the waist, pulled her in close, and they started to dance while Roberto stood by the record player, watching them with a smile full of affection and snapping his fingers in time.

But after one more twirl, Carlo stopped suddenly. He started to cough so hard he had to bend over in half, with his hands on his thighs.

Roberto lifted the needle and the record stopped with a scratch.

"I'll get you some water," Anna said, hurrying into the kitchen.

Roberto went to him and held him up by the shoulders. Carlo kept coughing with such violence that his face had gone red and his eyes were lined with broken capillaries. "Papa?" Roberto asked, worried.

"Here's the water," Anna said, coming back into the room with a full glass. She brought it to Carlo's mouth and helped him drink.

He drank it in small gulps, and then with a nod he pushed the glass back, as if to say that he'd had enough.

"It's over," he murmured finally, with a sigh.

"So I was right to say you're an old man," Anna said, trying to lighten the mood.

Carlo shot her a forced smile, went back to his chair, and let himself fall into it. As soon as he was settled, he pulled a cigar from the metal box on the side table and, still short of breath, lit it.

———

From that day on, Carlo's cough became a constant backdrop to the hot summer weeks, like a record spinning endlessly. He coughed at the beach on Sundays, when he went swimming, and would have to return to shore to catch his breath; he coughed during town hall meetings, sometimes so intensely that he was forced to stand up and leave the room; he coughed as he made love to Anna. A few times he'd had to break away from her embrace.

"I'm sorry, but I can't go on," he would say in a faint voice.

One day, his workers sent for him to talk about bringing the harvest up that year, with the heat they'd had. He'd gone to the estate but only managed to say a few words before being seized by a particularly violent bout of coughing, which seemed to never end. Luckily, Daniele was there gathering a few bottles to send as a gift to Mr. James, the clothing shop owner in New York. He immediately offered to drive Carlo home in his 1100.

Carlo had sunk into the passenger seat and rolled down the window.

"What's wrong?" Daniele asked, concerned.

"Oh, it's nothing," Carlo said. "It's this humidity."

"Did you go to the doctor?"

"Come on now," Carlo exclaimed. "Listen, did you think about my offer?" he asked, followed by another bout of coughing.

Daniele hesitated before answering. "Yes, I thought about it. Actually, I haven't made a decision yet," he lied. "You know, sometimes I wonder if this is really the kind of work I want to do."

Carlo made a disappointed smirk. "Oh, young people," he sighed with a wheeze.

Coughing fits exhausted him, made him feel perpetually tired and sleepy. After lunch, he often couldn't keep his eyes open and had to take a nap; in the evening, he'd collapse on the couch after dinner and Anna had to wake him up after turning off the living room lights.

"Carlo, come up to bed, come on," she'd whisper.

"You have to see a doctor," she balked one morning in August, while they were lying belly down on the bed in the gentle shade provided by the drawn curtains.

"It's probably just this air, with this sirocco wind that won't let you breathe," he mumbled, running his finger down the small of her back.

"Your doctor will tell you, if that's the reason."

Carlo exhaled. "You worry too much. Just as it came, so it will go."

"Carlo!" she exclaimed, annoyed by his stubbornness.

"Okay, okay. I'll go."

"When?" Anna insisted.

"This week?"

"No, tomorrow."

Carlo made a serious face, brought his hand to his forehead, and made a military salute. "Sir, yes sir, at your service!" he chuckled.

"Idiot," Anna said with a smile. "You're a real idiot."

———

The doctor was a balding man with a reassuring face. He had Carlo sit bare-chested on the bed and asked him to take deep breaths through his mouth.

"One more," he said several times, with his ear attached to the stethoscope. "Hmm," he murmured at last, before ordering Carlo to get dressed.

He sat at his desk, put on his glasses, and started to write on a piece of paper.

"Here," he said finally, handing it to Carlo, who took it and scanned it.

"I prescribed you an X-ray," the doctor explained. "Just to remove all doubt. Go to Dr. Calò. He's the best in Lecce. His clinic is at the hospital, he'll see you there."

The following morning, Carlo left home very early.

"You're sure you don't want me to come with you?" Anna asked as she sipped her warm milk on the bench in the garden.

"Don't worry, it'll be a quick thing," he said, and bade her goodbye with a kiss on the forehead.

He got into his 1100 and traveled the short distance to Antonio's house. He got out of the car, leaving the door open and the engine running, and knocked on Antonio's door.

His brother opened almost at once. He was wearing pants and a white undershirt.

"Remember what I said yesterday? Well, I changed my mind," Carlo said. "I don't want to go alone."

"No, of course not," Antonio said. "Just give me a minute to finish getting dressed."

At the hospital, after the X-ray, they sat in the waiting room. Carlo was casting nervous glances all around, at the dull green walls, at the chipped tiles on the floor, at the opaque glass on the large windows. "I've never liked hospitals," he said. "And this stench of disinfectant," he added, wrinkling his nose. "It's going to my head."

"I don't think anybody likes them, Carletto."

"Yeah," he murmured, still looking around. "Listen, Antonio . . . I'm sure it's nothing. He'll give me something, maybe some really strong tonic, end of story."

"I'm sure of it," Antonio said with a mild smile.

"Mr. Greco?" Dr. Calò poked his head out the door. He was a slim man with slightly hunched shoulders and an angular face, but he had lively eyes.

Carlo and Antonio stood up at the same time.

"Which one?" The man smiled.

"Me," Carlo said, raising a hand.

"Please, come in."

"I'd like to be there too, if that's okay," Antonio said. "I'm the older brother."

"If the patient is fine with that, I have no problem with it."

The doctor got straight to the point. There was a spot on his left lung, he explained, pointing at the X-ray.

Antonio squeezed Carlo's arm tight. Carlo stared at the slide with an inscrutable expression.

"There's no need to panic, Mr. Greco," the doctor assured him. "We'll start chemotherapy immediately. I have no reason to believe that you won't get better."

Antonio and Carlo got back in the car and remained silent until Lizzanello. But at the gates of town, Carlo stepped on the gas and turned onto the road to Pisignano.

"Where are we going?" Antonio asked.

"To the Great Oak Tree," Carlo said, his eyes fixed on the road and his hands stiff around the wheel.

The countryside opened up before them, lined with long drystone walls. When the Great Oak Tree loomed ahead, imposing, Carlo pulled over to the side of the road. They sat on the scorched earth and leaned onto the thick trunk of the tree. Antonio closed his eyes and squeezed Carlo's hand. They remained quiet for a bit, lulled by the sounds of the foliage rustling in the gentle breeze. Antonio opened his eyes and looked up at the thick weave of the branches.

"Do you remember Nino?" he asked with a little smile.

"Of course I remember."

Antonio chuckled. "I was just thinking about the time we brought him here and he climbed all the way up to the top."

"I nearly broke my neck getting him back. Risked getting a good beating from Papa."

"You and that cat had the same personality: playful and affectionate. In fact, you were his favorite."

"That's not true. He loved us both."

"Yes, but at night he would only sleep next to you."

"That's because you snore. You even snored as a kid." He chuckled.

Antonio pretended to be offended and playfully pushed him away.

"Nino," Carlo murmured with a smile, staring straight ahead. "The memories you just brought back . . ."

They remained silent for a few seconds, each immersed in his own memory of that beloved cat. It had been a carefree time of seemingly infinite happiness.

Then Carlo came back to himself. "I'll heal, Antonio, won't I?" he asked.

"Of course you'll heal."

"You're just saying that to make me feel better."

Antonio turned to look at him. "I don't want to hear you give up on yourself. That's not you. It's me, if anything," he tried to joke.

Carlo's eyes suddenly teared up.

"Hey!" Antonio exclaimed, shaking his arm.

Carlo closed his eyes and let out a single tear, which slowly slid down his face.

Antonio put his arm around Carlo's shoulders and pulled him in. "Don't worry. We'll get through this, Carletto. We'll get through this."

As expected, Anna reacted to the news in her own way. With Carlo she remained completely unfazed; she stared at him confidently and said, "The cure will work, and you'll be fine." Then she rolled up her sleeves and went into the kitchen, where she spent the rest of the afternoon making that which had always had the power to calm her down: pesto. That was how Giovanna found her—bent over the kitchen table pounding away with her mortar. She gently pulled out a chair, sat down, and watched Anna's strained face, tight lips, and wet, red eyes.

Then, without a word, she took the bowl with the pine nuts and passed it to her.

———

At the start of September, Lorenza and Tommaso returned from their vacation in Otranto, where they'd stayed in a summer residence belonging to Tommaso's former in-laws, the same one where he used to spend his summers with Giulia.

"Hi, Papa, can I?" Lorenza poked her head through the open door to Antonio's office. She was wearing a suit with a knee-length skirt and her hair was tied up in a bun. Her face was pale and gaunt, as if she hadn't gone to the beach even for a day.

"Lorenza! I didn't know you were back!" He welcomed her with a hug. "Come, sit down." He pointed to a chair. "How was it?" he asked, sitting in the chair in front of her.

Lorenza sat down and started to look around.

"I haven't been here in ages," she murmured. "Is that new?" she asked, pointing at a lamp on the desk.

Antonio turned around. "Not so new," he said. He looked back at his daughter as he crossed his legs and interlaced his fingers.

"Tell me," he said with a smile. "How was Otranto?"

Lorenza stared straight at him. "I'm pregnant, Papa," she said. "You're the first person I've told."

Antonio looked at her, surprised, then leaped up to hug her. "What great news!"

Lorenza remained motionless and rigid.

He pulled back. "What's wrong? You don't seem happy."

"Yes. No. I mean, yes, I am."

"So what's with the long face?"

"Nothing, Papa. Everything's okay. I'm just a bit tired."

"Your mother will be over the moon," Antonio exclaimed, sitting down again. "I can just see her."

Lorenza gave him a half smile that contained no trace of joy. "Yes, she deserves a bit of happiness," she remarked, standing up.

"Leaving already? You just got here," he said, bewildered.

"I'm going to tell Mom."

"Wait, I'll come with you. We can tell her together."

"No thanks, Papa. I want to tell her on my own."

Lorenza left the oil mill and reached the intersection where she would turn right onto via Giuseppe Garibaldi, which turned into her parents' street. She looked right for a moment but then took the road to the left—the one that led to Daniele's house.

21

Daniele opened the door and froze, watching Lorenza standing on his doorstep with a mixture of surprise and discomfort. He hadn't dared approach her in all those months; he'd promised himself he wouldn't interfere in her life, that he'd respect her position as a married woman and therefore "untouchable." Lorenza had made her choice and there was nothing he could do about it now. Yet in that moment, when he finally saw her an inch from his nose, he stepped back, as if in fear.

"You're not going to invite me in?" she asked, her voice cracking.

"I don't know," he said. "You shouldn't be here."

"Please," she begged him. Then she burst out crying, covering her face with her hands.

Daniele let her in, had her sit on the couch, and brought her a glass of water.

"It's okay, calm down, breathe," he murmured. He sat on the armrest, trying hard to keep his distance.

"Better?" he asked finally, after she put her empty glass on the table.

Lorenza nodded meekly, and then she looked up at him with eyes swollen with tears.

"Why are you here?" he asked.

She went to him. She put a hand on his cheek and caressed it.

Then she kissed him.

Daniele didn't try to stop her, nor did he pull away. He kissed her back, yielding to her, suddenly forgetting everything that wasn't Lorenza. They took off each other's clothing without interrupting their kisses. He laid his naked body on hers and right there, on the couch, they made love for the first time. Afterward, they remained in an embrace for a long time, naked and happy, and then, not yet satisfied, they did it again.

"This was how it was supposed to be," he whispered to her, stroking her hair. "If only you'd trusted me."

"I was furious. And afraid. Afraid of being alone forever, afraid you'd never come back."

He placed his lips on her forehead. "I know," he said.

"You know what the funny thing is?" she continued, sounding bitter. "I've never felt so alone as I have since I got married. It's not Tommaso's fault, he's a dear, very affectionate. But every time he touches me, I want to scream."

Then she confessed: She was expecting a baby, and it was the worst thing that could have happened.

Daniele pushed her away and sat up, with his hair still ruffled, and then he interlaced his fingers and pointed his eyes at the floor.

Lorenza looked down too. "Are you angry?" she asked in a whisper.

He ran a hand through his hair and jumped up. He filled a glass of water and drank it leaning against the sink, while Lorenza stared at him.

"No, I'm not angry," he said finally, in a faint voice. "I'm sorry for you, for your unhappiness."

From that day on, they continued to meet in secret.

He started looking for an apartment in Lecce, somewhere he could set up his studio and where they could finally see each other out of sight of the people of their town. It hadn't been easy to find a place. The ones he'd viewed didn't have the right lighting or were too damp or so run-down that he would have had to do a complete renovation, and he didn't have that much money. In the end, he came across an abandoned little house with three bedrooms and big windows in via Santa Maria del Paradiso, an alley in the Giravolte neighborhood, just around the corner from Porta Rudiae.

"My grandparents used to live here," a young man around his age explained. "I'm certainly not going to use it; I already have a place to live."

In the end, they'd agreed on an annual lump-sum rent, for the time being.

When Tommaso stayed late at the office, Lorenza would slip away and take the bus to Lecce. Although her pregnancy sapped some of her strength, she wanted to help Daniele and participate in his dream from the start; she'd clean the floor, degrease the windows, polish the doors. And when he brought over the Singer, his fabrics, and all his tools in his friend's pickup truck, she was the one who took care of organizing everything.

"And your box with the notebooks?" Lorenza asked as she stacked the rolls of fabric, separating them by hue.

"It doesn't exist anymore," he said. He told her about his argument with his mother, about the designs she'd stolen, of how he'd felt used, of how mean Carmela could be.

"I'm used to it. She'll never change," he said, saddened. "But I don't want to think about it anymore," he added, shaking his head. "It means I'll just have to sketch a new line, even more modern, something that even a woman in New York would wear."

Lorenza nodded sadly. "I think that's a wonderful goal. I'm sure you'll amaze everyone," she said with almost too much enthusiasm.

The truth was that she'd suddenly felt guilty, worried she'd missed a big clue as to what his mother had been up to. She'd realized that she'd been right about what she saw that night at her Uncle Carlo's birthday party. She *thought* Carmela was wearing one of Daniele's designs! But she'd immediately pushed away the thought and hadn't investigated further. *Maybe I should have,* she thought now. *I should have gone straight to Carmela to ask for an explanation.* But what was the point of dwelling on it now? And why tell Daniele, after all this time, especially now that they'd found each other again? No good reason at all. She decided to keep silent.

"We're missing a table, a mirror, chairs, a coatrack," Daniele said, looking around.

"You should have a sign made," Lorenza added. "I'd like to give that to you. It would mean a lot."

He looked at her and smiled. "Thank you. You're a darling."

She went to him, and he stroked her hair and then her belly.

"Do you know what my greatest wish is?" she said. "That this were your child."

He hugged her tight and then whispered, "I'd like that too."

———

Giada was born at home in mid-April 1949, after fourteen hours of labor. Lorenza's family waited on the other side of the door, except for Agata, who stayed by her daughter the whole time, holding her hand while the midwife told her to push. Tommaso kept standing up and sitting down again, unable to keep still.

Antonio kept putting a hand on his shoulder and saying, "Everything will be fine, you'll see. Eat something."

Anna and Giovanna alternated between preparing friselle with tomato and oregano in the kitchen and carrying out the midwife's requests whenever she asked for more clean towels or boiling water. Carlo came by but only stayed for a few minutes.

"I have to lie down," he said apologetically, looking tired with reddish bags under his eyes. Roberto walked him home, holding him up by the arm.

"It's a girl!" Tommaso exclaimed finally, his eyes full of joy. "I really hoped for a girl. My little princess," he said, gently touching her hands.

Exhausted, Lorenza fell asleep. Agata asked everyone to leave the room, laid the baby down in her crib, closed the curtains, and sat by the bed. Every so often, she'd use a handkerchief to dab Lorenza's forehead, which was beaded with sweat, or wet her lips with a bit of water, or quietly go over to have a peek at the little one. When Giada woke up and started to whimper from hunger, Agata took her in her arms and cradled her for a few moments.

"Granny's little love," she whispered with a smile. She opened the curtains slightly and leaned over Lorenza. "The baby needs to eat."

Lorenza grimaced. "I need to sleep," she grumbled, keeping her eyes closed.

"Nurse her and then go back to sleep," Agata said.

Snorting, Lorenza sat up in bed and Agata passed her the baby.

The first feeding turned out to be torture.

"Ouch," Lorenza kept complaining, her face contorted.

"Be patient, the first time is always like this. Then it passes," Agata assured her, sitting next to her on the bed.

"But it hurts," Lorenza insisted, pulling the baby away.

In the following days, it got even worse. Giada was constantly crying and screaming, day and night. Exasperated, Lorenza picked her up and cradled her vigorously, but this seemed to make the baby even more frantic.

"I don't know how to make her stop. She's driving me crazy," Lorenza kept saying to Tommaso, on the verge of tears.

He would get out of bed and say, "Give her to me, I'll try to calm her down."

"What do you think you can do?" she'd snort and start rocking the baby angrily again.

"Let me try," he'd answer, calmly.

And every time, as soon as Tommaso took Giada in his arms, the little one suddenly stopped crying.

"Praised be the Lord," Lorenza would sigh.

"But that's not right, my dear," Agata would reprimand her. She came by early every morning to relieve Tommaso. "Babies can feel it. They feel everything you have inside. And you, right now, have poison inside."

Lorenza hadn't seen Daniele since the day before giving birth, and she felt like she was going mad. She looked at her daughter and couldn't even muster a vague sense of love or tenderness; instead, she saw the pain of each feeding, the sleepless nights, the primordial fatigue, the acute cries that made her want to run away.

But whom could she tell about how she was really feeling inside? No one would understand. They would be indignant or think she was crazy. They would say she was broken.

Anna went to see her every day as soon as she got off work. She'd stroke Giada's little face, brush the little locks of hair off her forehead, and then sit down next to Lorenza.

"You look pale, ma petite," she said one day.

"Thanks, that much I know," Lorenza said rudely.

"Do you feel like talking about it?"

"About what? As you can see, I don't have much to say lately."

Anna turned to look at the crib and watched the baby sleeping peacefully. "Well, I wouldn't say that . . ."

"The truth is that I ruined everything, Auntie."

"You have a beautiful, healthy baby. It doesn't look like you ruined anything, don't you think?"

Lorenza looked irked. "I . . ." she tried to say, but then she stopped.

"You what? Go on, please," Anna prodded her.

Lorenza sighed, and then she stood up and went to look out the window.

"I don't know how to love her," she said without turning around. "I look at her and I don't feel anything. Sometimes . . ." She stopped. "Sometimes I wish she didn't exist. Then I'd be free." A tear streaked down her cheek.

Anna went to stand up from her chair and go to her, but something held her back.

Lorenza dried her face with the palm of her hand, then turned to Anna.

"You're not going to say anything? I know you think I'm a monster."

Anna looked at her, devastated. Where was that cheerful little girl so full of life, who was always so enthusiastic and kind and good? "I'm not thinking that at all," she said in a raspy voice. "I was just thinking about when you were little."

"I haven't been for a while."

"Yes, I know that."

Lorenza moved away from the window and slowly went to sit down in front of her aunt.

"I haven't seen Daniele in two weeks . . ." she whispered. Surprised, Anna tried to say something, but Lorenza stopped her. "Yes, I know you told me so. You warned me. It went as you predicted. Happy?"

"No, not at all," Anna whispered.

"I'm sorry, Auntie. I'm so tired . . ." She looked up and reached out to her. "Forgive me. It's not your fault."

Anna put her hand out and squeezed Lorenza's. It really hurt her to see her niece in that state, a victim of her own wrong choices. She felt a stab of pity for her, imagining her getting into bed with a man she didn't love, night after night. She felt incredible sadness at the thought that she could only be happy during the hours she stole from that life, in the secrecy of her love for Daniele.

"There is something I can do for you, if you want," she said finally. "I can have him come to my house. Tomorrow afternoon. So you can spend some time together, without interruptions. From there, you can be back here in a few minutes if Giada needs something. Agata will stay with her anyway, right? I'll come up with an excuse for your mother, don't worry. I'll tell her you need to relax for a few hours, that I have to cut your hair or something. As for your uncle, don't worry, he'll be gone all afternoon tomorrow. He has to inaugurate that new market area," she explained, making a dismissive gesture. "And Roberto will be with him. As for Giovanna, well, you can trust her."

Lorenza seemed to instantly bloom again. She flung herself at Anna and hugged her. "Oh, Auntie! You would really do that for me?"

Anna stroked her hair. "If it makes you smile like this, yes, ma petite."

———

The following afternoon, Daniele arrived at Anna's house in the throes of total panic. With his heart racing and his breathing labored, he knocked on the door.

Anna opened it and welcomed him with a smile. "Come, take a seat in the living room," she said. "Lorenza will be here any minute. Would you like a coffee? A glass of water? Something tells me you need one."

Daniele stepped forward awkwardly and sat on the couch. "Yes, maybe some water, thank you," he mumbled.

Anna went into the kitchen and Daniele looked around: the big fireplace, the paintings on the walls, the console table with the radio, the record player. He was struck by the absence of knickknacks and those thingamabobs that normally take over people's homes . . . *Ah, no, there is something,* he thought, spotting a papier-mâché doll on the mantel. He stood up and went to get a better look at it. It was a woman dressed in white and holding a basket of juicy red apples. There was a small chip on the side of her face.

Anna returned with the glass of water.

"Nice, isn't it?" she said, nodding at the doll. "I bought it a few months after coming here. The guy at the stand kept it hidden behind rows of dolls. And it was only because of that crack on her face, which made it different from the others. I've never been afraid of appearing different. That's why I still have it, after all these years."

Daniele nodded and smiled.

"Here you are," she said, handing him the glass.

Daniele took a sip.

Anna sat on the couch and patted the empty spot next to her. "Come," she said.

He took a seat next to her, still holding the empty glass.

"You know, I'm happy you're here," she said. "I've been wanting to meet you properly for a long time, talk to you a bit. It's strange, isn't it? Carlo, Lorenza . . . We have two people in common who are very important to us, yet we've never had a chance to chat, you and I."

Daniele's face seemed to instantly relax.

"Yeah, it's strange." He smiled, putting the glass on the coffee table. "I've spoken your name more often than my own," he chuckled. "I think Donna Anna are the words I've uttered the most in all my life."

Anna laughed too.

"I don't know how to thank you for today," he said. "When you showed up at my house yesterday, well, I was afraid you wanted to give me a piece of your mind. I . . . well, I wouldn't want you to get the wrong impression about me. I really care about Lorenza, and she cares about me, and . . ." He stopped short and looked down.

"And you were there first. Is that what you wanted to say?" Anna said gently.

He looked up at her, grateful. "Yes," he said. "Something like that."

Right then they heard a knock at the door.

"There she is," Anna said, and went to open up.

Daniele stood up and stared toward the entrance.

Lorenza walked in, panting, with an impatient look on her face. She ran up to Daniele and hugged him. He held her tight and buried his head in her hair.

Anna went into the kitchen, quietly closed the door, and went out to Giovanna, who'd retreated to the garden when she'd heard Daniele arrive.

After half an hour, they heard a key turning in the front door lock.

Anna quickly opened the kitchen door and ran in, followed by Giovanna. Daniele and Lorenza stood up from the couch, looking alarmed.

Roberto was standing at the door, holding up Carlo by an arm.

"What happened?" Anna ran to them and helped Roberto support Carlo's weight. He clearly wasn't capable of standing on his own.

Daniele rushed over to help them. Then all three of them laid Carlo down on the couch.

There was an expression of profound suffering on Carlo's face. Anna had never seen him like that.

"Carlo," she said, leaning over him. "What's wrong? What happened?"

He coughed and curled up on one side.

"He felt sick," Roberto said, his voice dense with fear.

Daniele knelt by the couch. As if only noticing his presence then, Carlo opened his eyes wide and whispered, "My boy . . ." Then he shifted his gaze to Lorenza, who'd remained motionless, unable to do or say anything.

Carlo closed his eyes slowly, with the grim expression of someone who has understood all too well.

This attack had been stronger than the others, Roberto explained. Carlo was just about to cut the ribbon to inaugurate the marketplace when he turned as pale as wax and was overcome by a cavernous, lacerating cough, like never before. Everyone gathered around him—someone held him, someone patted him on the back, someone screamed, "He's not breathing!" Roberto grabbed onto him until the last cough, when he spit out a large clump of blood.

"Go get Uncle Antonio," Anna said to her son. "We'll take him to the hospital right away."

"I'll go to Papa," Lorenza offered. Before leaving, she gave Daniele a disheartened look filled with longing and nodded as if to say *Tomorrow?*

Anna and Antonio helped Carlo into the back seat of the Fiat 508, and then Antonio got behind the wheel and took the road to the hospital.

Dr. Calò examined Carlo for more than an hour.

All Anna and Antonio could do was wait in the uncomfortable chairs in the sitting area.

Anna leaned her head back against the wall while Antonio hunched forward, his elbows on his knees.

She glanced at her watch. "How long is this going to take?"

Antonio looked at her. "I don't know," he said. "I just don't know."

"He'd never had blood come out before," Anna said.

Antonio nodded and looked straight ahead. He started to tap his foot on the floor.

She ran her fingers through her hair, sighing loudly.

"I'm scared, Antonio," she said. "I'm scared to death," she added, her voice trembling.

He hesitated, then placed a hand on her leg. She grasped it so hard she left nail marks in his hand.

"Me too," Antonio whispered.

The clinic door opened. Carlo came out first, followed by the doctor. They both wore the dark expressions of someone bearing bad news.

Anna and Antonio immediately stood up.

Carlo stared at them with the most desolate look they'd ever seen on his face. Then he took a few steps forward and without a word, opened his arms and pulled them in. Both of them together.

———

About a week later, Anna retrieved the warm-season clothes from the chest, hers and Carlo's, and emptied the wardrobes of the winter clothes, which she laid back in the chest in place of the spring ones. Finally, she gathered all of Carlo's light jackets, cool cotton pants, and shirts, and slipped them into a large bag.

She peeked into the bedroom to make sure Carlo was sleeping. When she heard him snoring, she closed the door and went down the stairs.

"I'm going to the seamstress. Can you stay here with Papa?"

Roberto looked up from a worn copy of *Romeo and Juliet*. He'd been chosen to play Romeo in the school play, so after he did his homework, he spent hours and hours each day reading and memorizing his lines. Sometimes he went up to his parents' room, lay down in bed next to Carlo, and kept him company while practicing.

"Yes, of course, don't worry," he said.

Anna tossed the bag over her shoulder and took the road to the dressmaker's shop.

When Carmela opened the door, the two women stood there and stared at each other for a few seconds. From the sadness in Carmela's eyes

Anna could tell that she already knew everything. As usual, it had been impossible to keep a secret in that town, and the fact that Carlo had taken time off from his role as mayor and from the winery had only served to confirm the rumors.

"Tràsi," Carmela said, letting Anna in.

Anna placed the bag on the table. In a firm tone, she explained that those were Carlo's clothes, and that she'd brought them to be taken in. They were at least two sizes too big now.

Carmela opened the bag and extracted the items gently, one by one, placing them on the table as she went. Anna had already fixed some pins to the clothes to indicate where it was necessary to shorten something or take it in.

"I know it's a lot of work," Anna said. "But I ask that you please do it as quickly as possible. I'll pay you double, if needed."

Carmela shook her head. "You see? It's remarks like that. That's how we know you are and always will be an outsider."

"Why, what did I say?" Anna frowned.

Carmela looked her straight in the eye.

"Around here, when one of us falls ill, no one would dream of making them pay, or making their family pay, for services," she said harshly. "Come back in five days and you'll find them ready," she added before dismissing her.

Carmela closed the door, annoyed, and went to sit back at her table. She put on her glasses and tried to go back to her work but couldn't. She shifted her gaze to Carlo's clothes and stared at them. She pulled a shirt from the pile; it was light blue with mother-of-pearl buttons. He'd been wearing it the day he showed up at her door again asking, "May I come in?" And she, like an idiot, had let him.

She brought the shirt to her face and sniffed it, closing her eyes: Carlo's smell, that mixture of spiced smoke and minty aftershave. She would have known it anywhere.

22

I have night's cloak to hide me from their eyes,
And but thou love me, let them find me here.
My life were better ended by their hate,
Than death prolonged, wanting of thy love.

Roberto was rehearsing his lines standing atop a ladder while Carlo, sitting in his armchair with a checkered blanket over his legs, tried hard to follow the text. Chemotherapy had caused all his hair to fall out, leaving him completely bald.

"How did I do?" Roberto asked.

"Fine, fine," Carlo said in a faint voice. "I'll let you know if you make a mistake." He coughed.

"You're tired. Let's take a break," Roberto said, stepping down from the ladder.

"Yes, just for a moment," Carlo said, placing the book on the table.

Roberto went to sit on the carpet at his father's feet and leaned his head against his legs. "Papa, I have to ask you something."

"What is it."

"What did it feel like when you met Mama? I mean, how did you know you were in love?"

Carlo thought for a moment. "I think I felt . . . like I was home. That I could show my most vulnerable side, knowing that she would understand, accept it and take care of it, and not use it against me. You know what I mean?"

Roberto nodded. "I think so."

"Why do you ask? Is there a girl you like?"

"So much, Papa," he said with a sigh. "It's just that I don't know if she likes me back."

Carlo smiled. "What's her name?"

"Maria. Her name is Maria. She plays Juliet."

Carlo chuckled and coughed at the same time. "Ah, it must be fate, then. But I promise neither I nor your mother will get in your way," he joked.

"Papa," Roberto said again, after a few seconds of silence.

"What is it?"

"I think I'm in love. When I'm with her, I feel like I'm home too."

———

Carlo was no longer leaving the house. Dr. Calò had been clear: He had to submit to total rest, avoid all manner of effort, and not push his luck with his already worn-out body. He'd been brutally honest: The tumor had spread in an unpredictable way.

"How long do I have left?" Carlo asked at the last visit.

The doctor's face darkened, and then he interlaced his fingers on his desk.

"I can't say. Just focus on getting better."

In those weeks, Anna didn't leave him alone for one second. She'd taken leave from work, for the first time in fourteen years, to be close to him. "Doctors can be wrong. They're human too, for Christ's sake," she kept saying. "You'll get better, I know it."

She refused to accept the possibility that he might not make it; she was convinced that Carlo's will to live would prevail over his illness. He wanted to tell her that she wasn't helping him at all, by being like that. He didn't want to be deluded by words of hope; he didn't want to evade reality to follow a mirage. He knew he would feel infinitely worse if he convinced himself that he could live longer than he actually had . . . The moment of goodbye would become even more unacceptable and harrowing. He wanted to say *Shut up, stop it, don't talk to me about all the things we still have to do together. Don't talk to me about the future. It hurts me, can't you see that it hurts me?*

Yet Carlo could never bring himself to do it, to tell her how he really felt. His heart broke at the idea that she, too, was trying to protect herself from the pain, to postpone it for as long as possible. He kept coughing up blood, feeling breathless, as if he had a boulder on his chest that he couldn't take off. He could see that he was only getting worse. Anna could see it too.

One day he asked her to send for the notary.

Her face clouded over and she crossed her arms over her chest.

"You're acting as if you're about to die for real," she said. "Stop it!"

Carlo tried to sit up in bed, but in vain. "Please, Anna, do as I ask," he begged her with a wheeze.

In the end, Antonio had to send for the notary, a dapper little man who showed up with a black leather briefcase and a freshly shaven face, judging by the little cut on his left cheek. Anna opened the door and barely acknowledged him. Then she went into the kitchen and slammed the door behind her.

"My apologies," Antonio said, embarrassed, leading the way up the stairs to the bedroom.

Carlo informed the notary that his brother would be present at the dictation of the will. Antonio locked the door, sat in a chair, crossed his legs, and clasped his hands together on his knee. This was perhaps the most difficult moment in his life, but he forced himself to seem strong, to be the rock on which Carlo had always leaned, to not show the anguish he felt inside. *I have to take care of him first*, he kept thinking to give himself courage. He knew his brother and he knew exactly what he needed; pretending that this wasn't serious wouldn't help him one bit. On the contrary, it would only exacerbate the fear and loneliness he was already feeling.

Antonio listened in silence as the notary took down Carlo's words. He was leaving the house on via Paladini to Anna, along with all the money. Roberto would inherit seventy percent of the Greco Winery and estate. The remaining thirty percent would go to Daniele Carlà for his "unshakable dedication, high profits brought to the winery, and the precious experience he'd gained, unequal to that of any other employee. Furthermore, he has earned my complete and unconditional trust. I'm absolutely certain that he will continue to make the winery prosper."

"With the hope," he added, "that Roberto and Daniele will manage it together in a peaceful and fruitful collaboration worthy of the two most talented young men I've ever met."

Antonio wriggled in his seat; he was about to say something, but Carlo nodded at him as if to tell him there was nothing to be done: this was how he was going to leave his estate to his boys.

But once the notary left, Antonio closed the door and let loose.

"How are you going to explain this to Anna?" he asked, genuinely shaken. "And how do you think Roberto will react? You can't go off with this massive plot twist. What if they start to suspect something? You can't let them find out this way, when"—he took a deep breath—"when you won't be able to explain yourself anymore. You can't do it, Carlo. You have to tell them right away, now."

Carlo turned his head away from Antonio.

"Or, please, change your will while you still can. For the love of God."

"You're worrying too much," Carlo said in a feeble voice. "They'll assume I was thinking about business, just business. Of the good of the winery, and of their future. I know Anna. I know my son," he concluded, out of breath.

"And what if you're wrong?" Antonio retorted, but Carlo interrupted him.

"I don't want to talk about it anymore."

Antonio sighed and placed both hands on the footboard, defeated.

Visitors started arriving in droves: winery workers, city hall colleagues, party allies, town council members. They all wished him a speedy recovery, advised him to not give up.

"We miss you."

"Don't worry, everything is proceeding as usual at the winery."

"Quit kidding around, we're looking forward to having you back."

"As soon as you're back, we'll pick up that project again."

"We'll talk about it when you're back on your feet."

Carlo always felt exhausted after these visits, overcome by the endless stream of empty words and absurd promises. Finally, he asked Anna not to let anyone in anymore. She had to send them all away, tell them he was resting, that he couldn't see them. He no longer wanted to see a single soul outside his family, he said.

"Oh," he added, before she closed the bedroom door. "But if Daniele comes, let him in. He can be here—he doesn't bother me."

Since Carlo had gotten worse, Daniele had decided to postpone the opening of his studio to take care of the winery.

"I owe him," he explained to Lorenza. Soon, he found himself replacing Carlo in all his responsibilities: He doled out the pay, negotiated with workers, gave instructions, checked deliveries, kept the books in order, ensured that nothing was delayed. Once a week, usually on Saturdays, he visited Carlo to give him a detailed report.

Carlo listened and nodded, pleased. "Very good. You're doing a great job," he said each time.

It was on one of those mornings that Carlo decided to talk to him about the will and the thirty percent he would receive.

"So you're prepared," he explained.

Daniele was stunned. "I don't know what to say . . . I . . . I wasn't expecting it . . . Why have you already written your will?" he asked, staring at him. "I want you to get better, Carlo, and . . ." His voice cracked.

"Come here, my boy," Carlo said, patting the bed next to him.

Daniele obeyed.

"I don't know if I'll get better," Carlo said. He was interrupted by a bout of coughing. "I want to take care of things while I still can. You understand, right?" he said, with a gasp.

Daniele sniffled and rubbed his teary eyes.

"I don't want to think about it," he murmured, shaking his head.

Carlo pursed his lips and placed a hand on his shoulder.

"Why me?" Daniele continued. "Does your son know? And Anna?"

Carlo stared at him intensely. Only God knew how much he wanted to tell him the truth. How much he wanted Daniele to look at him—just once; he didn't ask for more—with the eyes of a son. Yet he wasn't able to speak. The words died in his mouth, scratching his throat.

"Because you deserve it, my boy," he said instead. "You deserve it. It was my decision. Only mine. You don't have to worry about Anna and Roberto."

Just before Daniele left, Carlo asked him to promise him something.

"Anything you want."

"Lorenza," Carlo sighed. Daniele immediately went rigid. "I know what's going on, you know. And it's not okay, my boy. She's a married woman, she has a daughter. This thing will only bring trouble. To everyone. My brother would be terribly upset. Let her go; think of yourself. You'll find another girl to care for."

Daniele looked away. "I better go," he said, slowly standing up. "You focus on resting."

As he watched him leave, Carlo couldn't help but think back to the words don Ciccio had spoken that day, in the darkness of his bedroom: *Don't get any illusions that it'll work.* He'd been right.

———

Daniele left Carlo's house confused and dazed. Without knowing why, since he still hadn't forgiven her, he went straight to his mother's house. He opened the door to the dressmaker's shop and found her sitting at her Singer with her glasses halfway down her nose, held in place by a golden chain.

"My son is here, it's a miracle," she said sarcastically.

"Hi," he said coldly.

"You haven't come by in ages."

Daniele didn't answer and collapsed into a chair with a sigh.

Carmela stood up from the Singer and went to sit opposite her son. She slid her glasses off her nose and let them fall to her chest.

"Do you want a coffee?"

Daniele shook his head. "I just had one. At Carlo's," he said.

Carmela crossed her legs and rested her hands on the armrests. "And how is he?"

Daniele shrugged, looking afflicted.

Carmela swallowed. "What does the doctor say?"

"I don't know," he whispered. "But I don't think it's good, since Carlo wrote his will."

"Oh," Carmela said, surprised, and sitting up straight. "How do you know that? Those are private matters. Did his wife tell you?" she asked, scornfully.

"No," Daniele retorted, standing up. "He told me."

"And why would he tell you? What do you have to do with it?"

"I don't know what I have to do with it. I'm still wondering that."

She felt her heartbeat speed up. "I'm not following."

Daniele leaned on the table. "He left me thirty percent of the estate and the winery. Unbelievable . . . It makes no sense. Why me, of all people?"

Carmela stared at him for a while, speechless, as her thoughts piled up. She saw herself as a girl, Carlo, who was crazy about her and wanted her at all costs, the first time they'd made love, the tears she'd shed when he'd left her with that miserable letter, Daniele's birth, the rage she'd harbored throughout the years Carlo had been gone, the excitement she'd felt when she saw him again after all that time, the overwhelming emotion of returning to his arms, the lingering resentment after he'd left her for the second time . . . but more than all of this she thought back to don Ciccio's words.

In the end, he'll give him something. And it won't be a small slice of the pie. Trust what I say, I know how things go. Blood always wins.

She felt a small, almost imperceptible quiver of pure joy. She stood up and went to her son. She took his face in her hands and looked him in the eye.

"You must never again ask yourself that. Got it? Never again. You worked hard and you earned it. Nisciunu has given you anything as a gift. Nobody," she said.

———

On the evening of June 21, Anna carefully placed her and Carlo's dinner on a wooden tray and took it up to the bedroom.

"Bread and tomato, with plenty of oil, just the way you like it," she announced, walking into the room.

Carlo answered with a moan, without opening his eyes.

Anna put the tray on the nightstand and sat down next to him. "Let's eat something, come on, Carlo."

"I can't, I feel nauseous."

"At least a few bites, please."

He shook his head and opened his eyes. "I can't."

"Let's wait, then," Anna said patiently. "Maybe you'll be hungry in a bit."

"Lie down next to me," he said, placing his hand on the empty side of the bed.

Anna took off her shoes and slipped under the covers, curling up next to him.

"Where's Roberto?" Carlo asked.

"He went to the movies."

"With that girl?"

"What girl?" Anna exclaimed, raising her head.

Carlo smiled faintly. "The one he likes."

"And why haven't I heard about this?"

"Because you're jealous and you'd scare her away," he joked.

"Me, jealous? What nonsense!"

Carlo chuckled meekly, then closed his eyes again. "Keep talking to me, Anna. What movie did he go see?"

"I don't know, he didn't tell me," she said, with a knot in her throat.

"Does it have that Clark Gable of yours?"

"If that were the case, I would have gone to see it too, leaving you here all alone," she said, trying to make him laugh.

"Ah," Carlo said, smacking his lips. "Is he better-looking than me? You'd leave me for Clark Gable?"

She curled up in his arms and held him tight. "No. I don't like anybody more than you."

Carlo gave a hint of a smile. "That's how it should be, my love," he said. He started to stroke her face with the tips of his fingers. Then he opened his eyes and looked at her intensely.

"What is it?" Anna asked, smiling.

"I know what you were about to ask me, that day."

"When?" she said, amused.

"You wanted to know if I agreed with those men from the council, about the Home for Women," Carlo said. Anna opened her mouth to speak, but Carlo continued. "Do I think the idea is too modern for this town? Yes. Do I think you should set it up anyway? Yes, a million times."

Anna smiled and stroked his cheek.

"I'm sorry we haven't talked about it since," he added. "Promise me you won't give up on it."

"I won't give up. I'll get it done sooner or later. It's just that, at the moment, it's not at the forefront of my mind."

"Use our funds. Set up something private, without having to ask anyone for anything," Carlo insisted, but a bout of coughing interrupted him.

"Shh, no more talking," she said. "Try to sleep a bit."

They both closed their eyes and within a few minutes, they fell asleep embracing and with their hands interlaced.

The dinner on the tray remained uneaten.

The following morning, when Anna opened her eyes, Carlo was gone.

PART THREE

23

A Year and a Half Later

In the shaded bedroom, Anna opened Carlo's wardrobe and stroked the jackets hanging in a row, and then she gently took them in her arms and sank her nose into them, breathing in deeply. The smell of his minty aftershave was fading more and more every day. She closed the door and went downstairs. The little metal box with Carlo's cigars was still there on the side table. She lifted the lid; there were only two left. She pulled one out and brought it to her nostrils, smelling it with her eyes closed. Then she lit it with a match, puffed a few times, coughed, and finally rested it on the ashtray, allowing it to burn out while the smell of spice permeated the room.

She sat down on the couch and pulled her knees up to her chest. Carlo would have turned forty-seven the next day. *No doubt he would have thrown one of his memorable parties,* she thought. She looked around the silent room and imagined the scene: trays overflowing with food, crystal glasses brimming with Donna Anna, the music coming from the record player, the chattering and smiles of the guests, their evening gowns . . . but most of all him, Carlo, elegant as ever, with his infectious laugh echoing all around. If she closed her eyes, she thought she could hear it. She'd always hated those parties, the hordes of people that converged on her house, the mess they left behind; yet in that moment she would have given all the gold in the world just to celebrate Carlo's birthday again and to hear him say, at the end of the night, when they were finally alone and she was gathering plates and glasses, "Why, what a lovely party it was, wasn't it?"

Anna took a deep breath, trying to dissolve the knot forming in her throat. She stood up from the couch and headed toward her jardin secret, where Giovanna was balancing on a wooden stepladder, gathering the last pomegranates of the season and placing each one in a large wicker basket hanging from her forearm.

Anna crossed her arms in front of her chest and went to join her. "I'd say we have enough," she said, pointing at the basket.

"One more," Giovanna said, smiling. She picked a ripe red pomegranate.

They went back into the kitchen and sat opposite each other at the table, with the basket in the middle. They started to extract the seeds to make juice, gathering them in a bowl. Giovanna secretly popped a handful into her mouth every so often.

She never returned to the farmhouse in Contrada La Pietra. Someone with family in Vernole had told her that don Giulio was now the town priest and that he was "helping" an unfortunate young woman with blue eyes.

After Carlo's death, Giovanna's presence had been a true blessing for Anna. She'd instinctively known how to stand by her friend, which was through small but constant daily overtures. In the morning, in the immediate weeks after his passing, she had brought Anna her warm milk in bed, and then, in a calm tone, had invited her to get up, wash, dress, brush her hair. Initially, Anna wouldn't even react, so Giovanna would go, leaving her alone in the darkness. Then Anna had started to obey Giovanna's requests mechanically, almost robotically. Giovanna would help her into a dress or brush her hair, but never force her. Soon, she'd started to make a few timid suggestions, like "Shall we go to the market, since the pantry is empty?" Or "Do you feel like taking a walk, with this beautiful sun?" Or even "Shall we make pesto together this morning?"

She'd tried to alleviate the pain of Carlo's death by giving Anna what she needed most: the silence in which to let her memories decant. Just like in that moment, where she and Anna were shelling the pomegranates without talking.

Once the bowl was full, Anna stood up, laid a cotton kitchen towel on the table, and transferred the seeds onto it by the handful. She tied it closed and started to wring it, letting the juice filter through the weft of the fabric into a carafe.

"Maman, I'm back!" Roberto's piercing voice came in from the entryway.

"We're in here!" Anna said.

Roberto appeared in the kitchen and greeted them with a smile. "Just in time for fresh juice," he exclaimed, picking up the carafe and pouring himself a glass of the dark red liquid.

"Where did you go?" Anna asked, sitting down.

Her son flashed her a mischievous grin, identical to the ones Carlo used to make, and Anna's heart skipped a beat.

Roberto took one last sip, smacked his lips, and put his glass down.

"I was with Maria," he admitted finally. Then, as if he wanted to apologize for something, he bent down to plant a kiss on his mother's cheek. He also gave one to Giovanna, who blushed and bit her lip.

"Did you finish your homework for tomorrow?" Anna asked.

"I just need to do the Latin translation."

"Well go on, then, up to your room to study," she said. "I'll come up later and we can look at it together."

"Sir, yes sir!" Roberto laughed.

Anna shook her head, amused, and followed him with her eyes. Yes, despite everything, Roberto was still smiling. Carlo would have been proud of such a brave son.

Giovanna filled two glasses with juice and handed one to Anna, who lifted it and said, "Santé!" as the smell of the cigar burning in the living room reached the kitchen.

———

It was a dismal morning in late November, raining so hard that Anna was awakened by the sound of the water hitting the shutters. She pushed her sleep mask up to her forehead and raised herself onto her elbows, remaining there for a few moments to peer at the gray sky beyond the windowpane, obscured by the dense wind and rain. A pang of concern shot through her and she quickly tried to shoo it away, throwing off her blanket and putting on her slippers. She put on her blue silk robe and went down to the kitchen, which was darkened by the bad weather. While she waited for her milk to warm up, she tried to take a deep breath, but the air got caught in her lungs, as sometimes happened lately. She felt her heart beat faster and she instinctively brought a hand to her chest. Ever since Carlo passed, there were moments when she thought she could no longer breathe, as if the air had run aground somewhere inside her. She'd open her mouth wide and try to let as much air in as possible, but this didn't always work, and the matter caused her a great deal of anxiety. She became overwhelmed with the certainty that she would collapse on the ground, suffocated. Then, after a few minutes, everything would return to normal. Each time, the thought of it happening again and again frightened her.

She turned off the flame and poured the warm milk into her cup. Suddenly, the wind rattled the shutter on the French window so loudly it made her jump. Grasping her cup, she went to the window, looked out at the drenched garden, and drank her first sip of milk. She tried to take another deep breath and this time the air seemed to flow unobstructed. She brought her hand back to her chest and felt her heart return to regular rhythm, which calmed her. At least a little.

"Happy birthday," she whispered, staring at the rain, which was starting to thin out.

After getting dressed, she set the table for Roberto and Giovanna's breakfast and then left a note by their cups: *I went out early, don't worry.* Her watch showed almost seven o'clock. She threw her coat over her uniform jacket and adjusted her cap on her head. She went out into the courtyard, grabbed the handles of the Bianchi, and climbed on. She had no idea where she was going, but she couldn't stay in the house a minute longer. Not on Carlo's birthday. Not without him.

The streets were empty and an acrid and earthy smell filled the air. The Fiat 1100, still in the same spot where Carlo had parked it, was shiny and dripping wet. Anna shot a fleeting glance at what remained of the death announcement plastered on the wall by the door: strips of tattered, faded paper, writing that was now indecipherable. Only the C and the L survived of Carlo's name along with the drawing of a black cross on the top right. On the bottom, like a warning, one word remained perfectly legible: PASSED.

She started pedaling slowly, as the light rain stung her face. She passed Antonio's house and stopped. Beyond the curtains in the study, where he slept, the light was already on. She stared at the window and saw Antonio's silhouette against the light. She got off her bike, leaned it against the wall, picked up a pebble, and threw it at the glass. A moment later, Antonio pushed aside the curtain and saw Anna waving. His gaze softened and he motioned for her to wait. Soon after, he opened the door and went out to her, closing his coat over his pajamas but letting his slippers get soaked.

"What are you doing out at this hour?"

"Nothing. The rain woke me up," she said.

Antonio looked at her, pursing his lips. The circles under Anna's eyes had become darker in the past year, as if all her pain had gathered in one spot on her face.

"Yeah," he murmured. "It woke me up too."

"Can you hold me?" she asked out of the blue. "Please."

Antonio nodded and gently took her in his arms.

Anna rested her head on his chest and closed her eyes. "I don't know if I can make it through today," she said.

He rested his chin on her head. "I know," he said, with a knot in his throat that cracked his voice. "I know."

My Carletto is gone. Antonio didn't know how many times he'd articulated that thought. Hundreds, maybe thousands. It was the only way he could convince himself it had really happened. He hadn't even believed it when he'd watched Agata calmly and confidently dress his brother's lifeless body in his Sunday best, nor when he'd helped to carry the coffin on his shoulder from the church to the cemetery. Those moments were a blur, as if they had been a dream. The first time he realized Carlo was gone forever was the morning after the funeral, when he'd opened his eyes and that thought—*My Carletto is gone*—hit him like a punch, painful and inexorable. He'd just woken up in a world where his brother no longer existed.

"I couldn't breathe this morning," Anna whispered, without dissolving the hug.

Antonio sighed and started to stroke her back. "Give me a moment to get dressed," he said. "I'm going to take you somewhere."

He went inside and reemerged a few minutes later. Anna was waiting for him sitting on a step. The rain had stopped completely, and a faint light filtered through the clouds.

"Let's take the car," he said.

"Where are we going?"

"No questions. It's a surprise."

They got into the Fiat 508 and drove toward Pisignano. They rode in silence while Anna looked out at the sky, where a small rainbow had appeared.

Antonio pulled over by a drystone well. Just beyond it, the Great Oak Tree stood tall.

"What is this place?" Anna asked, leaning forward.

"Come," he said, getting out of the car.

He went up to the tree and placed a hand on the damp trunk. Then he looked up at the tree's canopy, thick and enveloping and still dripping with raindrops.

Anna joined him, looking at him questioningly.

"This is the Great Oak Tree," he explained. "It was our spot. Mine and Carlo's."

She frowned. "And why didn't I know about this?"

"No one did," he said. "We wanted it to be just ours . . . When I feel like I can't go on, when I miss my brother like air, I come here. Every time. I sit against the tree and I speak to him, as if he were sitting next to me."

Anna leaned against the trunk and crossed her arms over her chest. "Does it work?"

"For a bit," he said. "You know," he continued after a moment, "I think you need one too. A place where you can be with him. A place that brings you peace."

Anna shook her head. "There is no such place," she retorted, decisively. "No place I shared with Carlo can give me peace. His absence leaves nothing but a great void."

"Then fill it. The void, I mean."

"I envy anyone who can do that," Anna said. She kicked a little pile of wet dirt, which stuck to her shoes.

"Do it with your happiest memories," he said. "Carlo would want us to think about him with joy. He would want us to pop one of his bottles and toast to him, to his life."

Anna bowed her head and a tear rolled down her cheek.

Antonio rested his temple her on hers. "Today it's harder, I know." He dried her face with his thumb.

"You know, anytime I needed an answer, I knew I could find one in books. It has always been that way," she said, her voice breaking. "But this time . . ."

"This time you can't find it . . ." he continued.

"Right."

"I get it. I haven't been able to read a single page . . . As if I already knew I wouldn't find comfort. Yet there are writers who by yielding to their pain learned to talk about it with genuine honesty."

Anna let her damp eyes wander across the tree's canopy. "Curious, isn't it? That you found comfort here in the silence, in the absence of words?"

"Oh no, the words are there. But they're my own."

"The ones you speak to Carlo."

"Yes, the ones I speak to him."

She took a breath and forced the air out of her mouth. Then she glanced wearily at her watch. "I have to go to work, though I'd rather stay here all day."

Antonio smiled. "I'd prefer that too. Come on, let's go, I'll take you back." He put his arm around her waist and led her to the car.

As soon as he stepped back into the house, Antonio heard the clinking of dishes coming from the kitchen. He took off his coat and hung it up.

Agata, still in her robe, was washing the dishes from the night before. She turned and looked at him with her eyes still swollen from sleep.

"Where were you?" she asked. "The car was gone. And then I saw the bicycle outside . . ." she accused in a tone that fell somewhere between puzzled and bitter. She dried her hands on the tea towel.

Antonio sat down. "Yes, Anna came."

"And what did she want at this hour?"

"Did you forget what day it is?" he snapped.

Agata didn't respond. She turned her back on him and started to unscrew the coffee maker. "I know what day it is," she said finally. She rinsed the coffee grounds out of the moka pot, poured water into the bottom, then filled the filter with ground coffee.

"Then it's not really the time to make a fuss, don't you think?" Antonio said, standing up and heading for the door.

"Where are you going? I'm making coffee," she said.

"I'll have mine at the bar," he said, going out.

Agata watched him leave, one hand grasping the sink and the other on her hip.

She shook her head with a sigh, and then she screwed the moka pot back into position and set it over the flame.

She sat down and started to tap her fingers on the table. These days, her husband was all "Anna this," "Anna that," or "I'm going to see if Anna needs anything," he'd say, leaving the house early in the mornings. "Today Anna seemed a little better," he'd inform her with relief when he came home for dinner. Or "She seems thinner. She's not eating enough. We should have her over for dinner." In the weeks following the funeral, Agata had spent hours on end cooking for her sister-in-law and nephew, and even for "that Giovanna woman." She cleaned their house before and after the wake; she visited every day, offering to relieve them of all manner of burdens. Yet it was never enough for her husband. If he even noticed at all.

More than a year had gone by since Carlo's death, and no one had ever asked how *she* was doing. She cared about her brother-in-law; she really did. He had treated her with true kindness and always made her laugh with his constant jokes. Yes, Agata had shed genuine tears of sorrow for his death. Despite this, her mourning seemed invisible to Antonio and Anna; *they* were the ones suffering, the ones who needed understanding and comfort, the only ones who had *really* lost him.

"Oh, to hell with them," she burst out, roused from her thoughts by the gurgling of the coffee maker. She stood up, turned off the flame, and poured coffee into her cup. She drank it standing up, quickly, then went upstairs to get dressed. Like every morning, she was going to look after Giada while Lorenza and Tommaso were at work. *Thank God for that creature*, she thought as she ascended the stairs, gripping the handrail.

———

"They have to take the land by force," Carmine was saying, all fired up. He was leaning against the door to the back room, explaining to Elena why it was "right, actually sacrosanct," that workers occupy the land around Arneo, an enormous estate of tens of thousands of hectares between Nardò and Taranto. It was owned by a baron who'd been neglecting it. Ever since Carmine had joined the CGIL, the Italian General Confederation of Labor, he had started supporting the cause of the farmers and now he wouldn't talk about anything else. *Actually, he's never talked this much since I've known him*, Anna thought as she walked into the office in the middle of his little rally.

When the agrarian reform was approved that October, Carmine had come into work seething with rage and ranting against the government, which had completely excluded Lecce's territories from the liquidation law and the expropriation of uncultivated lands. Since then, he had done nothing but reiterate, day after day, that the workers needed to mobilize, to fight and force the government to include the Salento in its land allocation plans.

"Am I right, letter carrier?" Carmine asked her, turning toward her. In all those years, this was perhaps the first time they'd found themselves on the same side of an argument. The fact that Anna agreed with the farmers had suddenly altered the nature of their relationship; until then, Carmine had treated her coldly, even rudely. Now he was openly displaying a sort of sympathy mixed with kindness.

"Sure are," Anna nodded, placing her mailbag on the table. "Hoping that it's not just another empty gesture, though."

"Exactly!" Carmine exclaimed.

"Bah, I just don't get it," Elena grumbled. "It's as if you came to my house and told me that from now on it's going to be your house. Based on what, pray tell?"

"You'll have to get it through your noggin!" Carmine exclaimed, resuming his rally.

Anna watched them for a few seconds, then looked down with a sly smile and started to sort the mail. Tommaso and Lorenza arrived together soon after. He greeted everyone and smiled as usual. Anna noticed that Tommaso had recently stopped wearing the hat Lorenza had given him for Christmas three years before, and which he hadn't taken off until now.

Her niece passed her as she made a beeline for the telegraph office.

"Good morning, you!" Anna called.

Lorenza turned around. Her face was dark. "Yes, sorry, Auntie. Good morning," she mumbled, and then she crossed into the back room, squeezing between Carmine and the doorframe.

"We have to deal a decisive blow to the estate," Carmine was saying.

"God, you're still going on about that? Enough, for God's sake," Lorenza complained.

"You should listen to them too, kiddo," he scolded her.

"Excuse me, kiddo who?" Lorenza shot back.

"All right, all right, everyone get to work," Tommaso said in a conciliatory tone. Lorenza sat at her desk.

Anna watched him as she put her bag around her neck; wrinkles had appeared around his eyes and forehead, and his face showed deep exhaustion, making him look much older than his forty-three years. She felt a pang of guilt but quickly shooed it away.

Tommaso noticed he was being watched and looked at her. Anna quickly bowed her head and said, "I'm off. See you later."

She had just reached the door when Lorenza caught up with her.

"Wait, Auntie," she said. "Can I talk to you for a minute?"

Tommaso looked up again.

"Of course," Anna said. "But be quick. Walk me to my bike." When they were outside, Anna asked, "What is it?"

"Can I leave Giada with you for a few hours this afternoon? From three to five at the most."

"Are you going back to Lecce? To him?" Anna lifted an eyebrow.

Lorenza nodded. "Well?" she asked again. "Can you watch her or not?"

"Yes, of course. You know I'm happy to spend time with her."

Lorenza's face opened into a wide smile. "Thank you, thank you, thank you!" she said, giving her a hug.

Still smiling, she went back inside, and without so much as glancing at Tommaso, she sat back down at her desk. "What a beautiful complexion you have today!" she said cheerfully to Elena. "You look great."

Elana gave her a puzzled look.

"What do you mean, great? I didn't sleep a wink last night," she said. And then went on yet another rant to explain how badly her sleep had been damaged since the war.

Lorenza didn't hear a word; she was thinking about how in just a few hours, she'd be back in Daniele's arms. She hadn't seen him in six excruciatingly long days.

———

In mid-December, the shipment of Donna Anna, vintage 1950, was ready to leave the winery for New York. Daniele took care of it down to the last detail, adding to each crate a handwritten thank-you note and a bottle of Don Carlo, the Greco Winery's first red, which had been bottled in the first months of that year. Carlo, unfortunately, never had a chance to see it. It had been Daniele's idea to name it after him, and when he'd suggested it to Anna and Roberto, she'd taken his hand.

"He would have loved that," she said, her voice tinged with emotion.

Even Roberto teared up a bit before asking if he could try a glass. Daniele had filled a glass for them both, explaining how best to savor it.

"First, you swirl the wine in the glass like this, see? This is how to release the aromatic compounds," he said. "Then you tilt the glass at the nose to breathe the scent in more deeply."

"What do you smell?" he asked after a pause.

Roberto stuck his nose in the glass, then took it out and assumed a thoughtful expression.

"It smells like wine," he said finally, with some embarrassment.

Daniele and Anna burst out laughing, and then Daniele asked him to try again. "Can you smell the cherry, for example? Or the blackberry?" Roberto sniffed it again. "You should also be able to smell the pepper."

"Yes," Roberto said hesitantly. "But I only smell them now that you said it."

"The nose needs to be refined; it takes practice," Daniele assured him with a smile. "And now the taste test."

He took a small sip of wine and kept it in his mouth for a while, and then he swallowed it. "Can you sense that soft and velvety feel that lingers in your mouth?"

Roberto copied him and then nodded, but he didn't seem too sure.

"You'll see, in time you'll taste all these things," Daniele concluded, giving him a light pat on the back.

The days after Carlo's death had been very difficult for Daniele, and not just because of the pain of losing the man who had changed his life. He'd become certain that the will would bring discord, leading to fights and misunderstandings, and that his relations with the Greco family, *Lorenza's* family, would be irreparably damaged. He felt that if his mother had been in their place, she would have gone ballistic and opposed the will with steely determination. As he headed to the notary for the reading, he even considered renouncing that thirty percent, just to leave everything as it was and avoid muddying the waters. He'd practically tiptoed into the office looking like someone who was ready to apologize for something. He'd shaken Anna's and Roberto's hands as they sat next to each other, and then he'd sat in the chair left vacant for him. Throughout the reading of the will, he kept glancing at Anna and Roberto, wringing his hands, dreading the moment when the notary would utter his name. But Anna and Roberto's reaction floored him: They remained composed and silent, nodding every so often.

"If that's what Carlo decided, he had valid reasons. I'm sure it was for the good of the winery, and that's enough for us," Anna had assured him once they'd left the office. "Roberto has to finish high school, so until then, you will have to take care of it on your own."

To which Roberto, ruffling his hair comically, had said, "You'll have to teach me everything. I don't know the first thing about wine."

Daniele closed the last crate. "We're done for the morning," he told the cellar master—the one who'd taken his place when he was in New York—and shook his shoulder amiably. He glanced at his watch and wondered if he could still make the twelve-thirty bus to Lecce: he could draw for a few hours and then come back to the winery in the afternoon. He couldn't wait to finish a sketch he'd started a few days before. These days, he only managed to get to his studio a few times a week at most. The winery had absorbed him completely in the last year and a half. He kept working there because of his affection for Carlo, to honor the trust he'd put in him, but he'd also continued to pay rent on the studio, hoping to do both things. But lately, he'd been forced to admit that it was impossible. He sketched whenever he could, carving out time as he waited for Roberto to take on the fate of the winery. For the time being, the studio was at least helpful, being the place where he and Lorenza could still meet unseen.

He'd already climbed onto his black Taurus Lautal when he saw Antonio's Fiat 508 coming up the road, wrapped in a cloud of dust. He got off the bike, leaned it back against the wall, and went toward him.

"Good morning, Antonio," he said, bending to look into the open window.

"Were you leaving?" he asked.

"Yes, but don't worry," Daniele said. "I can stay a bit longer. Come, let's go inside."

Antonio got out of the car and followed him to Carlo's old office. Daniele closed the door and invited Antonio to take a seat. Then he took a big folder from the desk and handed it to him. "It's up to date as of yesterday."

Antonio smiled and opened the folder, leafing through it until he reached the last pages, as he did every week. He always looked at the logs and checked the accounting, insisting on treating Daniele like any other employee.

"The pay item is high compared to last week," Antonio said. "How come?"

"I granted a small raise," Daniele explained.

Antonio pursed his lips, dissatisfied, and sat back in his chair.

"Careful not to give in to them every time . . . If you raise the pay after every complaint, you'll lose all your authority with them. Be understanding but decisive, especially when saying no."

Daniele wanted to answer that those concessions seemed more than reasonable to him and that in general, he was on the side of the workers and their claims, even though the land belonging to the Greco Winery was not being contested. He, too, had been a worker once, and knew well how hard it was. He'd often thought that the pay was too low, but he'd had no power to change that until now. It was true that Carlo had never been an arrogant or despotic owner, unlike many of his peers—he'd always been available to listen to the pleas of his laborers and farmers, he sought their advice, he heard their complaints, and he never had a problem granting leave or time off. But Carlo was not one of them; no matter how hard he'd tried, he never would have truly understood them.

But Daniele could. He understood them full well. He knew it and the laborers knew it. He wanted to tell Antonio all of this, but he held back. He felt like their relationship was still precarious, and that the slightest hitch could destroy it. Antonio was kind to him, yes, but also distant; courteous but guarded. And then there were those times when Antonio would just stare at him, scowling, and Daniele, with a knot in his throat, would wonder whether he'd figured out about the affair. What would happen if he followed Lorenza and caught her coming into his studio? He didn't even want to think about it.

"Okay. I'll keep it in mind," he murmured, sticking his hands in his pockets.

Antonio stayed for another twenty minutes. He scrutinized the logs, redid the calculations, asked for an explanation of this or that. Daniele peeked at the clock and, with a hint of resentment, saw that he had missed the bus.

"Very good, I'd say that it's all set now," Antonio said finally, closing the folder. "I better hurry," he added, shooting him a furtive glance. "We're all invited to Lorenza and Tommaso's house for lunch today."

"Have a good lunch, then," Daniele said as they walked to the door, making a superhuman effort to smile.

———

Christmas Eve was exactly one week away, and that afternoon, Giovanna insisted on dragging Anna to Lecce.

"Let's go to the Christmas market. Please," she asked in an almost childish tone, like a whiny little girl. "I heard it's beautiful. Come on, come on, please!"

Initially Anna resisted, and then she begrudgingly agreed, but only to please Giovanna; she wasn't at all in the mood to look at ornaments and sequins, or to dive into a raucous crowd. The year before, she'd refused to celebrate Christmas, and she was determined not to do it this year, either. *Never again without Carlo*, she'd sworn to herself.

As she'd predicted, the fair irritated her; too many lights, too many people, too many smiles. Anna noticed every couple that walked by, especially those that held hands and seemed happy and in love. Giovanna seemed to only have eyes for the stands, especially the ones selling sweets. She wanted to try everything: candied almonds, mustazzoli, cupeta, purceddruzzi . . .

"Can we go now?" Anna asked for the umpteenth time.

"A little bit longer," Giovanna answered, but then immediately got distracted. "Look! Wooden trains! I've always loved those . . ." She grabbed Anna by the hand and dragged her to the stand.

They didn't get home until dinnertime, on the last bus, exhausted and with sore feet. As soon as Anna opened the front door, Roberto and Antonio popped out in front of her, smiling.

"Surprise!"

Anna looked to the center of the room and saw the great pine tree standing there, adorned just as Carlo did it. Without a word, she slowly walked up to it.

"Do you like it, Maman?" Roberto asked, rubbing his hands together. "It took Uncle Antonio and me all afternoon to set it up."

"He took care of everything," Antonio clarified with a smile. "I was just the assistant."

Anna picked up a little wooden angel with a missing wing. Carlo had always insisted on keeping it even though it had been broken for years and she always told him how ugly it was. "Who cares. It's unique," he'd retort. "And you don't throw away memories."

"Maman?" Roberto said again. "Well? Do you like it?"

Giovanna put a hand on her shoulder. "We just wanted to make you happy."

Anna sniffled and dried a tear.

"Take it down right now, please," she said, without looking anyone in the face. She headed for the stairs, but when she passed Antonio, she stopped and looked up at him.

"What were you thinking?"

Antonio looked back at her, bewildered, his damp eyes containing both pain and reproach. "I didn't . . ." he stammered.

Anna turned and ran up the stairs.

"Anna, wait," he said and tried to stop her.

But she didn't answer.

Silence descended on the room.

Antonio slowly went over to the tree.

"Come on, help me take it down," he muttered.

24

Four Months Later

Anna shot another impatient glance at her watch and saw that the hands were still at twelve twenty-five, just like when she last looked at it a few minutes before.

She asked Tommaso for the time, and after a quick glance at his watch, he told her it was twelve forty-five. She undid the strap, slipped off her watch, and turned the crown, bringing the hands to the correct time. She'd returned from her delivery route a while ago, yet she couldn't bring herself to leave. She was anxiously awaiting Carmine, who on that day had asked for a few hours off to attend the final hearing in the trial against the Arneo occupiers.

Sixty people, including laborers, CGIL leaders, and Communist party members, stood accused of "abusive occupation of lands." In December, two thousand local laborers had mounted their bicycles, loaded their work tools and a myriad of red flags onto their backs, and rallied to a war cry of "The land belongs to those who work it!" It had lasted no longer than a week, when the police chased away the laborers and burned their bicycles in an enormous bonfire shortly after the New Year. Anna's Bianchi

Suprema had been among them—she'd lent it to Marisa, the wife of a laborer from Copertino, a little town about fifteen miles from Lizzanello, who also happened to be Carmine's brother, Donato. Carmine had shown up at Anna's house on the morning of Saint Stephen's and asked her to lend her bike "to the cause," or rather, to Marisa, who was determined to follow her husband to the Arneo.

"She don't have a lady's bicycle. It was hard enough to buy Donato's, given his miserable earnings. Could you maybe lend her yours? Eh, letter carrier? I'll be sure to bring it back whole," Carmine had said.

Anna hadn't hesitated; she'd grabbed the handles of her Bianchi, which was parked in the courtyard, and given it to Carmine.

"I'll just have to deliver the mail on foot for a while. Like old times," she'd joked.

"Thank you kindly, comrade Anna!" he'd said, pleased.

When Carmine had apologetically informed her of the bicycle bonfire, he'd immediately offered to buy her a new one. Anna had refused.

"Don't worry about it," she'd assured him, putting a hand on his arm. "I'll buy it on my own."

He'd grumbled that it wasn't fair, that it was his job to pay her back, but she'd said, "It wasn't your fault. If anyone should be repaying me, it's the police."

The following day, she'd gone to the same bicycle shop that had sold her the Bianchi Suprema and asked for another one just like it. Even used would do, she'd specified. The guy, a short and very thin man in his fifties wearing a flat cap and pants that were one size too big, had managed to find her an identical model in just a few days, at half the original price.

"You got it for a steal, Mrs. Letter Carrier!" he'd said from his doorstep as she left, not before recounting the lira Anna had handed him in an envelope.

Finally, Carmine came in, limping slightly, and went to his desk. He looked distracted, somewhere between busy and pensive.

"There you are. About time," Anna said, standing up. "Well?"

He answered with a sort of grunt.

Elena, whose curiosity had been piqued, joined them, while Tommaso put his pen down on the desk and crossed his arms, ready to listen. He shot a quick glance at the telegraph office, but Lorenza remained glued to her chair.

"It could have gone better," Carmine began, sitting down. "They convicted twenty-five out of sixty. A 'symbolic sentence,' they called it, but a punishment it remains. They all should have been cleared. That's a fact."

"Meaning? What was the sentence?" Tommaso asked.

"A month in prison and a six-thousand-lira fine," Carmine said with a smirk.

"Gosh," Anna said. "The only consolation is that at least it wasn't all for nothing."

"Yes," Carmine sighed, leaning against the back of his chair.

The occupation of the Arneo had echoed across the national press; papers like *Il Paese* and *L'Unità* had written about it extensively, and Anna hadn't missed an article. They described the Arneo occupiers as heroes, "men covered in rags who, driven by the noble pursuit of cultivating the area, had laid siege to the estate." In the end, thanks to the struggle of those laborers, the province of Lecce had finally been included in the agrarian reform project, but it had been meager compensation, according to Anna. Of the 266,000 hectares vulnerable to expropriation, only 55,000 had been included in the transitional law.

"It will never, ever be enough," she'd said to Carmine. "Tensions are going to erupt between those laborers once they see who gets the land and who doesn't. How can a movement remain united with so much internal inequality?"

Carmine had agreed, getting even more fired up.

"This fight isn't over," he'd said like a true trade unionist, punching his palm with his fist.

Anna looked at her watch again. The hands hadn't moved. "What the heck?" she said.

"What's the matter?" Tommaso asked.

"My watch," she said. "It stopped working."

Tommaso shrugged. "Buy yourself a new one," he said with a little smile.

As she left the post office and got on her bike, Anna decided she'd take the watch in for repairs. She had no intention of trading it in; it had been *her* watch for the past sixteen years, for Christ's sake. Antonio had given it to her and it was the only one she wanted.

———

Roberto and Daniele were strolling through the estate, side by side. Daniele had rolled his sleeves up to his elbows and was wearing his trusty suspenders and work pants, while Roberto was in his blue school uniform, with the jacket and shirt. The farmers were bent over the vines, engrossed in their work, but every so often, someone would look up at Roberto and watch him. They were working on the vineyard's "shielding," Daniele explained, while Roberto listened attentively, holding his schoolbag in front of him with both hands.

"It means 'suckering,' which is to cut the extra shoots that pop up despite the pruning. They steal the nourishment and are sterile, so we remove them to keep them from weakening the plant."

"So many things to know," Roberto sighed, discouraged. He sat on a rock and placed his schoolbag on the ground. Almost every day now, Roberto would get off the bus from Lecce, where he went to school, and walk to the winery, where he'd stay for a few hours. He was almost finished with high school—only a few weeks left—and then he'd dedicate himself to his father's winery full-time. That was what he'd decided.

Daniele smiled and sat on the ground in front of him, then brought his knees up to his chest. "Come on," he assured him. "You'll learn quickly. Like I did. When I first got here, as a kid, I didn't know anything about anything," he said, making his point with a clear gesture.

Roberto seemed relieved and leaned back on the palms of his hands.

"Do you miss New York?" he asked.

"Sometimes," Daniele said. "That city is . . . magical."

"Tell me! I want to go too, one day."

"What do you want to know?" Daniele asked, smiling and resting his forearms on his knees.

"Well, everything. Like the girls," Roberto said, winking. "Are they like ours? And the skyscrapers: What's it like to look at them from below? Don't you get dizzy? Did you ever ride in one of those yellow taxis? And did you go to the top of the Statue of Liberty?"

"Hold on," Daniele cut in, amused. "I can't remember the first question."

"The girls!"

"Right. The girls. I wouldn't know, I didn't really look at them."

Roberto shot him a mischievous look, like someone who didn't believe him at all.

"I swear!" Daniele laughed. "I didn't even think about it." Then he looked down, embarrassed.

Roberto watched him for a moment. "You have it written all over your face, you know," he said.

"What?" Daniele asked.

"That you're in love with my cousin."

Suddenly serious, Daniele sat upright and pivoted on his hand, bringing himself up to standing. He rubbed his hands together to brush off the dirt.

"Gossip," he exclaimed, ruffling Roberto's hair. "Come on, let's go back to the winery. We still have to look at proposals for the new bottles."

"Sir, yes sir!" Roberto said. As they crossed the vineyard, he elbowed him in the side.

"What was that for?" Daniele chuckled.

"You didn't tell me about the skyscrapers."

"Oh, right. The skyscrapers. What is there to say . . . After a while you get used to them," he said with a shrug.

———

Every Thursday evening, Roberto and Maria dragged the console table with the radio into the middle of the room and placed it between the couches. At 8:58 p.m., the Rete Rossa station would air *Red and Black*, a variety show that Anna and Giovanna never missed.

For the occasion, Anna made pesto every Thursday night. Over time, the rest of the family had ended up joining the weekly event. They all had dinner together and once the program started, they scrambled to their seats on the couches.

"Can someone tell me what time it is?" Anna shouted from the kitchen. "If only I had my watch," she mumbled.

She'd gone to the watchmaker, but after examining the watch, he had looked up in defeat. "This one's a goner," he'd said. "Buy yourself a new one. Would you like to see some ladies' models that have just arrived?"

"No, thank you," she'd said curtly. She'd gone home, disappointed, and had placed the watch in a drawer in her dresser. And she still hadn't replaced it.

"Seven o'clock," Roberto shouted from the other room.

Perfectly on time, Anna said to herself. She started to pat the basil leaves with a damp cloth.

Giovanna was sitting at the table working on her chain stitches, double stitches, and single crochets. Recently, she'd become obsessed with crocheting. Her neighbor, the elderly woman who swept the sidewalk outside her door every morning, had taught her while Anna was at work. Giovanna had been practicing every day, for hours. She'd started with some simple oven mitts—there were two in the kitchen, with blue and yellow stripes—and then she'd challenged herself with a coin purse, then a few doilies for the bedroom, and now she was gradually taking on increasingly complex projects.

"It relaxes me," she said. "When I'm doing it, I don't think about anything else. It's so . . . comforting."

"Roberto!" Anna called out. "Go ahead and set the table."

Hand in hand, Roberto and Maria peeked into the kitchen.

"At your service!" he said, bringing a hand to his forehead.

Just like Carlo used to do when he was making fun of me, Anna thought with a pang of sadness.

Roberto pulled eight porcelain soup plates lined with blue flowers from the cabinet, while Maria fetched the forks from the cutlery drawer. Anna watched them furtively; she still didn't know if she liked that girl. It certainly wasn't hard to understand why her son had fallen for her, with her eye-catching looks and warm demeanor. She had long chestnut ringlets kept back with a headband, a little face with delicate features and rosy cheeks, and a petite and balanced figure. The phrases Anna had heard her utter most frequently were "Thank you," "I'm sorry," and "If you don't mind." By all accounts, she was adorable.

Yet Anna saw her persistent sweetness and politeness as a sign of lack of character, of excessive docility. She'd been perplexed, for instance, when Maria had announced that if Roberto wasn't going to college, she wouldn't apply either.

"I could be the secretary for the winery. I just want to be close to him," she'd said with a disarming smile, looking at Roberto full of love. Anna felt like all Maria wanted was to mold herself onto her son, as if she were made of clay.

"You're wrong," Roberto had protested, the only time Anna had brought up the subject. "Maria is not like that at all. She's stronger and more determined than you think. She has that particular brand of strength that comes from being calm and sweet. I want you to get to know her. Do it for me, please."

Since then, and only for the love of her son, Anna had not only kept her opinions about Maria to herself but also made an active effort to notice any redeeming qualities she might have. After all, if Roberto was in love with her, there must be something good about her . . .

She was about to add the pine nuts to the mortar when she heard voices: Antonio and Agata had arrived.

"No, don't close it, Tommaso's parking the car," Agata was saying to Roberto.

Antonio poked his head into the kitchen and greeted Anna cheerfully. "What are you up to?" he then asked Giovanna with interest, sitting down next to her.

"A summer shawl, in cotton."

"You're so good at it!" he said.

"More and more every day," Anna added proudly.

The front door closed and they heard little Giada's cheerful gurgles, accompanied by everyone's exclamations.

"What a delightful little dress!" Maria said.

"Nice, isn't it? I got it for her," Agata said.

"Do you like the dress Granny got you? Hmm, Papa's little love?" Tommaso said.

Giovanna smiled, dropped the needle and thread on the table, and went to the little girl.

"That smells nice," Antonio said, sticking his finger in the mortar.

"Hey!" Anna protested. "If you try that again, I'm going to crush that finger of yours!"

Chuckling, Antonio brought his finger to his mouth.

"It's delicious. As usual." Then he crossed his hands on the table and looked at Anna. It took him a few seconds to realize she was no longer wearing her watch.

"Why did you take it off?" he asked, furrowing his forehead and nodding at her wrist.

Anna stopped. "Oh, it stopped working. That con artist of a watchmaker didn't know how to repair it. I should buy a new one at some point," she said. "But I want *that* one."

"There's a little girl here who wants to say hi to Auntie Anna," Giovanna interrupted, appearing in the kitchen with Giada in her arms.

"There you are!" Anna smiled, continuing to work.

Agata erupted into the kitchen. "Is the water boiling?" she asked anxiously.

"I haven't put it on yet," Anna said, without looking away from Giada.

"I see. I'll do it," Agata sighed, looking extremely put-upon. She got up on her toes to pull the big pot down from the shelf.

They sat down to eat at eight P.M. Anna placed the steaming pot of trofie al pesto in the center of the table, and Antonio filled the glasses with Don Carlo.

Roberto and Maria were sitting next to each other, constantly giving each other little kisses on the cheek. Giada was in the high chair next to Agata, who was feeding her with a little spoon. On the other side of the high chair was Tommaso, who couldn't stop looking at his daughter as if in a daze, and then Antonio. Lorenza had sat opposite her husband. Anna and Giovanna were the last to take their seats. As usual, Giada was the center of attention, eliciting general hilarity with her made-up words.

"Fooculler!" she'd exclaim, pointing at the knife, and then she came out with a "gheen sauce!" when Agata took her first bite of trofie.

Everyone laughed except for Lorenza, who seemed even moodier than usual. She barely touched her food and was looking around as if she was listening to the various conversations when in truth, she could only discern a confused clamor. She couldn't stop thinking about the argument she'd had with Daniele the day before. It had been their first real fight.

They had developed a routine. Every Wednesday afternoon, she'd leave Giada with Anna, take the three o'clock bus, and join him in Lecce. She found him earlier that week sitting at his sewing machine, engrossed in his work, but as soon as she walked in, he ran toward her and in a flash, they united in a kiss that contained the full force of the kisses they'd repressed since their last meeting. They tore their clothes off and Daniele picked her up, holding her by the hips, and pressed her against the wall. She wrapped her legs around him and closed her eyes.

At five o'clock, a quarter of an hour before the bus would leave for Lizzanello—as usual, Daniele would take the following one—Lorenza had said, nervously, "Listen, I've been thinking about this for a week. Let's go to New York. You and me."

Daniele had stared at her, bewildered, then started to get dressed.

"Why are you reacting like that?" she exclaimed, surprised and irritated.

He tucked his shirt in and went to her. He took her face in his hands and in a low voice, said, "How can I? Drop the winery? Drop the studio? And your daughter?"

"I only care about being with you," she said.

Daniele lowered his hands. "You can't possibly think that. Of leaving Giada, I mean."

"It's my choice. It has nothing to do with you."

"How can you say it has nothing to do with me!"

"I think the real issue is that you don't love me the way I love you!" Lorenza screamed. "That's why you don't want to leave. The winery, the studio, my daughter . . . all excuses. If you really wanted me, you'd say yes. Right away, without even thinking about it!"

Daniele took a step back, put his hands on his hips, and stared at her. "Do you really think I don't love you? Really?"

"You're proving it right now."

"Just because I'm asking you to be reasonable? To think of your daughter?"

"Oh, go to hell! You know what? You just care about me when you get to slide between my legs."

"That's a cruel thing to say."

"I'm just telling it how it is."

Daniele had remained silent for a seemingly endless moment. Then he'd murmured, "You're going to miss the bus. Go, please."

I absolutely have to see him before Wednesday, Lorenza thought now. She pondered how to meet up with him. There would be nothing wrong with her showing up at the winery the next day; she could always say that she was there to talk to Roberto.

"Mama!" Giada said, reaching her little hand toward her. "Mama!"

Tommaso lifted her out of her high chair and took her to Lorenza. "Here's Mama," he said, putting the girl in her arms.

Lorenza put her on her lap and leaned back against the chair.

"Water, Mama," Giada asked.

Lorenza didn't move.

"Water, Mama," Giada said again.

"Dear, the child is asking you for water," Tommaso said a bit too loudly.

"Yes, sorry," she stammered. "Mama will get you some now," she said, grabbing the pitcher.

"Hey, here we go," Roberto announced, glancing at the clock above the fireplace. "Three minutes left." He turned on the radio and everyone took their places on the couches.

The couch on which Carlo always sat, the one by the fireplace, remained empty. Anna wouldn't allow anyone to sit there. Ever.

The voice of Mario Carotenuto bid a good evening to the audience.

———

Anna had been as clear as day: She didn't want any surprises, dinners, or celebrations of any kind for her birthday. She much preferred to spend the day alone.

"Actually, if you can, try to forget about it," she'd warned everyone.

The day she turned forty-four—that year it fell on a Sunday—she took her time and didn't get out of bed until late morning, awoken by the smell of tomato sauce and soffritto coming from the kitchen. Giovanna always added a lot of it whenever she made ragù on Sundays.

She took off her silk eye mask, put on her slippers and robe, and opened the door, then almost tripped over a red rose on the floor. Next to it was a small white envelope that said *Maman*. The note inside read:

Happy birthday to the biggest pain-in-the-butt mom in the world.

I love you,
Roberto

Anna pursed her lips and brought the note to her heart. Then she picked up the rose and went downstairs. She stopped at a side table with a bouquet of daisies, the ones she and Giovanna had gathered the previous afternoon, and put the rose in it.

She went into the kitchen, and after greeting Giovanna, she took the little pot and her cup out of the cupboard. "Did Roberto go out?" she asked.

"A few hours ago," Giovanna said. "He said he had to stop by the winery."

"On a Sunday?" Anna said, surprised, as she poured milk into her pot.

"He had to do something with Daniele," Giovanna said, shrugging. Then she looked at her, hesitantly, and finally said, in a low voice, "Can I at least wish you a happy birthday?"

Anna turned around and laughed. "Well, sure. Of course you can."

It was a warm and sunny day, without a cloud in the sky. As she sipped her milk on the bench, Anna enjoyed the heat of the sun on her face and thought that the only thing she felt like doing that day was getting on her bicycle and pedaling without a destination, alone and in silence. Maybe she would go all the way to the sea.

Back inside, she told Giovanna that she and Roberto would be having lunch without her that Sunday. "I want to go out, but I don't know when I'll be back. Do you mind?"

"As long as you have a lovely day," Giovanna said. "That's all that matters."

Anna planted a kiss on her forehead. "Thank you," she whispered.

Half an hour later, Anna left the house, mounted her Bianchi, and started to pedal slowly.

"Good morning, letter carrier," said a little old man, with a wave. He was the one who received weekly letters from his son, who'd gone to work as a mason in Turin.

"Happy Sunday, Mrs. Greco," said another man, doffing his cap.

"Hi, Anna," exclaimed two women who were chatting on a doorstep.

"Hey, no mail today?" joked a large woman who was shelling peas while sitting on the curb.

Anna returned every greeting with a slightly forced smile. When she finally turned onto the road to the beach, she sighed with relief. In moments like those, where she just wanted to be left in peace, she longed for the days when she was still a stranger in town—nowadays, she couldn't take one step without someone saying hello or stopping her for a chat. *Sometimes it's just so hard,* she thought. She passed by olive groves and fields lined with plow marks, all surrounded by long drystone walls. The silence she had sought finally enveloped her, like a silk mantle. After about ten miles, she reached a fork in the road and continued along a dirt path. The landscape around her changed and she immediately smelled one of her favorite scents: pines. They reminded her of her beloved pine forest in Bordighera, where the mountains plunged into the sea, and the naps she took there as a girl, lying on a bed of pine needles—when the sun beat down, the only way to escape it was to shelter among the conifers. Soon, the pine forest appeared before her, along with a sign that read BEACH. She got off her bicycle and pushed it as she ventured between the trees, breathing in deeply. Suddenly, she saw the white sand and blue expanse of the sea. Smiling, she leaned her bike against the trunk of a pine tree and ran to the shore. She quickly took off her shoes and linen pants and unbuttoned her white shirt. In nothing but her bra and underwear, she dove into the waveless water and then relaxed onto her back, with her arms out and eyes closed.

She realized that it was her first time swimming completely alone. During her summers in Bordighera, as a girl, she'd been with her cousins, who followed her everywhere; after that, Carlo had always been there. As with every time she thought of her husband, Anna felt a sudden pang in her chest and a shadow seemed to fall over her. Almost two years had passed since his death, and she still couldn't say what hurt the most: seeing the world go on despite his absence, or that she was getting increasingly used to the fact that he was gone. Every time she noticed that she hadn't thought of him for a whole hour, or whenever something made her laugh, she immediately felt a burning sense of guilt, a pang to the heart. *How long after the death of a love is it all right to laugh again?* she wondered.

She let herself sink under the surface of the water and held her breath for a few seconds.

When she reemerged and swam back to shore, she had no idea how much time had passed. She quickly dressed and found her bicycle. She rode home soaking wet while the warmth of the sun heated her arms and face, pinching her skin as the salt water dried.

She arrived at the gates of Lizzanello as the afternoon light was starting to fade. Before taking the road home, though, she stopped. *I'm pretty close to Contrada La Pietra,* she thought, looking to her right. *Maybe it's worth checking out the farmhouse . . . Who knows what condition it's in. I haven't been there in so long . . .*

She pedaled down the road she knew like her own pockets and soon arrived at the house. She pushed open the wooden gate, eroded by the rain and faded by the sun, and walked up to the door. It wasn't locked. She cracked it open and was immediately hit by a strong stench of fustiness and mildew. Everything was in its place, as if crystallized. She checked every room: cobwebs in the corners, layers of dust on the furniture, mold stretching across the walls . . . *I should at least come back and clean up a bit,* she thought. *Tonight I'll ask Giovanna if . . .*

An idea lit up her face like a flash. She looked around slowly and saw everything with total clarity. They could put a classroom with a blackboard and some desks in the living room; the big wall where the couch was had plenty of space to host a library; all they had to do in the kitchen was remove the cupboards and a few pieces of furniture to make room for some workshops; they could easily carve out a small dormitory upstairs . . . not to mention the land, which could accommodate a vegetable garden, even a pretty big one.

Why the heck didn't I think of this before? she said to herself. As everything took shape before her, a voice echoed in her mind. It was Carlo, saying, *Promise me you won't give up on it . . . Use our funds . . . without having to ask anyone for anything.*

She felt a knot in her throat. As always, her Carlo had been right.

She got back on her bike and rode home. As soon as she opened the door, the smell of ragù, which had invaded every room, enveloped her completely. She loudly called out to Giovanna but received no answer. *She probably went to see Giada,* she thought. *Oh well, we'll talk about it tomorrow morning.*

She sank into the couch in her damp clothes and with her hair still ruffled from the salty water. She let her eyes wander around the room, finally laying them on the table in front of her, where she noticed a little package wrapped in golden paper and a red ribbon. She leaned forward to pick it up, studied it for a moment, turning it around in her hands, and opened it, revealing a little blue velvet box. Inside was a wonderful watch with a rectangular face, a golden border, and a green leather strap. She gawked at it, picked it up, and stared at it for a long time. When she turned it over, she noticed a phrase inscribed onto the back of the quadrant.

With her heart beating, she brought the watch closer and read out loud:

To Anna from Antonio, for all the time to come.

25

That Summer

"What is it supposed to be, exactly?"

"Humph. A sort of school, they say."

"It's not a school. She says it's going to be a 'home.'"

"Doesn't she already have a home?"

"Yes, but it's a different home. A home for women."

"And what about us men?"

"Bah, what does 'for women' even mean?"

"That they'll be doing things. Women's things."

"I thought it was a school."

"I'm telling you, it's not."

Antonio was sipping his coffee behind the rope curtain at Bar Castello and couldn't help but overhear the conversation between the old men playing briscola.

"The letter carrier asked my wife, when the time comes, to show them how to make quilts," a man with thick curly hair cut in from the next table.

"See? I was right. It's a school. But for women's things," the first player exclaimed.

"I heard they'll be teaching how to read and write, and also history, geography, math," said another, stroking his long mustache.

"As I was saying. It's a school," the first player reiterated.

"Maybe, but I sure don't get it. Must be an outlander thing, I guess. Doesn't she know we already have schools?" mused the second player.

Antonio chuckled under his breath. It wasn't the first time he'd heard conversations like that about Anna's Women's Home. No one in town seemed to understand much about it. The only thing they knew for sure was that the letter carrier was about to "do something" with Crazy Giovanna's farmhouse. Some insisted she'd bought it for a pittance; others thought Giovanna had given it to pay a debt to her.

"She eats and sleeps on her dime," some said, smirking.

Others added, "Yeah, and before that she ate and slept on Carlo's dime, may he rest in peace."

Antonio placed his cup on the bar and walked out. The men went silent.

"Do you think he heard us?" the first player whispered, leaning toward another.

"It's not like we said anything bad," said the other, with a shrug.

"Good morning, gentlemen," Antonio greeted them, smiling.

"Good morning to you, Antonio," they answered in unison.

"What a happy coincidence," one said. "We were just talking about your sister-in-law."

"I heard, I heard," Antonio said, slipping his hands into his pockets.

"Well then, can you explain to us what this . . . thing is she wants to do?" asked the man with the curly hair. "My wife doesn't quite understand it either."

"I see," Antonio murmured, stroking his nose. "I'd say you're all right about something. This place will do a lot of things. But yes, it will only be open to women. It'll be a school for those who weren't able to study, but also a workshop for learning a trade, and a shelter for anyone who is struggling."

The men exchanged puzzled looks.

"In short, a place to help people. Nothing more and nothing less," Antonio concluded, and walked away.

But he heard someone whisper behind him, "Bah. Now I get it even less than before."

When Anna had so enthusiastically talked to him about her Women's Home a few months before, Antonio's heart had warmed. He was finally seeing that spark in her eyes that he knew so well and that he loved most about her. It was the same spark he'd seen when she'd decided to apply for the post office job, and when she'd started gathering signatures to give women the vote.

It was a spark of challenge to the world.

Anna's eyes hadn't lit up like that since Carlo had gotten sick. It had been a real relief to see her come alive from one day to the next, as she dove into a new project. And when Anna described it to him, Antonio had also felt a sense of pride. Only she could have conjured up such an idea, something that had never been seen before, and that could do so much for women.

"Let me help you," he'd said.

And he hadn't held back. Within a few weeks, he and Anna had cleared all the old furniture out of the farmhouse and loaded it onto wagons Antonio had brought from the mill, along with two of his beefiest workers. They replaced the gate and repainted the doors and windows. They pulled up all the weeds and marked the spaces for the gardens with picket fences. They repaired the leaks in the roof. Occasionally, as they worked, Anna and Antonio would find themselves looking at each other and smiling conspiratorially.

Sometimes Anna would stop and let her eyes wander. "Now I can see it even more clearly," she'd say.

"Have you considered putting all that hard work into your own house?" Agata would grumble when Antonio came home for dinner. "How many times have I asked you to buy some new furniture, eh? And to tear down this ugly wallpaper that your mother put up, may she rest in peace."

Whenever she started on her spiel, Antonio would let her rant, certain she'd stop sooner or later. But Agata persisted.

"No one in town understands anything about this, least of all me. What is 'Women's Home' supposed to mean? That woman and her inane ideas. And go figure why she always has to drag you into it."

Her rosary friends had barraged her with those very same questions at their recitation the previous Saturday. When Agata had arrived at her neighbor's house and sat down in the circle of women, silence fell. Then the ladies started shooting one another awkward looks.

"Cat got your tongue? Why did you all stop talking?" Agata had asked, frowning.

The neighbor, a spindly woman dressed in black, which highlighted her rosy skin and the peach fuzz above her lip, had looked at the others and finally found the courage to say, "It's just that we wondered how you were doing, whether this whole thing bothered you at all—"

"What thing?" Agata had interrupted, anxiously.

"This thing with your husband and your sister-in-law."

Agata had wriggled in her chair. "What are you going on about?"

"Please, don't misunderstand us," another had intervened, a large woman with very black hair. "Everyone knows it, that Antonio is helping her day and night, to set up this Women's Home no one seems to understand."

"When people don't understand something, it means it's wrong. My father always said so," said an elderly woman with white eyebrows and a raspy voice.

"Day and night now? Always exaggerating!" Agata had said. "He spends a few hours a day on it at most."

The women exchanged glances again.

"But why did she drag your husband into it, of all people?" the neighbor then asked.

"Exactly. If it's a women's thing, what does he have to do with it?"

"Even the signature drive, remember?" the elderly woman said.

"You're apparently forgetting that he's Carlo's brother, may he rest in peace," Agata said, making the sign of the cross. The others followed suit.

"And what does that mean? That now he has to take charge of her, too?" the neighbor insisted.

Yeah, she's not wrong, Agata thought to herself, with a sigh. Antonio was taking care of two families, his and his brother's. Since Carlo died, her husband was always running to help Anna whenever she needed something. *Oh, to hell with her, let her take care of herself! Damn her and the day she arrived!* Agata had thought many times, in a fit of jealousy.

Even so, she said, "You know how my Antonio is: He's too kind, and generous . . . But I'm very proud of him and of everything he does for our sister-in-law and nephew," she highlighted, hoping to put an end to the rumors once and for all.

"Of course he is! As good as they come. Always has been, since he was a child," the large woman agreed.

The others had looked at one another with an embarrassed expression and hadn't dared say anything else.

After a few moments, the neighbor had started in on the Hail Mary and the women followed her in unison.

Agata recited the prayers with her head down and her eyes closed, but between a Mater Dei and Ora pro nobis peccatoribus, she'd had to swallow anger and humiliation.

———

On that sweltering July morning, no one at the post office seemed to be in the mood to chat. The only background sounds were the clickety-clack of the telegraph and the tapping of Tommaso's pen on the documents he was reading. Carmine seemed deep in thought and was constantly touching his white beard; over the past few months, he'd let it grow beyond measure, frizzy and wild. Even Elena, who usually wasn't at a loss for words, was keeping to herself, as if she was annoyed by something. And Lorenza certainly wasn't any less bad-tempered than usual. Anna was sorting the mail, but even her mind was elsewhere; she was thinking that she had to procure not just a blackboard but also desks and chairs . . . things she couldn't exactly pick up at the corner shop. She would purchase everything else new—beds, sheets, clothes, seeds, gardening equipment, notebooks, pens, and all of the supplies they'd need for the craft workshop—but where the heck was she going to find furniture for the classroom?

There was another thing bothering her: the fact that Giovanna didn't want to be involved in any way.

"I still don't feel up to seeing Contrada again," she'd said as she worked on her cotton shawl without looking up. "But I'm happy for you, and your project is wonderful. Truly."

"I would like for it to become *our* project," Anna had retorted. From a certain standpoint, she understood her, but it drove her nuts that don Giulio still had so much power over Giovanna's choices.

It wasn't right.

Anna put the mail for the Greco Winery in a little bundle on the side; she'd bring it to Roberto later, at home, assuming he would be back for lunch. Since he'd finished high school, he'd thrown himself headlong into managing the winery and estate, as promised, showing a great sense of responsibility. *He sure is my son,* she said to herself with a smile.

She put on her mailbag and poked her head into the telegraph office. "Last-minute telegrams?" she asked.

Elena turned around to look at her and shook her head, pursing her lips; she looked tense and had reddish circles under her eyes. Her sleeping difficulties weren't news, but they seemed to have gotten worse lately.

"No, Auntie," Lorenza piped in. "Nothing new."

Lorenza didn't look great either that morning. Anna assumed she'd had another fight with Tommaso. The air of animosity in their home was so dense it could be cut with a knife. "I have a few minutes," she said to Lorenza. "Do you want to grab a quick coffee at the bar?"

"Yes," she said, pushing back her chair. "I could really use one."

There was an unsettling atmosphere in the square. The leaves of the great palm tree were so still they looked like they'd been painted onto the sky; the shop doors were all closed to keep out the heat; the two old men sitting on the bench and the four men in white undershirts playing cards at the bar looked worn and on the verge of liquefying.

Anna leaned her bike against the wall of the bar and sat at an outdoor table while Lorenza went to get the coffees.

"Tommaso seemed anxious this morning," Anna said, stirring her coffee.

"If he could just calm down a bit . . ." Lorenza said. "He's obsessed with that little girl; he worries about everything, even when there's no reason. And then it's always my fault if she cries, or doesn't sleep enough, or acts up . . ."

Anna sensed there was more but kept quiet.

"Not to mention this whole thing about Otranto. I don't understand why we have to go all the way out there every summer."

Anna lifted an eyebrow. *There's the real reason,* she thought.

"I told him clearly: This year I don't feel like it," Lorenza continued. "And do you know what he said? That I'm whiny and ungrateful. Me! Did I ever ask him for anything? He's the one who always decides where we go on vacation. Never once did he ask for my opinion."

Anna cleared her throat and spoke softly. "You don't want to be too far from Daniele," she said. "Is that why?"

Lorenza narrowed her eyes and shifted her gaze to the castle.

"It's only for two weeks," Anna murmured. "Do it for Giada. You know how much fun she has at the beach."

"There are beaches here, too," Lorenza snapped.

"Yes, but you have a house there, and it's a shame to keep it locked up. What does it cost you? Two weeks, Lorenza. Only two."

"It costs me a lot!" she exclaimed, increasingly irritated. "There are things you don't know, things that have happened. I can't leave him now. I can't," she said, shaking her head.

"It sounds like you're afraid of something."

"Obviously I'm afraid. He could find someone else and marry her. What do you think, that he'll be alone forever? That he won't tire of living like this?"

"And you think he'll find her precisely in the two weeks you'll be away with your family?" Anna asked, sarcastically.

"I don't want him to find her ever."

"You can't say that. You know—"

"It could all be so simple," Lorenza interrupted her. "If only we could leave here. Be far from everything and everyone. We could be so happy."

It was the first time Anna had heard her say something like that, and it worried her considerably. After a few moments of silence, she said, "Like Anna Karenina and Count Vronsky?"

"Yeah, just like them," Lorenza whispered.

Anna snorted, then rummaged in her mailbag for a few coins and put them on the table. "I have to go," she said. "But remember this: Anna Karenina paid for her choice very dearly. Think about it." And she walked away.

Lorenza leaned back against the chair. She knew the story of Anna Karenina; she'd read the book as a girl and remembered feeling great admiration for that romantic heroine. She'd been brave enough to risk everything to follow her heart. And even now, like when she was a child, Lorenza couldn't see anything wrong with that.

———

The following Wednesday, Lorenza brought Giada to her meeting with Daniele. On the bus, the little girl wouldn't stop whining because of the heat, rubbing her teary eyes with her little hands.

"Be good," Lorenza kept saying. "We're going to a nice place, to meet a dear friend of Mama's."

When they got there, Daniele was bent over his workbench, sketching.

"Here we are!" Lorenza exclaimed, forcing a smile.

Daniele looked at her and jumped to his feet, shifting his gaze between Giada and Lorenza.

Giada stopped on the threshold and stared at Daniele with still-teary eyes.

"Go on, come in with Mama," Lorenza prodded her.

Daniele shot her a bewildered look, and then he crouched by Giada and smiled at her. "Nice to meet you. I'm Daniele," he said, holding out his hand.

After a moment, Giada placed her little hand in Daniele's.

"Do you know how pretty you are?" he asked, stroking her little fingers. "I've never seen such a beautiful girl, I swear."

Giada brought a finger to her mouth, and without looking away from him, she smiled a bit and took a step forward.

Lorenza walked her in, pushing her by the shoulders, and closed the door with a sigh.

"Your name is Giada, right? Which means jade?" Daniele said.

The girl nodded.

"Do you know 'jade' is the name of a gemstone that has a beautiful color?"

The girl shook her head, amused.

"Come here, I'll show you one." He stood up and, holding the girl by the hand, he led her to the rolls of fabric. He pulled out a beautiful shiny green one. "Here. This is the color of jade."

Giada reached her little hand out and touched the fabric.

"Do you like it?"

"Yes," she said, happily.

"Then do you know what we'll do? We'll make a nice little dress. For you." He gave her a chuck on the chin.

Lorenza watched them the whole time with a pleased smile.

The two hours that followed were peaceful and lovely. Lorenza and Daniele took Giada's measurements, getting her to twirl like a princess, and then cut the fabric. He recovered some cuttings from a basket and fashioned them into hair bands that he then tied to Lorenza's head, to Giada's, and in the end, to his own, eliciting a delighted laugh from the little one.

Then Giada went to a corner to play with some pieces of fabric.

"Are you able to work?" Lorenza asked, nodding at the Singer.

"I'm trying," he said. "Since your cousin started full-time at the winery, I can come here at lot more often, at least."

"I'd really love to see the new drawings. May I?"

Daniele blushed. "They're just sketches." He leaned toward her and gently tucked a rebel lock of hair behind her ear. "But when I'm done, you'll be the first to see them."

"I can't wait," she said. She closed her eyes, sighed, and smiled. "I wish every afternoon was like this," she said.

Daniele smiled back. "Giada really is adorable," he whispered.

"Have you ever thought that it could always be like this?" Lorenza said, lowering her voice.

"Like this how?"

"Me, you, and Giada."

He stared at her as if he wasn't sure he'd understood.

"You said you'd never let me leave her," Lorenza continued. "Then let's take her with us. Would you do it then? Would you come away with me?"

Daniele stared at her slack-jawed, then cleared his throat and turned to look at Giada. "You don't know what you're saying," he said finally.

"You said it, that Giada was the problem," Lorenza hissed. Then she raised her voice. "I'm giving you a solution!"

Giada suddenly stopped playing and looked up.

"Take her away from her father? Her grandparents? Is that your solution?" Daniele said.

"At least I'm trying to think of one," she growled.

Giada started to sob, then she grabbed the fabric cuttings and tossed them in the air.

"Little one, what's wrong?" Daniele said quickly. "Is it because Mama seems angry? She's just joking! She just told me how happy she is to be leaving for the beach Saturday with you and your papa." Lorenza was about to open her mouth, but Daniele's harsh gaze was enough to stop her. "Isn't that right, Lorenza?" he said.

Giada stopped crying and stared at her mother.

Lorenza looked at Daniele with a mixture of pain and rage. "Yes, very happy," she said in a trembling voice. She quickly picked up her daughter and headed for the door.

"Lorenza, come back," Daniele begged her.

She didn't even turn around.

———

Anna was rushing to put her shoes on. Antonio would be there to pick her up any minute now.

"Be ready tomorrow morning at ten," he'd said, and she knew he was always on time. Anna had just taken two weeks off from work, and that day, they were going to an antiques dealer who lived in the country and who, according to Antonio's sources, possessed an old school blackboard.

"Sure you don't want to come?" she asked Giovanna.

"No, thank you," she said. She was sitting at the kitchen table with her needlework and a ball of pink wool in front of her, working on a pair of booties. "I'd rather stay here. And it's too hot to go out."

Anna looked disappointed. "As you wish."

Just then, she heard the horn of the Fiat 508.

"Here he is!" Anna exclaimed, heading out. "Bye, see you at lunch!"

Antonio was waiting for her with the window down and his arm draped over the door.

"You're the most insolently punctual person I know," Anna said.

"Punctuality is the virtue of the generous," he said with a smile.

As soon as they set off, the light breeze came in through the window and ruffled Anna's hair, releasing a delightful scent.

"Glad to be on vacation?" Antonio asked.

"Actually, I'm happy to have more time to dedicate to the Women's Home," she said. "You know, I was thinking about it last night. I'd like for it to be ready by the end of September. If I can get on with it in these two weeks, I can do it."

"Ah. Hadn't you decided on November?" Antonio said in bewilderment. "Why did you change your mind?"

Anna shrugged. "No real reason. The sooner it's ready, the better."

"Yes, but the end of September is little more than a month away. And I won't be here in the next ten days."

Antonio would leave for Otranto to join his wife and daughter, who had arrived there a few days before with Tommaso and the little one. Agata had offered to look after Giada. "So you can be alone with your husband for a bit," she'd said to Lorenza, without hiding her disapproval. Antonio had promised to join them after taking care of a few matters at the mill.

"I wouldn't want you to have to take care of it on your own. Shouldn't you wait?" Antonio continued. "What's the hurry?"

Anna put her hand on Antonio's, which was grasping the gearshift. "You're a dear, but don't worry about me," she assured him. "I think I can manage on my own."

Antonio became thoughtful and shifted into third. Anna pulled her hand away.

"I can stay," he said. "If you need me, I'll stay here. Really."

Anna turned to look at him. "What nonsense," she said kindly.

They drove for a few miles along a country road leading to Lecce.

"It should be here, after the well on the right, they told me," Antonio said, turning onto a side street. Soon they spotted a big tuff farmhouse surrounded by an orchard of almond and orange trees.

"I think it's this one," Anna said, leaning forward.

Antonio pulled over by a drystone wall and killed the engine.

They got out of the car and crossed the orchard. Antonio stopped and picked two almond shells from a tree, broke one in his molars, and handed the shelled almond to Anna.

"When we were little, right around this time, Carlo and I would go around the countryside stealing almonds and gorge on them," he recounted, breaking the second shell and popping the almond in his mouth. "One time, a landowner caught us and started to chase us with his hoe.

'You little wretches!' he yelled as we ran like crazy. Carlo turned around and made a vulgar gesture, and the guy got so mad he chased us all the way home." He laughed.

Anna smiled, imagining the scene. "I really would have loved to have known you as children," she said.

He smiled back at her and kept walking.

The wooden door to the farmhouse was ajar. Antonio poked his head through the opening. "Is anyone here?" he asked.

No answer.

"Hey there!" Anna shouted.

Silence.

They looked at each other for a moment, uncertain, and went in.

They found themselves in front of what looked like a huge market that had just been hit by a tornado. Antique furniture in various states of disrepair were stacked haphazardly throughout the room: oil lamps, gilded bronze jugs, wrought iron torch holders, statuettes of saints, cups of all sorts, teapots, wall clocks, fans, books, paintings, stools, dressers, chests . . .

"This is amazing," Anna exclaimed. "I wonder if he has one of those toiletry sets my grandmother used to use."

"What did it look like?" Antonio asked, coming over to her.

"You know, it was silver, with embossed handles," she explained. "There was a hairbrush, a coat brush, and a little mirror. As a girl, I played with them every afternoon for hours on end. I pretended to make myself pretty, like Granny."

"I imagine that wouldn't have been hard to do," Antonio said, looking around.

They suddenly heard a voice coming from behind.

"Who's there?"

Antonio and Anna turned at the same time. A man in his sixties with a long, tangled white beard was standing at the door, holding a pipe and looking emaciated.

"Please forgive us," Anna said. "We were just poking around."

"You must be Mr. Bruno," Antonio said, walking toward him with his hand out.

"That's me," said the man, shaking his hand.

"I'm Antonio Greco. Pleased to meet you. And this is my sister-in-law, Anna."

"Anna Allavena," she specified. "This place is wonderful," she added, with a big smile.

Bruno returned her smile, pleased. "What are you looking for?" he asked.

"I was told you have an old blackboard," Antonio said. "Well, we happen to be looking for one."

"You were informed correctly," Bruno said. "Come," he said, setting off. He led them to the adjacent room, where, between wardrobes, writing desks, a printing press, a plow, and a marble sink, there was a wall blackboard with a solid wood frame. "It's this one," said the man, letting out a cloud of smoke.

Anna crouched down to get a better look and stroked the smooth surface of the slate.

"What do you think? It looks like it would work, no?" Antonio asked her, crouching next to her.

"It's perfect!" she said. Then she turned to Bruno. "We'll take it!"

Antonio pulled some twine out of the trunk and they used it to tie the blackboard onto the roof, passing the twine several times through the open windows. Bruno watched them with interest, leaning against the doorjamb with his arms crossed. Every so often, he brought his pipe to his mouth and took a deep puff.

"Does it hold over there?" Antonio asked, poking his head above the roof of the car.

"Seems to," Anna said, and gave the twine a tug.

They got back in the car and had just turned onto the main road when they heard a thump.

They both turned around at the same time and saw the blackboard on the ground, smack in the middle of the road.

Antonio gaped at it. Then he turned to look at Anna. "Didn't you make a knot?" he asked.

"I was supposed to make a knot?"

They stared at each other for a moment and then burst out laughing. Anna was still heaving when Antonio opened the door and tried to put the blackboard back on the roof.

"Come on, stop it, come help me," he said, amused. But Anna's full and crystalline laugh continued to echo among the olive trees and spread around like pollen. And she realized that it was her first real laugh since Carlo's death. The first without the guilt, without wondering whether it was okay to laugh after losing the love of one's life.

Once back at Contrada La Pietra, they fixed the blackboard to the wall with long, thick nails. The opposite wall was now home to a spacious library. Until two weeks before, the shelves had hosted the mill's receipt archives. "I'll find another place for all these folders, don't worry," Antonio had said when he gave the shelves to her. The first two shelves were already taken up by Roberto's old schoolbooks, starting with the ones he'd used as a child, in elementary school. Soon, they would also have desks and chairs. *And then it will really look like a classroom,* Anna thought. Gigetto, the woodworker, had given her a very fair price for ten desks, ten chairs, and the ten bunk beds she'd set up upstairs.

"Don't worry, letter carrier. It'll all be ready by the end of summer," he'd assured her. "If you also need the mattresses, I've got a friend. I'll tell him to treat you well."

"I'd say we deserve a coffee right about now, don't you think?" Antonio said.

"Absolutely!" Anna said.

There was not a living soul in all the square; it looked like everyone had vanished en masse amid the scorching heat. Inside Bar Castello, also deserted, Nando was drying some glasses with a rag while the little radio on the bar played "Grazie dei fiori" (Thank you for the flowers), by

Nilla Pizzi, which had won the first edition of the Festival of Italian Song.

Nando placed two cups in front of them. "If I may . . ." he said, with some hesitation. "Try this almond syrup instead of the sugar." Without waiting for an answer, he took a bottle and poured a few drops in the steaming coffees. "My wife made it just yesterday, it's to die for . . . And it's on the house, of course!"

Antonio drank a sip of coffee. "Nando, it's delicious! Compliments to your lady."

Nando nodded with pride.

Anna was about to say that it was too sweet for her taste when Antonio started to sing softly along with Nilla Pizzi: "In mezzo a quelle rose ci sono tante spine, memorie dolorose di chi ha voluto bene . . . Son pagine già chiuse con la parola fine . . ."

Anna stopped with the cup halfway to her lips, staring at Antonio's mouth as it moved slowly, whispering the words to the song. Just then she felt a sort of jolt, right there, where her heart was.

"What's wrong?" Antonio asked with a smile, when he noticed he was being watched.

Anna quickly looked away. "Nothing," she said hastily, feeling her cheeks go red.

She drank the last sip of coffee.

———

The Greco Estate vineyard launched the 1951 grape harvest halfway through that August.

Daniele arrived in front of Roberto's house at five in the morning and rang the bell on his Taurus Lautal. "I don't want you to go on foot at that hour. It'll still be dark. I'd rather stop by and pick you up," he'd said the day before. When Roberto opened the door, still half asleep, Daniele greeted him jauntily and had him sit on the horizontal bar on his bicycle.

"You're sure you can still see the road?" Roberto asked, climbing on.

"I can see, I can see."

Every so often, along the way, if Roberto budged even slightly, the bicycle would swerve to the right or left.

"Oooohh!" he'd exclaim, afraid, holding on to the bar.

"Stay still, though!" Daniele would chuckle.

The laborers were starting to arrive in batches: on foot, on bicycles, and in carts drawn by donkeys. A few minutes after six, the sun finally appeared among the vines, lighting up the vineyard. The men scattered throughout the rows and began working at a steady clip, cutting the mature grapes from the plants and filling the baskets on the ground.

Daniele grabbed two pairs of shears and gave one to Roberto.

"Come with me," he said, putting a hand on his shoulder. He led him into the center of a row.

On those rare occasions when Carlo had taken him to watch the harvest as a child, Roberto had never seen his father join in with the workers, and he certainly hadn't started doing the same things they did. He'd take his son by the hand and walk through the rows, between the baskets full of grapes, checking that everything was running smoothly. Only once had he allowed Roberto to climb into one of the vats and press the grapes with his bare feet, along with the other children.

"Watch me," Daniele said as he cut a bunch of grapes off the vine in one clean motion. "Do as I do."

It was obvious that Daniele was used to joining the farmers and toiling along with them, during the harvest and more broadly. Roberto wouldn't have known which of the two approaches he agreed with the most, whether it was the benevolent but distant one his father espoused or Daniele's humble attitude. He trusted that he would find his own way sooner or later.

Suddenly, up ahead, a farmer intoned a folk song, spreading his light, piercing voice across the field:

E fior di tutti i fiori . . .

The others, from each row, joined in chorus:

Fior di lu pepe
Tutte le fontantelle so' siccate
Povero amore mio more di sete

They carried on, folk song after folk song, until nine, when Daniele called the break.

"I'm so hungry . . ." Roberto grumbled, touching his stomach.

"Come on, let's go into the winery and get some wine for everyone," Daniele said. "Then we'll eat something too."

They came out with two demijohns of Don Carlo, which the laborers passed from hand to hand, drinking in big gulps.

Daniele and Roberto squeezed in around one of the little circles the men had formed on the ground as they ate. One kid who was about Roberto's age softened two friselle by dipping them in water, spread some tomatoes on top, opening them one at a time, and covered everything with plenty of olive oil.

"For you," he said, handing one to Daniele and to Roberto.

"And the forks?" Roberto asked.

His request was greeted with a resounding laugh.

"Hah, the little lord wants a fork," exclaimed one man, chewing with his mouth open.

Daniele was looking at him, also laughing.

"What did I say?" Roberto said, confused.

"Tell me this," Daniele said, ripping off a piece of frisa soaked in oil. "Do you eat friselle with cutlery?"

"How else? My mother always made us eat it with a fork," Roberto said, as if he were saying the most obvious thing in the world.

"Try it with your hands," Daniele said, winking. "You'll see how much better it is."

Roberto joined his fingers in a pinching motion and tried to pick up a handful of friselle. *If my mother could see me now, she'd cut my hand off,* he thought, amused. He was about to bring the friselle to his mouth when a man arrived on a bicycle, out of breath and dripping with sweat.

"Daniele! Daniele Carlà! Daniele!" he was yelling.

Someone stood up and someone else looked up, but most kept eating as if nothing were happening.

"I'm here!" Daniele yelled, standing up. "What happened?"

The man on the bicycle stopped in front of him. He was still panting heavily.

"Drink something or you'll croak here in a minute," said a farmer, handing him the demijohn.

The man took a big gulp and then dried his lips with the back of his wrist. Then, his face tense and still out of breath, he said, "Your mother sent me. You have to go home immediately."

Daniele looked at him with concern.

"It's your father," the man said. "He's had a heart attack."

Daniele quickly climbed onto his bike and reached his parents' house, pedaling at breakneck speed. But when his Grandma Gina opened the door, sobbing into a handkerchief, he realized he was too late. His father hadn't waited for him.

26

The house had filled with the smell of chrysanthemums and of Carmela's jasmine perfume. Wearing a calf-length black dress and an organza veil that covered her face, Carmela remained sitting throughout the entire vigil, while a river of people offering their condolences passed before her. She played the role of afflicted widow impeccably, yet no one ever saw her shed a tear: not during the vigil, not during the funeral, and certainly not the moment they buried Nicola.

Toward Daniele she'd been, if possible, even more distant. She hadn't hugged him or given him a word of comfort. At least not until the morning of the funeral.

Daniele had walked into the kitchen to find his mother and grandmother drinking coffee.

"That coffin cost more than the church service," Carmela was saying in a scornful tone. "By the end, he was fatter than two pigs stuck together."

Daniele clenched his fists and screamed, "That's enough!," his voice trembling with rage. He ran out of the house, climbed onto his bike, and started pedaling frantically, wiping the tears from his face with the back of his hand. He couldn't stand it, that his father was being humiliated yet again. His whole life he'd watched him endure it in silence, unable to defend himself from Carmela's scorn, from her constant lack of respect, her dirty looks. And if Daniele ever dared to take Nicola's side, his father would block him, putting a hand on his arm.

"Your mother's right," he'd say. "I was wrong, I made her angry." Daniele had felt so much frustration as a child, watching that man make himself smaller and smaller over the years. *React*, he'd thought a thousand times. *Raise your voice! Get angry for once! She's the one who's wrong, not you! You're good, Papa.*

In church, during the service, he didn't even deign to look at his mother, even as she took him by the arm and rested her head on his shoulder, as if nothing had happened in the kitchen. Daniele kept his eyes fixed on the coffin, thinking back to all those times he hadn't gone to see his father, of all the meals they hadn't had together, of the chats between father and son that they could have had but never did; by reducing his visits to his mother, he'd also let his relationship with his father unravel. He'd tried everything to stem Carmela's presence in his life, to experience her in smaller doses, so small they couldn't hurt him. In his effort to keep her away, he'd ended up locking his father out too.

He missed his Lorenza terribly. He regretted having treated her so badly that afternoon at the studio. In the end, she had left for Otranto with her family, understandably angry and hurt. In those painful moments, Lorenza was the only person he wanted to comfort him, the one whose hand he wished he could hold.

He felt crushed under a boulder of sadness, alone in the world, even though so many people were attending the funeral and kissing him, holding him, hugging him . . . And then there was Roberto, who'd offered to help carry the coffin from the church to the cemetery.

"I know how you feel," he'd said with an expression of sincere regret, affectionately squeezing his arm.

Anna had been there since the vigil but only approached Daniele after the burial, taking him aside.

"Antonio left me the address in Otranto, just in case," she said. "If you want, I can let her know. Discreetly."

Daniele looked at her with a flash of hope in his eyes.

"I'd be so grateful," he said, with a sniffle.

————

Anna's telegram arrived in Otranto on a sweltering morning, while the family was at the beach. Only Antonio had stayed back on the veranda to read Alberto Moravia's new book, *The Conformist*; He and Anna had chosen it together as their summer reading, promising to talk about it upon returning from vacation. When the postman whistled from beyond the gate, Antonio immediately stood up from the lounge chair and went to him.

"A telegram for Antonio Greco," the man said, handing him the yellow envelope. Antonio turned it around in his hands and as soon as he read the sender's name—Anna Allavena—he ripped it open.

Daniele's father died of a heart attack. The funeral was today. I sent a wreath of flowers from all of you.

Antonio initially kept the news to himself, thinking it wasn't a good idea to ruin everyone's day, and that maybe, that evening, he'd find the right moment to break the news.

The others came up from the beach at lunchtime, ate on the veranda, and then Giada was put down for her afternoon nap while Tommaso and Lorenza pushed the dirty dishes to one side of the table and played cards. He was teaching her how to play tressette, explaining that the three had the highest value, followed by the two, the ace, the king, and so on. Every so often, Antonio would look up from his book to watch them. His daughter seemed unusually peaceful; over lunch she'd even laughed at one of her husband's jokes.

At sunset, Tommaso suggested to Lorenza that they take a walk along the seashore and she said yes. Antonio watched them walk away, side by side, feeling certain that the news of Daniele's father's death would cause that little bit of harmony they'd rebuilt to crumble like a sandcastle.

He waited until everyone had gone to bed before going out onto the veranda, committed to disposing of that telegram and pretending it had never reached its destination.

"What's that you've got there?" Lorenza asked, popping out onto the veranda. She was in her nightgown and her hair was all ruffled.

"Nothing," Antonio said, sticking the telegram in his pocket.

"If it's nothing, why are you hiding it?"

"You can't sleep?"

"Don't change the subject," she protested, frowning. "What's that envelope?"

"It's a message from the mill, nothing important."

His daughter crossed her arms in front of her and walked up to him. "Do you think I'm still ten years old? Let's hear it. What are you hiding?"

Antonio sighed, then slowly pulled the envelope out of his pocket and handed it to her. "I didn't want to ruin the vacation with bad news," he said, justifying himself, in a faint voice.

Lorenza shot him a reproachful look and slipped the telegram out of the envelope.

After reading it, she started going off the rails. She demanded that Antonio take her back to Lizzanello right away, in that precise moment.

"But it's nighttime. . . . Where are we going to go? Try to be reasonable."

"I don't give a damn if it's nighttime! I must go to him, he needs me," Lorenza yelled.

Antonio grabbed her by the arm and whispered, in an authoritative tone, "You have to go to your husband. He's the one who needs you."

Lorenza opened her eyes wide, stunned.

"Go back to bed, Lorenza. Don't make me angry."

She broke free. "You take me immediately, or I'm going on my own. Now. Even if I have to walk there."

The commotion ended up waking up Tommaso and Agata, who both ran downstairs as they heard the shouts.

"What's all this?" Agata asked, with a hand on her chest.

"Everything okay, Lorenza?" Tommaso asked, placing a hand on her back.

Lorenza stared at her father with fire in her eyes, waiting for him to come up with a plausible explanation.

"Nothing, don't worry about it," Antonio assured them. "Trouble at the mill," he added, waving the yellow envelope in the air. "I have to go down to Lizzanello tomorrow morning, but I'll try to be back by evening."

Agata sighed. "You're going to be the death of me!"

"That's why you were angry?" Tommaso asked his wife. "He said he'll be back tomorrow, don't worry. He's not leaving." Then he looked up at Antonio and smiled at him, as if to say that they they'd all gotten used to Lorenza's temper tantrums by now.

"I'd rather go with him, to make sure he comes back," Lorenza said. "Understand?" she added, turning toward her husband. "I'm going with Papa tomorrow."

———

"I can hardly believe it's true; we're almost done," Anna said, with her hands on her hips, looking around. In just a few months, Giovanna's farmhouse had been transformed, becoming everything Anna had imagined, down to the last detail. A wooden sign had been placed at the main entrance. It proudly said WOMEN'S HOME in black cursive. Anna had traced it herself in her clear and rounded handwriting.

Inside, the walls had been washed and painted white, giving the whole environment a fresh and clean feel; only the stovetop and sink remained of the old kitchen, to the right of the main entrance, along with the cabinetry and some shelves. The rest of the space was occupied by a large rectangular table surrounded by chairs and decorated with a bouquet of flowers. Against another wall were a sewing machine and a tall open wardrobe, which contained sewing kits and tools for working with papier-mâché and ceramics. Anna had explained to Antonio that the house would also be an atelier, whose products could be bought directly at the farmhouse or at the market. They would carry the label WOMEN'S HOME, and every lira earned would go directly into the pockets of the women who'd created the objects.

In the room on the left, where the living room once was, there was now a classroom with a blackboard, desks, and chairs. In the library, aside from Roberto's schoolbooks, Anna's favorite novels, which she'd brought from home, took pride of place—from *Madame Bovary* to *Wuthering Heights*.

Upstairs, the two bedrooms now hosted a dormitory with ten beds— six in one room and four in the other. Anna had even procured a few cribs.

The launch was due to take place about a month from now, on Carlo's birthday, at the end of November. That was what Anna had decided, in the end. Opening the Women's Home before then would have been impossible.

"Yup, we did it," Antonio sighed, standing next to her. But his face was clouded over.

"What's wrong with you today? It looks like your mind is elsewhere."

"I'm sorry . . ."

"It's just that you look so . . . I don't know. Sad, I guess."

"I have some worries, that's all," he said, shrugging.

"And may I know what they are?"

Antonio was silent for a few seconds. "Come with me. Let's get some air," he said, reaching for her hand. Anna took it and together they walked out into the garden. Antonio sat on the ground, pulling Anna down with him.

"Well?" she insisted, crossing her ankles.

"I'm sorry for Lorenza," he said after a few moments. "I thought her affair with Daniele was a thing of the past, but in truth . . ."

Anna swallowed but didn't say anything.

"I've watched her closely, in these past few months . . . I even followed her . . ."

"What did you do?"

"What I had to," he said curtly. "Do you know where she goes every Wednesday after she drops Giada off with you?"

Anna shrugged, then looked away and started to stroke the blades of grass. "I know that once a week she goes to visit that high school friend of hers, in Lecce," she lied.

"Well, if that's what she told you, then she told you a big fat lie."

"Where does she go, then?"

"To him. She goes to him every Wednesday. They meet in Lecce, in a place near Porta Rudiae," he sighed nervously.

"I still can't believe you spied on her . . ."

"But did you hear what I said?"

"I heard."

Antonio looked at her closely. "You don't seem surprised."

To which she stared back at him. "Because I knew from the beginning that it would end up this way. I told you so, don't you remember?"

"Anna, you have to help me," he said finally. "You have to talk to Lorenza. She listens to you. You have to reason with her, make her understand that it's all wrong. Stop her before she gets into trouble, before . . . I don't even want to think about it." He put his head in his hands.

"Calm down," she said, and she ran her fingers through his hair.

He looked up, with teary eyes, and let out his breath.

Seeing him like that broke her heart.

"Okay, I'll try to talk to her," she assured him, still stroking his hair.

Antonio nodded, and then he squeezed her hand in his, brought it to his mouth, and lightly kissed it. Anna felt herself go hot while a shiver flashed down her spine.

"Thank you," he said.

———

The inauguration was less than an hour away and Anna was walking back and forth without rest, wringing her hands. She was wearing a wool-and-silk cream-colored suit with a jacket fitted at the waist and a skirt that came down below the knee. She'd bought it for the occasion. There was a piece of paper in her jacket pocket on which she'd sketched a sort of welcome speech.

Every so often she'd stop, look at Antonio, and say, "What if no one comes?"

"They'll come, they'll come," he assured her.

In the workspace, Anna had set up a few refreshments, with the bottles of Donna Anna and Don Carlo that Roberto and Antonio had loaded onto the Fiat 508 and brought there that morning while out delivering the mail.

"Organizing parties and things like that is not exactly my forte," she grumbled, leaning on a desk.

Antonio smiled slightly, then went and leaned against the desk in front of her. "Carletto was good at these things," he said. "Can you imagine, if he'd been here?"

"He would have invited the pope," Anna joked.

"For sure," Antonio said, with a sad smile.

She, on the other hand, hadn't wanted to invite a single so-called clergyman. A few mornings before, as she was leaving Bar Castello, she'd run into don Luciano, who'd gone up to her with his arms wide open.

"Good morning, letter carrier," he'd said. "I was hoping to see you. Or I would have come looking for you at the post office."

"Looking for me? And whatever for?" she'd said, lifting an eyebrow.

"Well, for the blessing. We have to set a time. When should I come? The opening is this Thursday, right?"

Anna had looked at him bewildered. "What blessing?"

Don Luciano chuckled. "What do you mean! For your Women's Home, no?"

"The Home and I don't need any blessing to speak of!" she exclaimed.

The priest took a small step back, disconcerted. Two men sitting at a nearby table looked up from the three cards they were holding.

"Every new activity needs a blessing from our Lord," don Luciano had declared.

Anna smirked and got on her bike.

"Not mine, I'm sorry," she'd said, shrugging. And she'd left, leaving him in a lurch.

She checked the time again; it was just a few minutes before five, when people would start to arrive.

"What do you say we make a toast in the meantime, just you and me?" Antonio suggested.

"I say it's an excellent idea!" she said, clapping her hands.

They went over to the refreshments and Antonio picked out a bottle of Donna Anna and removed the cork. Meanwhile, Anna held out two glasses, smiling. He filled them both and took one from her.

"To the Women's Home," he said, lifting his glass to Anna.

She clinked her glass against his and added, "To us, who made it happen. Santé!"

"Santé," he echoed.

The first to arrive, at exactly five, were Roberto and Maria.

"Forgive us, Maman, we wanted to come sooner to help out, but there was a setback at the winery," Roberto said, planting a kiss on her cheek.

"My fault," Maria said, quick to apologize. "I messed up an order."

She immediately started looking around with her usual amazed expression; it seemed like every new thing was a reason for her to be completely enchanted.

Anna forced a smile and put her glass on the table. "Come with me, I'll show you," she said with a nod.

After a short while, Lorenza and Tommaso also arrived, followed by Agata with little Giada in her arms.

"And where's Auntie?" Lorenza asked.

"Upstairs with Maria," Roberto said. "Who wants wine?"

"I'll have some," Tommaso said.

"Oh, why not, I'll take a drop too," Agata said.

"Welcome," Anna greeted them, walking back into the room just then. Maria was right behind her, her hands interlaced. She immediately went over to Roberto, who wrapped an arm around her waist.

By quarter to six, no one else had arrived. A sleepy Giada was whining and rubbing her eyes with her little fists.

"The little one has to sleep," Agata said, cradling her in her arms. "We better take her home, no?" she asked Tommaso. "It's not like there's all that much going on here anyway."

"Yes, perhaps it's best," he said, standing up from his chair. "Lorenza, are you coming back with us?"

"Do you want me to stay here with you, Auntie?"

Although darkness had fallen, Anna was still staring at the fields outside the window, with her arms crossed in front of her chest. She turned for a moment and said, "No, ma petite, go ahead."

Antonio went over to Agata and whispered, "I'll stay a little longer." But his wife didn't answer.

As Lorenza was leaving, Antonio looked at her sternly.

"Bye, Papa," she said, holding his gaze.

"Bye," he said coldly. Then he closed the door and went to Anna.

"I told you no one would come," she murmured.

He looked at her dejectedly and put a hand on her shoulder. "I'm so sorry," he said. "I don't understand. There must be an explanation."

Anna hardened her gaze. "I don't give a damn," she said finally, decisively. "I'm going ahead with it anyway. Do you think I'm going to let a band of louts discourage me?"

———

The following morning, at the post office, Elena couldn't have been more apologetic.

"I wanted to come, I swear. But you have to understand. My feet are as swollen as sausages—how was I supposed to get all the way out there?"

"Don't worry about it," Anna said, without looking up from the letters on the table.

Even Carmine, as soon as he walked into the office, hastened to tell her that he was very sorry he hadn't been there. They'd called a last-minute union meeting—what was he supposed to do?

Everyone Anna ran into that morning seemed ready to slip her some excuse. As he served her caffè corretto, Nando told her he really wanted to be there, but then his wife had come up with one of her demands, and he'd had to tidy up the attic.

"When she decides that something must be done, that's it. It has to be done when she says and how she says."

"Don't worry, Nando," Anna said. "You'll have plenty of opportunities, if you want."

But what hurt the most had been Giovanna's absence. She'd hoped until the last minute to see her arrive at Contrada, but in vain. When Anna had gone home for dinner that night, Giovanna had asked, naïvely, "How did it go?"

Anna had retorted, "Do you even care?"

"Why do you say that?" Giovanna had asked, stunned.

"You even have to ask? I needed you there today, I needed you to be there for me. But you weren't. And what for? For *whom*? How much longer are you going to let that man win?" She'd gone up to her room, slamming the door.

A few hours later, Anna was in bed reading by the light of the lamp on her nightstand.

Giovanna gently knocked on the door. "May I? I have to tell you something." She walked into the room with her head down, biting her lip.

"You're right. I was wrong, I know. But you have to understand that I'm not strong like you."

"Yes, you are," Anna said, sitting up in bed.

Giovanna shook her head. "No, I'm not," she insisted. She took a seat on the edge of the bed and let her hands drop to her lap. "The truth is that I'm still afraid," she whispered.

"Of whom? Of that idiot?"

"No, not of him. I'm afraid of myself. Of how I might feel, of what I might experience. I'm not ready yet, that's all."

Anna sighed dejectedly and looked at Giovanna with tenderness. "You are strong, it's just that you don't realize it yet."

"Maybe. I don't know," Giovanna said. "But while I try to come to terms with it on my own, don't blame me for it."

"No, you're right," Anna said. "I'm sorry, too. Really." She reached her hand across the bedspread toward Giovanna, who took it gently, as if to say that everything was okay again.

———

Like he did every year in the first days of December, Daniele brought his Grandma Gina one of the first bottles of the new Donna Anna. The 1951 vintage seemed to be one of the best so far, thanks to the sunny but not sweltering summer and a few lucky showers that had freshened up the hotter days.

He knocked. "Grandma, it's me!" he yelled, knowing that Gina could hear less and less.

But Carmela opened the door, swaddled in her black widow's dress. "Look who's here," she said.

Daniele stiffened. "Grandma's not here?"

"Of course she is. Where else would she be?" Carmela said, opening the door wide. "Tràsi."

He walked into the kitchen and bent down to kiss his grandmother's wrinkly cheek. "Here you go," he said, placing the bottle on the table.

"Oh, how lovely." Gina cheered up. "Open it, please; I want to taste it right away."

Daniele smiled and pulled a bottle opener from the drawer; despite her seventy-something years, his grandma had never lost her thirst for the occasional nip.

"I'll get the glasses," Carmela said. "I'll try some too."

Daniele filled both their glasses, then asked his grandma to smell the wine's perfume. "What do you think?"

Gina breathed in deeply. "Seems good like always."

Carmela downed the glass in one go.

"Take it easy, daughter," Gina admonished her. "Hasn't your father taught you anything? Wine must be drunk slowly, slowly."

Carmela smacked her lips. "Good," she said, and poured herself another glass.

"I better go now," Daniele announced, stroking his grandmother's white, bristly hair.

"You're leaving already? You just got here!" Carmela grumbled, taking another sip.

"Yes," he said without looking at her. "I have to get back to the winery."

"Then what's Roberto there for?" she hissed. "You work more than he does."

"That's not true," Daniele said, defending him. "It's just that at the moment, we're taking care of different things. He's still learning, but he's doing it quickly."

"Perhaps." Carmela scrunched her nose and drank the last sip of wine from her glass. Then she reached for the bottle and turned it toward her.

"Donna Anna," she read, slightly slurring her words. "I'd like to see— now that you own part of the winery—when you'll dedicate a wine to your mother. Donna Carmela. Has a nice ring to it, no?"

Daniele sighed impatiently, then looked at his grandmother and said he really had to go now.

"You got nothin' to say?" Carmela burst out. "What is it? Don't I also deserve a wine from the Greco Winery?"

Daniele stared at her sternly. "No. I'd say you don't."

"Go ahead, honey," Gina said, trying to ease the tension.

"He's not going anywhere unless he first tells me to my face, clear and simple, what he thinks."

"Let it go," Daniele said, and went to leave.

"Oh, you're leaving? Go ahead, go," she said, waving her hand. "You're the spitting image of your father. Leaving is what you do best."

"I'll walk you to the door." With effort, Gina tried to stand up. But she was too agitated and couldn't move.

"No, wait." Daniele stopped her, without looking away from his mother. "This one I don't get. When, exactly, did Papa ever leave? He did nothing but tolerate you his whole life."

"Yes. His whole life. Sure," Carmela said, with a mirthless laugh.

"Honey, you better go now," Gina said in a trembling voice, taking her grandson's hand in hers.

But he didn't move. "Nothing. You can't even leave him in peace when he's dead. You just can't do it. You know what? You wanted to know what I really think? Well, I'll tell you."

Carmela looked at him daringly. "I'm listening."

"Do you know why I'll never name a wine after you? Because I can't even muster an iota of regard for women like you."

She narrowed her eyes and took a few steps forward. "And for that Anna, do you have regard for her?" she said through her teeth.

"Yes, so what?" Daniele said.

She came to within an inch of his face and studied him. "Yeah," she sneered. "Just as I said. Spitting image of your father."

"Shut up!" Gina yelled.

"Actually, I think it's high time I talk," Carmela exclaimed.

With a superhuman effort, Gina heaved herself against her daughter and tried to pull her back. "Shut up, vile woman!"

"Grandma, calm down," Daniele said, with concern.

"You Grecos are obsessed with that woman. It's like a disease," Carmela said in one breath.

Daniele turned to her and stared at her in bewilderment. Gina collapsed back onto the chair and closed her eyes, bringing a hand to her heart.

"What are you talking about? I don't understand," Daniele said.

Silence fell on the room.

It took a few moments for him to tie it all together.

And then, suddenly, with a jolt, Daniele knew.

———

Every afternoon after work, Anna would go to the Women's Home and spend hours there, hopeful and determined.

Most of the time, Antonio would keep her company.

"I don't like you being here all by yourself," he'd say.

"What do you think will happen?" Anna played it down.

"I don't know. But the thought makes me nervous."

So Antonio would leave the oil mill much earlier than usual and join her. For the sake of staying for as long as possible, he always found a small job to do: He'd set up some new books in the library, water the gardens, fix a shelf that looked a little unstable. He'd stay until darkness fell, and then say, "It's late. Let's go, I'll take you home." He'd escort her home as she pedaled ahead and he lit her way from behind with his headlights.

One early afternoon in mid-December, two weeks after the inauguration, Anna heard someone knocking and went to open the door, certain it was Antonio. But when she got there, she found a petite woman who looked like she hadn't eaten in a while. Her eyebrows were thick and dark, and her voluminous mane of curly black hair was streaked with gray. She was carrying a laden threadbare bag on her back, which probably contained everything she owned.

"I was told you can help me," the woman said.

Anna noticed a sort of archipelago of small crusts around the side of her mouth. "Of course, come in, sit down. I'll make you a coffee," she mumbled, in slight disbelief.

The woman's name was Melina. And she "turned tricks," she explained, staring at Anna as if to catch any hint, however imperceptible, of disdain. Anna didn't show any judgment.

Anna prepared the coffee and encouraged Melina to talk.

Melina told her about losing her husband in the war and of all the days her stomach had writhed because she had nothing to sink her teeth into.

"If the man is gone, so is the bread," she said.

"This is what they want us to believe," Anna said.

"I never went to school. I can't even write my own name," Melina continued. "I can't do anything. There's just this," she added, spreading her arms. "And it fed me. Until now." She leaned back in her chair. "But now this body is empty, flaccid, and men don't take pleasure in it anymore." She sighed and leaned forward. "I have to find work, and out there no one wants to give me any. I need your help. I'll learn anything—I'm a whore, not an idiot."

Anna watched her for a moment, then broke into a smile. "Well, I'd say you came to the right place," she said, getting up.

"One more thing," Melina continued, staying seated.

"I have a friend . . . Some scoundrel, I don't know who, got her in trouble and now she's expecting a babe. Her mother kicked her out and she has no place to live. Can she come stay here even if she's pregnant?"

When Antonio arrived a few hours later, Anna opened the door looking radiant.

"What is it?" he asked, smiling.

Anna took his face in her hands and planted a big fat kiss on his cheek.

"What was that for?" he asked, a bit concerned now.

"There's a woman in there," Anna explained. "And another one is coming tomorrow."

Antonio took her hand and looked her in the eyes. "I knew it," he said. "It was just a matter of time."

"Yes," Anna said. "Thank you for waiting with me." She squeezed his hand even harder.

In that moment, Melina popped out from behind Anna.

"Hello," she said.

"Hello," Antonio said, pretending he'd never seen her before to avoid arousing suspicion of their illicit meeting.

"Here she is," Anna exclaimed. "Melina, this is my brother-in-law Antonio. Antonio, this is Melina. The first resident of the Women's Home."

"Pleased to meet you," the woman said, with a hand on her hip.

"Pleasure is mine," Antonio coughed.

The following morning, before going to the post office, Anna made a detour to the big tree farm just outside town.

She walked into the nursery and looked around, noticing the lemon, almond, citrus, and pomegranate trees.

"How can I help you?" The voice of a man came from the right, surprising her. He was tall and sturdy, and he was rubbing dirt off his hands with a rag that looked like it hadn't seen water or soap in a long time.

"I'd like to order a Christmas tree," she said. "The tallest one you have."

The telephone rang for a long time before Anna went to pick up. She still hadn't gotten used to that irritating *ring ring*, which made her heart skip a beat every time. Roberto had given her the phone for Christmas. He'd pulled an ugly black Bakelite contraption with a dial and receiver out of a box and had asked her, all excited, "Do you like it, Maman? I bought one for the winery, too!"

"Who is it?" Anna answered curtly.

She heard her son laughing it up on the other end of the line.

"Roberto! What are you laughing at?"

"How can you still take so long to pick up?" he said. "Plus, don't say 'Who is it?' say 'Hello?'"

"And who decided that?"

"I don't know, but that's how it's done."

"Bah, me saying 'Hello?' Just like that? I feel like an idiot."

"As you wish, Maman," Roberto said, amused. "What are you doing?"

"What do you think I'm doing? I'm in a rush as usual: I just got back from work, and I still have to make lunch. They're expecting me at the Home for the two o'clock lesson."

"That's actually why I'm calling. I won't be back for lunch; I'll grab a bite here at the winery. So don't make anything fancy. I'll see you at dinner. Oh! And Maria's coming for dinner, remember?"

Anna registered the information and murmured, "Mm-hmm," and put the receiver down without saying goodbye.

"Who was that?" Giovanna asked, emerging into the living room. She was wearing the shawl she'd made. She hardly ever took it off.

"Who could it be? One of the two people who have our number," Anna joked. "Shall we make a quick pasta? I have to leave in less than an hour."

Giovanna nodded, then went to say something, but hesitated.

"What is it?" Anna asked.

Giovanna cleared her throat, then said in a faint voice, "I was thinking... what if I came with you today? To Contrada?"

Anna's face lit up with joy.

"But if I were to feel ... off, in seeing it, I mean, well, I'll want to leave right away," Giovanna specified.

"Yes, that's fine," Anna said. Then repeated, in a whisper, "That's fine."

———

Roberto put down the receiver, shaking his head. Phone conversations with his mother always ended the same way: suddenly. She'd decide it was time to put down the receiver and just do it.

"I'm going back down to the cellar," he said as he passed Maria's desk, which was piled high with papers.

Engrossed in her work, she mumbled a distracted "Okay."

Roberto went downstairs to the wooden barrels where the Don Carlo was still improving. It would take eighteen long months for the Greco Winery's red to be mature enough for bottling; by February, they'd be bottling the harvest from 1950. Those days at the winery were especially intense, but it wouldn't be long now. In the meantime, Roberto was working sixteen hours a day. He'd arrive at the first light of dawn and stay until evening, in part because by now, Daniele was much less present—entire days would go by before he'd stop by the winery again, and when he did come, he'd stay no longer than an hour.

Roberto couldn't say why, but Daniele seemed different lately: as if shaken by news, or maybe sad about something or someone? During one of his rare appearances at the winery, he'd tried asking him what was wrong, but Daniele had simply forced a smile.

"Don't worry about me, everything's fine, really."

Roberto didn't believe him, but he didn't want to press the matter. Even though, in truth, he did have an idea. He thought Daniele's distress had something to do with his cousin Lorenza. He'd started to suspect it when she came to the winery one late Wednesday afternoon, about a month before. It was only her second or third time setting foot there, at least since he'd been working.

"Cousin, to what do I owe the pleasure?" Roberto had greeted her. "Are you in the mood for a tipple?"

"Actually, I could use one," she'd mumbled, wringing her hands.

"Come with me," he'd said. In the short walk from the entrance to Roberto's office, Lorenza had looked around continuously, and once or twice she'd even jumped, whipping around after hearing steps coming up from the cellar or in through the gate. It had taken her a few good minutes, and a finger of the Donna Anna Anniversary that Roberto kept on his desk, to reveal the reason for her visit.

"Daniele isn't here, is he?"

"I saw him fleetingly this morning, but he didn't stay long," Roberto said.

"And he hasn't been back today?"

"No."

"Did he happen to say if he had any commitments in the afternoon?"

Roberto smirked and shrugged, as if to say he hadn't the faintest clue.

"I see," Lorenza murmured. She stood up suddenly, said goodbye, and headed for the exit. "Thank you for the wine."

———

Anna was going at breakneck speed while Giovanna struggled to keep up, even though she was pedaling as fast as she could. The bicycle had been her Christmas present from the entire Greco family.

When Giovanna had seen it, complete with a red bow on the handlebar, she'd felt a deep sense of shame, thinking about how paltry the little crochet works she'd packaged for each of them would appear in comparison.

Panting, she now took the road to Contrada La Pietra. Anna finally slowed down. As they approached the front gate, they both got off their bikes. As soon as Giovanna found herself outside her house again, she didn't feel at all *off*, as she'd feared. In fact, her heart immediately warmed. She thought that people probably felt this way upon seeing someone they'd once loved. She couldn't explain why she'd decided to return to Contrada on that day of all days, after all those years avoiding it, and despite the fear she still felt. Maybe it was because she was always alone now, since between work and the Women's Home, Anna was almost never home. Or maybe because, as Anna had said, she really was ready but hadn't realized it.

She stood there for a while, smiling as she looked at the farmhouse's new façade, with its aqua-blue door and shutters and a bouquet of brightly colored flowers on every windowsill. She slowly walked toward the front door, looking around in wonderment: how neat the flower rows were now, and how beautiful the gardens with all those colorful, juicy vegetables.

"'Women's Home,'" Giovanna read above the entryway. She smiled again.

Anna pushed the door open but then stopped. "How are you feeling?" she asked, somewhat anxiously.

"Fine," Giovanna said, peacefully.

"Really?"

"Yes, yes," she reiterated with confidence.

"Well, let's go in, then," Anna exclaimed.

The inside left Giovanna speechless. From Anna's detailed accounts she knew that there had been a number of changes, that she'd probably barely recognize her old home . . . but seeing it all in person was a huge surprise. She found herself in a completely new and special environment, which was now a house, a school, and a shop. It was a welcoming space full of light, where it was impossible to imagine certain ugly things taking place.

Anna took her by the hand and dragged her from room to room, barraging her with questions:

"Well, what do you think?"

"Do you like this?"

"And what about this?"

Then she introduced her to the four women who lived there. Giovanna thought she'd already seen Melina somewhere, even if she couldn't exactly remember when or where. Then there were Elisa and Michela, two sisters who were fourteen and sixteen years old respectively, orphans whose mother had died and who had never known their father. Up until a few weeks ago, they'd been in the service of the Tamburinis, but the lady had noticed certain glances from her husband—the "extremely respectable" Mr. Tamburini—and had summarily dismissed the girls, leaving them, with no home and no work. Finally, there was Elvira, twenty-two years old, with big blue eyes, who was pregnant. She was due in June, according to her calculations. She wasn't from around there, she explained. She was born and raised in Vernole. Hearing the name of that town, where don Giulio worked as a priest, Giovanna felt a jolt that was not lost on Elvira or on Anna.

"Do you know someone there?" Elvira asked.

"No, nobody," Giovanna answered.

With a smile, Anna asked them to take their seats in the classroom; the lesson was about to start. Giovanna went to sit at the last desk in the back, rested her cheek in the palm of her hand, and listened to Anna give her lesson while writing on the blackboard. The four women, especially the sisters, who seemed to be the most attentive, took notes. That day, Anna talked about verbal modes, explaining that they could be finite or nonfinite, and that for each one there were simple and compound tenses.

Giovanna was surprised to find how well she remembered that explanation; it was the same one Anna had given her many years before, in that very same room, when the two of them had read *Pride and Prejudice* together.

At the end of the lesson, as Anna assigned the homework for the following day, a woman with wrinkly hands arrived at the door, smelling of lavender. She was there to teach the women how to knit blankets, Anna explained to Giovanna, adding, "It's an ancient and precious art."

"Yes, my grandmother also made them, to sell. They were so colorful and beautiful. I really wanted to learn, but she never had the time or the desire to teach me. 'Run along, child, and don't pester me,' she'd say."

Melina and Elvira sat down in front of the lady, whose name was Pina, and began pulling balls of yarn and knitting tools out of a basket, along with the blankets they had already started. Giovanna slowly pulled up a chair and sat down next to them.

"Choose the three colors you like the most," Melina said to her, pointing at the basket full of balls of yarn.

Giovanna bent over and rummaged through the balls; she chose a nice bright yellow one, a turquoise one, and an orange one.

"Here are your needles," Pina said, handing them to her with a smile.

"Thank you," Giovanna said, happy as a child.

"Now let me show you some stitches," Pina continued.

The two sisters, who couldn't have been less interested in blankets, were peeking at the novels in the library with interest. Anna was guiding them in their choice.

"Maybe save this one for later," she said, taking a copy of *Crime and Punishment* from Elisa. Giovanna looked up at them. She remembered that book and its annotations well. It was the copy Antonio had given Anna, the one with the inscription saying that even the guilty deserve compassion.

"Here, take this, rather," Anna said, passing a different book to Elisa. Giovanna recognized it instantly; it was *Pride and Prejudice*.

I wonder if this young girl, like me many years ago, will wish she were Elizabeth as she reads the book, she thought with a smile.

Anna and Giovanna didn't leave until evening, just as the four roommates of the Home started on dinner; the two sisters set the table while Melina brought in an onion and a bunch of spinach she'd gathered from the garden and Elvira sliced the bread.

"See you tomorrow," Anna said.

"Oh, Elvira," she said then, turning back. "We can go look for baby clothes tomorrow, after the lesson."

Elvira nodded. "I swear that if it's a girl, I'm calling her Anna, like you," she said.

"Pray that it's a boy, listen to me," Melina cut in, cleaning the spinach.

While they got their bikes, Giovanna asked Anna if the knitting lesson would be held again the following day.

"No, Pina will be back on Friday," Anna said. "Tomorrow, a friend of Carmine's is coming for the first time. He works with papier-mâché."

Giovanna turned back and stared at the Home for a moment, thinking that it had been nice to spend the afternoon there. She couldn't wait until Friday.

———

The workbench at the studio in via Santa Maria del Paradiso was empty; the sewing tools, the notebooks with the black covers, the fabric swatches, the pincushions, the measuring tapes, the wooden yardstick, the scissors, the chalk, and the thimbles were all piled into a cardboard box. Next to it, on the floor, were the Singer, the iron, the rolls of fabric, and a wooden bust with no head or limbs.

Daniele gave the room one last glance to be sure he hadn't forgotten anything, and then he opened the door and started to load the stuff into the bed of the Ape motor van he'd borrowed from the owner of the Duomo Bar, one of the few people to have one.

"I'll bring it back tomorrow morning," Daniele had assured him. The guy had said that it was no problem, he could bring it back whenever he was done.

"So we won't see you around anymore?" he'd asked. "What a shame."

Daniele covered everything with a thick white blanket, which he then fixed with a rope. He went back inside, pulled the key out of his pocket, and left it on the table; the person who'd rented the house to him would come for it later. That was the agreement.

He headed out the door and closed it behind him without looking back.

Leaving the studio was only the first step; he still had to talk to Roberto and take care of things at the winery. Since that cursed day in his grandmother's kitchen, when his mother had revealed to him who he really was, in that cowardly way, Daniele had sunk into a deep sorrow. He'd holed up in his house and hadn't wanted to see anyone. He'd spent Christmas alone, in his little apartment, with his stomach in a knot and wishing he could disappear.

The goodbye he dreaded the most, and was putting off, was Lorenza. His decision to leave had taken hold slowly, over the past few weeks, but he'd become certain that it was the only possible choice. Staying and pretending everything was fine was a possibility he hadn't even considered. He knew himself, and he knew he'd never be able to look Roberto in the eye every day without telling him the truth. Nor could he continue to see Lorenza in the same way.

Carmela had tried to smoke him out more than once from his isolation. She'd knocked on his door, imploring him to forgive her; in tears, she'd begged him to open up, to talk. But Daniele had never opened for her.

"Your grandmother will die of a broken heart if you don't go to her," she'd said at one point. Daniele had continued to ignore her. Only once did he say something, from the other side of the door.

"Who else knew?" he asked.

"What does it matter?" Carmela said in a trembling voice. "Open up, my son, please."

"No. Answer my question."

He heard his mother sigh and waited in silence, stubbornly, until she answered.

He learned that both his grandparents knew and that even *Carlo* had known, but not always; he'd found out right before Daniele started working at the Greco Winery as a laborer. It had been his grandfather's idea, to send him to work there. He'd also been the one to "handle the situation" when she'd ended up pregnant.

"Did Papa agree to this?" he asked.

Carmela swore he did not; Nicola never knew anything, nor had he ever suspected it, she was certain.

"You should be ashamed of yourselves, all of you," he said. Those were the last words he would ever speak to his mother.

It was the first day of 1952 and hail had fallen from the sky.

Daniele had spent the following days lying in bed thinking obsessively about Carlo and the relationship he'd had with him. He tried to recall all the moments they'd spent together, his looks, his habit of hugging him for no apparent reason, the way he said "my boy," the time he told him he'd be sending him to New York, the moment he'd seen him again in Naples, just off the boat, the last time he'd spoken to him before he died, and the discovery of the inheritance he was leaving him. Now everything made sense.

He realized Antonio probably knew everything too, and *that* was why he always behaved so strangely toward him about Lorenza. He was afraid, just afraid. And then he'd thought about Roberto, and a silent tear had lined his cheek. *I have a brother,* he kept saying to himself. *A brother! Blood of my blood!* How many times, as a child, had he asked Carmela to make him a little brother, so he wouldn't have to play alone anymore?

"All my friends have brothers and sisters, why don't I?" he'd whine.

"Learn to make do on your own," his mother would say dismissively, every time.

And now he actually had a brother . . . and all the adults he'd trusted throughout his life had kept it a secret. His anger grew toward each of them. His grandparents and his mother had acted like puppeteers, manipulating his entire existence. And they'd taken advantage of Nicola's kind soul. His anger toward Carlo was the worst, because he hadn't found the courage, not even in the *end*, to break the cycle of lies.

And then there was Lorenza, his Lorenza. *My cousin,* he thought, shaking his head, as if he still couldn't believe it. He remembered the instant affection he'd felt for her when they'd spoken for the first time, many years before. He'd cared about her from the start, like that, instinctually. And then that caring had turned into love. Maybe he'd even loved her from the first moment and was only realizing it now.

And now? he wondered. *What's going to happen between us now?*

Telling her the truth was not an option. He knew Lorenza well, her impulsivity, her restless nature, and he knew she'd go straight to Anna, and then to Roberto, destroying their lives and undermining all the certainties they'd relied on until then. No, he'd thought, he couldn't allow that. Anna and Roberto didn't deserve that. *His brother* didn't deserve that.

He hadn't been able to touch Lorenza anymore. The first time he'd seen her since knowing the truth, when she came in for a kiss, Daniele had almost jumped back.

"What's the matter?" she'd asked.

"I'm sorry, Lorenza. I don't feel well today."

How could he make love to her, now that he knew?

Little by little he'd started to make himself scarce, staying away from the studio on Wednesday afternoons, leaving no trace. It had been painful, agonizing. He knew he was hurting her, and he felt terribly guilty. But he couldn't be with her. Not anymore. Which was why leaving had seemed like the only possible option. It would be painful, and it would remain so for a long time, but he felt that it was the only choice that would allow him to save everyone's lives. And that was what mattered.

Over there, in New York, he'd start over. With his sketches.

When he got home, he parked the Ape by the sidewalk and got out. *I better unload everything before it gets dark*, he thought, undoing the knots on the rope.

"There you are, finally." He heard Lorenza's voice behind him.

He turned around. "How long have you been here?"

"I searched for you everywhere . . ."

"I was busy, I'm sorry."

"Will you tell me what's wrong? If you don't want to see me anymore, just tell me. Don't treat me like this. Don't do it."

"I'm sorry," Daniele said again. "It's just that—"

"What do you have there?" she interrupted him, pointing at the cargo bed. Without waiting for a reply, she walked up to the Ape and lifted the cover with a single movement.

When she saw the entire studio crammed in there, she started to pelt Daniele with questions, which soon became recriminations and finally accusations.

"So you're running away? And when were you going to tell me? You did everything behind my back. Is there someone else? That's it, isn't it? Obviously, there's someone else. Cowardly as you are. You didn't have the courage to tell me, eh? You let me find out on my own. Who is she? Are you throwing me away, now that I'm no longer of any use to you?"

Daniele let her talk, but in the end, he lost his patience.

"That's enough! There is no one else. Stop it!" Exhausted, he ran his fingers through his hair.

Lorenza suddenly went silent. It was the first time Daniele had ever yelled at her.

"I'm sorry for raising my voice," he mumbled a moment later. "Come with me, please. We have to talk."

Lorenza walked into Daniele's house and he followed her, thinking, *This is the last time I'll see her, the last time I'll speak to her. I have no choice but to tell her the truth.*

She sat on the couch and crossed her arms in front of her.

"I'm listening," she hissed.

Daniele pulled a chair out from under the table and placed it in front of her. He sat down, leaning forward, and looked her straight in the eyes.

"I've made a decision," he began. "I've thought about it for a long time—"

"You're leaving me?" she said, cutting him short.

"You have to let me speak." He took a deep breath and continued. "My life, and your life, are a disaster. You're destroying your family. Giada is growing up with a mother who is always unhappy and angry, and I . . . well, if we go on like this, I'll never have a family of my own. I want . . . to stop here."

"You can't, I won't let you!" Lorenza yelled. "There is a solution, you know there is—"

"Lorenza," he said curtly. "I'm leaving."

"What does that mean? You're leaving? What are you saying?"

"I'm going back to New York. I'm leaving in a week. It's the best thing for everyone," he said, his voice cracking.

Lorenza jumped to her feet, furious. "You can't."

"This isn't something you can decide."

"No!" she shouted. "There's no way. I'm coming with you."

"You're not going anywhere. You're staying here. With your family. With your daughter."

"I go where you go! You're not going to New York without me."

Daniele stood up and paced nervously around the room. In the moment, he realized he couldn't poison her with the truth. He stopped and decided to say the only other thing that might quell her. It was a lie. But it was necessary.

"I don't love you anymore," he said, looking her in the eyes.

"It can't be . . ." she said slowly, in a trembling voice.

"I don't love you anymore," he said again.

And he felt his heart shatter.

———

"She's smart, she learns quickly," Anna was saying.

"I don't know," Antonio said. "How is she going to learn everything in so little time? I need someone in less than a month, not in a year."

"She can do it. I know it. Just trust me."

Antonio's secretary, Agnese, was about to retire, and Anna had suggested he hire Michela in her place. She was only sixteen, to be sure, but she'd watched her closely over the past few weeks and she'd noticed her lively intelligence and an unusual shrewdness for a girl her age. She worked hard during lessons and at the end, she always told Anna she wanted to "do more." Anna would always assign her another exercise and suggest more challenging books to read, which she'd do excitedly.

"I don't doubt that she's as smart as you say, but to learn what Agnese has been doing for almost twenty years in just one month . . . well, it doesn't seem realistic," Antonio said. "I need an experienced secretary."

"She'll become experienced," Anna retorted. "Let her shadow Agnese from the beginning, starting tomorrow. Agnese can then tell you whether she's getting it or not."

As he considered this, Antonio swung his chair left and right. Then he stopped. "So be it. Let's try it," he agreed, finally.

Anna clapped her hands happily.

"But know that you owe me," he added, waving a finger.

"I'll buy you a ticket to the movies, today," Anna said without missing a beat.

"You're asking me to the movies, madam?"

"Dummy," she giggled. "Anyway, yes."

"What's on?"

"*Umberto D.* It's by De Sica. They were changing the poster this morning, when I went by."

"It's a deal, then," Antonio said.

Just then they heard the clacking of heels in the hallway. It got closer and closer until it stopped suddenly and the door to Antonio's office was flung open.

"Lorenza!" he exclaimed, surprised.

"Hello, ma petite," Anna said. But she immediately saw that the girl was out of her mind. Her smile suddenly went out.

"It was you, wasn't it!" Lorenza shouted, moving toward her father.

"What?" Antonio asked, bewildered.

"What did you tell him? Did you threaten him?"

"Lorenza, calm down." Anna tried to stop her, coming closer.

"Who are you talking about?" Antonio asked.

"You know who I'm talking about! Don't pretend with me, don't even try!"

"Don't make me angry, Lorenza," he said, standing up. "I won't allow you to use this tone."

"Please calm down, ma petite," Anna intervened, placing a hand on her shoulder. "Your father has no idea what you're talking about. Can you explain it to him, please?"

Lorenza looked at one and then at the other. Then she started crying. "He's leaving," she murmured, looking at Anna. "Daniele is leaving. He's going back to New York."

"I don't know anything about that!" Antonio said. "I swear to you, Lorenza."

She stared at him for a moment, her eyes brimming with tears, and then she covered her face with her hands and started to sob violently.

"Auntie," she murmured finally, and threw herself into Anna's arms.

"Shh," she said, stroking her niece's hair. Then she looked at Antonio, who'd remained unmoving, standing behind his desk.

He just bowed his head.

———

"No, it's not that, it's that I would rather have learned it from you, and not my mother, that you're leaving for New York. I was a little disappointed, that's all," Roberto said as he watched the first crates of Don Carlo bottles being taken to the labeling department.

Daniele hesitated. "You're right," he said finally. "I should have come to you before anyone else. I should have known that Anna would tell you right away. I'm sorry."

"Gently," Roberto warned two men who were rather awkwardly dragging the crates along. Then he turned back to Daniele.

"Okay, well, it's fine," he said, with a little smirk.

"Shall we walk over to the vineyard?" Daniele suggested.

They exited the winery without talking. Daniele kept his hands in his pockets and Roberto kept his head down, but every once in a while, he'd lift it up to look around. The Tramontane wind was blowing especially cold on that late February morning, and the canopies of the trees on the road to the estate were fluctuating wildly.

"Are you leaving because of my cousin?" Roberto asked, breaking the silence.

"There's that, but it's not the only reason. I need a change of air. And I already knew it from the start, that I didn't want to do this all my life. I did it for Carlo, and for you," he said, his heart skipping a beat.

"I knew it. About you and Lorenza, I mean. Why did you play dumb when I asked you?"

"I don't know," Daniele said. "To protect her, maybe."

"You didn't trust me." There was bitterness in Roberto's voice.

Daniele stopped walking. "No, it's not that. You have to believe me. It's that . . . I didn't know how you'd take it."

"How should I have taken it? You're my friend . . ."

Daniele felt his stomach turn.

". . . and you can tell me anything. I wouldn't have judged you. I never judge anyone."

"Yes, this is true," Daniele agreed, with a slight smile.

They resumed their stroll.

"I'll miss you, though," Roberto continued.

Daniele put an arm around his shoulder. "I'll miss you too. A lot."

"When will you be back?"

"I don't know. Maybe when the next Don Carlo comes out."

"Hmm," Roberto grumbled, as if he'd understood that it was just a lie. "I think you won't be back at all. And how am I supposed to do this without you—"

"Of course I'll be back. And anyway, in these past two months you've managed the winery practically on your own, so—"

"And if I have to ask you for advice?"

"You can call me. Why else did you buy a telephone?" he said with a smile.

"Hmm," Roberto grumbled again, with his head down. Then he stared at him. "But you're sure you'll be happy there?"

Daniele did not respond right away. Then he shrugged. "I don't know. But I promise I'll try."

"See to it that you do, then," Roberto replied, with a fake tone of reproach.

They finally arrived at the estate, where the vines stood silent, devoid of leaves and color.

The white writing on the wooden sign had grayed and lost the sparkle from all those years ago, when Daniele had first set foot there. For a moment he saw himself as a kid again, standing there with his flat cap on his head and wearing suspenders to hold up pants that were a size too big for him. He saw himself looking at the vines and watching the Fiat 508 pull over by the sign. "Good morning, Mr. Carlo," he'd always say, lifting his cap.

Daniele walked up to the sign and touched the letters, one by one.

"We should really repaint this," he said to his brother.

28

A Few Months Later

When Antonio went down to the kitchen for breakfast, he found Agata bustling about, covered in flour. She must have gotten up very early, since the cake was already baking in the oven. "Smells good," he said, leaning down to take a peek. "It's been a while since you've made chocolate cake."

"That's what Giada wanted, so that's what I made," Agata said with a smile.

Antonio poured himself some coffee from the moka pot on the table and sat down.

"Do you want to lick the bowl before I put it in the sink?" Agata asked.

"You even have to ask? Give it over," he said. He gathered the rest of the chocolate cream with his finger and brought it to his mouth.

"Hmmm, so good," he said, pleased.

"Thank goodness," Agata said, satisfied.

Antonio took a sip of tepid coffee. Agata must have prepared it at least an hour before.

"Lorenza too, as a child, always wanted chocolate cake for her birthday." Antonio smiled.

Agata responded with a smirk, then took the bowl back and placed it in the sink, on top of a pile of dirty dishes.

"Let's hope she got out of bed on the right foot this morning, and that she doesn't ruin the little one's party," she sighed.

"Yeah, let's hope," Antonio murmured.

Since Daniele had left, in early March, Lorenza had become a bundle of nerves with a sunken face and withered arms. "I'm not hungry," she'd say, pushing away her plate every time they dined together.

She only ever spoke to Tommaso if it was strictly necessary, and in a tone that resembled a growl. One time, she had an outburst just because he'd forgotten to bring the olive oil to the table. Antonio had felt the need to intervene.

"Lorenza! That's too much!" he'd said. She'd jumped up from her chair and locked herself in the bedroom, slamming the door. Agata had tried to go after her, but Tommaso had stopped her.

"Let her go. At least we can have dinner in peace." That one sentence seemed to contain all of Tommaso's fatigue, Antonio thought. Maybe he'd exhausted his patience, or maybe he no longer cared what Lorenza did or didn't do.

Antonio had tried to speak to his daughter many times. He'd suggested they go on a walk just the two of them, he'd invited her out to dinner, to the movies . . . he'd even gone to visit her at the post office, but she'd always rejected him, withdrawing into an almost absolute, hostile silence.

"You're just happy he's gone, that's all you ever wanted," she'd said once.

Antonio had looked down, unable to deny it. How could he? As soon as Daniele had left, he'd released an enormous sigh of relief, thinking that maybe, finally, his daughter would forget him and in time, make peace with her husband, with her daughter.

Giada's little birthday celebration began in the afternoon, at her grandparents' house. The chocolate cake, covered in powdered sugar, was displayed proudly on the dining room table; on one side was a pile of dessert plates from the good china set, and next to them was the silver cutlery with the inlaid handles, which Agata only brought out for special occasions.

Giada arrived in her father's arms. She was wearing a pink dress with an organza skirt and a white velvet bow in her bob cut.

"Whose birthday is it today?" Agata said, grabbing her little hands.

"Giada's!" the little girl responded happily.

"And how old is she today? Tell Granny."

"Is this little performance really necessary?" Lorenza grumbled as she took her coat off.

"Show Granny how old you're turning," Tommaso said, placing the girl on the ground.

Giada lifted three fingers.

"Very good!" Agata cheered and then gave her a hug.

"Look, Granny made you a chocolate cake!" Antonio said, stroking Giada on the head.

Roberto and Maria soon joined the party. Maria walked in holding a box wrapped in a large red bow.

"Ooh! Who is that present for?" Agata asked Giada.

Sitting on the couch, away from everyone, Lorenza shook her head, as if to say that she couldn't stand her mother's silly questions.

With Maria's help, the girl started to unwrap her present.

Antonio turned toward Lorenza for a moment and, with a strict nod, asked her to join them.

"A doll!" Giada exclaimed, widening her eyes at a porcelain doll. It had blond hair, painted red lips, and a blue-and-white-checked peasant dress.

Just then, Lorenza came over and stuck her neck out just enough to peek, then went back to the couch.

"Auntie, that cake looks delicious," Roberto said.

"If your mother hurries up and gets here, we'll even be able to eat it," Agata retorted.

"She said she'd be a little late. She's teaching lessons at the Home," Antonio informed her. "But I'm sure she'll be here any minute."

"Let's hope so," Agata said, with a hint of disappointment.

Anna arrived about ten minutes later, apologizing for her tardiness.

"And Giovanna?" Antonio asked, closing the door.

"She stayed there. Her beloved knitting course is today," Anna said. "But let me wish a happy birthday to the most beautiful little girl in the world," she exclaimed, holding her arms out to Giada, who ran toward her.

"I have a present for you," she said, pulling a little package out of her pocket.

It was a round gold locket with a G for *Giada* etched on top.

"I had it made specially for you," she said.

"Thank you dearly, Anna," Tommaso said, with some embarrassment. "It's too much."

"Let's cut the cake!" Agata announced, clapping her hands.

Antonio sank three candles into the soft pastry and lit them. Everyone began to sing, "Happy birthday to you . . ." Giada went to blow out the candles, but Maria stopped her.

"Wait, you have to make a wish."

"But only think it, or it won't come true," Roberto added.

Giada thought about it for a moment, and then her eyes wandered to Lorenza, who was in front of her, on the other side of the table.

"I know what my wish is," she said, turning back to look at Maria. She blew out the candles amid general enthusiasm.

Anna took two slices of cake and went to Lorenza, who was sitting on the couch again. "Here you go, ma petite," she said, handing her a plate.

"No, Auntie. I don't feel like it."

"It's really good, you know," Anna insisted, sitting next to her and taking a bite.

Lorenza shook her head. "I feel sick just looking at it."

"I was thinking," Anna said, still chewing, "why don't you come help me out at the Home one afternoon? There's a new girl there, Giulia. She's about your age."

Lorenza nodded, but it was clear that deep down, she didn't care a lick about it.

"Well?" Anna prodded, putting her empty plate down. "Will you come?"

"To do what, Auntie?"

"To help me. I think it might do you good."

"Yes, of course," Lorenza responded with a sarcastic smile. Then she started to scratch at something under her shirt. But since the fabric wouldn't allow her to alleviate her itch, she pulled up her sleeve, revealing her arm.

Anna couldn't help but notice the scar from what seemed to be a cut. "What happened there?"

"Nothing," Lorenza quickly responded, pulling her sleeve back down. "I got distracted while cooking," she concluded, with a shrug.

———

Anna didn't think about that cut again until a few days later. It was a peaceful day at the post office, so much so that by eleven-thirty, she'd already finished her deliveries and was back at the office. She used the opportunity to do something she'd been thinking of doing for a while: open a postal savings account for the Women's Home, to which she would deposit a certain sum every month and which her residents could use freely to buy food, clothes, soap, cleaning products, and whatever else. Without having to ask her for money every time.

"You're sure about this?" Tommaso grumbled. "Isn't it best to start a reserve fund you can manage yourself, so you can control what comes in and what goes out?"

"They are not little girls and I'm not their mother," she retorted, lifting an eyebrow. "They don't need to be controlled. They need trust. And to feel responsible for their own lives."

"And what if whoever is authorized to use the account, for instance, tries to get smart? Takes out all the money and poof, disappears who knows where?"

"None of them would ever do that."

"How can you be sure?"

"I just am."

"As you wish." Tommaso gave in. "I just wanted you to be cautious. But the money is yours, so—"

"And I thank you," Anna said. "But I know what I'm doing."

"People are saying things, you know . . ." Elena interrupted them, poking her head in from the back room.

"Meaning?" Anna asked, turning around.

"That Melina . . . she's there, isn't she?"

"Yes. So?"

"But do you know what she does?"

"*Did*, if anything," Anna said, piqued. "Anyway, yes, I know. And?"

"It's normal that people should talk. They say the place has become a home for bad women."

"Who says that?" Anna said, irritated.

"Don Luciano, for example. But not just him," Elena said.

"Don Luciano." Anna chuckled. "Well, that doesn't surprise me."

"That guy knows whores better than anyone else," offered Carmine, who hadn't missed a single word of that exchange.

"You're such a gossip," Elena reprimanded him.

"As if you didn't know," Carmine said.

"Anyway, it doesn't matter what they say. Especially not don Luciano," Anna declared.

"Oh well, if you're fine with it, good for you," Elena grumbled. *Let her keep her home for bad women.*

"Actually, you know what?" Anna said after a few minutes, as if she'd been thinking about it that whole time. "I think I'll go tell him that to his face!" She swiftly walked out of the post office and crossed the crowded square, heading straight for the parish.

"In a hurry, letter carrier?" a man sitting on a bench shouted after her. It was the muscular man who worked the tobacco in that dilapidated house on the edge of town.

Anna didn't answer and continued undeterred. She found don Luciano in the churchyard with an altar boy in tow; he was talking to a small flock of faithful who had stayed back after the eleven o'clock mass.

Anna continued into the churchyard and when she got to don Luciano, she tapped him on the shoulder.

The faithful suddenly went silent.

"May I have a word?" Anna asked.

"Good day, Mrs. Letter Carrier," he responded amiably. "How can I help you?"

"Well, first of all, by not spreading false and vicious rumors about the Women's Home."

The faithful started to look at one another, as if to say *Who would want to miss a scene like this?*

"Experience has taught me that when rumors grow . . . loud, there is almost always a grain of truth to them," don Luciano said.

Anna would have gladly slapped him in the face. "There are also rumors about you," she retorted. "According to your reasoning, we should believe they are correct. *Almost always.*"

Meanwhile, some of the people from the square had come closer.

Don Luciano cast a glance at all those people, then looked back at Anna.

"You were insolent to refuse my blessing," he continued. "If you'd listened to me, you wouldn't have ended up with women of ill repute, and certain rumors wouldn't be circulating."

"And what is 'reputable'?" Anna said. "You? Who preaches charity and divine generosity but then slams the door on women like Melina? Aren't we all children of God? Apparently, you're saying that some are more children of God than others."

"That is absolutely not what I said," don Luciano protested, looking back at his faithful. "But a sin is a sin. It's not up to me to forgive them. It's up to God."

"Well, then I hope your God also forgives your sins," Anna said. "Because according to what they say, there are quite a few. Good luck, when you stand before Him." And she walked off accompanied by a rising murmur, like the buzzing of a swarm.

"Don't let her get to you, don Luciano . . ."

"Oh, if Carlo were still here, bless his soul . . ."

"She always thought she was better than everyone else, that outlander."

Elena and Carmine were leaning out of the post office doorway—it was obvious that they hadn't missed a single word.

"You sure gave it to him straight, eh?" Carmine said, amused.

"Not straight enough," Anna responded.

She went back into the office to get her coat and mailbag and left, still irate and with her heart beating fast. She climbed onto her bike and took a few deep breaths, trying to shake off the tension.

"What an idiot," she grumbled.

She pedaled away, completely absorbed in her brooding, until she realized she'd gone the wrong way. She was near Tommaso and Lorenza's house, so she decided to visit her niece, who hadn't been to the office in two days.

"She just has a bit of a cold," Tommaso had said, without looking up from his papers.

She rang the doorbell a few times before Lorenza came to open. When she finally showed up at the door, it took Anna one look to see that she hadn't stayed home because of a simple cold; she was extremely pale and had deep purplish circles under her eyes. And there were two bandages wrapped around her elbows.

"Don't worry, Auntie, I didn't try to kill myself, if that's what you're thinking," Lorenza said arrogantly, before Anna's dumbfounded expression. "Come in, but be quiet; Giada just fell asleep."

Anna stumbled inside.

"I think I need some water," she said, sitting on the couch. "Tommaso said you had a cold," she added, trembling as she took the glass Lorenza brought her.

"I asked him to say that. At the office. To my mother. To everyone," Lorenza explained.

Anna drank the water in one gulp and tightly squeezed the empty glass. "Now you're going to tell me what's going on," she whispered, staring at her niece. "I'm not leaving here until you talk. Or I'll go and ask Tommaso, and you know I will."

With a sigh, Lorenza sat down on the couch and without looking at her, she said, "They're just little cuts. Little innocent cuts—"

"Innocent? Are you kidding me?" Anna interrupted, incredulous.

"Yeah, what am I supposed to say? They make me feel better. But I didn't know the inside of the elbows bled so much, that's all."

"That's all?" Anna echoed. "You're telling me you think this is normal?"

"Normal . . ." Lorenza murmured, as if that word were unknown to her. "You know what's not normal?" she went on, with more energy, turning to look at Anna. "That Daniele disappeared into thin air. That I don't know how to get in touch with him. That I'm here and he's on the other side of the world. That's what's not normal, Auntie."

"That is no reason to . . . do what you're doing," Anna said, pointing at the wounds.

"I told you. It makes me feel better. At least for a while."

"But what you're saying doesn't make sense, Lorenza, do you not realize that? Someone needs to help you. You can't go on like this."

"Yes, help me, sure . . ." she said, looking up at the ceiling.

"Let me help you," Anna said, placing her hand on Lorenza's.

Lorenza straightened her head. "Oh yeah? You really want to help me? Then tell me where he is, where he lives."

"How am I supposed to know—"

"Find out. Even Roberto says he doesn't know . . . as if I were some idiot. I know they keep in touch, those two."

"And once you know where he is, what will you do then?"

"I'll talk to him, I'll write to him, I'll convince him to come back to me," she said with a shrug, as if it were obvious.

"That would help you feel better? To talk to him, I mean," Anna asked.

"Oh yes," Lorenza said with a smirk.

Anna thought for a moment. "Okay, I'll help you," she promised. "But you have to stop this, *now*," she said with a cracked voice, pointing at the bandages.

Lorenza did not respond.

———

It was just after dawn in early May when Tommaso, holding a sleeping Giada to his chest, knocked on his in-laws' door. Agata opened it in her dressing gown and with her hair gathered in a bonnet. As Tommaso walked in, he said in a low voice, "Bring Giada upstairs, please."

Agata stared at him in confusion. "What—" she tried to say, but Tommaso stopped her, indicating that they would talk, but not while the girl was present.

While Agata brought her granddaughter to the bedroom, Antonio came out of his study, tying his robe around his waist. "Tommaso, what's going on?" he asked, frowning.

"Let's wait for Agata," he said.

They sat down at the kitchen table. Tommaso pulled out a checkered sheet of paper folded in two and handed it to his in-laws. Antonio took it and opened it. Agata leaned in to read with him.

I'm fine. Don't look for me, was all it said.

It was Lorenza's handwriting, narrow and pointy.

Antonio and Agata looked up at Tommaso.

"What does it mean?" Antonio asked.

Tommaso explained that he'd found the message only a few minutes before, on the dining room table, when he'd woken up and gone downstairs. That was all he knew, other than that Lorenza had clearly gone out while he was sleeping.

Antonio stood up and started pacing back and forth, stroking his face.

"Did you have a fight last night? Was she angry about something?" Agata inquired.

"No," Tommaso whispered.

"How did you not hear anything?" Antonio burst out. "Someone leaves the house like that, in the middle of the night—"

"Calm down, Antonio," Agata said, putting a hand on his arm.

Tommaso rested his elbows on the table and put his head in his hands.

"It must be one of her episodes. You know what she's like," Agata tried to comfort him. "She'll be back."

"Maybe she went to that friend of hers . . . in Lecce," Tommaso suggested, looking up.

Antonio stopped dead and squeezed the back of a chair with both hands. How could he reveal to everyone, in that moment, that there was no such friend and there never had been? "No." He shook his head, decisively. "She's not there."

"She couldn't have gone far," Agata said.

"She could have taken the bus," Tommaso objected. "But I can't stay here without doing anything." He looked at Antonio. "Can we go look around the countryside?"

"Okay," Antonio said, doubtfully. "Let's try that."

Each with their own car and taking two different directions, Antonio and Tommaso set out. Antonio checked in every pagghiara from Lizzanello to Pisignano, then doubled back and headed south, toward the fields around the town of Castrì.

"Where are you hiding?" he kept whispering, looking around.

After wandering around in circles for more than two hours, he decided to return home.

"Anything?" Agata asked.

"I looked everywhere," Antonio said, tossing his car keys on the table.

"Maybe Tommaso found her," she murmured, wringing her hands.

Tommaso returned soon after. He'd pushed on until Lecce, he said, without even knowing where to look. Just then, he realized he hadn't alerted the office of his absence. He'd completely forgotten that he even had a job.

394 | FRANCESCA GIANNONE

"Yes," Antonio said. "They must think I'm missing at the mill, too."

"Go," Agata said. "You can't do anything else for now anyway."

"Maybe it's best if you go to Tommaso's when Giada wakes up. In case Lorenza should come back," Antonio suggested. "We'll join you later."

Agata nodded. "Let's keep this to ourselves for now," she warned as Antonio and Tommaso were leaving. "Maybe she'll be back tonight and we'll have made much ado about nothing. Tell your colleagues she wasn't feeling well. Anna too. Say that."

The wisteria at the entrance to Tommaso and Lorenza's house was in full bloom. Agata had always loved the smell of those flowers, and before opening the door, she stopped next to them and breathed in deeply.

"Now that's what I call a nice perfume," she said to Giada, who was in her arms looking sleepy. As she put the key in the lock, she wished she had a perfume that only smelled of wisteria.

She prepared some milk for Giada, gave her a few biscuits, and told her to start eating. "Granny's going upstairs for a minute, but she'll be right back," she said, with a caress.

She went up to the bedroom. As she waited for Tommaso and Antonio, a terrible idea made its way into her mind. With her heart aflutter, hoping with all her might that she was wrong, she went to the dresser and stuck her hand all the way to the back of the bottom drawer, beyond the folded towels. The light wooden box where Lorenza kept her jewelry was still there. Agata opened it, trembling, hoping, but it was empty. There was no trace of Lorenza's rings, bracelets, or necklaces. Everything was missing, even the locket with the G that Anna had given Giada for her birthday. Agata collapsed on the bed, struggling to hold back her tears.

That evening, at dinner, no one felt like eating.

"Where's Mama?" Giada kept asking.

"She went to prepare a surprise for you," Agata said. "She'll be back with a nice present, you'll see."

"But I don't want a present. I want Mama," Giada whined, rubbing her eyes.

In the end, Agata picked up Giada and brought her upstairs, staying with her until she fell asleep.

Downstairs, Antonio paced across the room. Tommaso sank into the sofa and stared into a void.

"She's not coming back," he whispered.

Antonio stopped pacing and looked at him. "I have to speak to Anna," he said.

Tommaso turned around. "Agata doesn't want anyone to know yet. Let's wait—"

"No." Antonio cut him off decisively, heading for the door.

All the lights in Anna's house were off, except for the one in her bedroom.

Antonio knocked on the door gently, but more than once, until he saw the light come on in the living room and he heard Anna's slow but confident steps—he would have recognized them anywhere—approach the door.

She opened it. She was wearing a blue silk nightgown and her face was shiny with cream. "Antonio? What happened?"

"I'm sorry, were you sleeping?"

"Not yet, but almost. Come in."

"Did I wake anyone up?" he asked.

"No, don't worry. I'm alone," she said, closing the door. "Giovanna stayed the night in Contrada, with the girls, and Roberto is at Maria's family's house for dinner. It's her father's birthday. Or her mother, I forget which," she mumbled, lifting an eyebrow.

Antonio stared at her and then pulled her into his arms, tucking his head into the crook of her neck.

"What's wrong?" Anna asked, concerned. She lifted an arm and put it on his shoulder.

"She's gone," Antonio exclaimed in a strangled voice.

"Who do you mean? Who's gone?"

She walked him over to the couch and held his hand while Antonio told her about the longest day of his life.

She listened to him with bated breath and eyes wide open. She imagined Lorenza writing *I'm fine. Don't look for me* before sneaking out of the house in the dead of night, along the dark and deserted street.

"Help me. Where can we look for her?" Antonio was asking her. "I just don't know anymore."

Anna slowly pulled her hand from his and just as slowly, she stood up. She took a few steps, covered her mouth with her hand, then stopped dead and looked at him. "I know where she went."

Antonio jumped up and went to her. "Where?"

Her eyes filled with tears.

"What's wrong? Why are you crying?" he asked, holding on to her arms.

"I did something . . . something stupid."

Antonio pulled away and took a step back.

"I gave her Daniele's address in New York. She wanted to write to him, talk to him, she was in so much pain . . ."

Anger and bewilderment crossed Antonio's face. "Why did you do it?" he asked in a hiss. "Why? I'd asked Roberto to never say anything. Ever."

"Roberto has nothing to do with it. I found it on my own. It was me," she replied.

"Why? Why would you do something like that, Anna?"

"You didn't see them, the cuts."

"Cuts? What cuts?" he shouted.

"The ones on her arms," she said, pointing at the inside of her elbows. "She told me they made her feel better—"

"What the hell is this all about?" Antonio yelled.

"I know, it's absurd, and I don't even really understand what it is, but you have to believe me, Antonio," she begged him. "The point was that Lorenza wasn't well. At all. And I was afraid for her."

"So?" His voice had become a whisper.

"She needed to speak to Daniele. I just wanted her to feel better. I didn't think that—"

"You didn't think," he said bitterly, cutting her off. "And you didn't consider." He took a few nervous steps through the room. "She's already at sea!" he yelled, widening his arms. "How am I going to get her back now? From where?"

Anna brought her hands to her mouth. "I'm sorry," she whispered.

"How could you not know?" Antonio continued, hitting himself on the forehead with his fist.

"I just wanted her to feel better," she said again in a faint voice.

"You should have stayed in your place!" he yelled. "She's not your daughter! She is not Claudia!"

Anna felt like he'd knifed her in the back. "What did you say?"

"Nothing," Antonio retorted, avoiding her eyes.

"I heard you," she said, coming closer. "Have the courage to say it again."

He made a movement as if to tell her to drop it and turned his back on her.

"Say it again," she hissed, pushing him to make him turn back toward her.

"You should have stayed out of it," Antonio said. "I'd asked you to get her to see reason, not to hand her a ticket to the other side of the world."

"I didn't hand her anything! I wanted to help her, like I always have."

Antonio closed his eyes. "You already knew everything, didn't you?"

"What do you mean?"

"You watched Giada every Wednesday, knowing where Lorenza was going." Anna looked away and tried to walk off, but Antonio grabbed her by the arm. "And you also knew that she'd leave. And you covered for her, and maybe you still are, aren't you?"

"No!" she yelled.

"Admit it!" She tried to escape his grasp, but Antonio squeezed harder. "You're a liar. I don't trust you anymore and I'll never trust you again," he added firmly, with eyes full of rage.

A flash of pain crossed Anna's eyes. "And you? How many lies have you told?" she screamed. "When did you ever tell Carlo the truth? When did you ever have the courage—"

Antonio let go of her arm. "What does Carlo have to do with it now?" he asked, dazed.

"You know," she said, still staring at him. Never in her life had she felt such a strong and uncontrollable rage. She felt like she was about to blow them both up, that she was about to turn to lava and leave nothing alive in her wake, yet she couldn't stop.

"Tell me: What's it like to pretend to be someone you're not? Antonio the *big brother*, Antonio the *honest brother.*"

"Stop it," he hissed.

"You want to know the truth?" she went on. "Carlo may have had many flaws, but at least *he* was authentic. He never hid himself. He was better than you, and you've always known it."

Antonio scowled and opened his mouth to retort, but then thought better of it.

He marched to the door.

"How relieved are you that he's gone? Now that you can finally be the center of attention?" Anna exclaimed, knowing that she'd hit him where it hurt.

Antonio stopped right there at the door. He turned around, walked straight up to her, and with all the strength he could muster, he slapped her across the face.

"Say that again and I'll kill you with my own hands," he said in a trembling voice.

Anna touched her cheek and stared at him in fear and disbelief.

Antonio clenched his fists and walked back to the door.

He'd already opened it when Anna whispered, "I'll never forgive you for what you just did."

He turned around. "Neither will I," he said.

He went out, leaving the door open.

Epilogue

August 13, 1961

"Grandpa, it's time for your medicine," Giada said in her squeaky voice, opening the door to Antonio's study. "Grandma says to come into the other room—she's already set it up for you."

Antonio was sitting at his desk. He turned to look at his grand-daughter. When she smiled like that, Giada looked so much like her mother it was unnerving. Sometimes, especially lately, Antonio would get distracted and call Giada Lorenza.

He hadn't seen his daughter since that May in 1952. But every year at Christmas he and Agata received a postcard from New York saying *Merry Christmas* with a lot of exclamation points. And only Lorenza's signature.

"I'm coming, little one," he said. "Close the door, please."

He waited for Giada to leave the room and then, hands trembling, he took the letter back out of the desk drawer. Roberto had brought it to him a few days before, in a white envelope that read only: *Antonio*. It was in Anna's precise and wavy handwriting: He'd recognized it right away.

"I have no idea what's in it. But I hope to see you at the funeral later," Roberto had said.

Antonio stroked the letter and read it once more.

Do you remember the book I was reading in Gallipoli? I think it was 1937, when we all spent the summer together in that lovely little villa that Carlo had rented. The book was Goethe's *Elective Affinities*. I was interested in the question it posed, the same one I was asking myself at that time: What happens to a couple of elements if a third one comes into play? Even then, as I've always done, I'd hoped to find the answer in a book. But that time, it didn't happen.

And do you know why? Because I had the answer right in front of me: It was you, who got up every day that summer as soon as you heard my steps (you thought I hadn't noticed?), who joined me on the veranda, and who sat down on the lounge chair next to mine to read with me. To be with me.

Well, I must tell you something: In these years of silence between us, I've continued to underline every book that I read, and to write my notes in the margins for you, even though I know you'll never read them again.

I know you've hated me. A lot. You never missed a chance to remind me, with your distant "hellos" whenever you ran into me in town, or the surly looks you'd shoot me from afar, or when you'd make me stop at the entryway at the mill and leave your mail with the secretary. You never even came to see the new location of the Women's Home in Lecce.

How much energy did you spend on hating me?

Too much, I know. The same amount I spent on hating you.

Know that I still haven't forgiven you for that slap. But also know that I haven't forgiven myself, either, for the poisonous words I said that night. And even so, I never considered coming to apologize.

The reason I did it only became clear to me recently. You know, an illness is like a key to a lock.

The truth, my dear Antonio, is that for all this time we've needed to hate each other.

It was the only way not to betray Carlo.

The truth, as you once said, is between the lines.

And do you know what's between mine? That I risked loving you more than I ever loved Carlo. And I couldn't let that happen.

Carlo didn't deserve that.

Now you know.

It went the way it was supposed to go.

At least I think so.

Anna

He suddenly heard a slight buzz coming from outside, followed immediately by the thundering voice of the priest, who began to recite the Eternal Rest above the whispers. Antonio put his weight on his armrests and pulled himself up with some effort. Slowly and hesitantly, he went to the window and gently moved the curtain aside with two fingers.

The coffin paraded before his eyes, held up by Roberto, Carmine, Nando, and another man Antonio didn't know, followed by a procession of dark clothes and bowed heads. Antonio narrowed his eyes and studied the procession: he recognized Roberto's wife Maria, Giovanna, Elena, Chiara on her husband's arm, Melina, and Michela, who'd been his secretary for a few months many years ago. Behind them were many, many other women he'd never seen before.

The coffin was topped not with the usual crown of flowers, but with Anna's cap, the one with the embroidered post office symbol.

In a flash, Antonio was back in the summer of 1934, on an afternoon in June. A hot wind was blowing through the deserted square and he was happy because his brother Carlo had finally come home. And then, out of the blue bus that had brought him back emerged the most beautiful woman he'd ever seen, with eyes the color of olive trees—eyes he had never been able to stop staring at. And maybe she'd noticed, because she blushed like a schoolgirl.

A sudden gust of wind, quick and strong, caused the cap to fly off the coffin and fall to the ground, right in front of his window.

Antonio trembled and quickly let go of the curtain.

Acknowledgments

My first thank-you goes to Lila and Babù, for being there for every word I laid on the page and for my every clickety-clack on the keyboard, unfailingly cuddled on my lap in winter and curled up at my feet in summer. Whenever my inspiration wavered, or when I grappled with a complicated scene, all I had to do to find the answers I sought was walk with them in the silence of the Salentino countryside.

Thank you to my sister, Elisabetta, my soulmate, to whom *The Letter Carrier* is dedicated. She has been a consummate reader since the first draft, and I know she cares about my characters as much as I do. Sometimes she might say, "Can you imagine what Carlo would have said?" or "He deserves one of Anna's cutting remarks."

I thank my mother, Claudia, for having jealously guarded Anna's memory; it was to her, Anna's favorite granddaughter, that our letter carrier passed down photographs, business cards, mortar and pestle, and everything else she held dear. Including her precious recipe for Ligurian pesto.

I thank my father, Franco, for his steadfast confidence in every project I undertake and for his unshakable support of my dreams.

I thank Ilaria Gaspari and her infectious enthusiasm, which encouraged me to continue even when the novel was still just an idea, a mere three pages.

A hug full of gratitude and affection for my editor, Cristina Prasso. It's thanks to her that *The Letter Carrier* found its home. I thank her for all the love with which she took care of this story, the meticulous attention she dedicated to it, and for having seen what the novel would become, even before I did. Working with her has been an honor, a wonderful journey I already feel nostalgic for.

A heartfelt thank-you to the Nord staff, for the warmth with which they welcomed *The Letter Carrier,* and for having held its hand and kept it safe throughout the publishing process.

I thank the Cantina Leone de Castris for the technical consultation. The Donna Anna is a loving homage to the Five Roses and its extraordinary story. Over the years, I've sampled more than a few wines, but the Five Roses remains my favorite. Irreplaceable.

A few necessary clarifications, before I finish: The town of Lizzanello described in these pages is a synthesis of a few villages of the Salento. I borrowed a glimpse from each of them, to reflect as best I could the landscape and the atmosphere of the lands; the people of the town that populate the novel are entirely the fruit of my imagination, so every reference to people who have actually existed is purely coincidental and involuntary; lastly, it's important to specify that the experiences of the Greco family were significantly altered and reworked for narrative purposes, and that the story I recount here is not their story.

Finally, my biggest thank-you goes to Anna, for having come to me. The last words she uttered, as passed down through my mother, were "I don't want to be forgotten."

You won't be. I promise.

ABOUT THE AUTHOR

FRANCESCA GIANNONE has a degree in communication science and studied in Rome at the CSC, the oldest European film school. She has published various short stories in literary magazines, both in print and online. She currently lives in Milan, but her heart is still in her native Lizzanello, a seaside town in the Salento region. She hopes to live there again one day.